THE
COMEDOWN

THE
COMEDOWN

a novel

REBEKAH
FRUMKIN

HENRY HOLT AND COMPANY
NEW YORK

Henry Holt and Company
Publishers since 1866
175 Fifth Avenue
New York, New York 10010
www.henryholt.com

Henry Holt ® and 🏛 ® are registered trademarks of Macmillan Publishing
Group, LLC.

Distributed in Canada by Raincoast Book Distribution Limited

Library of Congress Cataloging-in-Publication Data

Names: Frumkin, Rebekah, author.
Title: The comedown : a novel / Rebekah Frumkin.
Description: First edition. | New York, New York : Henry Holt and Company,
    [2018]
Identifiers: LCCN 2017045167 (print) | LCCN 2017035218 (ebook) |
    ISBN 9781250127532 (eBook) | ISBN 9781250127525 (hardcover)
Subjects: LCSH: Life change events—Fiction. | Families—Fiction. | GSAFD:
    Black humor (Literature)
Classification: LCC PS3606.R88 (print) | LCC PS3606.R88 C66 2018 (ebook) |
    DDC 813/.6—dc23
LC record available at https://lccn.loc.gov/2017045167

Our books may be purchased in bulk for promotional, educational, or business
use. Please contact your local bookseller or the Macmillan Corporate and
Premium Sales Department at (800) 221-7945, extension 5442, or by e-mail at
MacmillanSpecialMarkets@macmillan.com.

First Edition 2018

Designed by Meryl Sussman Levavi

Printed in the United States of America

10 9 8 7 6 5 4 3 2 1

for my parents
who deserve so much more than a book
here's a book

"The story reveals the meaning of what otherwise would remain an unbearable sequence of sheer happenings."
—HANNAH ARENDT

"Shit happens."
—ANONYMOUS

THE COMEDOWN

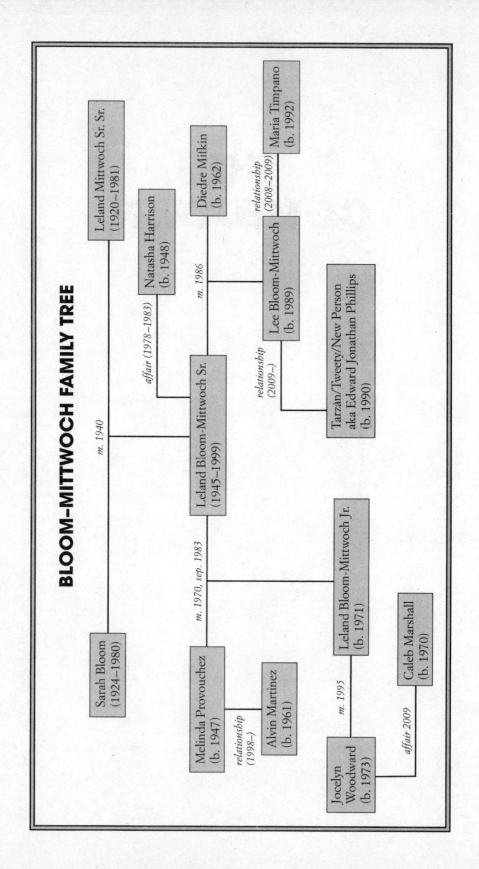

BLOOM-MITTWOCH FAMILY TREE

Sarah Bloom
(1924–1980)

m. 1940

Leland Mittwoch Sr. Sr.
(1920–1981)

affair (1978–1983)

Natasha Harrison
(b. 1948)

Leland Bloom-Mittwoch Sr.
(1945–1999)

m. 1986

Diedre Mifkin
(b. 1962)

Lee Bloom-Mittwoch
(b. 1989)

relationship (2008–2009)

Maria Timpano
(b. 1992)

relationship (2009–)

Tarzan/Tweety/New Person
aka Edward Jonathan Phillips
(b. 1990)

m. 1970, sep. 1983

Melinda Provouchez
(b. 1947)

relationship (1998–)

Alvin Martinez
(b. 1961)

Leland Bloom-Mittwoch Jr.
(b. 1971)

m. 1995

Jocelyn Woodward
(b. 1973)

affair 2009

Caleb Marshall
(b. 1970)

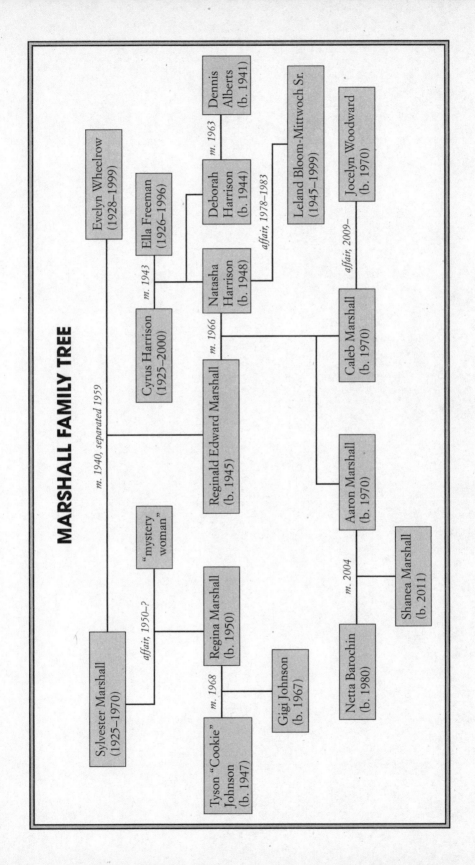

MARSHALL FAMILY TREE

Sylvester Marshall (1925–1970)

Evelyn Wheelrow (1928–1999)

m. 1940, separated 1959

"mystery woman"

affair, 1950–?

Cyrus Harrison (1925–2000)

Ella Freeman (1926–1996)

m. 1943

Deborah Harrison (b. 1944)

Dennis Alberts (b. 1941)

m. 1963

Natasha Harrison (b. 1948)

Leland Bloom-Mittwoch Sr. (1945–1999)

affair, 1978–1983

Reginald Edward Marshall (b. 1945)

m. 1966

Caleb Marshall (b. 1970)

Jocelyn Woodward (b. 1970)

affair, 2009–

Regina Marshall (b. 1950)

Tyson "Cookie" Johnson (b. 1947)

Gigi Johnson (b. 1967)

m. 1968

Aaron Marshall (b. 1970)

Netta Barochin (b. 1980)

m. 2004

Shanea Marshall (b. 2011)

PROLOGUE

May 8, 1999

Of those who've shut their eyes to the world with few or no regrets, it can be said both that their number is small, and that Leland Abdiel Bloom-Mittwoch Sr. was not among them.

At four in the morning on the fifty-fourth birthday he would've shared with his best friend, Reggie Marshall, Leland Sr. arrived in Tampa looking for a hotel. It didn't take him long to find one, the bright lobby of which wore several dark stories like a tall hat. From the road it had reminded him of a picture book of his youngest son's in which all the buildings had faces and spoke to one another; he liked that book, so he pulled in, parked, and removed his briefcase from the trunk. The kid at the front desk looked barely eighteen. She was rubbing the sleep from her eyes. He nodded at her with his best pitying face, set his briefcase on the counter, and asked if he could be shown a room.

"Yes you can," she said, sounding obviously dissatisfied with her station in a way he himself had once been. She clicked around aimlessly on her computer and the machine made a sound like small waves crashing. "I have four rooms available right now, all on the fourth floor."

"Does that floor have roof access?"

She looked both bored and confused by the question. "Yes, sir. Access to the roof is granted to any guest with a key." She turned her attention to a little machine by the computer. Leland Sr. made sure he wore an expression he hoped reflected what a bighearted mensch he was. She produced a key and handed it to him. "And now you've got a key. Your room number is 402. Did you need anything else, sir?"

He took the key from her gently and shook his head. "No thank you." Then he held it up next to his face and waggled it a little. "And thank you!"

Room 402 was well appointed: a single queen bed, a desk, a lowboy on top of which was perched a nice-looking TV. He turned on the TV and stopped on the station where a soothing female voice recited facts about the hotel as they appeared on the screen. Then he opened his briefcase. Emptied completely of the money, it felt lighter in every sense—its only contents now were his study Torah and the last twenty bag he'd ever buy. He keyed out a bump, inhaled deeply, and exhaled. It could've been better, that was true, but he was the beggar and not the chooser in this situation. He poured about half the bag onto the mahogany desktop and cut it up with his credit card. His blood, sludgy from the long drive, had begun to flow and his mind was restored to full operating capacity. Even room 402's many shades of beige looked brighter. Outside he could see the electric pinks and reds of a sunrise. Now was probably the time, he thought to himself, if ever there was one. He railed the rest, grabbed his Torah, and, his blood pumping, climbed the stairs to the eighth floor.

The door to the roof opened with a smooth click. He'd hoped for more fanfare or at least more resistance. When he thought about this moment on his drive to Tampa he'd imagined something special would happen to mark the occasion. He'd fantasized about getting into a fight with a bellboy, knocking over a food cart and then beating it down the hall while someone screamed "Call security!" But that was foolish. He didn't live in an action movie. G-d didn't live in an action movie. Moses could never have imagined a copy of his words would wind up on the roof of a Hyatt Regency in downtown Tampa so many thousands of years after he'd written them, and that they had was just testament to their long-enduring power. Leland Sr. wished he could've been chosen, called by G-d to write something like the Torah: long-lasting and capable of inspiring millions of people to greatness. But he hadn't been chosen—that sort of thing wasn't in his wheelhouse. This, what he was doing now, was the second-best thing he could've done in service of G-d. This had been in his wheelhouse from birth.

As he walked around the Hyatt's roof, knocking on the giant exhaust vent like a building inspector, tracing with his toe a set of fingerprints some workman had left in the concrete, he made a little movie in his head with scenes of all the people who'd loved him. There was his mother, Sarah Bloom-Mittwoch, the wild, pessary-using Berlinerin Ashkenazi who had gotten knocked up by his father in 1944, a full eight years after they'd escaped Germany, the European continent, and being gassed. He could see her in a Cleveland hospital on VE Day, pushing him out furiously while a nurse held her hand and promised her he'd already crested, that the pain would be over soon if she could just try to push a little harder. And there he was sleeping in the nursery with all the other newborns, Leland Sr. Sr. regarding him through the glass, crying, and biting down hard on his Turkish cigar as news of the Allied victory in Europe came over the speaker in the waiting room.

There was his first wife, Melinda, standing on the Kent State Commons in the white frock she'd since lost or thrown away, her arms extended, the features of her soft face quivering and bursting and bleeding into one another as his vision began to scintillate with LSD. There was Leland Jr. when he was three days old and still helpless, sleeping in Melinda's arms, both of them frozen forever in a rocking chair in the golden morning light that came in through the living room window. There was Natasha Marshall, Reggie's widow, dressed in her favorite peacoat with the collar that hugged her chin, sitting at her desk with all the books piled up on it. And there was Diedre, his gas-pumping Bathsheba in high-waisted shorts, wiggling her freshly painted emerald toenails—there she was on the sofa in their bungalow, the infant Lee suckling at her milk-engorged breast, his small fingers folding and unfolding in the air.

He thought how there was no way to know how long loving someone could last, or whether it was even a good investment to begin with. That's what kept people watching all those television soap operas. That's what kept people praying in shul. They wanted to know how the other people and things they loved would turn out—whether they'd be destroyed by them or loved back. He turned to regard the rising sun. Below, the streets were already beginning to fill with morning traffic.

True to the rabbi's prediction, the sunrise deepened to a violently dark purple. The clouds shifted apart. He thought he would faint. He thought he would drop dead. Every shameful, jealous, hateful thing he'd ever said or done in his life swam to the surface of his memory. His eyes watered with humiliation.

"This is too much," he whispered. "I'm unworthy."

From between the purple clouds emerged a Hand, palm upturned in compassion. "That's not true," the Hand said. "You are worthy."

"And Reggie?"

"Absolutely worthy."

He nodded, unsure if he should speak. The Hand remained hovering patiently over the city. Leland Sr. thought how incredible it was that this Hand had wrought the entire world.

Although he desperately didn't want to, he began to cry. "I thought the plan for me was unspeakable," he managed to say.

"So did Abraham when he bound Isaac," the Hand replied. "So did Job as he endured those plagues from the underworld."

Leland Sr. wiped the tears from his eyes with his sleeve. His face felt numb; from what, he couldn't tell. "What do I do now?" he asked, though he knew what the answer would be.

"Come to Me," the Hand said, making a beckoning gesture.

"And if I fall?"

"You won't."

About twenty feet stood between him and the roof's edge. Between him and the Hand—impossible to tell. He breathed in and exhaled slowly. Then he clutched the Torah to his chest, ran, and jumped.

MELINDA BLOOM-MITTWOCH, NÉE PROVOUCHEZ

(1947–)

1952–1967
Ohio

The last time her body hadn't been thought of as more than a poke-able and prod-able inconvenience—her face subjected to the disapproval of pink-lapeled Avon saleswomen, her feet too big to fit in the right pair of stilettos, her fat resistant to herb diets and massage belts and reducing creams—Melinda Provouchez had been a child of six. She would run up and down the little hill in front of her house, ten times, thirty times, out of breath and eager to conquer her territory. The hill sloped into a drainage ditch she pretended was a moat surrounding a castle. At night she watched the moon shine a long, white tongue down the length of Lake Erie and she thought about the big fish she knew lived down there with the lamplight growing out of its head. How could she harpoon it? She went to sleep dreaming of squirrels driving through the nighttime streets in cars they'd built out of acorns, sticks, and leaves. She drew pictures of her house and family and they vibrated with color. She showed them to her teacher at school, who wrote to her parents: Melinda has a very promising intellect and imagination.

When she was seven, her grandpa had poked her thigh during Christmas dinner and asked if maybe she shouldn't have that second helping of pecan pie. He'd never touched her before—they waved instead of hugging, she curtsied instead of kissing him on the cheek. He was sitting next to her and stuck his finger in her thigh's pale flesh, bare because she wore a stiff taffeta dress with layers of tulle underneath that made the hem ride up high past her knee. She looked up in panic but saw that everyone was laughing, her cousins, uncles, aunts, father, and mother. Only her grandma wore her grave, semipermanent mask of judgment: "Should you be treating her that way, Walter?" To which her mother responded: "Well, there's some truth to it."

So as she grew and came to understand who she was, where she was, and the other people around her, Melinda bore in mind the fact that there was some truth to it. Some truth she should be ashamed about. Her father was a well-respected man in the Lakewood community and in other parts of Cleveland, a supervisor at a factory where vinyl siding was manufactured for use in construction. He had a square neck exactly the width of his head and wanted sons, was irritated with Melinda until her little brother, Tommy, arrived a few days before her eighth birthday. Melinda's mother was less impatient, less boy-obsessed, but also less inclined to assert her opinions. If she agreed, then something "could be right," or "rang a bell." If she disagreed, she "didn't know." She was full figured, wore belted skirts and scooped-neck dresses like Elizabeth Taylor. Melinda's father seemed proud of how her mother looked, made a point of taking her out to the Italian restaurant in town on Thursdays—his one-day weekend—to show her off. Melinda had to spend this time holding a swaddled, frequently croupy Tommy and watching *Gunsmoke* on the couch while some knock-kneed babysitter talked to her varsity-letter boyfriend on the phone, interrupting her conversation only to complain to Melinda that the volume was turned up too loud. For whatever it was worth, Melinda also thought her mother had gorgeous proportions.

But when Melinda was thirteen, her mother's waist began to fill out. Her chin sagged and her breasts slackened. She ate two waffles with peanut butter and syrup every morning. Melinda didn't know why this was happening, and she also knew it was nothing to speak about. Their sunny house by the lake seemed darker, its rooms capable of being folded up and stored away like the hastily painted Nativity backdrops in the basement of their church. Her father began to stay out drinking with union members on Thursdays. Instead of fried chicken and Jell-O, her mother made Melinda and Tommy "healthy" dinners: green beans and ashen-colored meat loaves with a quarter-inch crust of ketchup baked on top. Dust motes appeared in every room, orbiting the yellowing spheres of her mother's milk glass lamps. Only Tommy, stumbling happily around in his fire-truck rompers, seemed to have no idea that something was going on. Melinda shook him off whenever he came to her with his plastic baggies of cowboys and Indians, telling him it wasn't a good time to play.

Something was happening to Melinda, too. Her father had inherited a book of German fairy tales, which she often paged through. She couldn't understand any of the words, but the pictures were horrific: a boy with severed thumbs, women in fancy ball gowns cutting off their toes to fit into a slipper. The worst was of a girl screaming while locusts swarmed from her mouth. Melinda kept the book under her bed and studied the words above the girl's picture: *Das junge Frauenzimmer.* She was too scared to ask her father what it meant. Her body had begun to creak and gasp and ache involuntarily—when she went to sleep, insects walked the lining of her stomach. The twitchy vibrato of a tight muscle was a locust batting its wings. The pain in her chest, the itchiness at her nipples: locust babies hatching from their eggs.

By Melinda's sophomore year of high school, her mother weighed two hundred and fifty pounds and rarely left the house. She cooked only pastas in heavy cream sauce and three-cheese casseroles. She let Melinda and Tommy drink Coke and orange juice instead of water in the middle of the night. At dinner—which even Tommy understood to be a difficult but necessary time—Melinda's father told her mother that she should be careful of her health. He eventually let it slip that people were talking about her. Melinda's mother did something she'd only done once before in Melinda's memory, on the day she'd said "Well, there's some truth to it": she folded her hands in front of her and stated an opinion.

"So what if they are?"

"So what if they are?" Melinda's father repeated, then looked at Tommy, who kept his head down and shoveled in his spaghetti. "So what if they are?" her father said again, and looked from Melinda's mother to Melinda.

Melinda, grown from a chubby child into a well-proportioned girl, chest buzzing with tension, looked at her father to confirm what she knew she would do anyway, which was agree with him. "Well, you should be ashamed," Melinda said. "If people are gossiping about you because of how you look."

Melinda's father pointed his fork at her and nodded vigorously. "Exactly!" he said. "Exactly!"

After that, Melinda's mother began to concede territory in their dark house to Melinda. She didn't knock on her bedroom door now at all—not to tell her about dinner, not to say good night—and never again turned on the TV in the family room while Melinda was reading. She hugged Melinda, but only if Melinda initiated the hug, and she stopped kissing Melinda on the cheek. For her part, Melinda ate less of her mother's fatty meals, stayed out on school nights with her boyfriend (to hold hands and smoke his father's cigarettes), and echoed her father's comments about her mother's weight. As her mother vacuumed the rug in the foyer, bent forward so her massive buttocks were vulnerable to Melinda's inspection, Melinda wondered if she shouldn't give second thought to that diet her father had mentioned. When her mother took a peppermint from the candy dish, Melinda asked her if she should be eating that. Melinda's grandmother had always said that a good child was seen and not heard. But now Melinda thought it was better to be heard and not seen: a beautiful, airy specter coaching her mother out of her sad life. A potential agent of change.

Once Melinda woke and caught her mother eating in the middle of the night. She'd baked a pie that afternoon and only Tommy had eaten a piece, complimenting her on its sweetness. Melinda had declined her mother's offer: she had an audition for the school play the next day, and she didn't want to ruin her complexion with sugar. Preaudition jitters had roused her from sleep, and she had gone downstairs for a glass of water.

And there was her mother in the dark, wearing her sack of a nightgown, licking the cherries from the fingers of her left hand as she scooped the pie crust with a fork in her right. Melinda flipped on the light.

Her mother looked at Melinda as though she'd just awakened from a dream. "What time is it?"

"Twelve oh seven," Melinda said.

"Hm," she said, and returned her focus to her plate. Melinda watched in revulsion as her mother raised the gooey contents of her fork to her lips, watched her swallow and sigh with pleasure. She went to the table and grabbed the fork from her mother's hand.

"Stop," Melinda said. "You weigh more than Dad."

Melinda had never seen this face on her mother before—wide eyes, a hurt and trembling lower lip—and wondered why she'd taken so long to show it to Melinda. She chewed the remaining pie in her mouth, made her face apelike by running her tongue over her top row of teeth. Then she scooped the rest of the pie with her hand and took another bite. Melinda grabbed the plate and pitched the remains into the garbage.

"Stop it," Melinda said.

Melinda's mother looked at her, chewing still. Her mother had cried at Rock Hudson movies, cried when Tommy "graduated" from nursery school, cried when her father hit a squirrel with the car—it would make plenty of sense for her mother to cry now. But she just kept chewing. She swallowed and crossed her plush wrists in front of her.

"Well, I don't know," she said. "It'll be hell for you someday, too."

Melinda ran from the room as though hexed. She hid under her sheets, hugging her knees. Her insides hummed with newly hatched bugs.

During her junior year of high school, Melinda underwent a growth spurt that made long, fat flippers of her feet and left a rash of pimples on her back. Her stomach swelled with fluid several days in advance of her period, with the result that she spent two weeks out of every month rotating among three cable-knit pullovers. She broke up with her boyfriend in the summer, and in the fall she took first place in the science fair for a project on laboratory behavior in dogs. Her father observed that she had a "brain for data" and asked her if she had considered becoming a secretary in an engineering firm. Tommy developed the obnoxious habit of reaching under her pullovers to tickle her stomach and telling her she needed to "reduce." When she asked him if it had anything to do with their mother, he shook his head and said he was just worried about her health. She applied to colleges, and Kent State offered her an academic scholarship. Her father drove her to campus on move-in day, singlehandedly carrying her heavy leather trunk up three flights of stairs to her dorm room.

At Kent State, Melinda monitored her body carefully. She ate only salads in the dining hall, drinking water whenever she felt hungry for something other than leafy greens. She had never been skinny, exactly, but she had never been fat, either: if she was careful, she could remain well proportioned, with hips and breasts that were frequently the envy of her suitemates. Eager to escape the suburban bread box of her childhood, she fell in with the hippie crowd, drinking dandelion wine and cheap beer, smoking grass in dorm basements, complaining about Nixon and Vietnam and "containing communism"—the pigs in the White House thought anything that wasn't capitalism could be sealed away like soggy leftovers. She kissed Jamie, who was leaving to join the Black Panthers. She participated in two hunger strikes to protest US imperialism. She met Leland.

Although most people in his circle were anarchists, he was the closest thing they had to a leader: a philosophy major and self-proclaimed "thinker." He always had drugs; people bought grass and magic mushrooms off him all the time. He walked around shirtless and barefoot, skipped half his classes but aced his finals. He was never not high, preferred turning on to going to protests, but he always managed to show up in time for the most exciting part of anything. Melinda thought his tastes ran more toward the tiny types on campus, but she'd thought wrong. He was obsessed with the way she danced, which she herself had always found awkward and kidlike. He called her "Sandra Dee from outer space." They dropped acid and she gave it up to him then, in his dorm bed, beams of light shooting out the soles of her feet. They started dating officially after that. She sent a photo of the two of them to her parents and mentioned that Leland had German heritage—which her father would approve of—but didn't mention that he was a Jew. Her mother wrote back: *You two make such a handsome couple.* Melinda nodded proudly at the compliment, ignoring the hot hint of guilt at the back of her neck. Her mother was right. They made a very handsome couple.

Spring 2009
Chicago

Nearly a hundred pounds heavier than her mother had been at her heaviest, Melinda watched as Leland Jr. slept in an industrial twin bed at Rush University Medical Center in Chicago, where he'd been hospitalized for three weeks following what doctors were saying had been a psychotic break. From what Melinda understood, he'd been touring a pharmaceutical factory, Cisco Drugs, someplace he had to be for work, and right in the middle of the tour he'd started hallucinating. He'd attacked the CEO (who had promised not to press charges) and slapped—or maybe punched, she didn't want to think about it too much—his own wife in the face. And, several minutes ago, he'd fallen asleep midconversation from some tranquilizers he'd been administered before Melinda started talking with him. Why they gave him the tranquilizers in the middle of the day—especially when she'd read on the Internet that tranquilizers could trigger catatonia, for which schizophrenics were apparently at risk—remained a mystery to her, and she didn't bother asking the nurses and doctors who spoke to her loudly if they deigned to speak to her at all, treating her as if she knew less about her son than they did. "Ma'am, your son is receiving the best care we can give him," one nurse told her, "and it makes it harder to provide him with that care when family members take their frustration out on us." They had taken a different approach with Melinda's daughter-in-law, Jocelyn. Patient, poreless, thin, doctors at least "understood her concern," and referred her to some hotline she could call for 24/7 support.

Her son had used his brief window of lucidity to discuss practical matters with her: whether people at work knew where he was, whether his front yard had been watered, whether Melinda wanted to leave the hotel and stay at their house. Melinda told him that was generous, but what she really wanted was to be closer to him, and going all the way out to River Forest and back every day without a car was a hike—*It's just the train to the green line to a bus, Mom.* In reality, she'd wanted to avoid the anxiety going on at her son's house: she'd spent an afternoon there when she'd first arrived in Chicago, Jocelyn rushing over to help Melinda every time she wanted to stand up or sit down, declining Melinda's offer to cook and instead ordering two sixty-five-dollar prepared vegan meals, spending two hours speaking with her lawyer on the phone. The hospital bill would be massive, she had said between calls, and they'd found some foreign substance in Leland Jr.'s bloodstream.

"It could be that the little brother and his friend poisoned him, and that triggered something." Jocelyn's young mind was already furred over with theories, Melinda could tell. "They've just been expelled for possession."

"Are you sure that's what it was?" Melinda asked, not particularly wanting to think about the little brother. The little half brother. "Have you talked to the doctors about how this kind of thing starts?"

But Jocelyn was now looking at the keypad of the only noncellular phone in the house, whispering to herself as though she were alone. "I shouldn't have pressured him like that. There was too much bad blood in the family. I should've seen this coming."

Her son wasn't sleeping, exactly—he was unrestfully unconscious. His jaw grinding was audible and his eyelids fluttered every few seconds in a way that made him look possessed. She flipped her phone open and saw that she had no new texts from Alvin—although that made sense, since he had a meeting with the school board. She closed her phone. Leland Jr. probably wanted her visiting hours to be over anyway. She mentally prepared herself for the walk from the hospital to the hotel, the sports bar where the college kids had accosted her earlier that day, already drunk at noon, pelting her with wadded-up napkins and asking if she knew what BBW stood for. She would call Alvin when she got to the hotel and give him the update he'd requested. She'd leave a long voice mail.

Leland Jr. grunted. She looked over at him and his eyes were open. He mewled like a child.

"Sweetie," she said. He didn't respond, which sent a horrible shock of adrenaline through her body. "Sweetie," she said again. "Leland."

He began to tremble.

"Leland."

He looked at her. "Mom."

"What is it?"

"Mom?"

She held his hand. He blinked a tear down his cheek. His voice was not his own.

"Mom, I'm a bad man."

"No! No, no. Oh, sweetie, no. Mr. Campbell said he forgives you."

"It's worse than that."

"And so does Jocelyn. They know you weren't in your right mind."

"It's even worse than that."

"What could be worse than that?"

"Something could."

Melinda blinked, watching him. He was the little boy with the gap between his teeth whom she'd failed to protect from his father. He was waking up in the middle of the night calling out to her, begging her to play "Desperado." He was always so nervous—he hadn't gotten a full night's sleep since 1979. That was probably why he'd gotten sick.

"I'm sorry," she said, shuddering with the realization that everything had been her fault.

He shook his head. "Mom, this isn't about that."

"About what?"

"It's about the briefcase."

"What briefcase?"

"Mom," he whined, "stop pretending."

"What do you mean?"

He grunted, rolled his eyes. "I took it from Lee and Diedre. It was locked and I never opened it. There might be money in there."

"I didn't know you even," she tried, but stopped herself. "Honey, you're imagining things. Please don't worry about it."

Then his face transformed: his eyes got huge, the tendons on his neck tight and large. His lower jaw out and rigid, he growled, "Believe me when I say what I did, Mom! For fuck's sake it was wrong what I did! Give it back!"

Then he held his head and screamed. She wanted to press herself comfortingly against him, but the scream was so horrible and not-his that she stumbled backward and nearly tripped. "Give it back to them! GIVE IT BACK!" he screamed. Melinda tried to tell him not to worry, that everything had been taken care of, but her voice sounded soft and pathetic in comparison to his. Two nurses pressed into the room behind her, one saying: "It would be best if you left."

So she left. She checked out at the front desk to the sound of her son screaming in protest against the nurse's harshly whispered assurances. As she signed her name on the visitors' sheet, the lower-right edge of which was dirty and curling, she remembered things she knew thousands of mothers before her must have thought about, standing in this very spot and signing their midwestern names—she read the three entries above her own: Pamela Joffrey, Louise Sheppard, Breanna Mullmann—as they applied cheap lip balm and thanked the bored secretary for the staff's (nonexistent) patience or sympathy or tolerance. She remembered how her child looked as he'd been happy (Christmas 1976: unwrapping a toy fire truck big enough to ride in), as he'd been sad (August 1983: after a fight with his father), and as she'd failed him (September 1978: in the car, silent, when she'd picked him up from school after he'd been sent home early for throwing a book). She scanned her memory for early warning signs of his illness. Had anyone even been thinking about mental illness in 1978? Kids played outside until they were tired, they came back in and did their homework and watched TV, you fed them, they went to sleep, and either slept through the night or awoke and required reassurance about the existence of ghosts or monsters. She had parented Leland Jr. on her own, protected his life, defended his passions. Had there been some new scientific discovery proving this wasn't enough? Would she herself have been better off being born later, giving birth to her son in the age of baby monitors and plastic-free cribs and organic teething rings?

But she was kidding herself. She wasn't some superparent who'd done the best she could with what she had. She'd smoked pot while she was pregnant. A lot of it. All the doctors in all the magazines said that was bad for any child. It was her fault he was the way he was. She'd known as far back as 1978 that she'd been at fault. She'd known on that day she picked him up from school after he threw the encyclopedia. Her worst fears had been confirmed on that day: he was his father's son.

She huffed a thick sigh in the mirrored elevator that brought her up to her hotel room. It was useless trotting out the woulda coulda shouldas, she'd always stressed that to Leland Jr. It was better to just understand everything in terms of good and bad luck. No real purpose to it all, just waves you either crested or were crushed by. Ever the pessimist, her son once asked her what you did when you got crushed by so many waves you couldn't even stand up to crest the good ones. "You pretend you can stand up," Melinda told him. "And then eventually you'll actually be standing." Then he'd asked, what if some deadly seaweed had just wrapped around your legs so tight and you just really couldn't stand up at all?

Bad luck was thick as thieves with their little family, of this much she was sure. Melinda could pinpoint the exact beginning of the end: late April 1970. She had been finishing up her communications degree at Kent State. Leland had graduated early and was working at Dog 'n' Suds. They were at a belated twentieth birthday party for Jeffrey Miller, whom they knew because he frequently bought grass from Leland. Crepe paper was taped to the walls and people roved around the room in cardboard party hats, eating cake off plates with Howdy Doody's face. Jeff was standing in the middle of it all dressed in an ascot and an old smoking jacket. "Welcome to your future, lovebirds," he said, offering them both flutes of champagne. "It's some snot-nosed kid's birthday party, and you're the chaperones." Melinda drank the champagne in one gulp and started seeing tessellating shapes that fit together to make a pocket watch, a complicated-looking thing that when viewed from far away was not a pocket watch at all but a globe, and then upon closer examination not a globe but the big, unblinking eye on the Masonic pyramid. A beautiful girl sat down next to her.

"Are you okay?" she asked Melinda.

Melinda nodded and pointed to where she thought Leland was standing. "My future," she said.

The girl smiled. "I'm Allison."

"My future husband," Melinda said.

Allison looked behind her and then back at Melinda. "Yeah, I think I know him." Her face soured. "Don't worry about him for now, okay?"

Melinda nodded. Don't worry about him. Light was coming off Allison's hair. Her hair was dark and thick, had those scented oils in it, went down past her shoulders. No makeup. She was beautiful and she didn't need makeup. Melinda tried saying that, but what came out of her mouth instead was the sound of wind in a tunnel.

"You're feeling it, right?" Allison nodded expectantly, her eyes wide.

Melinda nodded back.

"Is this your first time?"

Melinda was pretty sure it wasn't.

"It's fine," Allison said. "I'll stay with you. I'm going to ask you a question, okay? Have you ever thought about how each person in this country is like a gear in a grandfather clock?"

"Yes," Melinda said.

"Then it's like—I know you get me—then it's like a tyranny, right? Isn't that what's going on here?"

"Yes."

"With, I mean, I bet Nixon's going to threaten to invade Cambodia. And at this point who even agrees with him? Rogers? Kissinger? Even they know better. He's like one gear in the clock trying to take the whole thing over. And everybody's probably thinking: If he's the only one working and the rest of the clock is busted, then maybe it's the other way around, maybe the clock's working and he's busted. He's insane, and he's gonna make the whole machine fall apart, you know? Another example—"

Melinda tried to arrange the parts of her face so her expression suggested *Please, go on.*

"—another example is fucking J. Edgar Hoover. What do you accomplish by killing Malcolm X? Whom I liked better than King, by the way, he got straight to the point and King moseyed a little. But then what do I know, you know, since I'm white? Anyway, what do you accomplish by killing them other than proving you're some insane fascist sitting high up in his icy tower, trying to take over the world even as your little cabal's dwindling? It's like you're gonna end up alone, you asshole, you're all gonna end up alone. And what's worse is if we don't figure out something to do about it, then we're the broken gears, then the fascists still win, we all get pitched out in the same busted grandfather clock together. Emphasis on grandfather, you know?"

"Then we'd be useless."

Allison smacked her forehead. "Yes. Exactly! Exactly! You get me! What's your name?"

"Melinda Provouchez."

"Melinda Provouchez." She shook her head. "You're Jeff's friend?"

"I—" Catch-22: to explain herself she'd have to mention Leland again, but she'd been told not to worry about him for now.

"It doesn't matter, sorry, why you're here isn't important. You're on my frequency, I can feel it." She grabbed Melinda's wrist. "Have you ever thought about getting involved in politics?"

Melinda pictured Howdy Doody asking her: *Does politics mean lesbianism?* She laughed. Allison nodded deeply, as though Melinda had just made a lengthy and cogent point. "No, no, I'm feeling that. It's like, cheesy, right? It's cheesy to believe in anything when you're staring the pigs in the face and thinking: *Well, if we produced this evil, then it must be a part of us.* Which means we're going to become like it eventually. So why fight the inevitable?"

"I guess."

"But see, it's not like that!" Allison jumped up from her seat, her voice echoing as if they were both standing at the bottom of a chasm. "Seriously, it's not. You just have to be there with us. I'll show you."

And then Melinda made Allison "the most solemn promise ever" to come to all her protests.

◻

Not surprisingly, Allison was right about Nixon: on April 30, his bulldog face appeared on TV to announce the invasion of Cambodia. The protest was on the Commons the next day. Allison ran to hug Melinda as she saw her approaching. Jeff offered Melinda a sign that said BRING THE WAR HOME. They marched in a circle, screaming that war was murder and that it needed to be brought home. *Bring murder home?* Melinda had thought, but she didn't say it out loud. The protest was angrier than anything she'd ever participated in, but she didn't want to let on about that, so she screamed as loudly as she could. Allison pumped her fists in the air and told her she was a natural. Dr. Hoffmeier, whose entire American history class was marching on the Commons, stood in front of them, chubby arms crossed, smiling and shaking his head in a way Melinda could read as neither approving nor disapproving. Passing students paused to watch them, chant encouragement, take pictures. A small group broke off from their chanting circle, dug a hole, and buried a copy of the US Constitution, shouting that this was what Nixon had done to the real Constitution, he'd killed it last night on live television. Then Allison announced that there'd be another rally on Monday, same time, same place.

As she walked around campus on the days that followed, people watched Melinda as if she were a celebrity on vacation. She slumped down in her seat, pretended to ignore the attention, but really she relished it. She ate dinner with Leland in the boardinghouse where the two of them lived with twelve other scruffy boarders and listened to the landlady, Mrs. Donnovan, complain, as she usually did, about her daughters not understanding the value of a dime—"Do you kids not know that you save a dime every time you use the same lunch bag you used yesterday?"—and then kissed her future husband on the cheek, telling him she'd promised Allison and Jeff she'd get drinks with them in town. Leland gave her a long blink of his red-rimmed eyes and said he'd try to come by later.

"Melinda, *qué linda*!" Allison had shouted when Melinda walked in the bar. Jeff was next to her, leaning over a dark-looking beer and talking excitedly to a gaggle of guys on his right.

Melinda sat down next to Allison and for some reason felt compelled to rest her head on her shoulder. Allison combed Melinda's hair gently with her fingers and asked her how she'd liked the protest. Melinda said it'd been really great, it'd been far out, she couldn't wait until Monday.

"I'm so glad I found you," Allison said. "There aren't many people who're on this frequency we're on. Most people are down here." She held her hand below the seat of her chair, close to the floor. "They think they can solve problems with bullets."

Jeff turned around, and the gaggle of guys shifted to follow his attention. "Bullets?" he asked, his voice high and goofy. "That's no solution! What do you always say, Allison?"

She seemed game to play his straight man. "What do I always say?" She looked to Melinda, who did her part by offering an exaggerated shrug. "Oh, that's right!" Allison shouted. "Flowers are better than bullets!"

"Flowers are better than bullets!" he echoed, and the gaggle of guys echoed him. Someone ordered another round.

By the time Leland showed up, Melinda was sloshed. Her vision was accordioning and she was hugging Allison around the waist as they stood at the bar. Allison was trying to dance the Batusi, which everyone was telling her wasn't that different from the Watusi, but she insisted it was and said it had something to do with the arms. The music was loud, with a bunch of brass, the kind of stuff parents listened to. There were people in the bar who didn't belong to their group, older people who smelled like gasoline and leather. Everyone seemed to know the words to the song except for Melinda. Leland carefully peeled her off Allison and she put her arms around his neck. He smiled and told her she looked like she was having fun.

"I'm changing the world!" she shouted, spitting a little in his face, and laughed. He kissed her on the cheek and asked if she wanted to sit down. She told him she wanted to dance, so he led her through a four-step waltz he claimed his mother had taught him. She was nearly limp in his arms, letting him do most of the work. Her thoughts came barely punctuated. Allison and Jeff had disappeared somewhere and the lights flickered like before a thunderstorm. Someone pitched a beer stein at the mirror behind the bar. The bartender ducked, the mirror shattered, and a hoarse-sounding woman shouted, "Flowers, not guns!"

Melinda was forced up against Leland's chest as the crowd pushed past them, chanting and yelling like mashed keys in an untuned piano. A bearded guy took a hammer to the bar's front window. Melinda screamed "Allison!" but she was nowhere. Leland grinned at her. "Baby!" he said. She could barely hear him. She rubbed her temples, trying to cheat her vision into focus. He was mouthing the words *Baby, it's anarchy!* He grabbed her hand and they ran out in the street. Motorbikes were parked everywhere and people were heaving stuff through shop windows all down the block. Leland said something about how this was the logical conclusion to everything, and she asked him over the ringing in her ears what "everything" was. Then she called Allison's name again, a useless thing to do, and looked over to see that a cop had Leland pinned to the hood of his car, offering them a deal: they could either go peacefully with him and get off with a warning, or they could resist and get arrested.

Melinda and Leland went peacefully and were sent home after an hour at the station. Leland was revved up, delirious. In the room they shared, he told Melinda that America was falling apart, capitalism and democracy were crumbling, therefore it would be an excellent time to get married. *An excellent time to indulge in a capitalist institution?* she wondered, but she said nothing. Had Allison snuck out back with Jeff? Was Allison in love with Jeff? Leland began kissing her and she kissed him back. He unzipped her jeans and they had sex on the floor.

Governor Rhodes ordered the National Guard to Kent over the weekend. That familiar humming in Melinda's stomach returned, the sensation that she was being gnawed at from the inside. Her blood was feeding the bugs. Living was causing her death. She wanted to call her parents but she had no idea how she'd explain herself to them. They called her— Mrs. Donnovan knocked three times on her door, broguing "Ms. Prooo- voocheez! Telephone from Cleveland!"—but Melinda told her to tell them she had the flu. She needed time. She needed to find Allison.

Allison called her on Sunday night. "Oh, Melly, can you believe what's happening? The whole country's taking notice!"

"It's pretty amazing."

"It's bigger than any of us imagined. Did you ever imagine it getting this big?"

"I didn't."

"Rhodes thinks we're public enemy number one! And he's right! Peace is the enemy of fascism!"

Melinda knew from movies that every great revolution had its half- hearted sap who was always asking people if they really wanted to give up everything they loved for the cause—if maybe they could just rest easy knowing they'd come this far. Melinda was scared of Allison's tone, but Allison would probably hate it if Melinda were that sap.

"I'll see you tomorrow, okay?" Allison said. "I've got to go. We're planning."

"I'm sick," Melinda said.

"But this is history. You'll be there, right?"

"I'll be there no matter what."

"I love you, Melly," Allison said, and hung up.

The words stayed longer between her ears than Melinda would've liked. Her stomach lurched and she realized she'd forgotten to take her birth control. She opened her plastic clamshell: she hadn't taken any since Thursday. Her face slackened and she popped two pills at once. Then she sat cross-legged on her bed, paging through the copy of Antonio Gramsci's prison notebooks Allison had lent her.

She awoke the next morning with a raw throbbing below her navel. When she tried to shift her weight, her lower back protested. She checked for blood between her legs and found none. Leland was standing at the dresser, picking out a T-shirt. He told her he'd canceled his Dog 'n' Suds shift to go to the protest. What looked like a few grams of grass sat on the dresser in front of him. He probably figured he'd make more money at the protest than at work. Guilty, sweaty—their fourth-floor room was a heat trap—Melinda flopped onto her stomach and said she'd told Allison she was sick. She went back to sleep and was awakened hours or minutes later—she couldn't tell which. Leland was standing over her, pacing, explaining that the whole campus was swarming with militia and Jeff was dead, shot through the mouth. Allison was on her way to the hospital.

Melinda sat up in bed, innards howling. "She's dead, too?"

"I dunno, I didn't see it, I just heard it," he said in one breath. He sat down in the middle of the room and grabbed his knees. "It's gonna be slaughter." He looked at her. "We all thought they had rubber bullets, but they didn't."

She had the feeling that her entire life's progress had been lost in an instant.

She had to leave Kent. Her body was a bundle of raw nerve endings. There was only deadly quiet where her intuition had been. Her period never came.

She got her degree, married Leland, and they moved to Cleveland. For months, every major newspaper and magazine ran the picture of Jeff limp on the ground with the runaway girl kneeling over him, screaming. She didn't think about Allison: where she'd been standing, what she'd been wearing, how she'd felt when Jeff pitched the can of tear gas. Who'd shot her? Had she collapsed on impact? Melinda's body registered the child's kicks and little else. She grew larger without understanding that she was growing larger—her growth an extension of the child's will. She got her license and sold real estate and didn't think about Allison. And, for years to follow, the waves crashed over her until she could barely stand: the messy birth of her son, Leland in and out of NA, Leland Jr. cowering in terror of his father, the fight and the disappearance, her mother's death of a heart attack, her father's dementia, Tommy vanishing into a marriage with a woman who hated Melinda, her ensuing lonely period, her unpaid bills, her health, the briefcases.

The yellow briefcases.

He'd soldered one together and locked the other one shut, talking crazy about Reggie this and Reggie that and promising her that he would keep her safe. He'd taken both suitcases when he left. How could Leland Jr. have known about any of it? A new spasm of guilt shook her from the chest outward. She couldn't even begin to keep track of the ways she'd failed as a mother.

☐

She had come home from Rush and sat on her hotel bed, her feet throbbing as she undid her bra. Someone on TV was chattering about the Gaza Strip. Who had she been before he left her, she wondered. An automaton, a little aproned wife, the kind of woman Allison would've spit at. And when he finally lost his mind, she had spent her every day trying to keep him balanced—dusting the shelves twice, buying skim milk instead of 2 percent, unplugging the microwave in the middle of the night—all to keep from witnessing another outburst, to obtain another (usually empty) promise from him that he'd do something about his recidivism. If she was being perfectly honest with herself, she was frequently too stoned to notice how futile it all was. She should've known better than to think he couldn't sense her hypocrisy, demanding through her own haze that he "get help." And maybe he had been getting help, of a kind. She saw her son scowling from the driver's seat of her van during his last visit to Cleveland: "Where do you think he got all that money to snort up his nose? Honest employment?"

She bolted upright and called Alvin. One of few waves she'd crested in her adult life was Alvin Martinez, a fellow realtor. She'd met him the year Leland Jr. started work at Winn Maxwell. Fourteen years younger than her, Alvin had a seal-colored mustache and wire-brushed glasses, wasn't a fetishist but was pleasantly nasty in bed and completely devoted. So devoted that he agreed when Melinda suggested he leave ReMax rather than go public with—and thereby define, a hated word and practice of Melinda's—their relationship. And when she told him she'd never accept another proposal in her life, having wasted her youth playing house with a lunatic, he nodded gamely and said he hadn't planned on tendering one. She'd ignored the note of disappointment in his voice, offering to cut him free whenever he grew tired of their arrangement. Over a decade later, he still hadn't.

He picked up on the second ring. "Hello, love."

He sounded exhausted. When she asked him if he was, he promised he wasn't. She said she feared Leland Jr. may be psychic in addition to being schizophrenic. Alvin gallows-chuckled then apologized quickly.

"But in all seriousness," she said. Her tongue felt cottony: she took a Coke from the mini fridge and gulped it. "He knows about something he couldn't possibly know about."

"What is that?"

"Can you hear me?" she asked, but didn't wait for a confirmation. "It's a briefcase. Two of them."

"Uh-huh."

"Did I tell you about them?"

He said she hadn't. According to Leland, they'd contained "enough money to ruin all of us."

"Another one of his lies?" Alvin asked. "Or did they?"

"Did they what?"

"Contain enough money to ruin all of you? Jesus, how dramatic."

"I didn't look—I couldn't."

"Right." He sighed.

"I promised to keep it all a secret and he was so thankful. He stuck with the program for a while after that. Nothing happened so I figured it was all an act."

"What program?"

"The group meetings. NA."

"So it worked to entertain his delusions."

"Well, you know, who knows what he was mixed up in? He was so paranoid. He always kept these decoy wallets with fake IDs in them like he was going to be robbed. He wanted to build a decoy car out of wood. He told me having fake copies of everything was essential because his every move was being traced."

"Delusional ideas, love, that's what. They say schizophrenia can be hereditary."

"Leland isn't at all like his father."

She could almost hear Alvin shrugging. "Maybe you're right," he said, which was what he always said when he wanted to avoid a fight.

"The important thing is that—"

"What?"

She'd wanted to say "The important thing is that we weren't hurt." But that wasn't completely true. So she said, "It's just good that the police never had to get involved."

"A briefcase," he said, obviously attempting to shepherd her away from her memories. "That's symbolic. Like something in a dream."

"The way he spoke it didn't seem like a dream."

"Could be, but then you never know when someone's had a nervous breakdown."

"He said he knew I knew about it."

"Maybe in his hallucinations you did."

"It's just funny that there were actually briefcases."

"I know, love. But you can see how it's probably a big coincidence?"

She could. But then it would always be a big coincidence to Alvin, who'd lived his entire life in a world saner than hers. He came from a big family who sent detailed Christmas cards and loved Alvin from a respectable distance. Melinda promised to call him as soon as she had more information about Leland Jr.'s prognosis. She hung up. Alvin would want to worry with her, brainstorm recovery plans, help her vet doctors from afar. Play father to a son who could've been his brother.

Alone again, she took the numb, double-wide box of her left foot in her hands and attempted to rub it awake. Her doctor had recently warned that hers was the type of diabetes that would take her feet and vision quickly if she wasn't careful. She was supposed to keep her blood sugar balanced with a high-protein, low-carb diet, something she planned to do in two years when she retired. When she retired, she would special-order flattering dresses and go to the Shaker Heights farmers' market and rotate the selection of fruit and vegetables in her crisper daily. She would lose weight, which everyone except Alvin was fairly vocal about wanting her to do. There had certainly been a time when she herself would have wanted this as well. But now, after everything that could possibly go wrong with her flesh had gone wrong with it, promising to change it didn't make sense. She was living under a curse of bad waves—bad waves and bad news and bad luck—that much was obvious. Better to be a friend of fate than get on some desperate hamster wheel and sweat to death. A warm and uncomfortable current of electricity pulsed through her foot. She bit her lower lip in relief, closed her eyes, and started on the other one.

Against her closed eyelids was the specter of her son again, sound of mind and steering her van around a treacherous pothole in the road. What road? Was it in Shaker Heights? The 490? Was it a memory or a dream? "Wake up, Mom," he was saying, her handsome and capable son, pressing his thumb to the side of his chin. This was one of his habits when he was feeling tense. "He used you. I'm sorry to say this because it's difficult to hear, but he used you—he used both of us—and bled you dry and left us for dead. So why let him win?"

Tears slid from beneath her closed eyelids as the road and then the van fell away and her son shrank back to his pudgy child body, the space between his teeth widening. They were in his childhood bedroom in Glenville. He was pulling the comforter up to his chin. "Mommy," he said, "can you please tell me what you do when the seaweed takes your legs and you can't stand back up?" He'd been eight or nine when they'd last had this conversation. "You don't need to stand back up," she'd said, "because I'll lift you back up." How clearheaded she'd been that night! What a peaceful meal they'd all eaten together: vegetables (Leland Jr. cut them, she steamed them) and chicken Parmesan (Leland's mother's recipe). And they'd watched a movie on TV—a musical, *The Music Man*. No one was high. No one was even buzzed. That night was one of the few she could point to with confidence and say, "I started a family with the man I loved and it worked out." It had worked out. Or it had seemed to.

She put her bra back on, then her underwear, then her jeans. *I'll lift you back up*, she heard herself saying, *I promise I'll lift you back up*. He deserved her belief; she would find the briefcase for him if it was that important. She left the hotel and followed the Chicago Transit Authority's winding, transfer-filled path to River Forest, where she debarked the train at 11:09 p.m. (her phone's time, not hers) and walked the two blocks to her son's minimansion. The lights were still on. She rang the bell twice.

Jocelyn appeared at the front door, a giant, luxurious poncho-scarf wound around her tiny frame. Even in her own home, she seemed ill at ease. "Melinda!" she said. "What's wrong?"

"I'm sorry to be disturbing you," Melinda said.

"Disturbing me?" Jocelyn asked, and Melinda charged inside.

She turned on the light at the basement stairhead and surveyed the room beneath her. Contrary to her son's nature, the place was unfinished and disorganized. This was the kind of room she'd hide from prospective buyers if she were showing a house. She could see rebar in the exposed ceiling and tar splotches on the concrete floor. Jocelyn was tailing her, asking if she was okay, if there was anything she could do.

"I just need to see the basement," Melinda said. "For something for my son."

"Okay," Jocelyn said. "That's okay. Do you want to lie down first? Or I can come downstairs with you?"

Melinda ignored her. She went down the stairs and began looking for that damn mustard-colored briefcase.

Jocelyn's shrill voice came down the stairs: "Is there someone we should call?" *Better question, Jocelyn: Who was this "we" doing the calling?* Melinda shouted back up that she was fine and widened her search to a part of the basement that was especially dark and chaotic. Storage boxes chafed as she moved among them. One was sitting wide open, full of silverware she recognized from the Glenville apartment. Another box's tonguish flap lolled out to reveal a set of patterned blouses that were unmistakably hers. Both boxes had the word INHERITANCE scrawled on them. There was the wooden box with her grandmother's brooches. There were her old shoes, Leland Jr.'s GI Joes, the picture of the weeping Jews. She had the weird, light-headed feeling that this basement was where her son's dreams began, that the floor would give way to reveal his sleeping brain.

"Hello," said a male voice from the stairs. "Melinda?"

She turned around. The man was young, black, dressed in what looked like an expensive sweater and jeans. He wore the kind of frameless glasses her boss at ReMax wore. He had his hands on the banister as though he anticipated needing the leverage to back away quickly. "Hi," he said.

"Hi," she said back.

"I'm Caleb Marshall. Your son's attorney."

"Okay," she said. The name had ignited a pinprick of light in the depths of her memory. "Pleased to meet you."

She turned back to rooting through the mess. She heard Caleb descending the stairs, approaching, then he was standing behind her; she fell backward when she saw him up close, partly crushing a box of Christmas ornaments. He offered her his hand and she took it. The yellow light above them made dirty gems of the shattered glass.

"You're looking for something we've all been looking for," he said.

"What?"

His eyes softened, he raised his brows: she'd seen that same look of disgusted pity on so many faces before. "The briefcase. Jocelyn told me Leland can't stop talking about it."

"Yes," Melinda said, not knowing what else to say.

"If it helps you at all, I found it."

Her breath caught in her throat. "You did?"

Caleb nodded. "I hammered it open. Nothing but a couple of bricks and packing peanuts."

REGINALD MARSHALL

(1945–?)

May 8, 1973
Cleveland

The skyline over the buzz-cut prairie brush wore a glowing crown of electric fuzz as Reggie Marshall knelt on his right knee to address the bloody gash on his left. He looked up and there were Terminal Tower's yellow-dot windows, the spire that doesn't even come close to scraping the sky. He looked down and there was his knee broken open in the shape of a smile, his pants broken open, too, a smile within a smile. He touched the gash and winced so hard the pain made him drop to both knees, which hurt even worse. His whole body hurt like a motherfucker. Being him hurt like a motherfucker. He thought, *I'm the motherfucker who hurts like a motherfucker.* He thought, *Happy motherfucking birthday.*

He spun his head on its creaking neck-swivel so he was looking over his left shoulder, then his right. No one, but they still could've followed him all the way from the garage. And he was collapsed, crouching not twenty feet from the highway with his back to them, just begging them to run up on him. He was a pischer, as Sunny would say, which he thought probably meant your fool ass can't even remember to look both ways when you cross the street but in Hebrew-speak. Reggie put both hands on his head and dug his nails deep into his scalp, which he sometimes did to calm himself down. The right sleeve of his coat was torn up. A hollow-cheeked white man in a Cadillac drove by and slowed down to look at him like *We need to clean up these streets*, then sped off. If no one helped him, no one could find out what he was running from, and that meant much less of a situation. But if he was being honest with himself chances were small that he'd ever again walk into that apartment with the green tile on the ceiling, the apartment where Tasha had taken both his hands in hers and told him she wanted to spend the rest of her life with him. Six years after she'd told him that—just three months ago—he'd packed his father's old leather bowling bag with the four fake passports Sunny had made for him, five grand in cash, two of Tasha's old work dresses, a razor and shaving cream for him, and some jumpers and a picture book, *Baby Bear Is Hungry*, for the boys. That bag now stayed in the trunk of the sedan always. He was being realistic, not paranoid: shit happened in this business. He hadn't told Tasha about it because things like that disturbed her. She was sensitive and hard to read and he still wondered what she'd been watching for, staring soft-eyed out the window of her daddy's house on that first day he ever saw her. If he thought about it too hard, he got a tight little sadness in his chest. It sure as hell hadn't been him.

He could feel his heartbeat in his knee now, it was hurting so bad. His options were: (1) move back deeper in the grass and sleep there, or (2) walk west to Ohio City and find Sunny and tell him what had happened. Just below the skyline's chin was a chain-link fence crawling with weedy vines, keeping him from the Flats and the river and the rich white boats with bullshit names like SS *Salty Bottom* that were tied up to the dock. He could lean against the fence and sleep sitting up with his legs out in front of him, but now the gash was so full of dirt that even the air blowing over it stung so bad he had to bite the inside of his cheek to keep from crying out. He was a wimp about pain according to Tasha, and she would know because she'd given birth to twins in the bathtub at home. When he'd sliced his thumb chopping potatoes once, he had screamed so loud it woke Aaron the Brick up and got him crying, and even after Tasha had gone into the room to calm him down, Reggie was still dancing around the kitchen shouting about an ambulance. She had just clucked at him and said she hoped he never grew a uterus because that was what really hurt, he better fucking believe it. He had been so mad he had forgotten about his thumb and started in on a you-don't-take-that-tone-with-me lecture, the kind his father used to give. Then they both looked down at all the chocolate-syrup-colored spots on the floor and she looked back up at him like *Are you for real right now?* And she had been right. She had been so right.

Good Christ he missed her and it'd only been eight hours since he'd last seen her. He rose to his feet and stumble-jumped into the brush behind him, the grass whipping hard against his knee as he walked. He was lucky, actually. This whole thing could've gone a lot worse. He'd probably pissed off Shondor a little, but everybody pissed off Shondor. Shondor was born pissed off. Sunny would understand the situation. He was like the Shondor whisperer: if you did something dumb and you didn't know how to put it into words that wouldn't get you killed, you told Sunny and he'd make something up for Shondor and all you'd get was a slap on the wrist. One time a guy on the corner had gotten lazy and started letting junkies use in an alley a few blocks away; Reggie remembered the guy had these huge teeth like a cartoon horse and a permanent drip from blowing through Shondor's product. But luckily for the guy he was close with Sunny, they'd gone to the same temple growing up. Sunny told Shondor that he'd gone out to Glenville to see the guy and they'd fucked up the junkies and it turned out it wasn't Shondor's, it was Irish. And that calmed Shondor down and probably saved the guy's life. The guy told Reggie the whole story like he was preaching gospel. *I swear*, he kept whistling through his horse teeth, *I owe my life to Sunny. It ain't nobody else who'd put his neck on the line like that for me.* But then Shondor caught the guy in a smoke shop in Collinwood cutting fatties for his friends and he took him outside and shot him in the head.

Now all that stood between Reggie and the chain-link fence was a sick-looking tree. He watched the boats bobbing silently at the dock. He was about to sit down when the SS *Goodtimes* in front of him caught the reflection of some high beams. He took three steps back and kneeled on one knee again. The beams rolled across the riverbank, lighting up Reggie's torn right sleeve, his trembling hand. He ducked and threw himself back-first into the brush behind him, landing miraculously clear of any twigs or rocks. The mud was damp and thick and seemed to be filling his ears. He listened to the muffled sound of the truck's wheels. He thought about what he'd do if the truck stopped. It wasn't five-o in that truck, he knew, but it was probably the kind of redneck who'd kill to be one.

The truck stopped moving but the beams still shot light through the tops of the grass. Reggie tried to breathe less. He tried to count the number of windows in the skyline but it was too far away. He tried to remember the last time he'd been up close to Terminal Tower. It'd been when he'd taken Tasha to the West Side Market on their second date. He had bought celery, bell peppers, onions, and shrimp and taken her back to his place and cooked her gumbo. She had said he was a good cook and she wasn't expecting him to be one. His father was stretched out on the sofa that day, trembling and sweating, trying hard to pretend he didn't need his forty. Had his father met the boys before he died? It embarrassed Reggie that he couldn't remember. That was the sort of thing he should know.

Reggie's had been the last daddy standing in Hough, had only gotten locked up twice, once for less than a gram of grass and once for public urination. Reggie's mother used to call him "docile," which was the kind of word that made Reggie think of a deer or a dove. He was either happy or he was seeing withdrawal ghosts—the meanest he ever got was when his breakfast didn't come hot, and even then he just frowned and wouldn't talk to anyone for an hour or so. After Reggie's mother got taken away he made a habit of bringing Reggie to Hot Sauce Williams every Saturday. Reggie had liked watching him when the ribs were set down in front of him: his sleepy eyes got wider, his mouth smiled so his gums showed, his shaky hands tucking his napkin-bib into the front of his shirt. They had gone there so regularly that Lemaud Williams himself became friends with Reggie's father, calling him Sly because "I'm not tryna say 'Sylvester' every damn time I see you." It got so whenever they walked in the door Lemaud would walk out from the kitchen, wiping his hands on the towel in his apron, shouting, "Sly Marshall and Little Green Eyes are back!" The walls had been pink in there: whenever Reggie had a good dream as a little kid, even if he didn't remember anything in it, he always woke up seeing pink.

The truck finally drove off. Reggie exhaled hard and sat up. What the hell was he doing acting like a condemned man already? He bent his knee and inspected it in the moonlight. It was swelling up now, leaking still. He wasn't a condemned man. He hadn't used up his chance with Sunny. That was why he'd gotten as fucked up as he'd gotten—he was almost one of the guys as far as Shondor was concerned, he'd just run into a little trouble. Small-timers didn't run into trouble like this. Small-timers were disposable. Not Reggie. Reggie made bricks disappear. Shondor called him

Black Lightning, which Reggie hated at first but minded less when he'd heard guys calling Sunny the Schnoz. "The name's a compliment," Sunny told him. "It means he actually notices you." There was a lot worse in the world than being noticed. Why would you start anything if you're making 15K a year? Whenever he used to get mad at school, his mother would tell him never to bite the hand that feeds him, which was ironic since she'd pretty much bitten his father's hand right off and here Reggie was in a bunch of grass by the highway, not biting Shondor's hand. He dug both his hands in his pant leg at the knee and ripped it off. He tied it around the gash, whispering *motherFUCKER* the whole time because now it was Dockers against his blood and pus. If only his mother could see him now, hobbling back to the side of the road, breathing hard through his mouth because breathing normal somehow made the knee hurt more. She'd at least be impressed by his loyalty, probably raise those drawn-on eyebrows and say, "You starting to make your momma believe in God again." Now he could feel all the other places they'd fucked him up, the bruises on his sternum and right hand. The .45 was heavy against his belt. He still had that, at least. If he'd lost it, that'd be grounds for Shondor to end him.

He walked slowly, foot in front of foot, like his father used to walk right before he died. The skyline was still twinkling ahead of him—he was surprised by it. Why wasn't it giving up like the rest of the city? His father hadn't met the boys, Reggie remembered now. When Tasha was pregnant Reggie'd stopped by the place in Hough to tell his father the news, but his father had been on the floor when he walked in. He had rolled off the sofa onto his stomach. There were cornflakes sprinkled on his back and the Supremes blaring on TV. The cornflakes were damp with milk; the bowl was upside down on the sofa, still dripping onto his father's snoring head. "Dad?" Reggie had said, and his father didn't respond, didn't even move. "Dad!" he yelled, and his father's foot twitched, and Reggie felt small and pathetic the way he used to feel as a child, when his father would fall asleep on the sofa and his mother would smoke and stare at him like he was a stain she wanted out of the carpet. "Why did I ruin my life?" she'd ask him, and he'd say, "What you mean, Momma?" And she'd just shake her head at him, take a drag from her cigarette, and let the tears start falling behind her glasses. She had a rash across her nose and cheeks that never went away and always made her look angry. She said it was

Reggie who made her tired, but he figured out later it was her body attacking itself. His parents had been given bodies that hated them, made them grab for pipes and bottles—he'd done the same, he'd be lying if he ever claimed he hadn't. But they were worse and always had been. He only kept a little blow for special occasions because Tasha liked it, and he did knee-highs and sprints around the block and bench presses every morning. By the time Tasha was pregnant, he was stronger and sleeker than he'd ever been. When he found his father that day he had wedged his hands under his father's armpits and picked him up from behind, pivoted him, and sat him back down. "I was eating breakfast," his father had said, spitting milk as he spoke. Reggie asked him what else he remembered, but he just massaged up and down his left arm and stared into the obsidian of the now switched-off TV. The room had smelled like stale Schlitz and Maker's Mark. Reggie told him that this was the last straw, he couldn't keep on if he didn't go to a doctor or stop the drinking or both, and did he know that the whole reason Reggie came over was to say he was going to be a grandfather? His father turned to him and said, "A grandfather?" Reggie was hot with anger by then but not so much that he couldn't answer: "Yes!" Then he hung his head and whispered, "Goddamn," and his father wrapped his hand around Reggie's wrist like Reggie was a little kid again. That afternoon he made an appointment at the free clinic for his father but his father never went. Three months later, Reggie found him dead in the same position next to the sofa.

He'd always imagined Caleb and Aaron would grow up different than he had, with money and cars and the carefree laughter of rich white kids whose biggest problem was choosing where to go to college. He and Tasha already had a private school picked out for them, a Catholic kindergarten where they'd be taught how to count and spell before they turned four. They'd grow up to be twin doctors or lawyers. They'd have barbecues when Reggie and Tasha got old, the boys charcoal-grilling chicken while their children ran around Reggie's big backyard, Reggie telling some story about stealing soda or shoes or something as a kid, making his mother's temper into something batty and not dangerous, his father's drinking charming and not sad. The boys would laugh admiringly and Tasha would squeeze his hand. Caleb (he had always been more talkative) would say, "Dad, we're so glad we didn't have to deal with any stuff like that growing up." And Aaron would laugh and nod, pull his little daughter up onto his shoulders while she screamed "I'm too tall, Daddy!" because she'd be scared of heights, but he'd be such a good father that she'd trust him anyway. And Reggie would say, "It's true! Only in America could you start out like that and end up like this!" And Tasha would get her deep scholar's voice on and tell him to stop being so goddamned patriotic about a terrorist slave state. She was too smart for him and he knew it but she loved him still. Thank God she loved him still.

A car shot past him doing at least eighty if not ninety. Drunks shouldn't be allowed to drive—he could say this from experience. All those nights when he was a kid sucking down Wild Turkey, cruising around with Cookie and those other guys from the block: Rell, Kingston, Daevon. Miracle he didn't T-bone someone. Miracle he'd done all the things he'd done and still lived. He reviewed what he'd tell Sunny: he'd gone to the garage in Lakewood to find the guy Shondor wanted killed, found and killed him, hadn't counted on the guy's two friends being there. Then they'd tried to kill Reggie (specifically, Reggie scuffled with the one for his gun but ended up having to shoot him twice in the chest, then the other came at him with a knife, swiped hard at his arm, and tried to kneecap him but Reggie shook him off and killed him, too), and he'd done it all without leaving any evidence. They had clearly been foot soldiers, couldn't even handle Reggie between the two of them. It was pathetic how lazy their operation was run. He lived minutes from Little Italy and nobody was trying to stop him from picking off greaseball pawns.

Walking was easier as he got used to the pain. He passed the Cleveland Soapbox Derby track, its silver plaque looking blunt and knifelike without light to catch. He walked over the bridge above the flats, looked into the still-bright factory windows at the people in jumpsuits and goggles walking back and forth. One of them was looking out the window at him, and Reggie considered waving before the window went dark. It had to be at least ten o'clock, if not eleven. He had never understood how anyone kept a job like that: clocking in at nine in the morning or earlier, being forced to work overtime by a boss who wouldn't pay extra. If there was a way out of that hustle, why not take it? Tasha was always telling him to have compassion for people who didn't understand the boxes they were trapped in, and he tried to for her sake, but he couldn't see how anyone wouldn't want money if they had the chance to get it. Maybe people who'd always had it, people like the ones in Tasha's graduate classes who kept criticizing the "greedy bourgeoisie" and saying the world needed a revolution led by the poets. Whatever the fuck kind of revolution they were trying to start, Reggie had been getting rich the whole time. He'd gotten hired instead of killed by Sunny: could a poet do that?

He'd entered the city limits and none of the cars driving past him were slowing down to watch his crooked walk. When there was a gap in traffic he ran screaming in pain to the median, then ran from the median to the sidewalk and collapsed on the grass gasping, staring at the smoggy sky. The first time he'd kissed Tasha they'd been sitting on the Central Avenue bus headed east into the best sunset of his life, packed full of pinks and oranges and purples and blues: a sunset on acid. Tasha had told him Cleveland had sunsets like that because of all the factory fumes and he said that if he could watch sunsets like that for the rest of his life, he'd live right inside a steel factory, which made her roll her eyes and laugh. He knew he had her then, even though she was so far out of his league he couldn't see where she was standing.

He sat up and looked around him. A pack of drunk kids was walking up the street singing a song he didn't know—a bullshit folk song, probably. One of them stepped aside and parted the curtain of his hair, staring right at Reggie. The kid nudged him with his foot. "Hey, man," he said. Reggie lay back down. "Hey, man," the kid said again, "bad trip?" Reggie could hear the other kids snickering. The kid nudged him again, and then the nudging became a little kick. This one's lights are out, Reggie heard one of them slur, not the one who'd kicked him. He opened his eyes and now a girl was standing over him, white like the first kid, with worm-thin lips and fat cheeks. She laughed from deep in the back of her throat and made a sound like she was about to hock spit in his face. Instead he kicked her in the calves so she fell screaming to her knees, and when the long-haired one shouted "What the fuck?" and came at him, Reggie got to his feet in time to deliver a haymaker. Then he ran, the pain in his body gone, the kids screaming "Somebody call the police!" behind him. A helpless laugh escaped him as he ran. You really had to pity anybody stupid enough to believe in the police.

Detroit and West Twenty-Eighth: pink neon flickering the words MAS-SAGES OPEN at him. He got out his key and jammed it in the knob and the door came open in his hand. He was inside; the curtains were drawn, the room was dark. The back-room light was off. He reached for the switch next to the door and the Christmas lights along the molding snapped on to reveal the velour chairs, the girls' skirts and pasties laid out on the wood-and-leather tabletop, and, before he could even make sense of what he was seeing, the blinking red eyes of some wino. Reggie screamed and the intruder screamed, covering his face with a pair of raggedy-gloved hands. Reggie pulled the gun from his pants and cocked it, which made the man whimper "God no Reggie no." And then Reggie realized it wasn't a john or a wino: it was Leland Sr., the cokehead who always asked for Reggie by name.

"Jesus fucking Christ," Reggie said. "Why are you here? How did you get in here?" Leland Sr. shrugged and started blubbering as if this were the first time he'd ever tried talking. The only time Reggie felt bad about what he did was when he started to notice junkies deteriorating. When he first met Leland Sr., he'd been a skinny hippie with a days-old beard and some scrap-metal job and a wife with a kid on the way. Reggie didn't really pay attention to the people he met on the corner aside from how much money they had and whether they looked like liars, but Leland Sr. was like gristle in your teeth. He'd come up to Reggie and start talking and no matter how many times Reggie pushed him away his stupid ass would find a way back in an hour or two, yammering about how the president was a bitch and he couldn't refinance the mortgage on his house and how "medicine" made him stronger. Eventually Reggie just gave in and listened, because some days he was kind of entertaining and there was no getting rid of him once he got going. But Leland Sr. was the kind of stupid that couldn't take a hint, and he started to think he was Reggie's best friend. As in, he invited Reggie to dinner with his wife in what Reggie assumed was going to be a nasty Glenville two-bedroom, probably all dust-motey, the carpet full of cat shit, to which Reggie said, "Seriously, man? You inviting your pusher to dinner?" And Leland Sr. made some joke about *Guess Who's Coming to Dinner*, which made Reggie's skin crawl so much he slammed Leland Sr. in the jaw. The punch had knocked him down but he just stumbled up from the ground laughing, probably too numb to take a hint. Recently, Reggie would hide when he saw Leland Sr. coming, take a mid-afternoon hit if it meant avoiding Leland Sr.'s pasty speed-freak mouth.

"I got in through the front door," Leland Sr. said. "I picked the lock.

We share a birthday today, remember? I wanted to wish you happy birthday." Reggie threw his hands up. *When did I tell this hebe weasel motherfucker about my birthday?* he thought, but didn't say it. Instead he spun around so he was looking Leland Sr. in his sad-sack face and said, "I have business to do, man. You gotta leave."

Now he could feel Leland Sr. taking him in, his whole jacked-up self, so he moved to the other side of the room and pretended to be busy sorting pasties. "What happened to you?" Leland Sr. asked, and Reggie said, "It's better if you don't know." But Leland Sr. wanted to know—he was standing behind Reggie, breathing heavy on his neck, offering to fuck up whoever had fucked him up, until Reggie turned around and pushed him away. "I don't need your punk ass helping me!" he shouted. "You acting like a faggot!" That last part shut him up. Leland Sr. apologized and held his hands folded in front of him like a singer in a church choir, saying he didn't mean any harm, he was just getting desperate for a re-dose, his wife was making him see this headshrinker and it was driving him insane. "My whole goddamn life don't revolve around you," Reggie said. He began opening and rearranging the boxes on the shelf in front of him—water-damaged copies of *Hustler* and *Penthouse* mostly—hoping Leland Sr. would take the hint and just leave. But when he turned around the asshole was waving a hundred-dollar bill in his face. "I got this doing a favor for a guy at the Ford plant," he said, like Reggie gave a fuck. He sighed and grabbed the money. "Let's make this quick," he said, and Leland Sr. nodded, his face now like an obedient dog's. Reggie went downstairs to the basement, where the girls sometimes slept if they were going through a rough patch. There was one there that night, her greasy hair spun out sunray-style from her head, her face grimacing in sleep. Reggie would never think of touching one of them, but he knew the others did. He tiptoed past the girl to the safe in the back, opened the lockbox in the safe, and fished around for an eightball. Then he brought it upstairs and threw it on the table. "This is all we got left," he lied. "You gonna have to break that bill or take what I give you." Leland Sr.'s eyes got huge. He grabbed the bag, ripped it open, and dipped his pinkie inside. He snorted it up and did that two or three more times before his eyes got glassy and his head perked up on its grasshopper neck. "This feels Colombian," he said, and Reggie shrugged. "Honestly, man, can I just stay here for a little bit?" Leland Sr. asked. "My kid is sick and my wife is gonna be sitting up with him and if you kick me out I'll just go stand across the street." Reggie made a sound like a bull snorting. What was stopping him from breaking this stupid motherfucker's neck? He watched Leland Sr. do his sad little bumps. Outside a car rolled past slowly, bass pounding. There was something about him Reggie couldn't understand. He hated him, but hurting him would feel like kicking a stray dog. He had a philosophy that the kind of person who deserved to be on the receiving end of a barrel was also the kind of person who'd been on the firing end, and Leland Sr. had never been on the firing end.

"Just sit under the table," he told Leland Sr. "And be quiet." Leland Sr. started sputtering his thanks, offered as he always did to put himself on the corner if Reggie ever needed help. "Shut the fuck up, man," Reggie said. "You make one sound and I'll kill you." He remembered his mother telling him he was a promise breaker and that was why she hated him. She was halfway out of her mind by then, weeks away from being hauled off by the police. She was standing over Reggie in the kitchen with a knife in her hand. She was freebasing by then, the rash across her nose bright red and scabbing. The knife was the one he'd seen her use to slice the turkey's neck two Thanksgivings ago. Reggie was shaking in his undershirt, knees to his chin, tears down his cheeks. He was eight. He was asking into his knees, "Why am I a promise breaker?" He couldn't help it, he just wanted her to tell him so he could fix it. But every time he spoke, the whites of her eyes got angrier and she said, "You promised to love me and you ain't delivered on it!" Then she brought the knife down in the carpet in front of him and he jumped back and ran.

Leland Sr. crawled under the table and Reggie bolted the front door, then unlocked the door to the back room and bolted that, too. He turned on the single lightbulb and the room blinked into focus. Clients sometimes met girls back here—if it was a slow night, Sunny would turn it into a private room and one lucky john would get to turn a girl out on top of Sunny's mother's old kitchen table. Right now the room was almost empty except for some old shoes stacked high enough against the wall to reach Reggie's knees. He didn't want to think about whom they belonged to.

He sat down at the table and put his pistol in front of him. The clock on the wall said it was almost midnight. Reggie had been running late, but Sunny wouldn't have come and then left without seeing him. The idea that he would've made Reggie sweat a little. There was no reason for Sunny to

give him the money other than Reggie was loyal and everybody liked him.
Even the assholes who did nothing but bust people's faces for Shondor
thought Reggie was pretty stand-up. He was family. For the first time in a
long time, Reggie's knee screamed out and he squeezed his thigh to dis-
tract from the pain. He could feel his chest turning in on itself like the
hollow side of a spoon. Reggie thought of the girl trying to spit in his face
and replaced it with a thought about his sons eating Cheerios. Caleb always
picked them up one by one and Aaron just slammed handfuls into his
mouth. He suddenly regretted not bringing up a dub bag from the vault
for himself.

The back door opened and Sunny came in holding the briefcase, which
was stupidly canary colored and had all kinds of shit locking it up on top.
Reggie was relieved that Sunny had shown, but his face looked like the
stretched-back faces of those astronauts in the g-force machines on TV.
"Hey," Reggie said, and Sunny jumped and wailed, "What the fuck is
wrong with you?" Reggie shook his head, trying to look like *Don't start
something*, but he could never look that way with Sunny. Sunny, who came
across more as a needle-nosed accountant motherfucker than Shondor's
right-hand guy, with his button-down shirts and his high socks and the way
he had of putting so much waxy shit in his hair it looked like he got it
buffed at the car wash. Back when Reggie and Cookie were desperately
pushing their own grass on Scovill and East Fifty-Fifth, Sunny had come
up in a Cadillac one day to buy from them. Reggie, stupid kid that he
was, agreed and got right in the passenger seat. Then Sunny had a gun
in his ribs and as quick as he could Reggie whipped out his own gun and
shot Sunny in the shoulder. He still remembered being terrified of the
sound it made, and that little girl jumping rope outside the rec center
who looked through the car window dead at him. And Sunny, who
should've been weeping from pain, laughed. He'd looked from Reggie to
the little girl and asked him who his boss was. That was the start of the
whole thing.

But now Sunny wasn't looking the way he did in the car. He was small
and sunken. Reggie was starting to feel sick: Sunny's paler-than-pale face,
his own throbbing knee, the lunatic babbling away in the next room. "Were
you here earlier?" Reggie asked, and when he got no response: "Is that
the money?" Sunny nodded, staring at a place in the wall past Reggie. "Yes
what?" Reggie asked, but Sunny said nothing. Then he opened the brief-

case on the table. The bills were two stacks deep and wide enough to fill the entire thing. "That's it," Sunny said, then sighed and closed it. "I'm supposed to be dead." Reggie wanted to reach for the leather handle but held back. "What do you mean?" he asked, and Sunny began to cry. He thought it was a joke but the crying didn't stop. "My wife and kids," he said—Reggie had met all of them, Alma the Spanish girl and their two cinnamon babies, always squirming around, asking Uncle Reggie can we play Connect Four? He was surprised Sunny was capable of a woman like that, but then Sunny surprised everyone.

"Your wife and kids what?" But Reggie didn't really want to ask. Sunny shook his head and sucked his teeth. "Blown up in my car," he said, and shuddered so hard Reggie thought for a second he was having a stroke. "Blown up outside the dentist's." They both sat still, but Reggie could feel the room getting smaller. "It was meant for me," Sunny said. Reggie didn't hear much past "blown up." His first thought was to go home. Go home immediately: run if he had to. Fuck the money. But his second thought was, *Get the money, then go home.* He latched onto the briefcase handle but Sunny shook him off. "You're supposed to be dead, too," he said. "He's liquidating. He doesn't trust anyone anymore. I'm not supposed to have this briefcase still." Reggie wanted to know what the fuck it meant to liquidate a business like this but it didn't really matter. He tried again to grab the briefcase but Sunny shook him off, hard. "Come on, man," Reggie said, "I did the job, now give me the money." But Sunny was pacing back and forth, making these little hiccup noises. "He's basically my father," he kept saying. "He can't do this to me." Then he stopped. "I love him like a father," he said, staring Reggie dead in the face, his eyes huge and vacant. And then he brought what Reggie recognized as his favorite Beretta to his own temple. Reggie was on his feet, saying "Holy shit holy shit." He got the gun out of Sunny's hands and held it away from him. "Stop it!" he said, and then Sunny's little man-boy frame fell into Reggie's arms as he wailed. "You're so stupid," he said into Reggie's shirt. "It was supposed to be three guys there today. You're supposed to be dead. You know how I know that? I planned it. Shondor told me to." Reggie held him up and said, "You and me can get away. You got the money, I got a car, you can come with me and my family." Sunny snorted, the old laugh he did when one of the guys said something really stupid. "You seen too many movies," he said. "I'd rather be dead than be alive without my wife and kids." Then Reggie's jaw went crooked and he didn't feel any of the pain until he hit the ground and realized Sunny had punched him.

Reggie should've run when he had the chance. Tasha would've said fuck the money. His body hurt now so much he couldn't move. His ears were buzzing, making everything Sunny was saying a faraway hum. Like someone had hit a gong hard and then just let it ring and ring and ring. He remembered Cookie played drums in junior high. He got so good that they made him part of a program where he went on a bus to Shaker Heights to play in a youth orchestra, and one time Reggie went to see his show at the high school there. Cookie had done the same dumbass face he always did whenever he saw Reggie—tongue stuck out, eyes crossed— and Reggie was laughing so hard, because instead of doing it at the cor- ner shop or the gas station, he was doing it while wearing a suit on a stage full of white and Asian kids. The conductor said, "We'll be playing Prokofiev's concerto in something," and Reggie watched Cookie bang on the drum at the back of the stage, fast and loud and with perfect rhythm.

The last time he saw Cookie was four years ago. He had been trying to leave the woman he had his first kid with, a girl he kept calling "bossy" but who Reggie thought was calm as a swan. They were smoking at Reg- gie's place, trying to think of how to make more money. Reggie had just been fired by the postal service and Cookie was posted up on the corner. "Why don't you get back in it?" Cookie asked, and Reggie actually thought about it, the shit in his head making everything foggy. "Ay, it'll be like school days," Cookie said, his little cherub face scrunched up and laugh- ing. "It's like being sixteen again." The last thing Reggie wanted to be was sixteen again: making his father's rent, ripping up his mother's postcards from the crazy house. But who else was going to pay him? He was getting rejected everywhere he applied. He was in love with a girl and he needed to get paid.

He had officially been fired from the postal service for stealing from mailboxes, which he had never done. That was back when he was deter- mined to "fly straight" and "have a career." His route had taken him through Cleveland Heights, and every day he had to walk past the house of this ancient white woman who had a mouth like a toenail clipping all screwed up on the side of her face. Every time he pulled up into that neigh- borhood she was at her door staring him down, and once she even shouted, "I know why you're here and I can let the police know, too!" He tried to keep his head down, only speak if spoken to. But one day in that neigh-borhood, in a house several streets over, he noticed a girl standing in a second-floor window, looking out into the sky. She had been playing with her necklace, her one arm crossed over her stomach. He'd seen girls in Hough who looked a little like her, but none of them stood the way she stood, made that serene face she was making. She was more beautiful than all of them put together.

He parked and got out of his truck to deliver her mail, which he really didn't need to do because he could've just reached through the truck's win-dow, but he wanted to stand on her driveway and get her attention. He saw she'd seen him and was leaning forward to take him in, both hands on the windowsill, her face gentle and curious. He had waved up at her, chin to dumbass chest Cookie-style because he didn't know what else to do. She had laughed silently and waved back. She wore a sweater that showed her shoulders and a pearl necklace he'd later find out was made of something called Bakelite.

Every day after that he got out of his truck to see her. He did this even though she wasn't always there. Eventually she showed up every day, wav-ing like she'd been expecting him. Sometimes she'd point to her watch and shake her head, like *Look how late you are*. He'd point to his wrist and shrug: *I don't have a watch*. She'd laugh. When she laughed, she hugged her shoul-ders and turned a little from side to side. She was small, he could tell.

One day, she had walked outside and down the driveway. She looked at her feet even though he knew she knew he was watching her. She put her hands on the mailbox and smiled up at him. Then she stuck her hand out for the mail.

"I want to bring it up to the house personally," she said. Her first words to him.

"Who's living in that house with you?" he asked.

"My daddy," she said. "My momma. And my sister."

"Full house."

"Yeah."

They looked at each other a little longer, smiling.

"You go to school?" he asked.

"Yeah. Axel Renfroe College. It's one of the Black Ivies."

He nodded like he knew it, but he didn't. He could tell she saw right through him.

"My daddy teaches there," she said. "He's a professor of history."

"Would your daddy mind if I called you?"

She lost her smile for a second, and he waited.

"I'll be right back," she said. He didn't even know her name and she had left him standing at the foot of her beautiful driveway. He was about to drag himself back into the truck when she emerged from the house, skip-running down the driveway, a piece of paper in her hand. Breathless, she gave it to him. There was a phone number, and above it her name and a message: Natasha Harrison. Below the phone number was written: *Call after 7:00 p.m.!* Now, whenever she told the story, she was always saying she'd written something different. The message in that note was one of the few things they could never agree on.

He got fired the morning after that, the patchouli-smelling supervisor who'd hired him saying, "We should've known better than to take a risk on you, Reginald." That night he called the number at seven o'clock exactly.

Reggie was thinking about all of that while Sunny reached down to remove the Beretta and the .45 from his pockets. His eyes were up on the ceiling and his knee was oozing and a tooth had come loose from his jaw. *Damn, I should've just said no when Shondor asked me did I wanna do him a big favor for big money. Sunny's a fucking idiot if he ever thought he was family. I'm a fucking idiot for ever thinking I was family.* Then he was thinking of his real family, thinking of Caleb and Aaron in their matching cribs with the duckie bunting Tasha had picked out, thinking of Cookie and his goofy-looking daughter with Cookie's same busted teeth, thinking of his dead father and probably dead mother. Good fucking Christ he'd felt so small so many times in his life. Why, from the minute he was born, did so many people want him dead? What was so wrong with his being alive?

He wished things had gone differently. Out of his bloody mouth he whispered the words, "I wish things coulda been different." And then Sunny fired the .45 at his head.

LELAND BLOOM-MITTWOCH SR.

(1945–1999)

May 8, 1973
Cleveland

His wife thought he was a badly disturbed man, so he had agreed to sit in a room with someone he hated and talk about his earliest memory. And now here he was. The memory came from the year 1949 and found him standing in the kitchen behind his mother, listening to her tenderize a chicken breast with a stainless steel mallet. This noise was the loudest he'd ever heard associated with his mother, and the fact that he could only see her back—the carefully pressed Peter Pan collar of her dress, the knot of her apron, the shine of her shaved calves muted by panty hose—made him upset. In front of her like blank-faced cronies stood two refrigerators: one for meat and pareve and a shorter one for milk. He wasn't tall enough to see her arm raising and lowering the mallet: the sound could just as easily have been the result of something that was happening to her as something she was making happen.

Leland Sr.'s therapist was named Leonard Ulberg. He smelled like salmon and wore, for his extreme farsightedness, the kind of thick-framed black glasses that had gone out of style thirteen years ago. When Leland Sr. told him the memory, Ulberg leaned forward and said: "What does it feel like to remember?"

"It doesn't feel any way," Leland Sr. said. "It feels like a thought."

"What kind of thought, Leland?"

"About how maybe it was happening to her." He realized he probably shouldn't have told Ulberg this memory to begin with.

Ulberg folded his hands in his lap. "This was the first house you ever lived in, right? What was it like being in the kitchen of this house?"

It wasn't a house, it was an apartment, but Leland Sr. didn't see the point in correcting him. He shifted in his seat. "I don't know."

"Did you like being there?"

"No."

"Why not?"

Why the hell does anyone like being in his kitchen? Why was he being subjected to this, and on his birthday?

"I don't know," Leland Sr. said, and stared neutrally back at Ulberg.

The apartment had been in Cleveland Heights. They had moved there because his mother, Sarah, knew one other Sachsen-Anhalt family who lived in the area. The family's name was Brecht and every Friday and Saturday they went to temple at the Kinsman Jewish Center, which used to be mostly German-Hungarian and very frummie but had since opened its doors to any dedicated kosher-keeping Jews who'd escaped their home-town pogroms. The Brechts had two kids, Amos and Ruth, and they didn't get along that well with Leland Sr. and Leland Sr. didn't get along that well with them.

Cleveland Heights may have been called the Heights, but it wasn't, and just one of the ways you could tell was by the quality of the grocery store. The place was small and dirty and had a flickering light in the meat aisle. Leland Sr.'s mother spoke with irritation about the old Negro man who was always trying to fix that light, carrying on about how the manager must've hired him out of charity because the Negro man always did things too slow and bungled the job. She was happy when the manager fired him and hired a Jewish veteran with a missing eye who fixed the light the day he started. The grocery store made Leland Sr. depressed, even as a little kid. His mother always bought gray-looking meat just because it was blessed by a rabbi. The little circles of salami he couldn't have looked so tender and delicious.

"What were you thinking about just then?" Ulberg asked.

He'd been thinking about food he couldn't have as a child. A polyp of ill will exploded in his brain. "Well, I feel better!" he barked.

Ulberg laughed his Austrian gallows-laughter. "If only it were that easy, huh?"

Leland Sr. laughed back harshly. "No. No, it's not." He half rose. "But would you mind if I just use the restroom quickly?"

Ulberg gave him a neutral look. "Go out my office, take two lefts—it's at the end of the hall."

Leland Sr. did as he was told. His brain was itchy and hot and he regretted neglecting it for so long. What he was thinking about now was the Kinsman Jewish Center and the fat face of Amos Brecht as he shoved Leland Sr. down the stairs one Shabbat. Leland Sr. couldn't have been older than seven. He'd been crying and bleeding from the knee. Sarah had run to him without saying anything to Amos, who stood at the top of the stairs, picking his nose. It was Mr. and Mrs. Brecht's place to punish him. Leland Sr. couldn't remember if they had. He couldn't remember what had happened to Amos, either. He'd probably gone off to law or med school and then returned to the Heights to practice. The Brechts were known for driving Amos and Ruth hard, even though they were both stupid kids.

Leland Sr. entered a stall in the bathroom. He removed a small, tightly wound, and almost empty baggie of medicine from his coat and then removed his keys from his pocket. He opened the baggie and dipped his house key in and brought the ridged end up to his right nostril to do a little bump. He did another one at his left. As he was doing this, the door opened and Leland Sr. could see the loafers and ankles of a pair of Farah slacks. He stopped midsniff. He should've been panicking, but he was thinking instead about the little roll of skin between the bottom of Amos Brecht's head and the top of his neck. Leland Sr. needed at least four bumps for this to work and didn't really care what the loafers and slacks thought of him. He flushed the toilet once. Then he got down on his knees and made sounds like he was dry heaving. He collected spit in his mouth and let it drop into the bowl. He made sure to gag on the spit a little before releasing it. If he could've produced a wet fart, he would've. The loafers and slacks paused by the sink; there was the sound of running water. Leland Sr. flushed the toilet again and then again. The loafers and slacks left, not doing what they had presumably come to do. Leland Sr. stood up and arranged things for his third bump. He sniffed it up, right nostril, and said under his breath: "Fucking Brecht." Then he did his fourth, left nostril, and sucked on the tip of the key. The key wasn't enough, so he broke

a little rock in the baggie with his pinkie and ran it over his gums. He left
the stall and looked at himself in the mirror. He picked at his nostrils. He
doused his face with hot water until it was pink. Then he dried it with a
paper towel. He tilted his head backward, using the angle to get a view up
his nose. He sniffed once more and left the bathroom.

When he returned, Ulberg said: "You were in there a while."

"Well, yeah. I was thinking."

"Thinking about what?"

Leland Sr. could answer this one truthfully. "Amos Brecht."

"Who's Amos Brecht?"

"He was the son of my parents' friends."

"Was he your friend?"

"No. We went to temple together."

Ulberg nodded, considering this. "Why wasn't he your friend?"

"I dunno. He shoved me."

"He shoved you."

"Yep."

"How did you react?"

"I cried."

"What else?"

"Nothing else."

This wasn't true. Leland Sr. had held the grudge until Purim 1954. This
was four years before Kinsman was sold off and became the Warrensville
Center Synagogue, when the Purim celebration had still been in a shabby
little banquet room where the adults got drunk while the kids acted out
the story of Esther and Mordecai on a thin "stage" that was just two mess-
hall tables flush against each other. Leland Sr. was playing Haman. Ruth,
thin-haired and sow-looking, was playing one of Esther's attendants. Amos
had gotten the role of King Ahasuerus: all he had to do was pretend he
couldn't fall asleep, which wasn't a problem Leland Sr. guessed Amos ever
had. Leland Sr. liked wearing the ugly Haman mask and hearing the noise
of the graggers whenever his name was announced. He played such a convincing Haman that the rabbi pulled him aside and promised him the role
again next year.

After the rabbi complimented him, Leland Sr. went outside in his
Haman mask to where the other kids were playing. They were all wearing
their coats and kicking the dirty snow; some had started a game of chas-

ing one another with sticks. Amos and Ruth were playing together, still in their costumes under their coats. They were climbing the concrete steps to the back door and then taking turns jumping from them, seeing who could jump the farthest. Inside, the adults had gotten loud and were making dinner noises. Leland Sr. went up to Amos and tore his paper crown from his head.

"Hey!" Amos warbled.

Leland Sr. stamped the crown into the snow. Ruth backed away, sucking nervously on her finger.

"I'm Haman!" Leland Sr. shouted. He climbed to the top stair. "I'm Haman!" he shouted again. He'd gotten the other kids' attention by now. It was strange to say "Haman" and not hear graggers and booing.

"You messed up my crown," Amos said.

Leland Sr. began delivering his lines: "I'm Haman and I order an execution of all the Jews in Persia!" Then he jumped off the stairs and onto Amos, who was too stunned to move, and they fell down together. The other boys gathered in a circle around them; a few of the girls ran away and one started crying. Amos tried as best he could to block his face, but he was horrible at it. Leland Sr. was moving too fast for him to scream or cry. He held Amos's arms back and kneeled on his biceps. Then he punched Amos's face a few times, once hard enough to break his nose. Then he slapped him. The girls who hadn't run away were screaming and the boys were chanting. After some more slaps, Leland Sr. became dimly aware that there were adults outside, and that Amos had succeeded in letting out a huge sob.

Leland Sr. was pulled off Amos and then Leland Sr. Sr. was holding him. Mrs. Brecht helped Amos off the ground and was holding him in her arms. Leland Sr. kept on kicking.

Leland Sr. Sr. yanked the Haman mask from Leland Sr.'s face and threw it down. He kneeled in front of Leland Sr., who was crying by now: "No son with my name should ever behave like that."

Sarah and Leland Sr. Sr. had, after the incident, worked tirelessly to win back the trust of the congregation. Sarah quickly sent the remainder of their hamantaschen to the Brechts. Leland Sr. Sr. allowed the rabbi to separate Leland Sr.'s desk from the other children's during Hebrew school. The Brechts pretended to understand but grew distant. Leland Sr. was stripped of his role as Haman (it went to a skinny kid named Louis), reduced to wagging a gragger with the adults until he became a bar mitzvah.

Ulberg's office was now noticeably brighter.

"Do you know why you were referred to me?" he asked Leland Sr.

Leland Sr. laughed. "By my wife."

"We both know who asked you to come to me, but why did she do it?"

Leland Sr. shrugged.

"I don't think she knows why herself," Ulberg said. "But can I hazard a guess?" He didn't wait for Leland Sr.'s response. "Because you seem to have a problem with drugs. And you're at what we call the 'high bottom' right now. You haven't lost your job, you haven't lost your wife and son, you seem to be doing relatively okay financially. But maybe you know you can't stay at the high bottom forever. Am I right?"

Leland Sr. focused very closely on Ulberg's face, which was looking plush and wattley in the same way Amos's had. Leland shook his head and smiled pleasantly.

"I can't stop you doing what you're doing, Leland. That's your choice. But I can help you figure out why you're doing it. For this to work, you'll have to help me out a little, too. You'll have to tell me some things about your life."

"Yeah, I'll tell you whatever you need to know," Leland Sr. said.

"Great," Ulberg said. "I think we can make some progress here, Leland."

Leland Sr. drove home, drumming the steering wheel to the tune of "Nobody Wins." As he drove from west to east, the houses started losing their paint, the stores gaining typos on their awnings. When he got home the boy was asleep in his crib and Melinda was reading a book. When she saw him she smiled and started to ask the question and he said: "Completely unaffordable."

"What?"

"That was . . ." He looked at his watch. "That was one and a half hours. That cost me fifteen dollars."

"But there's ways—"

"Not really," he said, and went into the kitchen, hoisting his pants. He felt tremendously clearheaded and powerful, and with this feeling came— as it often did—the fear that it would be gone soon. He ate an apple from the crisper. Melinda hadn't stood to follow him.

"So you're giving up?" she asked.

"You know it's my birthday, Melinda. We should be getting cake."

Unfazed, she repeated her question.

Leland Sr. turned to face her. "Yep."

"It sounds like you never even wanted to try it."

"It sounds like you're a psychologist, too." He smiled at her flirtatiously. She did not smile back. "It's not going to work financially," he said. "I'll fix it another way."

"If you don't see a shrink, the family's not going to work at all."

This statement was designed to send an ordinary man into an emotional tailspin, but it didn't work on Leland Sr. "I doubt that."

"Leland, you're sick."

"Yeah?" He sat down next to her and took another bite of the apple. "How so?"

"You—" She put her book down to gesture, but her gestures were inexpressive—most of them involved repeatedly describing a globelike shape in midair. "It's like, you sometimes don't know what's real and what's not. You were on acid most of the time in college, you've been high since I've known you."

"And you?"

"Not as much as you."

"Even just once is enough."

"And I think—well, I really think those drugs made you different. You get mad and sad in ways you didn't before."

Leland Sr. looked at her squarely. "I can get mad and sad the way I used to," he said. "Just say the word."

This disarmed her enough to make her laugh. He saw the fault line and pried at it, grabbing her knee. "Is this how I used to be?"

"No—Leland, that's not what I'm talking about."

"What are you talking about?" He began massaging up her thigh. She tried to stop him. Leland Jr. coughed loudly from his crib.

"He has the croup," she said.

"What were you talking about?"

"You getting better." But she was smiling now; he'd won. "I just think that maybe if you talked to these doctors they could help you."

Leland Sr. now had his hand on her inner thigh. "Plenty of hippies did a lot more drugs than I did."

"Well, yeah, but I care about you doing them, not the hippies. There was an article about Timothy Leary in *Time* last week." She looked at him and her face seemed softer, smaller, like the face of a child seeking approval.

"We promised no more of that, right? You know, we promised when I got rid of all the grass when Leland Jr. was born."

She was fond of saying this. It made them better parents, in her ultra-humble opinion. And of course it was a self-soothing lie: he could still smell the grass coming from her dresser drawer. He could smell it on her as she cooked dinner. "But the kid got high, whether you meant him to or not," he reminded her.

Melinda had given in to Leland Sr.'s hand. She had uncrossed her legs. He was nearly up to her crotch.

The boy woke up and began screaming. Leland Sr. withdrew his hand, slumped back in his captain's chair, and ate his apple, watching Melinda hurry into Leland Jr.'s room. She returned with the boy in her arms. He was red in the cheeks and his nose was mottled with dried snot. She held him on her hip.

"You're getting a little big for your crib, aren't you, baby?" she asked.

Leland Jr. shook his head, still screaming. He was already two years old but he barely talked. She pointed to Leland Sr. "You see Daddy? Wanna say hi to Daddy?"

Leland Jr. shook his head again, slowed the waterworks to a trickle, and began to hiccup. He looked at Leland Sr., who waved.

"Do you wanna go to Daddy?"

Leland Jr. stuck his fingers in his mouth and hugged his mother around the neck. Leland Sr. looked at them both. The boy had instantly undone all his work.

"You can't just talk your way out of this," she said, running her hand over the back of Leland Jr.'s head. "You don't see yourself when you get this way, but I do. And look, you've already scared Leland Jr."

"I haven't scared him. He doesn't remember anything."

"He remembers you throwing plates." This had been her trump card for the past three months, the plates incident.

"One plate."

"It scared him."

Leland Sr. shook his head. "What's for dinner?"

But his question was useless. She'd gotten combative again and could not be distracted. "Don't try to change the subject! You have to go to the shrink, Leland."

"Do I have to bankrupt the family, too? Because that's what's going to happen."

"We can afford it."

The boy was screaming again.

"For fuck's sake," Leland Sr. said. He went into the kitchen. She followed him this time, the boy a human shield on her hip. "What's for dinner?" he repeated.

She was silent. He opened the fridge in search of deli meat they didn't appear to have. Predictably, she spoke first.

"You are going to do this," she said.

He stopped searching but didn't face her. This would give her the impression that he was building to a pique, but really he felt nothing. "This is just another hippie fad," he said. "Just because you see it in the movies doesn't mean it's going to work."

"If you don't do this, you won't be setting any kind of an example for your son."

He slammed the fridge closed and turned to face her. "You want my son"—he used his entire hand, palm up, to gesture to the boy—"to grow up to be the kind of guy who has to go talk to some fat old faggot about his problems because he can't handle them himself?" He'd matched his son's decibel level and then quickly exceeded it. "You told me to try it, I tried it, it didn't work. Enough!"

"You have to work at it, not just try!"

"You're the fucking expert! You win!" Leland Sr. went past her, out of the kitchen. He saw his coat on the captain's chair and grabbed it. Leland Jr. was now coughing through his screams.

"You're upsetting him," she said.

He put his coat on. He knew it wouldn't do him any good to get angrier. She'd started to cry a little and her grip on the boy had gone slack; she had to walk over to the couch and set him down. The boy got stiff and angry without his mother to claw onto and he sat there shivering, snot running down his upper lip.

Leland Sr. pointed his car in the direction of work: Cleveland Scrap, down by the stockyards. It was his birthday after all. If no one was going to do anything nice for him, he'd do something nice for himself. The shop was closed for the night but maybe guys would still be hanging around playing poker. They were a small outfit, run by Mickey, a wide-faced Czech guy whom Leland Sr. had gone to school with since the fourth grade. Mickey dropped out of school after the ninth grade and got a job at Republic Steel, then got fired from that for stealing machine parts and did something—Leland Sr. couldn't remember what—that led to him spending a year in juvie. When he got out of there, he flipped enough cars to open his own scrap shop in the stockyards and got all his friends jobs. The summer after Leland Sr. graduated college, he gave Mickey a call and asked for one.

"College wants a job at my scrap shop!" Mickey's voice was high-pitched and cigarette-rough.

"I just want a job," Leland Sr. said.

"Why don't you come down to my office for an interview, College?"

Coming down to Mickey's "office" meant burning a fat jay on the bank of the Cuyahoga right next to Republic Steel. It was the part of Leland's life before he discovered medicine when everything felt slow and messy. Melinda was still upset about those kids getting shot on campus. She was at home pregnant with swollen feet, probably studying for her real estate exam. He was already trying to think of ways to leave her that wouldn't hurt her feelings, but he still loved her and would probably feel bad if he didn't see their child being born.

If only he could've beamed into the future and seen himself still working at that shop three fucking years later. Leland Sr. Sr. and Sarah had expected him to do something useful with the philosophy degree, become a lawyer and spend at least three years "getting established" before he got his wife pregnant. But he hadn't done either and now they barely ever spoke to him. Sometimes they sent money, sometimes they sent holiday greeting cards, occasionally Sarah called him and asked him if he had any plans to stop renting and buy property.

After one of these horrible phone calls, he'd wandered into the back room at Scrap, where Mickey and all his juvie friends were playing cards after clocking out. He had seen Mickey pressing his face close to the table with a tiny chunk of straw in his nose. He had watched Mickey slap his cheeks and laugh and pound his chest, pass the straw to the guy sitting next to him. Leland Sr. sat down—eventually it was his turn. He'd only done mushrooms, acid, and grass before. He bent down close to the table and got halfway through the line, then stopped. Mickey called him "college pussy," so he finished it. How could he explain to his mother the way he felt after that, like his brain worked as it had always been intended to work? How could he describe the way the room looked, the way his thoughts moved, the big, bright faces of all Mickey's juvie friends shouting about how smart and funny he was? She'd never understand. Instead he told her that he'd never buy property and she should get used to the way his generation was living.

Halfway to the shop he remembered Mickey was out of town until Thursday and so redirected toward Ohio City, toward his friend Reggie. When he thought of people like Reggie, people who'd realized about the healing power of medicine and had resolved to make their livings outside of conventional capitalism, he got excited. He saw hope for the future—his future. They shared a birthday, V-day babies both, basically twins. Except Reggie didn't have a father who'd cried and chain-smoked Turkish cigars in the hospital waiting room, a father who got so emotional that the only name he could think to give his newborn son was his own. Leland Sr. imagined Reggie's father as Reggie but meatier, a John Wayne type who never took no for an answer. As was the case with Leland Sr., Reggie's draft number hadn't gotten called, though Leland Sr. guessed he probably would've burned his card if it had been. He hung out with Reggie on the curb whenever he could. Sometimes he talked to people for him, got them to cough up more money when Reggie did his count at the end of the day and found he was running short. Reggie even let him come back in the massage parlor where he worked, especially if it was winter— Leland Sr. never had a good coat because the cold didn't bother him, but Reggie would always tell him to come in so he didn't freeze his ass off and scare away customers. Then Reggie would go to the basement and Leland Sr. would get to sit on the velvet couch in the front room surrounded by girls who wore aprons over their pasties and bikini bottoms and flitted around him like exotic birds. They even smelled beautiful: peach and grapefruit and honeysuckle perfume, occasionally a hint of well-washed bare skin. There was one named Meesha who flirted with him every time he was there. Once she even went to the bathroom with him and took her apron off free of charge. She said she was doing it because she felt bad for him, and when he asked her why she only shrugged and kissed him on the cheek. Maybe special people who understood him could read the truth on his face: the life he'd made before medicine was inferior to the life he'd made after medicine, and he was trying to loose the chains of the former so he could live in the latter. He thanked Meesha and told her she wouldn't have to feel bad for him much longer.

He parked four blocks from Reggie's usual spot, paid the meter, and started walking. He hadn't seen Reggie in almost three weeks and he'd begun to worry. He'd been buying from a gray-skinned guy in the massage parlor who called himself Lev; whenever Leland Sr. asked about Reggie, Lev just shook his head. It was getting cold already—every year it seemed to happen earlier, or else he was just feeling it earlier. It was almost discouraging to think about how much he'd changed and how little the world around him had, how slow everything moved in comparison to his brain. He felt bad for everyone who lacked his supersensing powers, and he felt bad for Reggie because his coworkers didn't care about him. In his dream world, there'd be a government agency that dispensed medicine in glass bottles like the milkman's. Every American would have the option of turning on for free; if they didn't want to, they could just pass it along to their neighbor. That was the problem with Melinda—she'd turned on and turned off, left behind what could've been a beautiful life. She'd never struck him as the kind of girl who wanted two kids and a two-car garage, but people changed. Especially women.

By the time he got to Reggie's spot, his thoughts were running too fast for him to keep up, and there was what felt like dirty water pooling in his forehead. He never realized how badly he needed to re-up until it was right on top of him. He walked up and down the street: Reggie wasn't there. He called Reggie's name and an old woman across the street yelled at him to keep it down, it was a weeknight.

"I'm looking for my friend, ma'am!" Leland Sr. shouted back. "I haven't seen him in three weeks! Wouldn't you be worried about a very dear friend of yours if you hadn't seen him in three weeks?"

He was sputtering by the end of the sentence, spitting into the street. The woman's eyes got wide and she turned and pushed her little cart of knickknacks fast away from him. Reggie was nowhere, but the kids who bought from him were skulking around in front of the Cash and Carry on the corner.

"You seen Reggie?" Leland Sr. asked one of them, a pale blond girl named Tina or Teresa with sticky-looking bangs. She turned away from her boyfriend, a shade darker than Reggie with a sharp chin, and spit on the ground in front of Leland Sr.

"Yeah, I seen him," she said.

"When?"

"The fuck you mean when?" she asked, and her boyfriend grabbed her hand and laughed. Then her eyes got big. "Oh, damn," she said.

"What?"

"Oh, I know what's happening here. He's avoiding you."

Leland Sr. laughed. "Sure," he said. "Believe what you want to believe."

"No, seriously, man," her boyfriend chimed in. "You annoy the shit outta him. He told me."

The girl covered her mouth with her hands. "You're not getting high anymore, Big L?"

Leland Sr. could feel the dirty pool getting bigger. "Don't call me that," he said.

"What? 'Big L'?" The girl cackled, the sound like a knife to his inner ear.

He turned around and walked off. If they couldn't behave like actual human beings, he didn't owe them his time. Actually, all bad behavior was just human behavior—truly good behavior would have to be superhuman, the kind you could only achieve on medicine. Instead of living out a shitty nightmare of earthly dependence, begging for your weekly paycheck and your groceries and your whiny family and your messy house, you could be a supersenser like Leland Sr. You could be the kind of person who saw all the system's hypocrisies and rejected them. He saw, for instance, that humans only felt they needed to be governed because they told themselves so—everyone was perfectly capable of rational self-governance. Look at all those tribal cultures in Papua New Guinea: they didn't need a president telling them what and what not to eat, whom and whom not to fuck. People only believed in families because they felt they had to. What was wrong with letting a child make decisions for himself—why have a mother and father hovering over him constantly? Why commit yourself to only one woman for the rest of your life? Why go to college and study books and take tests just to win a paper-pushing job to support that woman and her children? A job where you'd probably end up writing some forms or deposing some evidence or stitching up some skin so the world could keep on turning all average and unquestioning and calm like it had before. A job where you'd do your best to make it more difficult for people to live out-side the normalcy coffin—where you and your clients would keep on arm-ing police officers and paying taxes and electing bureaucrats who didn't give a fuck about your lives but made it sound like they did. Only he and the few others like him could see above the fray.

The light was off in the massage parlor and the door was locked. He tried the door on the side, then the one in the back. All locked. This was a first. He went back around to the front and knocked on the window.

"Lev!" he shouted. He looked at his dark reflection in the glass, the golden halo of the streetlamp behind him. "Lev!" he shouted again. A car passed behind him, honking its horn as it crawled away. Did he know that guy? He was starting to feel very bad. He banged on the door, tapped on the window. He thought about smashing it but thought better: the last thing he needed was some pig telling him he wasn't following the order of the law.

"You've been through this," he whispered to himself. "You remember last Easter?" Holy fucking God did he remember last Easter. Melinda insisted on dragging him and the boy to church and he'd sat there think-ing he had about two hours of sermons to endure but he'd really had four. Goyim loved their sitting and chanting and tithing. He hadn't had any medicine since early the night before. By the time he started feeling it, he'd already gone outside three times for a cigarette. By noon his skin was crawl-ing and his thoughts were turning to suicide: jumping from the balcony, sharpening the cross on the pulpit and falling on it, breaking the stained glass and slitting his wrists with the shards. A faraway part of his brain knew these thoughts would disappear once he got his hands on his medi-cine, but all the closer-up parts of his brain felt them as incredibly real. He was sweating and digging his fingernails into his kneecaps. Melinda gave him a tight-eyebrowed look. When they got home, it felt as if there were pebbles under his skin. He went to the box he kept under the boy's crib (formerly at the back of his sock drawer, in his glove compartment, on the highest shelf in the closet). He was praying he'd still have at least a dub's worth left, but he had nothing. He'd had to drive all the way to Ohio City, biting his nails bloody, praying that this would never happen to him again. He'd barely made it to Reggie's spot, his sight flickering on and off. Reggie let him re-dose right there, less than three feet away, whispering the whole time that Leland Sr. was an idiot for not planning ahead and he should feel really fucking lucky Reggie was a kind person.

Remembering that Easter was a mistake: now he couldn't stop thinking about it. He tried the doorknob again, harder than he had the first
time. It was times like these that made him miss Judaism, the faith of his
childhood. A religious man would be able to cross his arms over his chest
and say, "The door will open for me when the time is right." They actually believed shit like that, and it usually worked for them. Maybe the deal
was God was only real if you believed in God, so you made Him and all
the benefits of covenant-ing with Him real just by opting in. It was like a
pyramid scheme if pyramid schemes worked: Leland would tell two friends
about how great God was and they'd tell two friends and all of them would
reap the many and various benefits of being religious Jews. That was more
how Christians worked, though. Jews didn't want you telling two friends,
because those two friends may not be special enough to be Jews. Meanwhile some of the most heinous, snot-filled, vengeful motherfuckers
he'd ever met were somehow special enough by birth. Amos Brecht, the
Hebrew school teacher Mr. Chertoff who'd slapped him in the mouth,
those stipple-skinned gangsters who blew people up with car bombs.
Unnecessary violence would not be part of a world where everyone took
their medicine, that was something Leland Sr. knew absolutely 100 percent
to be true. It was both exhausting and infuriating how far ahead in time
he could see and how incredibly slow people would always be in catching up. In his more generous moments, he could tell that the problem
wasn't even a lack of love or respect—Melinda, the boy, Mickey all listened
to and cared about him, all would probably be torn apart if he turned up
dead—it was a lack of understanding, a smallness of mind. Everyone he
knew (except for maybe Reggie and a few other guys who hung out at the
massage place) was living in a tiny, concrete-lined world of pleases and
thank-yous, where sidewalks were for walking on and streets for driving
on, where the most electrifying thing in their lives was TV. How could
they be expected to listen to him, to treat him with the same patience and
compassion with which he'd treated them? How many times had he sat
awake listening to another one of Melinda's nightmares about the girl
who got shot at Kent State? How many times had he risen from bed to
coddle the boy while he screamed his skull-rattling screams at three in
the morning? How many times had he gone to the Ford plant to cut deals
that edged out Mickey's competitors? And how did they repay him? With
niceties, with their pleases and thank-yous. Never by just listening to him.

Desperate times, desperate measures. He dug in his pocket for his penknife, which had been a gift from his father on the night of his bar mitzvah. He couldn't even remember the name of his Torah portion anymore. It'd had something to do with building an altar or binding a book. Probably Deuteronomy. His mother had cried the entire time. His father's face had been hidden in a cloud of cigar smoke. The rabbi said something like "Young Leland surprised us all with his studiousness at the very last minute." Mr. Chertoff was sitting in the second row, arms crossed, the wrinkle between his eyebrows forming the trunk of the tree and his forehead wrinkles its branches. He was daring Leland Sr. to fuck up, which Leland Sr. didn't. Sometime after the service and before his party, his father took him aside and gave him the penknife. "Don't let your mother see this," he said. "She'll sweat right through her blouse." At that point Leland Sr. Sr. looked the way he'd look until Leland Sr. left the house for college: his leonine face jowly and fat, his nose infected with blackheads, his lips constantly cracked. Leland Sr. remembered looking into that face and finding it hard to believe he'd ever been frightened of it.

He stuck the blade in the keyhole and torqued the lock (pin tumbler, typical) until he heard a click. Then he wedged the knife between the door and its frame and the front room was his. He turned on the Christmas lights and looked around the place. It was depressing without the girls. Why did they let places like this get so dirty? He thought he could hear bugs scratching across the linoleum behind the desk where the johns got their room tokens. But maybe that was just the sound of his ears trying to work: they were dry, as was his nose, as were his eyes. Your average person couldn't hear bugs' feet unless they were basically straw-sized. Leland Sr. could, though. But maybe not for much longer if his brain stayed dry. He looked in the boxes on the shelves: condoms, underwear, condoms. Some newspapers and magazines. On the floor: thong sandals. Under the massive leather-top table in front of the window: garbage bags, empty beer bottles, a belt with an extra notch close to the tip. Leland Sr. had been renotching his belts, but in the opposite direction. In the past two years he'd lost thirty pounds he couldn't regain even if he'd wanted to. Next to Melinda in bed he found himself in a Jack Sprat–type situation, which he resented. He tried the door to the back room: locked. He was fishing for the penknife again when there was an urgent jamming of keys in the front door. He flipped the back wall switch and the room went dark again; he shrank until he was on the ground with his knees to his chest. In stumbled a silhouette who looked nearly bald against the orange light shining in through the curtains. A familiar-looking silhouette. Leland Sr. stood up, about to speak. Then the lights came on again.

"Fucking Christ," he heard Reggie say. He could only see the top of Reggie's head because he was blocking Reggie's face just then with his hands, suddenly ashamed that this was how they were seeing each other after three weeks. "How did you get in here?"

But Leland Sr. didn't need to explain, at least he didn't remember needing to. He and Reggie had a cosmic understanding.

"I thought you were dead! I haven't seen you in a month."

Leland Sr. lowered his hands and saw Reggie was already busy looking through boxes. "Not dead, just working," he said. He turned around and the lower half of his face was covered in dried blood, his bottom lip and nose busted. He had the post-fight glassy eyes, the ones Leland Sr. always used to get when he was trying hard to deny the amount of pain he was in. Insult to injury. Leland Sr. could feel his heart rate accelerating. He wanted to do for Reggie what Melinda did for the boy: clean his wounds and kiss him on the forehead.

"Who did that to you?"

Reggie looked at him like he was an alien and then kept on digging in the boxes. "It's better if you don't know," he said.

This was very wrong. This whole situation was very fucked up and wrong. "No, it's better if I do." Leland Sr. stood and went to Reggie's side of the room. "Seriously, I'll fuck that guy up for you."

He saw the muscles in Reggie's shoulders relax. "You'll fuck him up for me?"

"Yeah, of course." The pebbles under his skin were growing into stones.

Reggie snorted. "You're acting like a faggot," he said softly, not without compassion. He turned around to face Leland Sr., who didn't flinch. Insults weren't a problem for him because they were typically made out of fear. Reggie's face was in bad enough shape that being scared would make sense. He looked at Leland Sr. looking at him, then wiped his mouth off with the bottom of his shirt and said, "Just wait here, all right?"

Time should've passed slowly then, but it whipped by. Reggie returned with much less than an eighth of medicine. Leland Sr. gave him a hundred dollars and told him to keep the change.

"Are you sure?" Reggie asked.

Leland Sr. nodded. "Happy birthday. You look like you need a little good luck."

Reggie pocketed the bill and tossed him the half eightball and told him to wait in the front room. He limped into the back room, switched the light on, and locked the door behind him.

Leland Sr. had a snowcapped pinkie in his nose by the time the door clicked shut. He was thinking both that his brain's wheels were greased and how unfair it was that guys like Reggie who were fundamentally good and caring got beaten up. That was another thing that would be different in a world where everyone took their medicine: the goodness of people wouldn't be overlooked. Yes—he did another bump—yes, he'd thrown a plate in frustration when Melinda first proposed he go to the shrink. If pressed, he'd admit that it was wrong of him, but then he'd been angry that she wanted him to spend money on a shrink, and even angrier that she'd accused him of having "delusions." Ignoring the fact that he wasn't delusional—that he was probably the least delusional person now walking the planet—how delusional did *she* have to be not to see his goodness? He saw hers! Through her tears, her nastiness, the mornings she stumbled back into bed covered in the boy's puke and shit, he still saw the same ruddy-cheeked woman whose big heart busted open when she turned on, who could describe better than he could the hills and vistas of the human subconscious, and who could return from the mind's farthest reaches refreshed instead of exhausted. If people took their medicine, they'd instantly see all the motivations for other people's actions. There'd be no more misunderstandings, no more beatings, no more death.

It was funny to him that maybe he'd come up with the idea for world peace sitting under a table in a whorehouse. Great minds don't necessarily do their thinking in great places. Although—he was laughing hard now, squeaking in between gasps—this was a pretty damn great place. The less-than-an-eighth was vanishing in his hands. He could hear Reggie talking to someone in the back room. When had someone else come in? What was Melinda doing with the boy right now? Probably putting him to sleep.

Leland Sr. stood to kill the lights and he heard something smack. He was still and tried to turn off his thoughts so he could hear the smack again. Nothing. He waited a long time and nothing. He got a little more medicine in his longest nail and held it to his nose. Then a gunshot and a second one right after.

Ears buzzing, Leland Sr. dropped the non-eightball. Reggie was in that room. The door was locked. He threw his body against it, kicked it. His brain felt hot enough to turn water to instant steam. No talking coming from behind the door. He remembered the penknife: he took it out of his pocket. He opened the door: Reggie was on the floor, eyes closed, bleeding from the side of his head. Another guy was on the floor next to him, a little Peter Lorre–looking guy Leland Sr. had never seen before. The right side of Peter Lorre's head was gory, bloody, open. He was holding a gun in his right hand, another in his left. Leland Sr. kicked the gun from his right hand. He started crying. He should've seen this coming. Then he glanced across the room and saw on the table ahead of him an open briefcase, and in that briefcase rows and rows of bills.

NATASHA MARSHALL, NÉE HARRISON

(1948–)

1954–1965
Cleveland

She felt—perhaps wrongly, but then Daddy had inculcated in her a nasty rhetorical habit of hypothesis-testing and second-guessing—that she'd been marked from birth for something magnificent. Her earliest memory was of lying on her stomach, her legs in the air behind her, smelling of the dime-store baby powder Momma always seasoned her with, reading a *Plain Dealer* headline aloud: ALL FORCES TOIL TO CLEAR CITY; SOLDIERS CALLED IN. It was Thanksgiving and blizzarding and she'd been alive for what amounted to a fraction of a second in history's grand scheme, she herself already a grand schemer as she sounded out the headline again and looked up at her awestruck momma, who rewarded her with a little knot of cookie dough and then asked Daddy if he knew Natasha could read. "She was born reading," he said, and that became the truth.

Natasha had an older sister, Deborah, who had a lanky body and a thick halo of hair that would, over the years, break two of her momma's best combs. Natasha understood early on that she and Deborah were not meant to be friends. Deborah enjoyed television, roller-skating, and magazines, the sorts of things Natasha's mind ran too fast to appreciate. A little sister usually sat on her big sister's bed and looked on in wonder as the big sister applied makeup or filed her fingernails or danced to an LP, but Natasha was no such little sister. She stood skeptically in Deborah's doorway and grilled her with questions about fractions, parts of speech, the presidents. She recorded Deborah's insults and demurrals in an empty notebook to show Daddy, who encouraged her to persist no matter what kind of names her sister thought up to call her. "Get a good answer out of her, Tasha. Make sure she's paying attention to that free education she's getting." Natasha mostly ignored her momma's suggestions that she give her poor sister a rest.

She woke up before sunrise every day and felt the great thing coming closer. She read about the girl who'd traveled to Russia to hike the Ural Mountains alone, the teenage millionaire with twenty patents, the sixteen-year-old concert pianist who'd played Carnegie Hall and published best-selling books of poetry. She read about the movie star who'd gotten her big break as the Farm Hills Girl in an oatmeal commercial. She listened to *Quiz Kids* whenever it came on the radio, acing the English, history, and mythology sections and embarrassing herself with her performance on the math section. She studied the lives of great men and noted their earliest achievements: Dr. King got his doctorate at age twenty-six (she teased Daddy about this because he'd gotten his at thirty-two), John F. Kennedy was twenty-seven when he got the Purple Heart, Chuck Berry was twenty-nine when "Maybellene" came out. In order to be great, she'd have to make her contribution before the age of thirty. Easily done. She sometimes wished the bar was set a little higher, just so she could justify the time she spent planning it all out.

Every morning Daddy drove Natasha and Deborah to school and then proceeded to Axel Renfroe College, where he taught history and where Natasha planned to study after she graduated high school. While Deborah steamed up the window with her halitosis and then drew pictures in it, Natasha slyly tried to decipher from Daddy what he thought her contribution to the world would be. She did this by starting up a conversation about homework or current events. Once Natasha and Daddy fell into a rhythm private enough that Deborah resigned herself to silence, Natasha would start monitoring Daddy's responses for clues:

"Do you think it's true what you **read** about the Alamo?"

"Think carefully. You reach a conclusion almost as fast as you can **read** a **page**, Tasha."

"Answer's in one of the **books** in your room."

"Not enough **published** on the topic, I'm afraid."

There was the chance, she acknowledged, that she was just hearing what she wanted to hear. But she liked to think that Daddy was dropping these hints intentionally, two steps ahead of her as always. She'd been born reading, so her contribution would have something to do with books.

Their house was full of books, all Daddy's. His study boasted the most in one place. His chair stood on four cinder blocks and so did his desk—he claimed the height helped his mind work. When he sat at the desk he looked like a judge presiding over his bench, the two cedar bookcases behind him forming a grim tribunal. The one on his left contained his history books on the topics of his interest: the Mexican-American and Civil Wars, the Adams presidencies, the evils of Manifest Destiny. The one to his right contained his literature collection: bound volumes of the transcendental poets, the thick tomes of the industrial-era realists, the heavy and slight experimentations of the high modernists. A quarter of one shelf was reserved for a collection of prose and poetry in Russian, which Daddy had learned to read in graduate school, and which included Dostoevsky's *The Insulted and Humiliated*, from which Daddy had gotten Natasha's name. The rest was written in English, and the subject was America's violent past.

Natasha made no secret of her preference for Daddy's right bookshelf. By the time she was a sophomore in high school, she'd torn through it. In the dustier volumes she wrote margin notes with a red pen, responses to Daddy's undergraduate scribbles: *Yes, but did you consider that she'd just had an abortion?* and *The meter is evidently **not** trochaic* and *Who died and made you king of the meatpacking industry?* She knew he'd probably never see them. She didn't know if she wanted him to. She had a favorite, Herman Melville, and she debated everything about him with Daddy at the dinner table. Deborah and Momma either picked at their plates in silence or had conversations of their own. The few times Deborah tried to interrupt them, Daddy told her to please wait until he was finished. By the time he was, the dinner plates had typically been cleared and everyone was staring into their emptied pudding cups, thinking of all the things they still had to accomplish between dinner and bedtime. Finally, Daddy would turn to Deborah: "What was your question, Deb?"

The time Natasha spent with Momma went slower than normal time. One afternoon could have diffused into several, the hours luxurious. Momma let Natasha and Deborah lick cookie batter from spoons while she wandered from one end of the kitchen to the other, checking on the chicken in the oven and the collard greens on the stove, describing to them her plan for a meal that wouldn't materialize until hours or possibly days later. Her gentleness was at odds with the way the house usually worked. Deborah and Natasha stopped arguing and sat in reverent silence as Momma paced the kitchen preparing dinner; when they were very little, they'd waited patiently as she massaged extra-virgin olive oil into their scalps before bath time. Daddy gratefully scarfed down everything she cooked, praised her to everyone he knew, wondered aloud how the family would have gotten by without her. She was the daughter of Arkansas sharecroppers, late to reading and writing, practical minded. At nineteen she followed family friends to Cleveland, where she was hired to clean tables in the Axel Renfroe cafeteria. On the first day, a twenty-two-year-old Daddy looked up from the corned beef and hash sandwich he was eating and through the little window where the dirty trays were deposited for cleaning made brief eye contact with the pretty young cafeteria worker. He tried to make a habit of not prolonging his meals, finding eating to be a tedious distraction from worthier projects of the mind. But meeting Momma's eyes made him feel a way he'd never felt before in his life, so he lingered over that lunch for her entire afternoon shift. Her version went like this: "I was washing dishes and I looked up and saw this boy in glasses looking at me, and I didn't want to be rude, so I smiled at him."

Although Natasha didn't typically enjoy people who distracted her from thinking about the great thing she would contribute to the world, she enjoyed every second spent with Momma. Granted, she had to spend those seconds in moderation—immersing herself entirely in Momma's world would make her slow, compassionate without meaningful cause. But there was no reason not to take time away from Melville to wander the kitchen with Momma as she set timers and whipped cake batter. There was no reason not to accompany Momma on the occasional outing: to the grocery store, to the fabric store, to visit her friends in the neighborhood of Hough. Going to Hough was Natasha's favorite for two reasons: the first was that Deborah refused to go, and the second was that whenever Natasha opened her mouth the people there thought she was a miracle. They told her to take good care of herself, she was destined to make everyone proud, and asked Momma what she'd done to get a miracle child. What was it, because so-and-so is pregnant right now and wants a baby like yours. Daddy called people like that "common"—he said science had killed religion and he had no idea why someone would believe in ghosts and magic luck charms and voodoo spells "invented out of fear and boredom on some plantation"—but Momma didn't agree. She never went to church, but she read the Bible and had nailed a little wooden cross above her half of the bed. She was of the mind that God worked in mysterious ways, and that the world was full of good-luck tricks to curry His favor. So she took queries about Natasha's growth in earnest, trying to remember if she'd slept on her side or her back during the pregnancy, if and when she'd baked with cinnamon or cardamom, what the weather had been like on the day Natasha was born. Natasha had not yet decided if she wanted children, but she knew they'd only come after she wrote a book about *Typee* if they came at all, after she herself had set sail for the Marquesas Islands, living among savages as Melville had. Then maybe she would return to Cleveland and have children with someone deserving of her time and intellect, an accomplished man who himself had traveled and studied and shared her curiosity about greatness and how it was achieved.

The Joneses, whom they often visited in Hough, were the clan Momma had followed out of Arkansas. At their head stood Patreese, thin in all her bright Sunday dresses, widowed, ten years Momma's senior. She wasn't necessarily envious of the fact that Momma didn't live in Hough so much as she was curious about it. What was it like being married to a born-and-raised northerner? Patreese said she'd met people like him who didn't even consider themselves black folks, were always trying to say how nobody besides them had any self-respect. "Does he have enough self-respect for you?" Patreese asked, ribbing Momma, smiling, patient anger in her voice. Momma smiled back and never answered. Patreese had a daughter, Demetra, who had a two-year-old boy. While Momma spoke with the mothers, Natasha would babysit, trying to get the boy to waddle to her, rushing to him before he could fall. She liked the way he smelled, and she liked the way he cooed when Demetra picked him up: when the two looked at each other, there was an exchange of light between them that made Natasha curious and then embarrassed. Joyce, their next-door neighbor, had three baby girls and would sometimes bring them over and pay Natasha twenty-five cents an hour to watch them, too. She sat in the living room surrounded by big-eyed children, a clueless heap of them drooling and crying and pulling at her socks, Momma and her friends in the next room talking about the things they missed from Arkansas, smoothing the hems of their dresses and saying, "It's just more of the same here and they promise you it's different." Natasha felt important, indebted to these women and their children, like she was the once-in-a-generation phenomenon who would prove to them all that it didn't have to be more of the same.

She graduated high school early and started at Axel Renfroe a few months before her seventeenth birthday. Her class schedule was Chaucer and Newtonian physics in the morning, then lunch and American history in the afternoon. Daddy had told her that this fall would begin the most important years of her life, and that she would need to treat every lecture and assignment as vital to her survival in the world. She did, or she tried to—she found that Daddy's words in her head had the damning effect of making her mind wander and then worry about wandering. She understood that she'd have to do twice the work in order to be half as good as the rest of her physics class, which was a bunch of engineering majors gunning to be anointed teacher's pet. And the homework was dull: when she tried to do it, she thought about everything else. The sex in *The Miller's Tale*, a line of Melville's poetry: "Beadle of England / In formal array— / Best fellow alive / On a throne flung away!" She stared out the window and mumbled: "Here's to thee, Hal." More pressing: the tense pain in her chest that she worried might be an incipient heart attack. Poor fat old Falstaff. Her figure in the mirror in her room. Was she too thin? Deborah would know how to fix that, but after so many years of keeping her distance, there was no use in asking her—even if a metaphysical cannon shot them both into some parallel universe where Deborah actually wanted to help Natasha, she was more likely to be out with her boyfriend anyway, a white high school dropout named Dennis who drove a motorcycle and smelled like wax. Daddy didn't know about him, and Momma didn't like him.

The day that she first saw Reggie, she was trying to solve her physics problem set but couldn't focus. She was thinking instead of Melville tied up by Polynesians: hapless Melville licking his wounds as a witch doctor attempted to kill him with a curse. Maybe it was her faulty reading of the literature, maybe Daddy would correct her if she bothered to run the idea by him, but Melville had always seemed less invested in splitting the world into opposites than in reporting on human helplessness. Were the Polynesians so evil and Melville so good, or were they doing to him what a whole army of European explorers would've done to them in a heartbeat? And Ahab—why read about him if he was just a heartless madman, if he had (presumably) nothing in common with the reader? Natasha would hunt the white whale if given a chance, absolutely she would, she wouldn't care at all how she looked to her crew as long as the thing she wanted most in the world was within her reach. She tightened the ribbon on her dress that gathered right beneath her bust. She sat down, then stood up, then paced the room. The second question involved turning gravitational potential energy into velocity. She looked out at the sky, which was boring, then down at the ground. There was someone at the end of her driveway. A mailman, a new one. Younger than the old one but probably older than she was. He reached out of his truck, a handful of envelopes and magazines: his shoulders were wide. She stood in the window looking down at him, running her hand over the necklace of Bakelite pearls at her collarbone. He parked his truck and got out. He walked around the nose of the parked truck slowly, opened the mailbox, and slid the mail in. He waved at her and she waved back. It was a little weird, what he was doing: usually the mailman just parked the truck and delivered the mail through the window. It was strange to see something different, especially in their neighborhood, where everything had been the same for as long as she could remember. The rare deviation from routine coming the few times their garage door got graffitied with slurs, which Daddy had to scrub off before anyone could see—but even that kind of thing happened with enough regularity that she wasn't surprised by it anymore. The mailman was something else. Like a car driving backward or a bald eagle eating a hot dog. She laughed, and he got back in his truck and drove away.

He was back the next day. She watched for him. He parked, got out, and put the mail in the mailbox just like he had the day before. He was a little tall for his uniform; there was a gap between his socks and the hem of his pants where his ankles showed. He looked up at her and she made herself as visible as she could in the window, pressing her nose against the glass. Something from a dim fold in her brain said she was being reckless, she should be focused on catching up in class. She was seventeen—her life was full of promise, her potential was limitless—and she was pressing her nose to her window so a mailman could see her. She walked away to finish her problem set.

After that something shifted inside her. She couldn't admit to it because she didn't know what it was, but it was pressing at her insides like she'd swallowed something sharp. When she went to Hough, she kept an eye out for the mailman. When she visited Demetra and Joyce, she imagined them in their aprons at Chuckee's Drug Store. Had she been there before? She hadn't—Momma was always promising to take her there for a sandwich and then having second thoughts. Had she ever looked at a waiter or a gas station attendant or a street cleaner the way the mailman had looked at her? She hadn't. She'd once said "excuse me" to the janitor at her high school and he'd moved his bucket and mop out of her way, saying nothing in response. What did they have to say to each other? What did she have to say to the mailman? She felt warm and a little uneasy whenever she saw him. She felt distracted. She had the suspicion that she'd been thinking about things wrong.

In the morning she went out to collect the mail from the mailman. He seemed surprised to see her, smoothing the front of his shirt like he'd come underdressed to a ball. His eyes were green. He asked if he could call her and she took the mail from him and ran into the house, head light-feeling, a smile tickling the corners of her mouth. She threw the mail on the table and found a scrap of paper. Then she remembered that Daddy usually shut himself in his study around seven o'clock, which meant he wouldn't want to bother with the phone. She wrote *Don't call until 7:00 p.m.!* beneath her name. She brought the piece of paper out to him and he took it from her, made it an excuse to catch her fingers briefly in his.

When she went back inside, Daddy and Momma were sitting at the kitchen table, an envelope torn open between them. Daddy was waving its contents around and speaking strongly—yelling, Natasha realized. Momma had her hands in her lap and was looking at the pile of unopened mail. When he saw Natasha, Daddy smiled in a way she didn't recognize. He said, "Well, well, look who's here." Momma looked at Natasha pleadingly, but Natasha wasn't used to taking directives from Momma, so she said, "I just ran outside again because I thought I'd missed some mail." Before the sentence was out of her mouth, Daddy showed her the piece of paper, which was her midterm grade report. "You're making a C in physics," he said. Natasha tried to say that she'd fix it before the end of the semester, but he slammed his fist on the table. He asked Momma what she thought was so useful about distracting Natasha from her studies by taking her to babysit in the ghetto. He asked them both how either of them expected anything good to come out of the family if they were letting Natasha's talent go to waste. He asked what was the value in laziness and time wasting. Momma said she didn't think of it as time wasting, and he stood back and grunted and smacked her in the face.

Moving fast-but-slow like in a nightmare, Natasha took the stairs to her room two at a time, listening to Momma try to get a word in edgewise. The sharp thing she'd swallowed shifted in her stomach. She felt like puking it up, but that was impossible. She lay on her bed and thought how Momma would obey Daddy. She listened to him pacing and roaring downstairs and thought how Deborah would obey him, too. But she wasn't like them.

March 26, 1983
Cleveland

On her birthday, she woke up in her bed in the Central apartment and looked out the yellow-edged window and realized she had turned thirty-five overnight. Momma always said she was a difficult baby—after twenty-six hours of labor she'd come out in the middle of the night, wide-eyed and colicky for the first two months—but she'd been worth it. The boys had been born in the afternoon after a few hours of labor: Tasha always attributed her good luck to Reggie's genes. A man who loved her that much couldn't possibly give her children capable of hurting her. Daddy on the other hand hadn't understood Momma well enough to love her. It had taken Tasha years to see it, but she saw it clear as day now. Momma was some homespun oddity to him, the human rod he'd used to ground the lightning of his (less than superior) intellect, the prop he trotted out to avoid accusations of self-hatred. She could hear him running the argument in her brain. Yes, he may have been a capitalist who believed in dressing well and "seeing across differences," but he had taught at Axel Renfroe and married a country woman. What kind of Uncle Tom would do that? Tasha turned on her stomach, exhaling her stale breath into the duvet. A fork-tongued Uncle Tom. An Uncle Tom who would speed up whenever he drove through East Cleveland, who would probably have sped up driving by the building she and her boys lived in now.

The place had been Cookie's before he left Cleveland to live with his wife's family in Georgia. It was supposed to have been a temporary haven for Tasha, someplace she could go to gather her thoughts and keep the boys safe after Reggie had disappeared. Back then, Cookie thought the people who'd come after Reggie would be coming after her, too, but then they all got blown up or their throats slit or whatever happens to drug dealers when they become useless to one another. It had been all over the papers at the time but she couldn't bring herself to read any of them. When she couldn't find Reggie—when nobody could find him—living in Central had turned into something more permanent. She found out through friends of Cookie's that the last person to see Reggie alive had been a white junkie named Leland. They knew this because he was on the street talking about it to everybody. Tasha hadn't kept up with the news after that: two types of blood in the back room, a bunch of car bombs that had gone off in East Cleveland, someone who named names and then disappeared or was disappeared. What it amounted to was Reggie had vanished and the cops wouldn't look for him—he was presumed dead, or more likely they'd killed him themselves. What it amounted to was she had to pay the city of Cleveland thousands in restitution or be found guilty of conspiracy. And then that white junkie showed up on her doorstep one day begging to come in for a coffee and crying about how sorry he was for her loss. She should never have let him in.

The last time Daddy spoke to her, she'd been packing up the dishes in the University Circle apartment. He had called to say that the family wished her the best but could not support her foolish decisions any longer. "We warned you about that boy," he said, "but your refusal to listen has resulted in your own ruination." Then he hung up. Momma called periodically when she knew Daddy wasn't listening. One time she called and her voice sounded so broken apart that all Natasha could think of was the time Daddy had slapped her in the face.

"It was when you left the PhD program for the boys," Momma said. "I think that's when you started losing Reggie."

"I didn't lose him," Natasha said, exasperated.

Momma's disapproval hummed at the edges of her overcorrected grammar. "The least he coulda done was keep you all safe."

"He did keep us safe!" Tasha protested. "And he kept us well fed. He did the best he could with what life gave him."

"Daddy wanted more for you, is all," Momma sighed. "All the time he's been saying that to me."

What did he want, really? Tasha spending a lifetime at Cleveland State among fellow PhD candidates who didn't look like her, forced day after day to defend her "alien" point of view? A life spent in front of a lecture hall full of plump white faces, watching them count the minutes until the end of her lecture? She wanted Melville only, Melville without all the trappings of having to be Tasha-Marshall-interested-in-Melville. Deborah, on the other hand, had married her dropout and moved to New Jersey with him, where he had a few cousins he had said were going to help him become a policeman. He ended up a janitor at Princeton University instead. His biggest claim to fame was cleaning the office of some math professor who solved some impossible equation and won a prize for it. When Deborah did call, she'd say "Dennis put down new carpeting in Professor Milo Andritt's office!" like Tasha was supposed to care. So she pretended to, and when Deborah's voice took on a sad lilt and she asked, "You still staying at that place in Central?" Tasha said yes, pretending that it was intentional. Now, every month when they spoke, Deborah offered to send a chunk of her secretary's salary, and every month Tasha accepted. She knew her sister must secretly delight in this: the former fuckup helping the wunderkind out of poverty. When Tasha and Reggie had been taking Momma and Daddy to the opera, Deborah barely picked up the phone. But the minute Tasha's husband disappeared, the phone was ringing off the hook. Everyone but Momma had betrayed her. Only Momma deserved to know the truth, so one day, exhausted from years of lying, she told her.

"Momma," she had said, feeling shame and pity and anger at once. "I didn't lose him. He was already gone."

"What are you talking about?"

"He dealt drugs. Isn't it obvious from what they said in the papers?"

She waited, eyebrows raised, for Momma to react. Silence, then the kind of ragged breathing that comes before a faint.

"I thought it was a gunfight at the massage place and he got caught in it," Momma said in a small voice.

"Please, Momma." Natasha was aware that her voice had a scolding lilt. "You know better than that."

The line went dead.

She'd been without him almost a decade now but still reached across the bed for him. On this birthday, she'd taken her morning shift off from Hero Sandwiches and her afternoon shift at the grocery store. Nowadays she walked to work in a shower cap and housecoat, barely paid her bills on time, let her hands and face get ashy in the winter. She was no different from anyone else, and she'd been wrong to think she ever was.

□

Thinking about Daddy's exceptionalism now made her sick with anger. She hated his fake judge's bench and his stupid patrician face, the gold wire-framed bifocals he'd always cast his eyes over in search of her. Whenever he got bored and needed a devil's advocate to banter with, an opponent to beat in chess, he'd stare over those bifocals and call out, "Where's my little matryoshka doll?" Natasha couldn't keep herself from remembering it. Here I am, Daddy, unwashed and dysfunctional. Happy now? Where had he come off thinking either of them were special? He could have spent a lifetime acting white and white people would still call him boy and give him their dinner order or suitcases to carry—she'd seen it happen too many times, seen him grit his teeth and correct them with politeness she knew even then they didn't deserve.

She'd awakened that morning with a Tabasco-furry, unclean taste in her mouth. Dust motes hovered around and above her, eddying in the warm current of her breath. In the room down the hall, one of her boys was spinning one of her records. It was faint-sounding because he was trying to sing over it without knowing the words. It had to be Aaron, because Caleb would never sing loud enough for anyone to hear. Her blood ran cold for a second: was it a school day? She sat up, turned to the wall calendar behind her bed (a gift apropos of nothing from Deborah, March's picture a green-and-blue hummingbird dipping its needlelike beak in a giant, vulvic petunia). It was a Saturday. She collapsed in relief. Now that her body was awake, it was beginning to hurt again. The muscles in her lower back were constricted and tender to the touch, the ones on the left side so knotted that the pain shot all the way down her leg. She turned on her side, but it was no better there. She listened to Aaron singing. It was the Gap Band, "You Dropped a Bomb on Me." He was trying to sing the background vocals, too—she could detect a little falsetto. If he sang like that in public, people would start saying the things about him they always said about boys who'd grown up without fathers. She kneaded the back of her thigh with her fist. At least it wasn't Rick James.

She stood and went to her dresser, found the pair of gold conical earrings Reggie had given her as a second anniversary present. Both her feet were prickling with nerve pain. If she could've afforded a visit to the doctor, she would've had him run every diagnostic test in the lab—she needed a full-body tune-up, an oil change. She stood for most of the day every day, and when she finally sat her back seized and spasmed, insufferably tight whether she was hunched or arched or somewhere in between. There were sores under her toes that wouldn't heal, a hardness at the bottom of her stomach that kept her from fully digesting anything but greens cooked to a grayish paste. She was surprised whenever she confronted the mirror to see a young-looking face staring back. If she stood far enough away, she looked twenty-six still, or twenty-four. But a few steps closer and there were her weathered cheeks with their dilated pores, her glassy eyes, the tiny hairs at the base of her chin.

She'd always known the outlines of her husband's work, but for legal reasons had kept her distance from the specifics. She held nothing he'd done against him. She'd watched him get fired from the postal service way back when they'd first started seeing each other, had sat around with him for the year he couldn't get a job. Not even Mr. Hafez at the corner store would hire him—not even the Chinese couple who ran the gas station in Glenville. Sunny was the first person who didn't hate him, who paid him regularly and in full, who respected his talent and intelligence. Another thing Daddy would never understand was that it took talent to do what Reggie did. Talent and athleticism and some of the quickest thinking she'd ever seen. He was always one split decision away from a bullet to the chest. He kept his guns in a safe box under some loose tiles in the bathroom floor. She hated it at first, and she told him as much. They fought about it. He told her he'd been locked up three times as a teenager: possession with intent to distribute, stealing something he hadn't stolen, and loitering. He'd tried following the law but the law just followed him until he felt like he was being hunted. There was no legal good life, so why not live an illegal good life now that they'd been given the chance? Natasha countered that maybe it was a good life, but the cost was too high. Better to live humbly and stay alive than live well and die. But she couldn't change his mind, and nothing bad ever happened to them. There was a chance he'd been right. She loved him too much to leave him anyway.

When the boys were a year old, she had heard him coming up the stairs to their University Circle apartment as she was putting them to bed. And before he saw her coming from their bedroom to greet him in the hallway, she saw the blood on his shoes, saw his coat flap open to reveal the butt of a pistol. He had walked carefully into the kitchen, expecting her to be asleep. She went back to their bedroom without saying anything. She never saw those shoes again.

He was a good father. He was better than any of the fathers she'd known, her own included. He had cried for nights after the boys were born, guilty that he hadn't been the one kneeling over her as she strained in the bathtub during their delivery. He'd slept on his side facing her, the boys in between them screaming instead of sleeping—whenever he could, he'd carry one of them in each arm to the living room and sit on the couch with them so she could sleep. For months, she'd shuffle into the kitchen around dawn and see his snoring profile, the cradle-soft heads of Caleb and Aaron pressed against either armpit. He noticed their personalities before she did: the way Caleb would laugh and point his fat index finger at birds and trees and houses, giggly and inquisitive; how Aaron observed the world from his stroller with his little arms folded over his stomach like a stoic Mafia don. He'd take them to the park on Mayfield where all the Italian kids played, and not even some craggy *nonna* with her yellow-white hair and golden rosary could help commenting that Caleb and Aaron should be in commercials on TV. It was something about Reggie's smile, his confidence. Tasha knew he had enemies in Little Italy, but he played civilian so well nobody ever bothered him. She felt safe walking with him anywhere, even after Cookie had drunkenly told her one New Year's that Reggie was Cleveland's Most Wanted Man. She figured that was some kind of macho contest stuff—who can anger the most people and still manage to stay alive?—but it turned out Cookie was right.

□

I can't go on. I must go on. She was at least smart enough not to be hypnotized by Beckett's literary nonsense. She stood up and was confronted with a wave of exhaustion so strong she considered staying in bed for the day. She shook off the doubt and began dressing herself. Now her thoughts were proceeding in an awful circle—her mind was eating itself like an ouroboros, likely because she had nothing better to do. She thought that her brain in most any other body would surely be zippering an expensive skirt in a big house in the World of Consequence. Who, when being tailed by a security guard in a department store, thought of the space both she and the guard occupied as Cartesian, her place a coordinate on a graph and his a separate, encroaching coordinate? Who gulped down the poison in the water more enthusiastically than Tasha, named for a crazy white person in a novel?

If she kept thinking and thinking and thinking like that, she wouldn't make it through the day. And she had plans that day, embarrassing plans with Leland that the boys couldn't find out about. Year five of these plans (on and off, to be fair to herself), and she'd managed to do a decent job of keeping it from them both. She'd wait until they were older and just come forward with it, tell them bitterness can rot a person inside out, ask them to imagine her viscera turning blue-black and her tongue drying up inside her head. She'd say, "Sometimes seeking revenge against the world by whatever small means available is the only cure for the inner rot." Leland was her revenge against the world, the last person over whom she held power, who could be made to feel a fraction of her own pain.

The Gap Band LP was done and still spinning, making the dense, fuzzy noise of empty wax. She went into the living room and turned it off: Aaron was nowhere to be seen. She went to her desk, where two different Melville companions lay open on either side of her typewriter. The second companion was opened to an earmarked, scribbled-over essay by Ellyn Marmeloy, a professor of American literature at Dover College in Ontario. Ms. Marmeloy had made the definitive argument for "Bartleby the Scrivener: A Story of Wall Street" as the Freudian counterwish of the Rather Elderly Man who narrates it. *Secundum* Marmeloy, the Rather Elderly Man isn't recounting the story of the eccentric scrivener formerly in his employ— he's remembering a dream he himself once had, one in which his ego is divided between Bartleby and Bartleby's worried third-person observer. Since he has always been of the mind that "the easiest way of life is the best," the Rather Elderly Man is supremely (arguably even sexually) satisfied by Bartleby's failure to function—his real desire isn't for Wall Street success but for grand and transparent failure.

It was an excellent essay, at least in Tasha's opinion. The essay in the second companion was a rebuttal to "I'd Prefer (Not) To: An Ego-Splice in 'Bartleby'" by an obscure scholar named James Hefnow, a man who'd made a career of arguing unsuccessfully against Marmeloy. Tasha hadn't read his essay closely—he'd asserted something along the lines of "Marmeloy lacks a nuanced understanding of the concept of the counterwish"—but she had read Marmeloy's ad hominem rebuttal, "A Very Modest Proposal," in the *Journal of Melville Studies*. "Hefnow is an intelligent and accomplished man who nevertheless cannot recognize an error in his own logic," she'd written. "He requires the victim of his attempted *reductio* to explain its absurdity to him." Tasha had written her own rebuttal, one about how Bartleby was the Rather Elderly Man's spiritual guide (Philemon to the boss's Carl Jung) instead of some defective aspect of his ego. The essay also fleshed out what she recognized as Melville's distaste for capitalism—in such a system everyone eventually loses sight of their humanity, becomes their work, etc.—and invoked Dickens's Scrooge and his three cautionary spirits. It'd taken four months to write and she had felt something stir in her as she worked that she had thought was long since dead. She'd sent it to Marmeloy. No response, which of course she'd expected; probably better that way.

The real question was whether Marmeloy had even read it. Or whether she'd given it to some student worker or department secretary to read. Daddy had always had all his mail forwarded to the history department secretary at Axel Renfroe, an acrylic-nailed woman named June who read and summarized for him the angsty queries of future students, the threats from irate parents, the tedious requests from far-flung colleagues. Was June still at Axel Renfroe, or would she have retired by now? And if she was still there, had Daddy told her to throw out all mail from someone named Natasha Marshall? June might have remembered the name—Daddy spoke rarely enough of his personal life that June probably thought Tasha was named Teesha or Tiana or something—and asked him if he was really serious. She could see him nodding solemnly: "Yes. A grave trespass has occurred against my family's honor."

"A!" she called. There was a noise like a shoe kicking the wall at the end of the hallway, then silence. "Aaron!" she called, not liking the reedy way her voice sounded. She lit a cigarette from the pack on the dinner tray in front of the TV. There were two fewer than had been in there yesterday, which she knew was probably Aaron's fault, but for which she could hardly blame him. There emerged from the room at the end of the hall not Aaron but Caleb in his usual oversized shirt, smiling, his hands behind his back.

"Momma," he said.

She arranged her face to look happy. "Hi, baby," she said.

"Hi," he said, and sputtered out a little laugh.

"What're you laughing about?" she asked.

He shrugged. "It's your birthday, so I got you this." He produced from behind his back a long-legged frog body and she jumped away. He followed, wagging it in front of her until she realized it was a rubber toy. Then she remembered how small he was in comparison to his brother (they were both thirteen but Aaron seemed seventeen and Caleb eleven), how strangely he dressed, how often he came home from school bloodied by kids stronger than he was. The shameful facts of his situation formed a hot compress around her skull. She wanted to cry for him, for her, for their doomed future.

"The fuck is that?" she said instead. "Why would I want this? You better grow up, Cee. After all I've done for you."

He stumbled back, shocked. "Momma, it was a joke." He pulled something out of his pocket and put it in her hands: a digital watch.

"It's the Casio C-80 calculator watch," he said, his voice buoyant again. "It's all these articles about it in *Popular Science*, it's the watch of the future. I thought you'd like it because it has a calendar in it, so you won't have to use the paper one Aunt Deborah sent you."

She cried then. "Cee," she tried, then hiccupped.

He hugged her; he wasn't yet as tall as she was. "Momma, you thought I'd get you a goddamn frog for your birthday?"

"Cee, where'd you even get the money?"

"I saved up some, and A gave me some, and he let me pick it out," he said. "So it's from both of us that way."

"How long you been saving up?"

He shrugged.

"Can you still take it back? Can you still get your money back?"

He was already buckling the watch around her wrist. "Nah," he said. "It looks good on you, though."

There was no way to express how sorry she was. She kissed his head, held him as though shielding him from shrapnel. He let her do it for a moment, then pushed away. "I gotta breathe, Momma, Jesus," he said.

"Where's your brother?"

"He went out with some of the guys. He said to tell you happy birthday and he wants to cook dinner."

The clock on the wall above his head read one twenty-seven. She didn't want to say what she said next, but she did anyway: "Can you go out with him? I need to clean around here."

"On your birthday?"

"Look at this place. It's long overdue."

"I can help you clean. I can start on our room."

"No, baby. You already did more than enough."

Something strange passed between them, a ghost or the shadow of a ghost. The feeling left her cold.

"All right," he said. Then he got his coat from their room and left.

Now she'd actually have to clean before they got home. The living room alone was a mess of yesterday's dinner hardened on plastic plates, Aaron's stained white T-shirt and Browns jersey, stabbed-out cigarette butts, a pyramid of Dixie cups Caleb had built for some reason while watching *Knight Rider*. She pulled the couch from the wall, her back spasming in the process. A single condom still in its wrapper, not the brand she used. A wiry ball of her own hair, crumbs from pizzas the boys had eaten. She picked up the hair ball and threw it out. There was a knock at the door and she opened it.

He had dressed up: a checkered button-up, slacks, a leather tie, and a belt on its tightest notch. His skin was gray and he was shining with sweat, the hair at his embarrassing side part already damp. In one hand he held a silver tin, in the other a yellow suitcase. He looked like a villain in the comic books Deborah used to read. He leaned in to kiss her and she leaned away.

"Did I do something wrong?" he asked, looking genuinely hurt.

She pulled him in and closed the door, pointing to the tin. They sat at the kitchen table and did bumps—it was bad, and she could feel it all accumulating in a brain pocket just above her left ear, but she kept doing more because at least she was feeling better than she'd felt this morning. He explained to her, as he did every time he saw her, that he was more in love with her than he was with his wife and that there was nothing stopping him from leaving Melinda and being with her forever if she'd just admit that she loved him back.

"The problem is I don't." She watched in semidisgust as he snorted up a two-inch line from the table's surface.

"But I think you do," he offered. "The way we fuck, I really think you do."

"You're wrong," she said.

They fucked. It was serviceable. It was better than serviceable, if she was being honest: it was redemptive, a convenient place to release her anger. She finished. As always, she looked away from him, closed her eyes tight, and tried her best to conjure Reggie's face, and if not his face at the very least his eyes and forehead, or his beard and chin, any piece of him that her memory conceded to make available to her on short notice. He materialized briefly and she felt she'd held him—fucking Leland always did this to her—and she sighed with relief. She would take this wherever she could come by it. She knew how Leland felt, desperate for a dose.

When they were done and sitting naked next to each other, he pulled the goddamn briefcase he'd been carrying onto the bed and told her that it contained almost a quarter of a million dollars, a present for her. She laughed, then felt bad for laughing. This was like the time he loped into her apartment claiming he could hear other people's thoughts. Or the time he took both her hands in his and told her he was being wiretapped by God.

"It's for you," he said. "It's for the boys, and for your birthday. It belonged to Reggie. I can't keep it anymore. I'm leaving."

She made to open it but saw that it had been soldered shut. The anger started in the back of her throat. She shoved it away with her naked shin—it was heavy, with what she didn't care to know. "I don't want your garbage," she said.

"But did you hear what I said? I'm leaving."

She lit a cigarette. "And I don't want your garbage."

He swallowed; his tumorous Adam's apple bobbed. "Natasha, I'm leaving because Cleveland is no longer safe for me, not with knowing the things I know. I'm going south, to Florida."

She sighed. It had been almost ten years since Reggie had disappeared and still Leland was talking this way. "Why Florida?"

"I saw an ad for it in a travel magazine. For Orlando." She grunted, and he persisted. "The beauty of this country is you can go anywhere and remake yourself completely. I've been speaking a lot to my rabbi, been speaking to him about God, and I really think that you could try to speak with him, too, we could look into getting married and living in Florida, where we'd be safe, where the boys would be safe, I really do think of them as my own—"

She hit him. She didn't realize she'd done it until after she'd done it. He doubled over, swearing, both hands at his cheek, the knobs of his spine visible above his head.

"I'm sorry," she said.

He shook his head. "No, no, you were right. You were very right. The boys aren't mine, they're Reggie's. Spiritually they are mine, maybe, or will be after you take this money from me."

"It's not money in there," she said, tired of him, ready to be alone.

He looked at her as if she'd just informed him he'd eaten poison. He lifted the briefcase, shook it, slapped it. "There's money in here, just sealed up for safety. You don't know what I've been through, Natasha. If you won't come with me, then take the money. If you will come with me, then you can also take the money in a way, it'll be our money to have, just safer in Florida, but you'll absolutely have to let me know either way, I'm leaving forever this week. I can't be with this briefcase alone anymore."

Now, despite herself, she'd begun to question her own disbelief. Beneath the delirium and mania there shone in his eyes a recognition of some external threat. Or was she just losing her mind? How much time had she spent with him in this bed, smoking while he told her his theories, denying his requests to be loved back?

She clucked her tongue.

"I'll take the money, Leland. How about that?"

There was a beeping noise, a loud one. Leland stood up, exposing his hairy thighs and wormlike dick, his whole shrunken body. "What's that?" he demanded. "What's making the noise?"

She had no idea. It was coming from the nightstand where she'd put her earrings. Then she saw the Casio, its screen flashing 3:30 3:30 3:30.

"This damn thing my son got me," she said, pressing at random the buttons on its face. She looked up at Leland, then out the window, then again out the window. She screamed, pulled the covers to her chest. It was Aaron, face and hands pressed to the glass pane. Through the sheer curtain she saw he wore a black shirt with the words *You're just a sucker M.C.* printed in white, a shirt she'd never seen him wear before, could see his hands tighten and rise as fists from the glass. Leland looked out the window and flinched away, sat down naked in the corner.

Tasha's throat went dry. Her vision blurred. "I'm sorry, baby!" she shouted at the window, but Aaron's face was set in a tight rictus of anger. She never imagined he'd look this old this young, be this capable of a grown man's outrage and grief, and she feared for him. She looked down at the bedspread, rubbing her eyes. When she looked up again he was gone.

DIEDRE BLOOM-MITTWOCH, NÉE MIFKIN

(1962–)

Orlando

What had been happening in Diedre's life prior to the summer of 1985, the month of July, when he drove up to the Shell where she worked in his 1976 green Ford Pinto, dressed in resort-owner pants and a guayabera, pupils massive behind a pair of expensive-looking Ray-Bans? She had been living with her girlfriend Trish in an efficiency above Sol's Delicatessen in Orlando. Trish who worked at the same Shell as Diedre but who earned more money because she also waitressed three days a week. Trish who played drums in a hardcore band called Damocles Anthem that was moderately famous in the Orlando underground scene, playing places like Club Space Fish and D.I.Y. Records. Trish who confirmed the stereotypes about girl drummers dining at the Y: all of them had something to do with rhythm and persistence, and Trish had both.

When she met Trish, Diedre had been eighteen, the frizzy-headed child of southern Jews with an Irish obsession so strong they'd decided to name their only child after a mythological Celtic queen known for her misery. Diedre found the name embarrassing, especially since they couldn't even be bothered to spell it right: in all the books it was "Deirdre," and all her schoolteachers automatically wrote it that way, apologizing when she corrected them.

Her mother was a stenographer, the tight-lipped, brittle-boned daughter of a Jacksonville cantor, a woman who'd grown up wearing wigs and swimming in mikvehs and thinking she was inferior to men until she disobeyed the cantor by attending the ice cream social where she met Diedre's father. Her father was a bow-legged, thick-chested frummie-turned-semiapostate who could maybe be seen as handsome in the same way the movie gangster Jimmy Cagney could be seen as handsome if he also drove a produce truck. They lived in a one-and-a-half-story ranch in a row of identical one-and-a-half-story ranches, the three of them bonded by their unusual last name and their weekly trek to Congregation Ohev Shalom and divided by nearly everything else.

Diedre's mother had decided to spend the Reform second half of her life working furiously to make up for what she'd missed in the Orthodox first. She bought herself two nice dresses, one twill and the other houndstooth. Every Thursday after work, she changed into the twill and drove back out to the Denmark Café, where she hobnobbed with a gaggle of wealthy goy housewives who'd been there since noon, drinking coffee with nonfat milk and sharing a single scone among the four of them. Diedre's mother had been given Semitic blood but non-Semitic features: an ovoid, olive-complected face with heavy lashes and a small nose, a Mediterranean beauty that Aryans didn't seem disturbed by. Although she rarely understood what they were talking about, she was always polite, laughing at the appropriate times and learning to correctly use their expressions: "weekday window-washer" and "all the bread, none of the butter." As a consequence, she became a member of two or three "prominent" book clubs and a sewing club. When the clubs hosted their socials, she wore the houndstooth and a necklace of Bakelite pearls.

Diedre's father, disinvited from all club socials after making what he thought was a joke among friends about one goy's curtains maybe not matching her drapes, had decided to spend the second half of his life retreating inward. He was a small, hairy man who perspired through his shirt at the underarms and nipples and had a gap between his front teeth that Diedre had inherited. He was lovable, and his lovability was in large part due to his smiling unawareness of his own self: his odd-smelling produce truck, his hairline receding in the shape of a bird in flight, his arcane jokes that came poorly translated from their original Russian. Whereas Diedre's mother proved a social asset at school, Diedre's father was her Achilles' heel. This was difficult for Diedre, because she had known from an early age that she was one of those girls who would always worship her father, who would look for a boyfriend with his same self-assured brawn, his same sense of humor.

▢

After school Diedre was typically shut in her room, forcing herself to at least stare at her homework before she swept it off her desk and set to work cutting up and resewing her jeans, tearing pictures out of magazines, and listening to the Buzzcocks. It was while spinning "I Don't Mind" that she pierced her ears with a sewing needle and a rubber eraser. Pete Shelley's voice brought her back to earth; he of all people wouldn't care if her piercings weren't perfectly symmetrical. At school she wasn't a person but a deadly combination of traits—a freak who was also stupid, averaging Cs and Ds in most classes except English, which was a C-plus. She was saved from complete ostracization only by her mother's prominence. She had no friends, just people who acted friendly toward her: a tight-knit pack of burnouts, a few proto-goths, the occasional skinny lone wolf who entered her orbit for a few weeks only to drift away after she acknowledged him. She wasn't beautiful: her hair grew in crimped and uneven patches of frizz, there was the gap between her teeth, her feet were splayed, her chest flat. In a restaurant on her sixteenth birthday, a waiter had called her "sir." In those years, she was painfully aware she had no obvious talent, no way to legitimize her existence. She bought pain pills and weed off the burnouts. She smoked the weed at night and ate the pain pills in the morning so at school she always had the distant, heavy-headed feeling that her eyes were tunneling into her skull.

By her senior year, it was clear to everyone in the Mifkin household that Diedre would not be the first among them to go to college. Her mother was disappointed and her father was pleasantly indifferent. She got an after-school job at a diner called Mayman's with the understanding that she'd work there until she could afford secretarial school. She was a "pre-server," cleaning tables, mopping the floor, and hastily delivering customers their plastic tumblers of water before the real waitress (it was usually Shirley or Dayna during Diedre's shift, both chain-smokers, both happily married) came over and sweetly inquired after people's orders. Pre-serving, with its dirty mop water, its crumbs in the cracked linoleum, its hair balls and shit stains in the bathroom, was good enough for her. The few times she needed to fill in for a missing server, she found herself gagging at the smell of the twice-baked, Crisco-thick food; she hated acting polite to kids who spat their straw wrappers at her; she hated the way people began eating the minute she set their plates on the table, the way they couldn't afford anything more than a grunt when she came by five minutes later to ask if everything had been lard-slathered to their satisfaction. She got reedier in those early months working at the diner, subsisting mostly on Popsicles and stalks of celery, declining her father's creamy blintzes in favor of sticks of chewing gum. Soon her clothes hung from her body and she felt as though she'd finally accomplished something.

One day she returned from her ten-minute break having burned a fifteen-minute jay, her eyes star-clouded, and saw a pale brown girl with premature crow's-feet, tight black ringlets, and tiny teeth sitting at the counter and drinking a cup of coffee. She smiled out from under her frummie-looking fedora, making obvious the chip in her right front tooth. "Can I get some service?" she asked.

Diedre nodded and tied her apron around her waist. She took out her notepad. She noticed the girl didn't have a menu, so she got her one. The girl smiled, showing her unnatural teeth. She took the menu, opened it, skimmed it, and closed it. She looked at Diedre.

"I'm Trish," she said.

Diedre nodded and began to write that down, then stopped. Trish laughed.

"Do you like it here?"

Diedre hesitated before answering. "They work us hard."

Trish glanced at the menu, then back at Diedre.

"But we all need to eat," Diedre said. "We all need to put food on the table."

Trish laughed again.

"What kind of food can I put on your table?" Diedre said, trying to say it like a joke.

"What kind of food can you put on my table?" Trish asked, and Diedre nodded briskly, trying not to laugh because the way she'd said it, it sounded like it could've meant something else. She was like her father trying to make conversation with a pretty woman. Would you like your Korall melted? Your roll buttered? Trish bit her lower lip.

At the end of Diedre's shift, they were kissing in the stockroom. Trish's plump lips and tiny teeth made hard little pills of Diedre's nipples. She stuck her head under Diedre's shirt. Diedre made gasping noises without meaning to. She had only been kissed once before, by a lone wolf named Benny Hopgood in a science classroom after the final bell had rung. The kiss—chaste, brief, lips on lips—was nothing compared to what Trish was doing. If Trish noticed that Diedre couldn't exactly follow along, she never let on.

After that they saw each other all the time. Trish had been kicked out of her Catholic parents' house for what she called "being a trashdyke," so she lived with four other kids in a trailer down a swampy road at the edge of town. Two were the Doherty brothers, speed-metal freaks from the Everglades who were missing teeth from a combo of drugs and semi-pro boxing. Another was a girl named Sophie Lin who sat on a bean bag behind a massive curtain of hair and smoked purplish kush from a hookah whenever she wasn't working at Hollywood Video Rental. And the fourth was a guy who said his first name was Raymond and claimed to have no last name. Raymond's uncle was in the Hells Angels, which meant the trailer got an infusion of tina every couple of months.

Trish's bed was a cot in a room she shared with the Dohertys. When they were gone—and they almost always were—Trish and Diedre snorted tina and fooled around, doing things Diedre had previously read about in magazines but now understood perfectly under the ecstatic influence, every part of her body magnetized to Trish's touch, her crotch slobbering the minute the tina unfurled its glittery petals in her brain. Trish had blindfolds, eighteen-inch toys, boundless energy, no past. All she revealed about her parents was their religion and their willingness to kick a sixteen-year-old kid out of their house. Diedre didn't even know if Trish was from Florida or not, if she had siblings, if she'd graduated high school. In the glorious early days of their relationship, none of it mattered. Not in the smoke-dense world they inhabited together, where Sophie was always asking them to guess the title of the song she was humming (it was usually unguessable) and all six of them piled onto the couch to watch *Dallas* after heating their respective frozen dinners in the Dohertys' sauce-spattered microwave. Diedre could see herself spending the rest of her life with Trish, which was pleasantly shocking considering she'd always imagined herself eventually settling into a version of her parents' tired routine with some hairy-backed guy from their congregation. That was the beauty of Trish: she was completely left field. If Diedre's mother even met Trish, which

Diedre hoped she never would, she wouldn't even think, *I bet this lesbian's sleeping with my daughter.* Diedre's father might pull Diedre closer to him if they saw Trish on the street, urging Diedre to stay employed so she wouldn't have to resort to "turning tricks like that one." (Anyone poorer-looking than him was a "that one.") It wasn't so much her parents' hypo-thetical disapproval she was getting off on—it was their very real dumbness.

Diedre moved out of her childhood bedroom and into the trailer, sleep-ing splayed across Trish on the cot. Eventually Diedre's mother started agitating for a visit, so Diedre and Trish hatched a plan to find some real estate of their own—the Dohertys' boxing practices and Raymond's one-man jam sessions were proving to be too much, anyway. They moved into an apartment above a delicatessen, a dusty efficiency owned by a one-eyed landlord who claimed to have acquired his condition in Vietnam. When Diedre's mother finally made good on her threat to visit, they hid all of Trish's toiletries in the cabinet under the sink, praying Diedre's mother wouldn't start rummaging around. Bewilderingly, she seemed pleased with what she saw.

"Well, it's cozy," she said, pulling a checkered dress of Trish's out of the closet. She swatted dust from it, frowning. "You've got some interest-ing new clothes."

"And all this without a college degree," Diedre said, which her mother ignored, floating across the room to inspect the curtains.

After two years with Trish, Diedre finally got beautiful. She kept on try-ing to starve herself but her body revolted, sending her to the fridge in the middle of the night after a Popsicle-only day, insisting she gorge on cheese and peanut butter and chocolate. Her breasts filled and so did her hips. At first she was embarrassed about it, cinching her jeans in hopes that making an equilateral triangle of her butt would prevent anyone from noticing. But Trish noticed—for a while, it was all she talked about. "Something to hold on to!" she said, grabbing a cheek in relief. "I loved you then as much as I do now, but it was harder to show it." Soon Diedre understood what she meant. Even on tina Trish had been delicate, using only the tip of her tongue, holding Diedre at the hips as though she were teaching her to float on her back in the shallow end of a pool. Now she pulled and squeezed every item of skin that wasn't flush with Diedre's bones. They were louder and wetter and finished quicker. Diedre realized her tooth gap was sexy instead of embarrassing. She grew her hair out long, bathed it in tea tree oil, and knotted the silky strands in a bun at the top of her head. She abandoned the triangle and wore tight leggings and tank tops that showed everything. She switched from black lipstick to mauve, and she pierced the cartilage of her right ear from the point nearest her head to her earlobe. She began to get stares from men, all types of them: college football players, office workers, panhandlers, grocers. Trish put her hand around Diedre's waist as they walked down the street. Sometimes Trish cleaned up, too, zipped herself into a strapless cocktail dress and sprayed her hair and wore a black plastic choker. Then all the creeps on the street would start cheering for the two of them to kiss. And instead of flipping them off, they did. They kissed in front of the creeps, on the bus, in the stockroom at the diner. When Dayna caught them in the back hallway, Diedre was fired and they both got jobs at the Shell. Trish had said they'd have to work double shifts if they wanted to save up for their wedding. It was hard to tell if she was joking.

A few months later, Trish made another announcement: they were giving up tina because they needed to "get serious about life." Diedre had no idea why this was happening, and spent days exhausted by her own cravings. Noodle-kneed, she asked Trish what the fuck she meant by getting serious about life. Trish—who didn't seem to miss tina—responded patiently that they weren't kids anymore, they'd barely used that much anyway, they needed to schedule their time on earth better. Diedre couldn't take it; she never got it out of her system completely. She woke up and went to sleep with splitting headaches, grinding her teeth, sick to her stomach. Trish started going back to the trailer to fool around on Raymond's drum set, Sophie on bass, Raymond on guitar, one of the Dohertys singing vocals. At first they just played Black Flag covers, but then she started to write songs. Most of them were about what it felt like to be on drugs. A few of them were about a "lizard-eyed girl" Diedre assumed was her. She watched Orlando's weirdos crawl out of their basements to headbang to Trish's songs. She was always stoned in the front row, trying to make eye contact with her girlfriend to confirm whether a particular song was about her, getting jostled by the sweaty, muscled moshing behind her. The shows got more frequent. Trish wound through the crowd in search of talent scouts or small-time record producers, shaking hands. They'd wind up at the Florida Hospital cafeteria afterward, gorging themselves on veggie burgers (Trish no longer believed in eating meat), making conversation with all the pale-faced straightedge kids about whether Morrissey and Johnny Marr were fucking.

Diedre began to spend more time home alone. She thought maybe she was being punished for getting hot. She was getting hetero attention—the kind of attention they'd both vowed to disavow. Maybe it was because Trish didn't like being in competition with a bunch of muscular assholes who probably wanted to drive her girlfriend around in their beaten-up cars and take her to shitty concerts. When they went out to eat after work, Trish began to do things like peel bills from the roll in her pocket, insisting that Diedre didn't have enough. When Diedre complained about the blender being fritzy, the broom's bristles being frayed, the radio's antenna being bent, Trish replaced them all, happy to play the part of breadwinner. She left Diedre gifts on the kitchen table: a gram of weed, a turquoise necklace, a shubunkin goldfish. Diedre named the goldfish Patti and watched her swim around in her glass bowl, her belly scraping the rainbowed pebble stuff at the bottom. Two weeks later, Patti sprouted knobby growths on her forehead and her swimming became confused, one fin paddling frantically while the other remained flush with her side.

"There's no such thing as a fish doctor," Trish said, stooping to see through the murk in Patti's bowl. "Maybe there's some food we can give her to get it to go away."

"Vets look at fish."

"Vets don't."

Diedre pulled the tendrils curling at her hairline, a habit she thought she'd kicked in high school. "How do you know?"

Trish smirkingly kissed the top of her head. Patti swam into the side of her bowl and bounced backward like a piece of flotsam, blinking slowly.

"I think she's going blind," Diedre said. "I'm gonna change the water."

"You think fish years go faster than human years?" Trish asked. "How fast do you think a fish year goes?"

"I don't know."

Diedre changed the water, plucking gnarled Patti from her habitat and letting her flop and gasp for a few seconds in the sink. Two days later, Patti was floating on her side at the top of the bowl. Diedre poked her and watched her fins twitch, her nut-sized brain sending the remainder of its electricity through her dying body.

She stepped back. Tears were gumming up her mascara. What was she, five years old? Would she hold a funeral in the toilet bowl, ask Trish if there was a fishy heaven? Sirens mewled in the street, sending an unwelcome burst of noise through the apartment's single window, reminding Diedre that she was—she always was—completely alone. Back in the day she would've occupied this time with tina or coke or Trish's body. Trish could be out there fucking someone else right now, a groupie from a concert. She had plenty of groupies, guys and girls, but the girls were more attractive: tan, toned, multiple piercings, straying from their boring, ponytailed boyfriends to thrash their heads in the front row. But maybe Trish was trying to really mess with her, which meant she'd probably be fucking one of her rangy, tattooed guy groupies. Maybe she'd fuck him and come back smelling like Coors and his hand-rolled cigarettes. Maybe she'd come back with gonorrhea or HIV. Or worst of all: maybe she'd come back with a record deal.

Diedre turned on the TV—*60 Minutes*—and maneuvered to sit on their bed, her eyes never leaving the screen. Her father would say she was letting the situation get the "bladder" of her and that she needed to relax, take deep breaths, "let it all out." Downstairs, someone was arguing with someone else over an unpaid bill; she turned up the volume on Mike Wallace, who was talking about a nationwide increase in child kidnappings. There was nothing satisfying to listen to, but she was too tired to get up and spin an LP. Once upon a time, Trish would've done that for her. Now she was spending her time on earth better.

Diedre picked at a patch of scaling skin on her shoulder. She cupped her left boob, then her right. She looked over at Patti, kneaded her shoulders in embarrassment, looked away. She could just as easily go out and fuck someone, too.

The door clicked open and in walked Trish, eyes distant, jeans rolled up at her ankles in a way that made her look like an alt-farmer. She set down her drumsticks, took off her coat, lit a cigarette, took an initial puff, looked over at Diedre, took a second puff.

"Hi, babe," she intoned around the cigarette. Diedre hugged her knees. "What did you do today?"

"I had today off."

Trish ignored the answer, pulling pieces of paper from her backpack, arranging them on the kitchen table and shuffling them around as though she were within inches of breaking some Soviet code.

"What's that?" Diedre asked.

"Hm?"

"What's the papers?"

Trish made what sounded like a noise of acknowledgment, but sleepier.

"What's the papers?" Diedre asked again.

"Something for the band."

"What for the band?"

"We're going on tour."

"Where?"

She shrugged. "Just Florida."

"Like where in Florida?"

Silence, paper shuffling, tar-thickened air. "Daytona Beach."

"Patti died today."

Trish looked up. "How?"

"I feel pretty bad about it."

"How?"

Diedre hadn't anticipated needing to provide a backstory. She stood, got the bowl from the dresser, and brought it to Trish, who looked into it and then back up at Diedre.

"The water's clean," Trish said.

"I mean, yeah."

"It was dirty like the day before yesterday."

"Yeah, but I changed it."

"Maybe you changed it too late."

"You think that's why it happened?"

Trish shrugged, poked at Patti, then took the bowl from Diedre and set it down on the kitchen table. She stank of the Dohertys' hand-rolled cigarettes and her own unwashed smell, a mustardy, rubbery perfume that clouded at the nape of her neck and under her arms. She cupped Diedre's chin in her hand and pulled her in for a kiss, landing on her lips in a way that bruised, and then shook Diedre's head no, no, no.

"You don't want to be kissed?" she asked.

Diedre pried herself from Trish and stumbled away, rubbing her cheeks.

"That's maybe the one thing that could make you cuter," Trish said. "If you didn't want to be kissed all the time."

Diedre slept poorly that night, her limbs freezing, her head hot, folding herself into a fetal ball to accommodate Trish's snoring and sprawling. She rose at dawn and watched the sun creep upward, stretching by pressing her hands into the tense small of her back. She was almost four years deep into a life with a woman who her mother (now attending Christmas luncheons and fantasizing about a rhinoplasty, according to her father's latest update) and her father (still driving the produce truck, still making his fatty blintzes in a time and place where people would kill to be thin) thought was her roommate. She imagined waking up four years from now—she'd be twenty-seven!—and listening to Trish's throaty snores, smelling the mustard under her arms, heating up frozen dinners, and wondering where in this great state of Florida Damocles Anthem would play next, but mostly thinking about how expensive the vodka would be at the after-party.

It was June or July and she was sweating in her Shell jumpsuit, her sleeves rolled up, her hair a bandannaed mess of knots and flyaways, her cheeks a livid red from overwork. It was a Sunday, she knew that much, because Trish wasn't there: Sundays Trish worked at Denny's until four o'clock. Sundays Diedre could unzip her jumpsuit and roll it down, drink a glass of water from the cooler outside the convenience store like this without Trish constantly reminding her to zip up.

She was doing exactly that when the Ford Pinto pulled up, her supervisor barking at her to get on that pump because she was pretty and he looked like a good tipper. She chugged the last of her water, pulled down her sunglasses, and made her way to him, the sleeves of her jumpsuit flopping at her sides. The driver of the Pinto watched her approach, the familiar widening of the grin and arching of the neck. She could see behind his sunglasses a pair of thick-lidded eyes. They darted vertically (the length of her body), then horizontally (between her and the convenience store). He looked at her over his frames and she saw immediately that he was a little old. Not the frightening, elderly kind—the interesting, adult kind.

"What's your name?" he asked.

She pulled the nozzle from the pump, tightened the main valve, and unscrewed the cap on his gas tank. "Diedre."

"Pretty name," he said. "You certainly took your sweet time saying it."

Annoyed, she kept working in silence. Then she remembered the tip. "It's an Irish name," she said. "I don't know why my parents chose it."

"What's your last name?"

"Mifkin."

"So you're a Jewess?" He hissed the last syllable.

"Russian, yeah."

She could feel him watching her work. As his tank filled, she made her own assessment of his body: average height, hair graying and receding, the skin behind his unbuttoned collar rooster-colored, his forearms pale.

"You're a northerner," she said.

"On the money."

"What's your last name?"

"I have two," he said. "Bloom-Mittwoch. My mother was too much of a fighter to give hers up."

She nodded.

"Mittwoch means 'Wednesday' in German," he offered.

"Oh," she said. "I took Spanish in high school, but I can't really speak it."

He sniffed and rubbed his nose, and it occurred to her that maybe he partook. He looked both rangy enough to know where drugs were and rich enough to be able to afford them. She hadn't been properly high in months.

"My girlfriend's gone for the weekend," she said.

This had the effect she'd intended: he took off his sunglasses and looked her up and down again. "You've got girlfriend trouble?"

"Yes."

"Can I ask what's wrong?"

The pin on the nozzle clicked. She took it out and screwed the cap back on his gas tank. "I dunno," she said, unaware that her life's course was about to change again. "I guess I'm just not in love with her anymore."

May 16, 1999

The day of Leland's funeral was brutally humid, which she didn't know if he would have liked or not. He was the type to be totally indifferent to the weather: he could've smiled through a hurricane and broken china on a sunny day. Maybe that had been part of what was "wrong" with him, what the doctors and Rabbi Kamzin had recently been warning her about, but she hadn't seen it that way. He'd been reacting reasonably to an unreasonable world, was how she saw it. Her father used to say the same thing about her way back when she had refused for three weeks straight to go to school. So Leland wasn't bothered by the goddamn weather. One less thing to worry about, in her opinion.

Kamzin had already called the house twice that morning. She had ignored both calls. She didn't want to wake up into her widowed reality again. Lee was sleeping at the other edge of the king bed she'd once shared with his father, snoring softly after a fitful night. She'd rolled across the sheets—stained by now with her food, the ash from the many squares she'd smoked, her spilled beers—to comfort him, to whisper in his ear that he always had her, and that she planned to stay around for a very, very long time. She couldn't remember what she'd been doing when Leland jumped. Probably she'd just been getting home from the bank, unlocking the screen door and walking in on Lee sitting cross-legged in front of his cartoons, surrounded as he usually was by empty cans of orange Fanta. That was wrong, though, because they were saying he'd jumped early in the morning. She'd been asleep, or going to sleep. She'd probably been buzzed, but not as buzzed as he'd been. She laughed, and Lee shifted in his sleep. At least he'd gone out high.

She had been in love with him, or maybe she'd been in respect with him. They had a mutually respectful arrangement: he'd been through what he'd been through, she'd been through what she'd been through, their pasts didn't count and their future seemed manageable, if not bright. They'd gotten married impulsively, after a night together in his Orlando hotel room with two bottles of grain liquor and a bag of cocaine. He gave and gave instead of giving and withholding as Trish had; she'd missed being high so much that when she was finally high again she felt like she was soaring. He seemed bent upon satisfying her cravings, delivering to her whatever it was she wanted. They'd talked about everything, every moment of their lives prior to that night in the hotel room—she'd told him about losing her virginity, trying to get high from an empty whipped cream can, an evening during her freshman year of high school when out of boredom she stuck sewing needles into each of the fingers on her left hand. She'd told him about Trish locking herself in the bathroom, about how her parents didn't know she'd been a lesbian. He told her about his ex-wife, Melinda, who'd insisted he was a lunatic, and his son, a boy he'd named after himself who didn't take after him at all, and their sad little apartment in Cleveland, a city he called the Mistake by the Lake. He told her that he'd been raised a Jew and had neglected Judaism to his extreme disadvantage. She said she felt the same—she didn't know if she really did, but she knew she'd been wrong the whole time to pretend she was meant for anything else—and after they got their photo taken at the Elegant Enchantment Wedding Chapel she vowed never to do anything churchy ever again.

They went to Kamzin's congregation every Saturday after that, this incredibly frummie place called Chaim Sheltok where she had to sit with the other women behind a cheesecloth and where she would often stare up at the flaking picture of Jerusalem on the domed ceiling. She could see the outline of Leland's head a few benches in front of her, could see him bow forward in prayer, adjusting his kippah and tallit. As a little girl she'd been disciplined at Ohev Shalom for trying to wear one of the kippahs she'd taken from the wicker basket at the front. Trish would've thought something like that was funny and stupid. But when she told Leland he got a tight-lipped look on his face and said, "Well, it's Halakha." Trish was pure anarchy, but looking back at it now, she saw that Leland had been anarchy with a Jew's sense of purpose.

He'd turned Diedre on to the idea that her life could be an arc instead of a series of jagged happenings. With Leland she could grow up to be someone who actually impacted other people instead of being impacted by them. Before she'd been a gap-toothed kid who shrank at the sight of authority and relied on the louder, powerful, more impressive people to make decisions for her. Now she was the loud, powerful, more impressive person. She'd gotten married, gotten a job as a bank teller, bought a bungalow with her husband in a swampy town twenty miles outside Orlando called Heimsheim, gotten (sort of) clean, gotten pregnant. Sure, she drank a little bit, smoked a little bit, did a bump or two on special occasions, but Lee came out fine, came out kicking actually, proof she was capable of producing life. She knew this was the family Leland had always wanted, a good Jewish family full of love and tenderness and mutual support. And he'd found a matriarch in Diedre, a Sarah to his wandering Abraham. If she thought about it, she felt flattered that he'd traveled so long and far in search of her. When he first held Lee, Leland said, "Now *here's* my son." The family in Cleveland had been a dry run, preparation for his real family. Now Lee was the gap-toothed kid too skinny to defend himself and Diedre was alone in the world with him.

She smoked a cigarette, then rolled and smoked a blunt, watched her exhalations break apart as they reached the ceiling fan. The phone rang, and Lee turned onto his back and mewled. She thought how funny it would be to call Trish and tell her everything that had happened. If she had Trish's number still, which she didn't. Last she'd seen of her was a lengthy profile in an issue of *Maximumrocknroll*, which Diedre got delivered to the house. It was Trish, Sophie Lin, and two guys Trish had used to replace Raymond and the Dohertys, all arranged so Trish was standing with her legs apart and smirking, holding her drumsticks in one hand and a cigarette in the other, the rest of them behind her. She looked bonier than Diedre remembered her, her clavicles sticking out and the muscles in her neck stringy. The headline was: "Damocles Anthem Is Changing How We Think About Hardcore." Diedre couldn't read the whole article—not because she was jealous, which she knew for sure she wasn't—but she did get to the part where Trish was described as "a woman drummer-vocalist whose Mexican background hasn't gone unnoticed in the white-as-milk hardcore scene." They'd signed a record deal, had a debut album called *Baby Bottle* or *Baby's Bottle*, Diedre hadn't read very closely—she had to cancel her subscription after that. But that'd been almost five years ago. She was sure Trish was famous, but not like Rage Against the Machine famous, not even Botch famous. She was in that sweet spot where all the money was on its way but had not yet arrived, where talking to Diedre would still be reasonable. They used to prank call bars asking for someone named Tits Lavender, a joke they loved so much they'd sometimes answer the phone with "Tits Lavender speaking, may I ask who's calling?" She imagined calling Trish wherever she lived now—New York, probably—and asking for Tits Lavender. Maybe she'd get an agent or a producer or a lover on the other end, someone who'd pull away from the receiver and go, "This girl's asking for a Tits Lavender?" If they knew Trish, they'd know better than to hang up right away. It was funny, Diedre thought, how two very similar people could start out in the same shitty place and one could end up so much better than the other. Trish had at least tried to make sense of the world, make the things she'd done in it meaningful. Diedre just hated the world, and that motherfucker hated her right back.

Now Lee was awake, which seemed to be frightening for him. He was looking up at her smoke trails, blinking tears out of his long-lashed eyes. She was at least 50 percent sure he'd turn out to be gay, just from the soft way he walked, the pitch of his voice, the pair of blue satin shorts he always insisted on wearing in the summer. And now here he was lying on his back crying as she imagined he would someday in the bed of a boyfriend, or possibly a girlfriend before realizing he wanted boyfriends, crying quietly as he remembered this very moment on the morning of his father's funeral when his shitty mother was too stoned to comfort him.

"Baby," she said, pulling him toward her. He stayed a lump. "Baby, how are you?"

He sniffed and shook his head.

"Oh, me too, baby. I feel the same way." She hugged him and he stayed inert.

"How come nobody tried to stop him?"

They were making horrible eye contact now in the morning half-dark. The phone rang again, which made him jump.

"Ignore that," she said. "I'll call him back when we get up."

"I bet a lot of people had the chance to stop him," he said.

Did he mean Diedre? There was the fight they'd had the night before he left, when she said he'd have to quit the "medicine" because it was making him paranoid. He'd been bingeing that week, hadn't been to work in days, and she figured it was another one of those if-you-don't-come-in-today-don't-bother-coming-in-tomorrow situations. Whenever he got like this she just hid his shit or did it all herself, tried to get him to spend a day or two getting clean. She'd never seen anyone consume yayo with the enthusiasm he did. Not even the Dohertys and Raymond had devoured enough crank to match Leland's appetite. He breathed it, would bathe in it if he could. It was a lot, even for her. When she hid it, he'd storm into their room raging, then sobbing, then begging. It didn't matter, though: he always knew where to get more. She hid it the day before he left and when the fight and his paranoia had escalated, she remembered thinking that all of her friends had known when to stop partying. She'd told him that and had stormed out of the room, put Lee to bed, and gone to bed herself. Those had been the last words she said to him.

"It's hard to know when someone is suffering like that, what they need," she said, hearing in her own voice how much she was bullshitting. "Daddy was suffering so much, and not even you or I knew how bad it was."

Lee made fists and pressed them into his eyes. "I did!" he wailed.

Eventually she got up to take Kamzin's call, which was about the logis-

tics of the shiva and what should be said in the eulogy. No one would see
the corpse because of the way he'd died—his horrible new form had
been revealed to Diedre alone on a steel gurney at a morgue in Tampa.
Aside from the kaddish they weren't going to have much of a Jewish
burial, because the corpse had to be transported (outrageously expensive)
and then prepared for burial (also outrageously expensive; she didn't
know whether it was a part of grief to wish he could've at least died closer
and less gruesomely), and then she had to pay for the funeral and for
Kamzin to put together a eulogy. What was he going to say? Leland had
hardly been a pillar of his community. The best he could do was manage
to be hated and loved at the same time.

□

The nicest dress she owned was part pleather, so she had to wear the
second-nicest, black suede she'd inherited from her mother. Lee had a suit,
thankfully—Leland had purchased one for him for shul, arguing that he'd
be able to wear it on his bar mitzvah, as if he wouldn't grow at least five
inches in the next four years. Then again Lee seemed to be the kind of kid
who'd stay small his entire life, so there may have been some logic to
Leland's strategy. They combed their hair together in the mirror, Lee's lips
tight.

"How're you feeling, baby?" she asked.

"I'm not feeling any type of way," he said, his voice tired as Kamzin's.
"I just wanna get this over with."

The synagogue was empty when they got there, Kamzin busy in his
office. Diedre noticed the chipped paint on the domed ceiling, the droopy-
faced angels rushing to the feet of the guy who'd built the synagogue; she
couldn't remember his name but he always looked so young in the painting. Then she looked twice: had the painting always been of him? She could
be remembering it wrong, of course, but hadn't it been of Jerusalem when
they first started coming to services? Kamzin emerged from his back office
in his comically tall kippah, dabbing at the corners of his mouth with what
looked like a cloth napkin.

"I thought we'd have to throw together a service for you, too," he said
to Diedre. "The way you didn't pick up your phone this morning." He
adjusted his tie, his cuff links, caught sight of Lee's pale-with-grief face.
"I'm sorry for your loss."

People began to trickle in: Leland's boss, a few of her friends from the bank, a woman whose son was friends with Lee at school, some older members of the congregation. One man told Diedre that Leland's singing had been beautiful, and she didn't bother reminding him that Leland never sang. Just before the service was about to start, a young man wandered into the chapel and started talking to Lee, who was greeting mourners at the front door. Diedre had never seen the man before in her life: he was tall, maybe ten years younger than she was, black, well dressed, squatting in front of Lee like a grade school teacher on a field trip, listening patiently while Lee explained something, then looking when he pointed back at her. She waved, and he made his way toward her.

"Diedre, Lee's mom?" he said, extending his hand. "I'm Caleb Marshall. From Cleveland."

"Nice to meet you," she said.

His brows knit, unknit. Diedre was waiting. "I'm so sorry for your loss," he said. "Did he not tell you about me?"

She searched her memory for stories of Cleveland. All she could think of was the nasty ex-wife, the disobedient son. "I'm sorry, I don't think so."

This appeared to be very disturbing to Caleb Marshall, who sighed and threaded his fingers together. "Okay then," he said. "He, well, he paid for my college and law school. I'm very grateful to him."

Diedre tried to suppress a laugh but couldn't. "I'm sorry, is this a joke?"

"This absolutely isn't a joke." The small crew of mourners were beginning to look at them—his voice had changed—but Diedre didn't care. "He paid me back in money he owed my father. He wanted to make up his family's debt to ours." He paused, raised his eyebrows. "Your family's debt to ours."

"My husband used to carry those cheap plastic wallets," Diedre said. "At any given time he had less than a dollar in each of them."

The young man looked angry. "I don't see how that has anything to do with . . ."

Kamzin appeared in the main chamber, waving his hands like the building had caught fire, saying something about how they had to get things going before it got any hotter.

"I'm sorry, I don't know about the debt," Diedre said. "You're welcome, of course, but it sounds like we knew two different men." She left Caleb standing in the lobby and went to grab Lee's hand.

The burial plot was smaller than she'd remembered it being. Maybe it was the shabby gaggle of mourners, the way Kamzin cleared what sounded like a fist-sized piece of phlegm from his throat before reading scripture Diedre didn't recognize, but the whole affair felt pathetic. She remembered how the two of them used to watch Lee play in the sprinkler from the porch, Leland shirtless and drinking a tallboy while she wore the Pixies T-shirt she'd bought for him and smoked a blunt, her legs crossed over his, math rock blasting through the windows of the house. She remembered how he'd turned around during services to blow kisses at her behind the cheesecloth, how thrilled she was that they got away with being Jews by day and rock stars by night, how not a single member of that congregation suspected she went home and practiced air guitar on her bed and snorted yayo and made fun of *Dateline* with her husband, a man for whom she suspected she'd always had a place in her heart but hadn't realized it until the day at the Shell when he was right in front of her. Now the memories came faster: Leland in a pair of workman's gloves digging the palmetto bugs out of the gutter, Leland shaving Lee's hair into a Mohawk and telling other congregants that Lee had done it himself, Leland wading into the swamp behind their house to wrestle the alligator Lee claimed he'd seen in there. She closed her eyes, dizzy from a cocktail of loneliness and guilt and self-pity, and when she opened them again she saw Caleb glaring at her over her husband's coffin. He'd been joined by a tallish white man and his supermodel-looking wife. Diedre didn't know these people. It wasn't supposed to be an open funeral for the entertainment of anybody who just happened to be walking by. Her son was trembling at her hip, wiping his nose with the back of his hand. The supermodel was looking everywhere but at Diedre, and the man, her man—Diedre saw that he had the same high forehead as her late husband, the same thick eyebrows. A little "oh God" escaped her mouth, and Kamzin stumbled in his speech, went on.

She'd known practically as soon as she could think that she had been destined for a strange life, but she'd had no idea she'd been destined for the humiliations she felt later that day before her husband's shiva began. How was she, a greasy-faced Florida teenager, supposed to know that at some point in the future her husband's son from a previous marriage would come to her husband's funeral and demand that he be able to "see" the house before the shiva started? All those nights spent waiting home alone for Trish to get back from her shows, those afternoons spent massaging her swollen ankles while pregnant with Lee, those mornings spent counting old men's sleeves of change in her bank teller's uniform—how could she have known that this would happen to her? Furthermore, how could she have known what to say? The son was stronger-looking than Leland had been, taller, clearly richer. His wife had gone back to the hotel while he followed Diedre home in his rental car. She agreed to it because he wore an expensive suit and threatened to sue her if she didn't comply. What was she supposed to do? The minute he arrived, he spun around the room, his eyes bright with anger.

"He lied to you!" he yelled, sweating in his suit. "None of this belongs to you. My attorney has proof."

"Who's your attorney?" Diedre asked. It was all she could do to fight back.

But he didn't answer, just rummaged. He took nothing that Diedre had purchased with her own money, nothing that belonged to Lee—just the odds and ends that Leland had arrived with from his previous marriage: a locked-up yellow suitcase she'd never asked him about, a few paintings from the wall, a wooden box of jewelry he claimed belonged to his mother, a box of old deeds that belonged to her as well. He told Diedre he'd already claimed possession of the car. Now that the old man was dead, he said, all these things would be restored to their rightful owner.

"Take what you need and do it fast," she told him. "You're traumatizing my son."

Lee was sitting on the couch, pretending to watch TV, but he was really watching Leland Jr. wander self-righteously around the bungalow. This would surely be a moment he'd be stuck reliving, Diedre couldn't help but think, one of the thoughts he'd have at her own funeral: *My mother didn't even give two shits about the lunatic who stole stuff from our house on the day of my dad's funeral.* After Leland Jr. had gone, she held her hand out to Lee but he ignored it. She asked him to come into the kitchen with her and eat potato chips, but he shook his head. She begged him to just help her cover the mirrors, but he said he was "busy." She gave up. She had her limit, and she'd reached it.

She went into her bedroom and closed the door. Soon guests would be arriving with potato salad and candied carrots. She'd have to act natural, like nothing had happened. Lee would be catatonic on the sofa, bingeing on cartoons. She figured she had about fifteen, maybe twenty minutes to get a little stoned and change out of her dress, which was tight in the chest, and into "mourning clothes." She packed a bowl and closed the blinds. On the shelf above her bed she kept all the cassettes she'd bought but had yet to listen to. Among them was *Baby Bottle*, the title designed to look like it had been spelled out in spilled milk. She put it in her Walkman, put on her headphones, and skipped through the tracks until she got to one whose bridge she partially recognized: "getting looked up and down / by the lizard-eyed girl." She lay on her singed bedspread, crossed her ankles, and listened to Trish sing about her.

AARON MARSHALL

(1970–)

March 26, 1983
Cleveland

The light was pouring in through the window slats in the room he shared with his brother. They were looking less and less like each other, especially now that Aaron had three or four inches on him. He had to wake up but he didn't want to. He had places to be. He had to put on his shirt and go through the motions of another day in the city of Cleveland in the neighborhood of Central and he didn't want to. Everybody had their limit. He was tired.

He was almost thirteen and he already knew that the world had been built against him. What other proof did he need? His friends got frisked after school for no reason, teachers told him he had "potential" but was "acting delinquent," his mother was sleeping with the ofay who'd probably murdered his father. His friend Andre had a country mom and whenever they had Aaron over for dinner she called everyone at the DMV where she worked an ofay. Aaron liked it because lots of people who heard him say it didn't know what he was talking about, and he didn't want his enemies knowing what he was talking about. And he had enemies, plenty of them.

It was a Saturday morning, their mom's birthday, and Caleb was still asleep. Typical. Their mom was going to see the ofay today, probably: they'd been seeing each other for a while now and it made Aaron so angry and humiliated he didn't even want to bring it up, the way it felt like a curse to think about a nightmare. That was about to change. He sat up in bed and grabbed his new shirt off the floor, the one he'd worn yesterday and the day before that and the day before that when he bought the new Run-D.M.C. tape. He sat up so his feet were shoulder-width apart on the floor and brought his hands together as if in prayer and then pulled them apart and brought them together again. He looked up at the ceiling. Water stains. A lot of people, elders, would tell him he was spoiled: he had a roof over his head, his momma fed him every day, he had clothes and shoes and went to school. Sometimes he saw his mom's face in the morning, the grayish bags under her eyes, and he tried to think the way the old people thought. But then he'd think of the ofay's stupid shiny little face and the rage would come.

Caleb liked school, in his expected dumbass fashion. He never missed a day. Even the time he got beaten so bad Aaron saw in his mouth that one of his molars was dangling from his gums, he just spent part of the day in the nurse's office and tried to go back to science class with a wad of cotton shoved in the gap. Like that wasn't going to get him beaten again. It was a cycle, Caleb saw it: you acted like a little bitch and then you got treated like a little bitch and then people saw how you got treated and kept on treating you that way until you did something. He could only keep rescuing Caleb for so long, until people started treating him like a little bitch, too. That day wasn't far off, actually. He'd been walking with Andre and some kid had asked him if they were fucking. As if that were a perfectly logical question. Then he laughed—Aaron had never seen the kid before—and pointed at them, saying to his friend, "Too many faggots in this mafucken school." The kid was the skinny, horse-faced kind who was all fronting and no substance: the only thing Aaron had to do to shut him up was stomp his left foot. But still. Two years ago, nobody would be saying anything like that about Aaron and Andre. A year ago, even.

He lit a cigarette he'd stolen from Andre. He spit the smoke into the center of the room, where it lingered in a hot cone before evaporating. Caleb coughed a little in his sleep but didn't wake up, just rolled over on his other side and kept snoring. He slept too much and snored too much, that was his problem. What kind of person got told by the shittiest kids in school he was going to get "annihilated" the next day and then went home and did his homework and fell asleep like nothing was going to happen?

That was how he got his tooth punched out, because he slept on that instead of telling Aaron, and then Aaron had to basically rush in there like the fucking paramedics. It was his sleepy, school-loving ass sitting in geometry class two months ago while Aaron cut and went back home to get some tapes and cigarettes for a girl he liked, her name was Mychelle but she wanted him to call her Meeches, and he'd seen the ofay's car out front, gone upstairs to their apartment, and heard his voice behind the door. He couldn't believe it since the car hadn't been there for almost a year and he thought she was done with him. Aaron broke in through the fire escape and lay under the covers in his bed listening to his mom and the ofay talk about the day his father died, listening to the ofay describe a back room and a guy named Sunny and talk about what Aaron was surer and surer was a fake fondness for yayo. He had heard the ofay say, "And then he was lying on the floor and they took him away somewhere. I tried not to move," and his mom telling him she'd heard enough. The ofay reminded her that she was the one who'd asked to hear it again. His mom just sucked her teeth. And while all this was happening, where was Caleb? The same place he'd been two years ago when Aaron had first caught their mom and the ofay: sitting in school.

The story of his mom and the ofay never got easier to believe. The ofay claimed Reggie Marshall had wanted him to check up on his family. As if Reggie Marshall would even bother fucking with a guy like that, let alone making him a godfather with his dying breath.

He wanted to respect his mother. He really wanted to. He knew she'd been smart, and when she was young she'd wanted to teach college, and because she'd fallen in love with his father her parents didn't talk to her. Now she worked shit jobs and they got food stamps and they lived in an apartment that, she told him over and over, was nothing like the one he'd been born in. He sometimes saw her still trying to read after a shift at work. She had lots of books and notebooks and an old typewriter that had been a gift from grandpa way back when. Aaron read what she wrote after she went to sleep: "Capitalism is the motivating force behind Bartleby's death wish." He had no idea what she was talking about, and the word "Bartleby" sounded so stupid it got him mad: why the fuck should she be doing this instead of finding a better job? But he respected her for trying, he guessed, and he respected her for being with his father, who he saw in pictures had been the kind of guy who ruled a city like a combination of Michael and Vito Corleone, young but hard, never green a day in his life. That was until the ofay and his lies muddied everything up. He knew his father was still alive somewhere, hiding out to keep them safe. He knew it better than he'd known anything in his life. But he still hated it, because it was worse to grow up without a living father than with a dead one. Why had he done this to them? Why had he faked his death without even sending a letter? A small part of his heart bucked and strained against his ribs: *I'm alone! I'm all alone!*

He finished the cigarette and put it out in the Coke can next to his bed.

"Cee," he said. Caleb didn't move. "Cee. Caleb."

Caleb turned on his back and made a little snore that sounded like Andre's dad's cat. Aaron went over and poked him in the stomach. His eyes blinked open, wide like a baby's, and then narrowed when he saw who it was.

"What do you want?" he asked.

"Wake the fuck up, man," Aaron said.

Caleb closed his eyes and sighed. "It's not even a school day." He grabbed his dumbass digital alarm clock off the shelf, looked at it, put it back. "It's not even ten a.m."

"I have to tell you something," Aaron said.

"Tell me it in two hours."

Aaron pulled the covers off Caleb. "Get your ass out of bed."

Still sleep-fuzzy, Caleb stood and grabbed the covers out of his hand, then threw himself back on the bed. "Who the fuck are you? Moms?" he asked. "Go smoke your cancer sticks outside or something, smells too much like your ugly ass in here."

Aaron went outside, slamming the door a little—not that it would wake anyone up. He sometimes thought about how if they were still cave people he'd be the only one alive in the family, or if he was generous they'd only be alive because of him: he was always awake and he could spend all his time guarding them and fighting off predators while they slept their long, lazy hours, dreaming nonsense dreams they'd probably wasted whole weeks of awake time trying to describe to him. He'd never had a dream in his life. Every time he slept (and it was usually brief), he just got plunged into darkness like a man buried alive, pounding at the ceiling of his coffin until he could wake up again. He hated sleep, hated staying still, hated anything that left him defenseless. If he could, he'd spend his entire life awake.

But being in a body was some fragile bullshit he'd have to tolerate forever: being in a body that could get broken, with a mind that could get hurt, with a face that got spat on and talked down to.

The living room was empty, as he'd expected. The TV was still on, playing a Western, so he turned it off. He thought about cleaning the room and then realized that he wasn't going fast enough: he had places to be, and he wasn't trying to spend his whole day pretending like his mom wasn't constantly betraying him. Caleb still called her Moms but Aaron gave up calling her anything. It had always been something about her, the way she treated him. She liked Caleb more because they could talk about math and books and whatever else Caleb gave a shit about in school. Every time she found a cigarette in the house, or weed, it was always Aaron's fault right away—even the times it was Caleb's. And since Aaron had grown this past year, she always walked at a little distance from him when they went out. She hugged him softer and looser, too, and there was a weird, stiff way she moved whenever she'd had to lift him when he was little, like she was lifting something too heavy for her to carry. Plus the things she did didn't make any sense. She had a big, wide forehead and bright, always open eyes, and when they were really little she smiled a lot and told them to believe that everything in the world was going to work out fine for them. Who believed that? She would tell Caleb when he got another A or found ten dollars on the ground outside their building or got kissed by a girl at school that he got lucky and there was a pattern to everything and he was being watched out for. Not God, she always said, we don't believe in that religious nonsense. We're not like other people. But weren't they just like other people if they replaced "God" with "something watching out for you"? And that something clearly hated Aaron from the start, because the only people who had his back were Andre and a few other guys, maybe Meeches if she liked the tapes he gave her.

Then Aaron remembered the watch. He went back into their bedroom, where Caleb was already snoring again. Caleb had wanted to get her something nice for her birthday for once instead of the usual Bisquick-for-breakfast-handmade-card thing he (and Aaron, sort of) did every year. He'd wanted to get her a Casio, which Aaron thought was ridiculous. But Caleb was obsessed with it, was tearing out the pages of a bunch of nerd magazines and storing them under his bed. He even went into the store in Tower City and the guy there told him he was only allowed to use one coupon per purchase. So Aaron, because he guessed he was actually an idiot, started feeling bad for Caleb. He got a bagful of shake and old oregano from Andre's house and sold it to a bunch of white college kids for fifteen dollars. Between that and all the money Caleb had saved up in his sad little piggy bank (Aaron used to have an identical one but he'd smashed it years ago trying to get five dollars out for candy), Caleb got to buy the fancy Casio and look like the perfect son. "I'll say it's from both of us," he said, but Aaron didn't really care.

Now he got the watch box out from under the bed and started messing around with the instructions, which were printed almost too small for him to read and were numbered and boring. He found the part for setting an alarm and set it for when he'd get back from where he was going. Then he got dressed the rest of the way, slid into his knockoff Nikes, and looked at his face in the mirror. The edges around his ears were busted. The watch said it was ten twenty-three. He had time to go to Smitty's if he wanted a haircut.

Then he was on his bike wearing his best clothes and he felt a little dumb but he knew it was worth it for Meeches. There were three girls on the corner of Central and Fifty-Fifth as he rode by, all of them had honey hair but were talking in Mexican accents, and the one with the big thighs called out to Aaron, "Where you going?" and the rest of them laughed like it'd been a dare. He imagined her thighs in shorts, then in panties, then he felt bad about it for some reason because he was going to talk to Meeches about the tapes and he was already blowing this shit in his head. He biked east, toward Hough. A few guys were walking across the street arguing, trying to sound gully, and one of them watched Aaron pass on his bike like just biking there was wrong. He biked over a package of Funyuns and a box of crushed Parliaments. He biked over a losing lotto ticket and almost lost his balance running over a baby shoe. It was the morning, he reminded himself, and a Saturday, which meant that Daevon was probably working, had probably been sculpting old men's hair for the past three hours already.

Aaron liked Daevon because Daevon used to be friends with Cookie Johnson, a little round-faced guy who was Aaron's dad's best friend back when they were all kids in the sixties. Daevon wasn't like other old folks, who were constantly reminding Aaron that "Cleveland's changed" and that "a lot of people put in a hell of a lot of work just to make this place somewhere you can live." He was a little old—probably the same age as Aaron's mom—but he looked young, and he acted young even though he always had a mustache and a beard and an outdated Afro. He called Aaron "Big Fry," which Aaron wouldn't let anyone else call him. He cut Aaron's hair in exchange for a nugget of weed every now and then, which he said he just couldn't give up. He had a little daughter named Priscilla who lived with him half the time and in Glenville with her mom the other half. She was six or seven, and whenever she came to visit the barbershop Aaron always got a deck of cards off the shelf to play Go Fish with her. She was smart for her age and told him all about how she wanted to be a doctor when she grew up. Aaron had always wanted a little sister he could protect, a smart kid who'd wake up at the same time he did and make the same kind of friends and stay loyal to them until she died. He could say which boyfriends were good boyfriends for her to have, could tell her how to not fuck around with people who wasted her time, could make her promise when she got rich to let Caleb's useless ass borrow her money. He had a feeling that Priscilla wanted to get rich as much as he did, and that both of them would be the kind of rich people who'd come back to Cleveland and build schools for all the kids there. Or open a really nice office doing whatever they were doing and hire all their friends so nobody was working at the dollar store or the gas station or the high school cafeteria. Once he got rich, he was going to get himself a penthouse in New York City and marry a girl who, if she wasn't Meeches, at least looked as good as she did, and then he was going to come back and give everyone else the money they'd been trying to get their whole lives. Priscilla had similar dreams. She told him she was going to be the first girl doctor to invent a fake heart that worked just as well as a real one.

"I'm gonna get richer than my daddy is right now," she'd always tell Aaron over cards. And Daevon would smile and laugh and say that wouldn't be too hard.

Aaron biked faster, liking the idea of getting to spend more than an hour at Smitty's, liking the fact that there was a smart little sister there waiting for him. Cars were whipping past him now, faster than usual, it felt like. A cop car followed at his back, its siren whining, then passed him. For once they had something better to do than stop him and ask him to empty out his pockets. There were more girls on the sidewalk, walking with boys: none of the pairs were touching except one couple, the girl hanging

The Comedown □ 115

off the boy's arm and the boy kicking a rock along the sidewalk really hard, so they had to take lots of steps to catch up with it. He was focused as hell on kicking that rock. Aaron wouldn't care about some dumbass rock if he had that girl hanging off his arm all the time. The girl had her hair wrapped up in two buns on her head. She was wearing shorts even though it was kind of cold, and they were short enough that the hoodie she was wearing almost hung over them.

A little red building with a little red sign: SMITTY'S SEAWAY BARBERSHOP. He never asked why it was called that. There was no sea, there was definitely no way to the sea, and fuck if he knew who Smitty was. He locked his bike up out front and watched through the window as Daevon bobbed and wove around the head of a customer. When he walked in, Daevon looked up, then back at the gumby he was sculpting. "Big Fry," he said. "You got a date?"

It was like Daevon knew everything. "I dunno," Aaron said. He slunk into the room, trying not to make eye contact with the guy getting the gumby. Priscilla was nowhere in sight.

"Sure acting like you do. I remember how your daddy acted when he first met your momma."

Now Aaron was interested. He took a chair and Daevon got one of the other guys to take over the gumby. He cleaned out the electric razor. "You want moisturizer, Big Fry?"

Aaron shook his head. "Places to be."

"Ay!" Daevon laughed. "Called it."

"What about my daddy?"

"What you mean, what about your daddy?"

"You were saying he acted some type of way when he met Moms." He felt fake letting it slip out like that, but he couldn't help himself.

"Oh yeah." Daevon took the razor to Aaron's edges, describing how his daddy used to look: tall and thin with a beard that he could grow before any of the rest of them could, wearing the old blue button-downs he stole from the post office even after they fired him, driving the Caddy he and Cookie souped up in Cookie's friend's garage. Back before he was a powerful man with powerful connections, when he was still another broke kid hustling to get out of the neighborhood, he was obsessed with Natasha Harrison, who had the meanest parents in Cleveland. They wouldn't let her eat or sleep or anything without their permission, according to Aaron's daddy. They had him over for dinner once, decided he was a "delinquent," and kept her trapped in the house until she ran away.

"But before that," Aaron said. "What did he do before she ran away?"

What didn't he do? He snuck over to her house at midnight and threw little pebbles at her window and she leaned out to talk to him. He worked every odd job there was to scrape money together so he could get her a pair of shoes, a necklace, a coat. He couldn't get hired anywhere "legitimate" so he stopped trying. He didn't spend any money on himself. He brought gifts to her at her college—Daevon had to drive him there a few times when the Caddy broke down. He sold whatever he could get his hands on so they could get an apartment together. He flipped cars, herb, LPs, hats, liquor. Until he met Sunny, that is.

Aaron loved this part of the story. "How did he meet Sunny?"

Daevon hadn't been there, just heard the story from Cookie. According to Cookie's memory, he and Aaron's daddy had been working the block when some white guy drives up in a DeVille and asks for a half gram of smack. Which they don't have, because neither of them fucks with that stuff. The white guy—he's little, he looks kind of like a doll with heavy eyebrows and a big forehead—gets out of the car and shoves a gun in Aaron's daddy's side. He tells him to get in. Cookie does something he'll always regret: he runs away, back to his place, where he sits and cries for an hour, thinking his friend just got shot. When that's over, Aaron's daddy's banging on the door and Cookie opens it and Aaron's daddy wants to know what the fuck is up. He also says the guy ended up being decent, had even hired him. A salaried position. Cookie has no idea what to say— "congratulations" didn't exactly seem right—so he asks him what the work will be. Aaron's daddy just grins and says, "More of the same." Cookie can't believe it. He's just happy to see his best friend alive.

"I would be, too," Aaron said, totally unable to help himself. "What happened after that?"

If Aaron was smart, he should know what happened after that: Aaron's daddy started making real money, he got the girl he always wanted, he rented her a nice apartment in a nice part of town. And the girl gave birth to twin sons.

"She gave birth in the apartment, not the hospital," Aaron said. "Me and Cee were coming so fast she didn't have any time to get to a hospital."

"You know your own history better than I do, Big Fry," Daevon said.

"But you know stuff I don't know." He hated how desperate he sounded. "You know stuff about, maybe like what my daddy was doing when I was really little?"

Daevon bit down on his lower lip and shook his head. "Your daddy wasn't around for long when you were really little."

"I mean—I mean before then. Like when I was a baby."

The door to the back room opened and out bolted Priscilla, carrying a GI Joe in each hand. She wrapped her skinny arms around Aaron, who tried to hug her back without shifting too much under the razor.

"Momma got me these," she said to Aaron.

"Where'd you put the other guy's shoes?" Daevon asked. Priscilla shrugged, then hunched closer to Aaron.

"Daddy, I'm showing my friend," she hissed, which made Daevon laugh.

Aaron didn't hear them; he was thinking about his dad. He'd had time with his dad and he'd been too small and stupid to be aware of it. He'd been held by his dad, burped by his dad, but he'd never actually said a real word to him. The idea was making him sick.

When he looked up again, Priscilla's face was in his. "What you thinking about?" she asked.

"Nothing."

"You're lying."

He looked at her face, her eyes big and dumb and young.

"I'm not lying," Aaron hissed. "Go play over there."

Daevon stopped the razor. "I'm not giving you a haircut with you talking that way to my daughter," he said, his voice suddenly stern, and for a moment Aaron felt alone the way he imagined Caleb did when he had to find a place to sit in the cafeteria.

"I'm sorry," he said, but it was to Priscilla's back: she'd already gone across the room and was making up some story about how the GI Joes had to escape out the window.

They finished out the haircut in silence. Aaron looked in the mirror and he didn't even look like his dad: he had his mom's forehead and eyes, her nose, her lips. He didn't have her hands (she always said she had "long alien fingers," but he didn't know if he had his hands: they were slender and short, something he'd always been self-conscious of). His hair was looking good, but that was Daevon.

"Big Fry," Daevon said, rubbing some thick something that smelled like his mother's aloe gel in the curls at his ears. Usually Aaron told him to skip this part, but he felt too dumb to do anything about it. "I know you're having a hard time, but you can't take it out on my kid."

"I'm sorry."

"It's fine. We're all going through what we're going through."

And then he was outside Smitty's feeling much smaller than he'd felt when he came in. He looked behind him, through the glass door: the clock on the back wall said it was a little past eleven. If he was right about how his mom's day was going to go, she was probably just waking up. He got mad again, and then at Caleb—everything he'd been through in this fucking day already and their lazy asses were just waking up—and biked, little-feeling, east on Hough, across MLK Drive. He was supposed to meet Meeches in front of the Museum of Natural History at noon, but she was nowhere. It'd make sense if she stood him up. He imagined her waking up and thinking about him, another neighborhood dumbass without a father, another in probably a long line of them who'd tried to get with her. He sat down on the grass, holding his ankles. He did what he usually did whenever he felt like this, which was to start thinking of all the ways he could get rich. He could become a landlord. He could make music like Run-D.M.C., except he didn't have any talent or rhymes. Used-car dealership. Find Sunny's boss and get a job—his boss was probably dead, but maybe there'd be someone else who had taken over. And then when he was rich he could buy a car and buy a house for his mother and Caleb to keep them both away from the ofay. He could give Daevon a gold watch.

"Ay," a girl's voice said.

He looked up: Meeches. She was standing leaning back on one leg, her chest out, her arms crossed. Her hair was short and blond. He wanted to touch it but he knew she'd never let him.

He stood up. "Hey," he said, then corrected the pitch of his voice. "Hey."

She laughed. "Hey."

Things might get better, he realized. At the very least the day could get better. She had said she liked all the tapes he gave her, "It's Like That" and the *Wild Style* tracks. She let him hold her hand. And when they sat in the little gazebo house right in front of the museum, she told him all her friends said he really liked her. He could feel his cheeks heating up.

"I do," he said. Then, remembering what Daevon had said: "And I'd buy shit for you."

She laughed and drummed her chest with her fingers. "You'd buy shit for me!"

Why was she laughing? Now he was thinking about Smitty's again, about Priscilla. How many times was he going to fail in a single day? There should be a fucking limit.

"Yeah, I would," he said.

"With what money, A? Your momma work at the grocery store."

Now his cheeks felt this-can't-be-happening hot. He'd spent weeks asking about her, trying to get friends of friends to give him information. What he knew was her dad and mom were married, they owned a house in Central, her dad worked as a manager at Macy's. That's how come she had the good hair. He was just the tallest kid in their grade. That was why she was sitting here with him. He ran his elbow, hard, into a beam of the gazebo. She jumped back from him like he was about to detonate.

"I gave you all my tapes already!" he said. "What the fuck more you want?"

Now she was clutching pearls she wasn't even wearing. She stood up, backed out of the gazebo. "You insane," she said. "My friends told me you'd be like this."

He thumped the beam again. The roof of the gazebo shook. Meeches was walking away from him, holding her hands out in front of her. "I'm telling everyone about you," she said.

"Go tell them!" He almost added "bitch" to the end, but knew it would make him feel bad later. She was too beautiful anyway. He wanted his tapes back. He wanted them back so bad; it hurt in his head like he was holding a deep cut open to zero-degree wind. She walked, then ran away from him. He folded his hands across his stomach and then folded over them like he was trying to keep warm. He hated her so much. Why couldn't he stop watching as she ran, thinking about how her calves moved and thighs clapped and how her shoulder blades shifted back and forth under her sweatshirt?

He got on his bike and dragged himself back up Hough, not really seeing where he was going. The hill was more punishment, and he didn't even know what he did to deserve it. Be born? Miss his dad? Hate his dad for not writing to them, for leaving them and not caring? What the fuck was he supposed to do? He biked fast as he could past Smitty's, back onto Fifty-Fifth, down to the liquor store where the two old drunks, one light-skinned and one dark-skinned, were sitting as they always did, talking about Cab Calloway and the war and whatever the fuck else Aaron didn't have the time to listen to. He threw his bike down so hard it shook them out of their conversation. They wanted to know what he wanted. He pulled ten dollars from his pocket and asked if either of them wanted to get him a bottle of bourbon.

Drunk, he biked back home feeling tilted so close to the ground that he was basically riding sideways. A church somewhere chimed two thirty, then three o'clock. He hated himself. There was no person on earth he hated more than himself. He biked past a car wash playing "I Want You Back," biked past an old woman yanking on the arm of a little boy who screamed. Maybe if he hadn't said what he said to Meeches, they'd be sitting there in the gazebo still. Maybe he'd have his hand up her shirt by now. If he hadn't gone to Smitty's, he wouldn't have thought about his dad buying shit for his mom, he wouldn't have said what he said. But then he would've had busted edges, so there really was no winning. Caleb was probably still asleep. He pushed one pedal, then the other, his feet thick and numb like they'd been dipped in cement. Fuck if he was ever talking to her—ever looking at her—again.

He threw his bike down in front of the complex and stalked around to the back, the first floor. His mother's bedroom window faced east; he'd see it first when he turned the corner. At least he wasn't going to be taking shit from her anymore.

May 8, 2009
Los Angeles

He'd met his wife, Netta, at a protest in Chicago. He had been almost thirty then, and he'd decided to be done with Cleveland for good: his mother had gotten a teaching job somewhere in Canada and his brother was finally living out his messiah dream as Lawyer for the Poor and his dad hadn't come back from the presumed-dead, so Aaron saw no reason to rot in Cleveland with all the other kids from the block. He hustled enough to get a car, cheap but not humiliatingly cheap, packed a bag, and left. The only person he told was Andre—none of the girls he was seeing, not his manager or coworkers—and that was just because they lived together. He left a note on his dresser that said, "I left and I'm trying to never come back, good luck, A." He'd had a straight job working as a fry cook at a place called Hotwater Kitchen, and on his off time he and Andre sold kind bud to their friends and shake to their enemies. He made enough money doing both to live independently of his mother, to pretend he wasn't thinking about what could have been in that damn yellow briefcase.

Even now, rising from his bed as Netta remained asleep beside him, setting his watch to remind him about a game of golf he'd promised Ted Schulman, brushing his teeth and looking at the bougainvillea dripping like heavy eyelashes over the window, he was thinking about the briefcase. He was thinking about it because his mother's sixty-first birthday had been roughly two months ago. He had no intention of calling her—he hadn't spoken to her since he was eighteen—but every year he found himself wanting a little more to hear her voice. He was curious how it had changed. Maybe she'd get on the phone sounding old and cigarette-hoarse, like that friend of hers Demetra who had that weird giant-eared kid who tried to play with him and Caleb, or she'd get on sounding all rich with a Canadian accent, and he'd get to match up the woman she was with the woman she used to be and see how quickly her fakery crumbled. She'd want an apology. He didn't want to apologize for anything—didn't think he needed to.

Ted Schulman wanted to talk to him about buying up a bunch of public housing in Lynwood and turning the buildings into single-unit dwellings. Aaron would try to steer him toward a property in Inglewood, an abandoned warehouse adjacent to a weedy lot, but knowing Ted, Aaron figured he'd probably laugh and shake his head. He called Aaron "Boy Scout" a lot, as in, "Boy Scout here's trying to save the neighborhood. Is it your liberal wife? Does she realize you're part of the problem?" In this case, he'd make the argument that luxury condominiums in any failing neighborhood will just attract the kind of businesses white renters like to frequent, and then United Colors of Benetton will be replacing Mom & Pop's Fried Chicken and some other developers will get their hands on the public housing and make the killing Ted could be making. "It's the way of the world!" he'd probably say today on the golf course. "So why not cut out the middleman and just make happen what you know's gonna happen anyway?" Aaron always tried to put up a fight, but he knew Ted had a point. It was the way of the world, and he was a part of that way.

Netta was the reason he was trying to save public housing anyway.

Having grown up in public housing, he hated it—hated how it felt living there, how people treated him for living there, how the other people there were always trying to beat him up and rip him off. Netta hadn't come from money either, but her parents had at least been able to afford a small apartment on what seemed like the white side of Chicago. He'd stayed there with her for about a year, working a job he didn't care about, meeting her college friends, eating her father's cooking. She had told her parents Aaron was the son of immigrants trying to pay for college and they bought it. Sometimes her father even came in to check on him in the cot he was supposed to be sleeping on in the study room across from Netta's. He always spent the first part of the night there and then a little bit of the morning. He met Ray, an acquaintance of hers from her high school days, at a party after one of her gallery openings. She was getting famous in the Chicago art scene by then, even had a little blurb and a profile in the *Sun-Times*. Ray, light-skinned and goofy-faced, had made it out of Chicago on a scholarship to Howard, was a loyal Omega Psi Phi who liked to get high and show Aaron his old step routines. He called Aaron Biscuits 'n' Gravy, Biscuits for short. Aaron never knew why Ray liked him so much, but he counted it as one of the biggest blessings of his life: Ray was a real estate agent and he gave Aaron all his old exam study books, even showed him a copy of his old exam results that he'd managed to shake down some lady at the testing office for. Aaron took the Illinois exam without stepping foot in a classroom—without even getting his GED—and passed and he and Ray started showing houses together, mostly middle-income places to young couples looking to start families in Albany Park or Ukrainian Village. They worked for a real estate office called Blanicks LLC, then started their own team when they could afford the office space. Then Ray got poached by a development company in LA called Onyx and asked if Aaron wanted to go, too.

Netta had never been a booster of the real estate career, but she hadn't exactly been complaining about the money: they had their own place now in the kind of neighborhood where white people with office jobs picked up their dogs' shit in little plastic bags. But it took some time to get her there. He had caught her one night in her office, drawing hands on a gigantic sketch of an old woman. She was obsessed with this old Dionne Warwick song her mom had on vinyl, "I'll Never Love This Way Again"—he'd set it on the record player her father had given her and started it playing.

She'd turned around, looked him up and down, and smirked. "What does your fool ass want now?" That's when he had kneeled down and opened his hands to show her the candy ring he'd bought at the pharmacy. "I love you," he had said—he said it almost every day now. "Will you marry me and move to LA?" She put her charcoal down and stood up from her desk, approaching him. "I'll marry you," she'd said, "but I can't promise you anything about moving to LA." It took him a year, but he had managed to convince her.

Now he was stepping in the shower, staring into its giant buffed brass showerhead as the mineral-tasting water rained down. He'd gotten used to all kinds of things in his life just to fit in at Onyx. He had to ask Ray for a "cigarette" instead of a square, had to pretend he knew what a cheese plate was and that it didn't give him indigestion, had to go golfing and jogging with Ted Schulman in parks full of people who didn't look like him. He had to spend hours in a sauna on a corporate retreat and nod when Ray and Ted asked him, "Are you sweating out all your inflammatory toxins?" He had to pretend that nothing made him lonely, but he'd always been good at that. He could pretend anything if he was getting paid enough. The shower water was pelting him in the forehead, too cold, but he needed to wake up. He scrubbed himself with a loofah, something Netta knew about before he did. Sometimes she rubbed her temples and told him she felt like a sellout because she was making art for the very people Aaron was displacing from their homes, and he should seriously consider leaving Onyx. She'd been doing this more and more in the months since she'd gotten pregnant—when they'd first moved there, she was in love with him and confident he was going to bring down the system from the inside. He hadn't wanted to tell her that nobody could bring down the system because you can't "bring down" something you're a part of. She'd gone to a fancy college, gotten a bunch of people telling her how good she was at drawing, gotten gallery shows where rich people bought her art. It's easier to think you're going to be a revolutionary when everything's going your way. But she was beautiful and patient and compassionate, and his kid was growing inside her, so he wasn't exactly going to sit around lecturing her on who she was and who he was and why she should just stop bothering him about it all.

The shower lasted longer than he'd meant it to. He got out, the room still steamy as he shaved. His beard grew quickly; if he slept in he had stubble.

He didn't want to think about golf with Ted, so he looked at his reflection. He was taller than he'd once thought he'd end up being, darker than his mother, his features sharper than hers. He told himself this was all his dad's genes. He was starting to look the way his dad used to look in those photo albums his mother made, sitting on the couch in jeans and no shirt, holding Caleb in one arm and Aaron in the other, his chest carpeted with hair, his smile huge and white. Aaron was sure he had his dad's eyes and forehead now that he was done growing. And he definitely had his chest and biceps, there was no question about that. He was his father's son. Somewhere there was an inheritance waiting for him. Somewhere they were celebrating his birthday.

He couldn't remember now if he'd been thirteen, fourteen, or fifteen. He'd been young, at the very least, and angry and drunk worse than he'd ever been since. He'd set a trap to catch his mother fucking the ofay. He could've just walked away—that would've been humiliating enough. But a drunk kid is going to run inside the apartment, inside the bedroom, and try to beat the shit out of that cowering ofay. And instead he's going to get the shit beaten out of him, get restrained by his own mother, and when the ofay finally limps away, whining about how he was just trying to do good and he could call the cops if he wanted to, the drunk kid's going to look his mother in the eye and say that she's a disappointment to the family. And she's going to tell him that if she's such a disappointment, he can get by without his inheritance. And he's going to ask what the fuck you mean "inheritance" and she's going to make to open the yellow briefcase on the bed behind her, but he's going to first, he's going to stomp on it and kick through it because it's soldered shut and flimsier than it looks, and when he finally does he'll see that it's just full of a bunch of books written in a weird scribble language she'll angrily tell him is Hebrew. And then the drunk kid's going to ask whether this is proof enough that the ofay is stupid and a murderer and how she feels fucking around with the ofay who murdered her husband and she's going to say no son of hers would talk to her like that and she's going to throw him out of the house and he'll slink back a week later and things will never be the same between them.

But over time Aaron saw that the ofay couldn't have been stupid, just insane—how else could he have gotten away with a crime like killing Aaron's dad and then lying about it for decades? And even on the off chance it wasn't the ofay himself but some other ofay—Sunny or Sunny's boss—how could a pure dumbass get out of there alive? A lunatic maybe, but not a dumbass. Which explained Aaron's feeling that there was a real briefcase somewhere, with real money. And maybe his dad was alive and had it. Or maybe it wasn't a briefcase: maybe it was a house in Honolulu and his dad had been trying to reach them for decades. He had told Caleb his theory once, back when they were living in that house in East Cleveland with all of Caleb's nerd friends. Caleb was probably high on benzos (he always was back then), and he'd said, "You a sucker if you think his body didn't get ground up by a trash compactor. You know how them violent crackers work." He said it with half-open eyes and a flat face, like Aaron was the dumbest student in second grade. Aaron couldn't remember punching him, but he could remember crying alone in his room upstairs, flexing his aching hand, feeling embarrassed that he was who he was and would have to go on being who he was until he died. He thought about not waiting to die, but he remembered he wasn't weak like Caleb—fuck if the world was going to make him hang himself. It sure as hell was giving him the rope, though.

He got to the office early, and it was quiet; none of the interns were there, none of the secretaries. He sat in his corner office, looking over a few project proposals, proofing a few deeds, mostly playing blackjack on his computer. Around ten o'clock the office started filling, the junior agents taking their seats at their cubicles outside his office window, the secretaries adjusting their headsets, Ray meandering back and forth from the water cooler, waving at Aaron every time he passed. Aaron waved back, then stared at his screen, pretending to be busy. He was getting sick of Ray. He'd started cheating on his wife with a girl half his age who worked at the In-N-Out, and he kept on taking Aaron through the drive-thru there on lunch break to see her. And she was beautiful, disgustingly young, Puerto Rican, had baby deer eyes, and wore a choker. Aaron was sick of seeing her and sick of hearing about sex with her and especially sick of Ray telling him that if he wanted to tap that he could, just say the word. When his phone beeped right before lunch, he left out the back exit and drove to the golf course.

Something about the day had made him numb. It was a bad idea to schedule golf for this day. Netta was probably just waking up—she went to bed late and woke late, a habit from her twenties Aaron thought she'd grow out of—and would probably text about how much she missed him and would he mind picking up some pineapple on his way home. She always wanted to buy something new, try something new—it felt as if she couldn't make it through a day without spending money she didn't need to spend. His phone buzzed: it wasn't from her. It was Ted, asking him if he wanted someone from the course to caddy or if he was fine on his own. At a stoplight Aaron texted back: *I'm fine on my own, thanks.* Ted Schulman had a bright red bulging face and made three-quarters of a million dollars a year before taxes. Aaron made half that. "If you want the commission, you've gotta be aggressive, Boy Scout." He'd been A, Big Fry, Biscuits 'n' Gravy, Boy Scout. Who the fuck even called him by his real name anymore? Netta.

He wasn't looking forward to golf, because he'd get beaten again and Ted would use that to convince him that the public housing didn't need to keep standing and he'd end up having to personally go down to Lynwood and tell the tenants they were being evicted.

His vision began flashing white: he blinked and it went back to normal, then flashed white again. By the time he pulled into the golf course parking lot, blinking couldn't bring it back. Pain ballooned at the front of his head and he gritted his teeth to keep from crying out. He had a flash of Priscilla running around Smitty's Seaway Barbershop, singing about how she was going to be a doctor someday. He wondered where she was now, if she was happy. He saw Netta turning over on her pillow, opening her almond eyes to smile at him, undoing her ponytail and kissing him. He saw Meeches at school, sucking on the nib of a pen. How many girls just like Meeches had he had to fuck with before he found Netta? But really, deep down—how different was she from Meeches? She had to be. She had to be different from his mother, her stern liar's face.

His phone was buzzing on the seat next to him, but he was hurting too hard to look at it. He waited it out, listened to it buzz a second time, a third. Ted was losing his patience. Or Netta had found a spider. He rubbed his eyes and his vision returned, but the migraine was still bulging at the edges of his skull. He flipped open his phone. Three missed calls from Caleb Marshall: 12:57, 12:59, 1:03. Then a text: *Dad's alive.* And another: *I'm so sorry. You were right.*

LELAND BLOOM-MITTWOCH JR.
(1971–)

1977–2009
Cleveland

Of the many fist-clenching memories provoked in Leland Jr. by a visit back to Cleveland, the most offensive was one he couldn't even claim. He had been six years old when his mother had tearfully confessed and the older he got, the better he became at imagining the event (events, if he was being honest) with memory's width, length, and depth.

His mom and Leland Sr. in 1970, at home and at parties, dressed in the idiot garb of their times, his mom's stomach round with him, Leland Sr. doing what he knew how to do best: snorting or smoking whatever was snortable and/or smokable in his immediate reach. Leland Jr. imagined his mom inhaling deep—no doubt at Leland Sr.'s urging—out of one of the eight six-inch glass bongs Leland Sr. had collected in college. Then Leland Jr. followed the smoke down her windpipe and into her bronchial tubes and into (he knew from sleepless hours spent on WebMD), the lungs' parenchyma, where the alveoli would've pumped the corrupted oxygen into her bloodstream and then into his own. Time after time after time she'd done this without thinking, mother and son getting high together, his little fetal self becoming asthmatic and forgetful. His blood and body and amnion foggy with her indulgence, his barely formed eyes bugging, his veins constricting. He didn't hate her for it—he hated his father.

She'd made the confession following an incident in 1978, which

Leland Jr. wished he could forget, during which he had for some reason thrown a volume of the *Encyclopedia Britannica* across his second-grade classroom and into the fish tank. Even after it had happened he had felt like it'd been someone else, a mediocre kid, one with freckles and a sour smell and stupid eyes. He knew fetuses exposed to marijuana could grow into aggressive kids with low test scores: he'd read at least one, if not two, studies about it.

Ms. Tarski had treated the whole thing as a code-blue emergency. She had kept Leland Jr. after class and called his mom. His mom was at the school in under fifteen minutes, looking stricken when she walked through the door. Ms. Tarski had preserved the crime scene, and she let his mom look long and hard at the book and the fish tank and Leland Jr., who by then was crying and saying he was sorry and he didn't know what was wrong with him or why he did it.

Leland Jr. had sat on the floor and begged his mom not to punish him. Then he begged that if someone had to punish him, at least let it be her and not Leland Sr. His mom, who seemed to care zero whether Ms. Tarski saw her crying or not, began to well up and said of course he would not be punished. *It's all my fault, sweetie—that much is clear as day.*

"Do you know why Dad sleeps so much?" she had asked in the car on the way home.

Leland Jr. hadn't thought that much about it because he tried not to think that much about Leland Sr. "He's tired," he said.

She nodded. "Right. He's trying to make a change. He had a very hard time when you were a baby, but he's making a change now. And it's not easy for him."

He looked up at her and she seemed mountainous, and he didn't think it made sense that kids were supposed to grow bigger than their parents. (And when he finally did outgrow them, he vowed he would accept no sum of money to be seven again, when he was under the thumb of the detoxing and retoxing Leland Sr., when Dad Needed the Apartment to Rest after Work, and no matter how strung-out and exhausted he seemed he could still catch you making noise in your room or in the hall and throw you hard up against the wall if chances were Mom wouldn't hear.)

"Well"—and his mom started crying, and she had done a miniswerve that made Leland Jr. grab the edges of his seat and crane to see over the dashboard—"I had a few difficulties, too. Not as bad as your dad, but a few."

And then she explained to him how, had she known then what she did now, she would not have smoked grass back when she was pregnant with him, and how he had to understand that it was not uncommon with her and Dad's friends, that a lot of people were doing it, and a lot of them didn't know what kind of effect doctors were suggesting it had on children. (*How miraculous*, he told himself after every session of self-righteous Googling, *that I wasn't born with a hole in the heart or neonatal retinopathy or an incapacitated brain*.) She was so sorry, and when they got home she let him have ice cream before dinner. And he understood the reason she was doing this was that there was something wrong with him.

The day after he'd thrown the encyclopedia had been a Saturday, and when he woke up at eight thirty, he still didn't know what grass was, unless it was the greenish-brownish kind you occasionally saw outside, which he found hard to believe. He knew only that it was something punishably bad and kids couldn't be around it, so he figured he might find it on *Fat Albert and the Cosby Kids*, where Rudy was always doing something kids weren't supposed to be doing. But that morning's episode was useless, because it was just about Heywood being too nervous to admit he needed glasses, and the only thing Rudy really did was play on the baseball team and make fun of Heywood for being such a lousy hitter. His mom had let Leland Jr. eat just bacon for breakfast and told him she had to leave to see a client early but to please try and not wake Daddy and when she got home they'd talk about school. He ate the bacon out of a bowl by himself on the couch and watched the *Jackson 5ive*, which was even less capable than *Fat Albert* of offering him an answer to the grass question, and by nine thirty, when on TV it was just two men in sport coats saying they'd predicted how the Browns would do against the Jets tomorrow and it was Under Lock, So Gentlemen Start Your Betting, Leland Jr. could hear Leland Sr. moving around in the big bedroom.

Leland Jr. got up quickly and shut off the TV and then went back to the couch. He heard Leland Sr. say "What the hell?" and call out *Melinda* twice. Leland Jr. thought about going to his room, but there were fewer escape options there. The best thing to do was leave the house but that would involve opening the front door, which always made noise. He pulled his knees to his chin and his stomach constricted and went sour. He counted out one hundred and twelve seconds during which all he did was imagine he'd gone deaf, and he did a hopeful projection of his deafness onto the entire house. Nothing made any noise because nothing could hear the noise anything else was making, and he imagined that the deafness hit Leland Sr. so hard he couldn't even remember what it was like to hear at all. He took a bite of bacon and shuddered.

But just a few seconds later, there was Leland Sr. walking around in the kitchen, skinnier than a normal man should be, wearing just briefs and a T-shirt. All Leland Jr. heard in his head was a weird soft ringing, and he focused his eyes hopefully on his kneecaps.

"Where's your mother?" Leland Sr.'s voice broke Leland Jr.'s illusion to pieces. "Where is she?" he asked.

"I don't know. Showing houses."

Leland Sr. turned on the TV and then sat down next to him. "When will she be back?"

"I don't know."

The answer obviously hadn't satisfied him. "How're you doing?"

"Fine."

"Mom told me you got mad in school."

He froze, terrified. How would he know about this? Did he care?

"I don't know anything about that," Leland Jr. said. "I'm gonna go outside."

Leland Sr. laughed. "I don't think so." On TV now they were talking about another car bomb.

"I think I'm going to go outside," Leland Jr. tried again.

It seemed like Leland Sr. wasn't listening. Leland Jr. started to get off the couch. "Don't go outside," he said, still looking at the TV. Leland Jr. sat back down.

"How do you think Danny Greene stayed alive so long?" Leland Sr. asked.

"I don't know."

"*I don't know.* You've been saying that this whole time. Make a guess."

"He was smart."

"That's right." Leland Sr. smiled. "He was a real modern-day Robin Hood. You know why you can't go outside?"

"No."

"You'll get blown up, that's why. They'll kill you like they did Danny Greene—you saw that on TV. Or like they killed your dad's friend Reggie."

Leland Jr. nodded.

"You know who's really murdering everyone?"

Leland Jr. shook his head, which made Leland Sr. snort.

"Of course you don't. It's cops. Crooked cops. There's actually no such thing as a straight cop. They're a gang. A violent gang."

Leland Jr. nodded.

"Tell me why you got mad in school."

If Leland Jr. hadn't understood his reasons in the blind and furious moment he had flung the book, he understood them even less now.

"I don't know."

"I don't know isn't an option."

Leland Jr. knew he had to make something up. But he was a horrible liar, having been taught by his mom and Ms. Tarski never to lie. But would they allow him to lie if not lying meant he said *I don't know* again, which wasn't an option? He rooted around in his brain for something that was not a lie.

"Mom said it was a behavior problem because she smoked grass when I was still in her stomach," he said.

This had been a horrible thing to say, and he knew it as soon as he said it. Leland Sr. went very stiff and stood up. He went to the front door, which he dead-bolted. Leland Jr. imagined the hallway outside the door, the pink-and-white carpet and the walls that always smelled like paint, and beyond them the big glass door that let you outside. The front yard. The street.

"We're going to have a conversation and we're going to make sure no one can sneak up on us while we have it," Leland Sr. said. "We're gonna make sure no one can spy on us."

Leland Jr. felt an electric feeling, like his brain was trying to show him one last good time before he died. He jumped over the back of the couch.

"What the hell are you doing?" Leland Sr. said. He picked Leland Jr. up under the arms and brought him back to the couch cushions. He smiled, which was more disturbing to Leland Jr. than if he'd been sneering. "My dad, your grandpa, who you never met, he was not very nice to me when I misbehaved, but he did not get physical with me. He did not hit me, he was just silent to me. I would rather that he had hit me a little. Wouldn't you?" He gave Leland Jr. a gentle smack on the cheek. "That's better than the silent treatment, isn't it? Why are you shaking?"

"I'm not shaking."

"Yes you are. I'll explain why Mom said what she said. She doesn't understand how the world works. You're lucky I do. You're lucky you've got me to explain it to you. Grass is what people call marijuana, and the police and the government made it illegal. Did you know that?"

Leland Jr. shook his head.

"It's not bad for you, but they think it is. It's harmless." He sighed and stared ahead of him, and Leland Jr. thought for a second that he'd forgotten about the conversation. "I haven't had a drop of anything in two weeks, not even coffee, and you think I'm happy about it?"

"I don't know."

"The answer is I'm not. I'm very unhappy about it. A normal man doesn't sleep fifteen hours a day. A normal man is gainfully employed. I need medicine to function as a normal man, but the kind of medicine I need is outlawed. A society in which this happens is not one that's right. Do you understand? Mom thinks I have no right to medicine. This is a well-meaning idea, but it's very foolish."

Leland Jr. felt suddenly very ill.

"Just don't do it again." Leland Sr. smacked him on the other cheek, and it stung more this time. "See? That's better than the silent treatment. That's all you've earned, okay? You can do it to me if you like."

Leland Sr. offered his cheek and scrunched up his eyes. It remained one of Leland Jr.'s biggest regrets that he had been shaking too hard to hit his father back.

Early April 2009
Cleveland

Piloting his mother's Town & Country across Shaker Heights to Woodward's Foods, his regret that he hadn't smacked Leland Sr. was stronger than ever. Fists tight around the wheel, he was only half listening as she read aloud her list of necessary items. They were at the stoplight before the Woodward's when she got to sauerkraut and Leland Jr. said, half to stop the word stream, "If the special occasion is just my visit, then you shouldn't be getting all this." It seemed like she was trying to impress him. Which, he thought, regarding her sitting next to him in the car (flowered sweater, triple chin, the smile of a child in blissful transit), was in itself miles from being impressive.

"The occasion isn't just you," his mom told him. "I haven't made something nice in a while."

Inside the store they drew the kind of polite stares rich white people give when they're disgusted by something. His mom was not a disgusting person, and she did not deserve stares. She was just large. She was Rubenesque. She carried approximately 313 pounds on a five-four frame—they had remeasured this morning, to her protest. She had to waddle sometimes—she was waddling a little now, using the shopping cart as a sort of walker—but she should never be the object of anyone's disgust.

Seriously? Leland Jr.'s cinched face inquired of a man looking at her with zero social decorum.

The man, spooked, turned his brushed steel frames toward the melons.

"What are we going to get first?" Leland Jr. asked.

But she was quiet; she'd felt the man's eyes, too. "I don't know," she said blandly.

"What's first on the list?"

"Yogurt," she said.

"Okay." He began to steer the cart. "Dairy aisle."

His phone registered a text with a soft chime. It was from Jocelyn. *Are you home yet, babe?* She wanted to talk. He repocketed his phone and looked up. A woman had stopped to watch his mom's graceless passage down the dairy aisle.

His mom passed her and began to lower her upper half into the dairy case to grab a yogurt. Plain, as Leland Jr. had insisted. He approached the gawking woman.

"Excuse me. Ma'am?"

She registered his words with shock.

"I'm talking to you," he said.

"Yes?" she managed.

"Do you see that woman?" He pointed to his mom.

She nodded.

"Were you staring at her?"

She tried to shake her head but it came out like a tremor.

"That woman is my mother," Leland Jr. said. "Do you think she's blind?"

She shook her head more thoroughly.

"Correct. She's not. And she can see you staring. So stop."

He didn't wait for the woman to acknowledge what he'd said. He turned around and grabbed the side of his mom's shopping cart, into which she'd placed two cartons of maple yogurt. He removed them and exchanged them for two cartons of plain.

Why this staring? Wasn't something like 60 percent of America obese? Likely every self-satisfied shopper in this Woodward's had seen—or been related to—someone of girth. Maybe they themselves had been guests of honor at some Weight Watchers 100 Pounds or More Party, holding their size-twenty-four pants up over their size-twelve frames. These assholes are so quick to forget the fat they've lost. He assured himself that if he were some size-twenty-four who'd somehow whittled himself down to his current twenty-nine-inch waist, he would've felt sympathy for those who continued to suffer as he had. He would've felt a sense of kinship with them, and he would've had no problem stepping out into the middle of the aisle in Woodward's—in any grocery store, not just Woodward's—to help them move their carts or retrieve items from the topmost shelves.

The phone reregistered Jocelyn's text. He unlocked the screen so he wouldn't have to keep on receiving the reminders. His mom had found her grocery list and was checking it using the lowermost subsection of her trifocals.

"Why do you still live here?" he asked. "Why don't you ever seriously consider living in Chicago closer to me and Jocelyn?"

She looked at him with an uncharacteristic quickness. "That's a long conversation, honey. Not the kind we'd start while grocery shopping."

"I'm just asking."

"A move like that right now wouldn't be practical, exactly."

He sighed. They had this down to a catechism. "Yes it would! You're retired."

She shook her head. "The next thing on here is arugula."

"I don't understand why you don't make the move, Mom. What is there for you out here?"

"You know," she said.

"No, I don't."

"Memories."

No other widow-divorcée thought this way, he was pretty sure: sitting in her ex-husband's mental dreck, keeping herself single for no apparent reason beyond a physiognomic flaw that could easily be fixed if she wanted it enough.

And who'd taught her to hate herself like this? Who'd taught her to think this way? She'd grown up with privilege, no siblings but a younger brother, ostensibly supported by her parents. She'd done well both socially and academically at Kent State. She was smart, capable. She had been at one point very beautiful.

Leland Jr. regarded her as she shook some arugula into a bag, her face hanging forward in heavy folds. According to pictures, she'd been short and curvy when she was young, the majority of her weight in her butt and hips, almond-eyed, her hair dirty blond. She had had a habit of smiling pursed-mouthed so it looked as if she thought the photo was a joke. In the Kent State yearbook, there's a photo titled "High Ambitions!" where Leland Sr. is playing the electric bass with a jay between his lips—somehow the yearbook adviser didn't care about this?—and she's golden and innocent standing next to him, banging on a tambourine. And then a twelve-year codependent joke of a marriage, no official divorce, his suicide, and here she was, the poster child for diabetes and hypertension. Leland Jr. could pinpoint the exact moment the transformation had begun: he'd been thirteen and she'd been thirty-four and Leland Sr. had exited their lives without warning. She'd started eating. One morning before school instead of eggs and oatmeal Leland Jr. had come downstairs to buttered white toast and bananas and peanut butter; she'd eaten half the jar before he'd gotten up. Then there were thick lasagnas, frequent ice cream sundaes with chocolate syrup, bags of chips hidden behind the toilet. Leland Jr.'s new method of intervention was stocking her house with vegetables and gluten-free bread so she'd have no option but to binge on health food. But she was wily—during his last visit, he'd found a bag of Lay's under the sofa.

Jocelyn sent another text: *Can you please just call before I take two hydrocodone and go to sleep?* Her back pain must be raging again. She'd been stressed for the past two months: a client at Lefébvre was giving her trouble. But he also suspected that she was reporting her pain as more severe than it actually was and the real problem was just that she couldn't sleep.

"Mom?"

She'd moved on from bagging the arugula and was scanning the produce aisle. "Honestly, honey, I've been shopping here like you told me and it doesn't get any easier to find anything."

"Mom, I have to make a phone call. It's Jocelyn."

She nodded.

He went up to the checkout aisles and called Jocelyn. Despite her obvious annoyance, her voice sounded thick and relaxed. She'd taken the hydrocodone.

"You know what I was thinking?" she asked.

"What?"

"Maybe you could make up with Lee."

"Lee Bloom-Mittwoch?" he asked.

"Yes," she said. "Who else is named Lee?"

"Are you kidding?"

"You're in Shaker Heights."

"They live in an apartment somewhere. They don't live here. We're in your dad's store getting groceries."

"Leland," she said, her voice flat. "He's eighteen years old. He's hurt."

"He's a fucking punk!" Leland Jr. said, and lowered his voice when he got stares. "This is what you wanted to call me about?"

"I just thought it'd be a good idea."

"I'm not gonna do that. You read that e-mail he sent a year ago."

"It'd help you release some anger," she said as if she hadn't heard him.

"Stop getting involved, babe," he said, barking "babe."

"It was just an idea I had. Take it or leave it."

She sighed thickly, as if he were a slow but obedient child. "I'm trying to put you out of your misery."

"Okay. Put me out of my misery. You just compared visiting him to having me put down."

"You can't even call him 'Lee'!" she said, and hummed in exasperation. "It's just 'him'!"

"I don't want to talk about this. I'm with Mom."

"I bet she'd be pro this idea."

"Go to sleep," he said. He hung up on her and regretted it but not enough to call her back. He found his way back to the produce aisle.

"Who was that?" his mom asked.

"Jocelyn, Mom. I told you."

She sighed. "Oh."

An angry shiver shot down the back of his neck. "You know what she was calling about?" he asked.

"No," she said.

"She was calling to suggest I go see Lee while I'm in town."

She nodded.

"He sent us an e-mail a while ago. He was obviously fucked up when he sent it."

"Don't swear in public, honey."

"I'm sorry," he said. He held his phone in front of him with both hands. "He was asking for 'assets.' He thinks I owe him. I forwarded it to Jocelyn; I had no idea she'd respond to it."

"What did you say back?"

"To the e-mail?"

"To Jocelyn just now."

"I said of course I wouldn't."

He felt increasingly justified in his decision to hang up on Jocelyn. At Leland Sr.'s funeral ten years ago she'd held Leland Jr.'s hand on the flight, but when they'd gotten there she'd spent an uncomfortable amount of time smiling at Lee, who was a grubby-faced nine-year-old in a child-sized magician's suit holding the hand of the stepwitch he'd crawled out of. Grosser even, the stepwitch had wept off her pancaked-on makeup, and Jocelyn had offered her a tissue, and after that Jocelyn had gone back to the hotel, leaving him to deal with all the legal business. Leland Jr. hadn't had the patience to explain to Jocelyn that, though appearances may be deceiving, these were not people who deserved her compassion: these were people who indulged in their habits of self-destruction with the same hedonistic joy Leland Sr. had. At least Jocelyn had the decency to reassure Leland Jr. that he was justified in doing what he'd done, rooting through their house to take back what was his: the jewelry, the paintings, the silverware and china, the car, the old yellow briefcase that was locked shut.

But now here they were back to square one, and it was Jocelyn who was e-mailing grubby little Lee, who was actually not so little anymore. She'd even offered him an internship or something with Lefébvre. What she didn't understand was that the Bloom-Mittwochs' disasters didn't look like her family's, couldn't be solved with ex post facto acts of guilty charity. The lives of the Bloom-Mittwochs had been strange and wretched for decades. The best he could do was distance himself and his mother from the rabble.

With the Town & Country's ample behind packed with groceries, the car heaved home, favoring the passenger side. He bit his lip very hard. His mom was inflicting a lite rock station on them both.

"I'll make a vegetable roast for us," she said. "And there's going to be *St. Elmo's Fire* on cable, with Emilio Estevez. So maybe we could watch that."

"What's a vegetable roast?"

"Something healthy." She was lost, staring out the window. "Emilio Estevez always reminded me of you. I think you look like him."

"Mom, I don't look like Emilio Estevez."

"You're not doing yourself any favors when you deny it." She smiled up at him. "You're handsome in the same way."

"Mom?"

She was silent.

"Maybe let's bring up the topic of moving to Chicago again."

"Okay," she said.

"Right now," he tried, but stopped, and had to swallow hard before he started again. "Right now Cleveland and Shaker Heights are kind of like a toxic waste pool. They're like a pool you have to wade around in. And the toxic waste is all the stuff you've dealt with in your life."

"Leland—"

He ignored that. "And you have an opportunity—I've talked to Jocelyn and she thinks it's right—that might allow you to be with us in Chicago."

She snorted, which she sometimes did when she was not in a good mood.

"Sweetie, I'm sorry." She turned to him; her face, deformed by age and weight, could only approximate the look of concern she used to give him when he couldn't sleep without that damn Eagles song. Or when he was in high school and so throttled by his own perfectionism that he'd settled into a four-year-long bad mood. "Is it too hard for you to be here?"

"Mom!" he found himself shouting, almost barking. "I just think you should move on."

"Move on from what? I have friends here. I have people who love me. There's Alvin, for one."

"Ah good fucking lord, Mom! Is he worth it? Is he worth *this*?"

He did a top-down gesture that encompassed the whole of her, and her face was pure horror before she turned to the window.

They didn't talk for a while until he said, "That's not what I meant."

And then: "It's like he has his hands on you from beyond the grave." They ate dinner in silence (the "vegetable roast" turned out to be a casserole that was mostly cheese and noodles with a few green peppers, but he was too dogged to comment), watched *St. Elmo's Fire* in silence. When he finally went to bed, he lay on his back across the covers, phone in hand, ready to spend the better part of the next hour composing an e-mail to Jocelyn. She didn't know how to solve the problem, clearly. The solution was getting his mom to move to Chicago.

His phone dinged. He checked it immediately, expecting it to be a text from Jocelyn, but it was from Scott, an analyst and sometime jogging buddy, and the content was just: *NAV predicted +4 by end of week.* Work. The mutual fund that employed Leland Jr. was planning to invest in the development of a bipolar I antipsychotic that could also be prescribed for depression/anxiety. Leland Jr. and two other team members had done most of the research: it was being synthesized at a lab in Mississippi called Cisco Drugs, the generic name was teraflin (no trade name yet, obviously), it had a chemical structure that looked like a child gymnast doing a back-flip. So far it had tested well among female and male bipolars ages thirteen to twenty, and it was going to be branded as a "kids' drug." It had all the benefits of lithium with the side effects profile of Ritalin, and everyone on Scott's end was very excited about it. Scott had just the other week referred to Leland Jr.'s team's discovery of teraflin as "visionary" and "endlessly profitable."

Leland Jr. had never asked himself why the issue of his mom, and not the issue of assigning market value to intangibilities like "biotechnological growth," was what seemed to be demanding so much from him. He on more than one occasion had lost himself in the shine of some senior partner's calvity during an executive board meeting, wondering why his mother hadn't remarried and whom she'd seen since Leland Sr. left her.

She'd stayed single all Leland Jr.'s adolescence: her only thoughts seemed to be about his father, who would sometimes send her letters detailing how she'd failed in their marriage. Letters that compared her unfavorably to Diedre, the stepwitch, compared Leland Jr. unfavorably to the squirming baby boy also named Leland (Lee for short). Leland Jr. was in college by the time the Lee letters started rolling in and she'd saved them all. He had to believe she'd stayed single out of masochistic loyalty to Leland Sr. Or was that just the mind of the teenaged solipsist? Had she, he sometimes wondered as the project manager walked investors through ten screens of infographics, really gone ten years without sex? Twenty? He remembered when she'd just begun gaining weight and was looking ample and healthy in a way he could best describe as "rural," she'd had a lot of very long conversations with the butcher during which he'd smiled wetly. Now there was this "friend" Alvin.

The thought that really dogged him—that had prompted a handful of Winn Maxwell JägerThursdays and corresponding guilty 10Ks on the treadmill the day after—was that he was not a step ahead of Leland Sr. as he'd always believed, but two steps behind. That was Leland Sr.'s legacy: setting traps. And the trap of Leland Jr.'s life had been his masterpiece. Leland Sr. had let him believe he'd won, but that was only because the mysterious other shoe hadn't dropped. He might have known from the moment he dared Leland Jr. to hit him that Leland Jr. would be his greatest adversary, would be the one fucking person in the world who begrudged him the codependent clemency he needed to stay alive. Now he thought it could have been because of Leland Jr.'s hatred of him that the warped old man had left. Leland Jr. had grown up, acquired cojones, and started slamming doors in Leland Sr.'s face and calling him (in both casual conversation with his mother and less casual conversation with the man himself) an idiot, a druggie, a burnout, and, when he acquired the vocabulary, a fuckup, a piece of shit, a woman-hater. And if it earned him the occasional brain boxing—so what? *I'm keeping this name just to spite you*, he often thought. *I'm obliterating your legacy and making it my own.*

Still, Leland Sr. appeared to have lain down and taken Leland Jr.'s abuse, which Leland Jr. found eerie if he thought about it too much. Besides throwing him a very occasional punch or shove, the most he'd done was call him "ungrateful" in those letters, and "impossible son material" and "very unlike this new child, Lee, who does love me very much, and who I believe better deserves my name." Which meant, of course, there had to be another shoe about to drop.

What is it and when's it gonna drop? Leland Jr. wondered, phone still in hand, staring at the gold stars either his mom or the previous owner had stenciled onto the guest bedroom ceiling. And is there any way I can possibly prevent it from dropping? If he was being rational, he'd just dispel the idea as superstition—it was a mental chore that could be carried out as quickly as the readjustment of a cuff link or the stirring of cream into coffee. But thinking about his family made him irrational. When thoughts like these dogged him, the go-to solution was to loudly "fuck" Jocelyn (who had to be gotten into the mood for this kind of thing, which was its own bureaucratic process), or bang his head once hardish against the wall if Jocelyn could not get in the "fucking" mood, or watch tasteless porn, his morning memories of it typically dim (he was once disturbed to discover his browsing history betrayed a fascination with breathplay bondage). If none of these were sufficient, then he'd do this comforting thing where he stripped to just his pants or underwear or sometimes got completely naked and folded himself up between the side of the toilet and the bathroom wall to meditate and possibly cry. He felt foolish when he did this but he knew it was (1) practical, because an occasion like this was usually concomitant with JägerThursdays, and it helped to have the toilet nearby, and (2) soothing, because since childhood he'd found fitting himself into small spaces (closet shelf, the space under his bed, the washing machine when he'd been very little) proved a huge relief to his nervous system.

He stared at his phone's screen and turned it off. He was accustomed to taming his insomnia with midnight runs, and he'd brought along his Nikes and mesh shorts. His mom's house was a highly insomniac site for him. He breathed deeply, tensing and flexing his ab muscles, and sat up in the bed. Dressing for running carried for Leland Jr. the same duty-bound gravitas as dressing for work: lacing up his running shoes meant he was about to do something of equal import to what he usually did after double-Windsoring a tie. He cracked the window. It was a nice enough night.

Outside, he ran spellbound, shirtless, low-frequency vibrations beginning in his ankles and ending in a forearm twitch. He'd set his watch to track his distance and was feeling sluggish for the first two miles—the route took him past the elementary school and Chagrin Boulevard—but then he hit his stride after mile three, at which point he'd arrived at the Highland Park Golf Course. Scanning the premises for insomniac retirees, he jogged up to hole one and then downhill to hole two, which was in a sand trap. Unwilling to stop running but wanting to think, he jogged the perimeter of the sand trap. Why did he even bother visiting this place? He flashed on the face of the strange young man at the funeral ten years ago, the supposed beneficiary of Leland Sr.'s generosity. Now Leland Jr. remembered, though he didn't particularly want to, how the young man had driven Jocelyn back to the hotel while he had followed Diedre back to her musty bungalow.

Maybe the other shoe had already dropped.

No, no. That was paranoid thinking. That was Cleveland talking, not him. The young man hadn't fucked his wife, his mother's belongings were still in his house, the locked-shut briefcase could contain whatever he wanted as long as he didn't open it.

Leland Jr. jogged faster, the first fartlek of his run, leaving the golf course behind him. It wasn't Jocelyn's fault, that much was true. Or at least it wasn't completely her fault. Even though they'd agreed not to have children (a sore point for his mom; for her mom, too), she still sometimes acted like a mother. He'd catch her casting recklessly about for something to stanch her bleeding heart. She settled on ridiculous causes. Dangerous ones, sometimes. Like once she'd suggested to him that they go on Craigslist and pretend to "order" prostitutes who—she claimed she could tell from the photos—were trafficked children, and then they'd sequester those children in their house and call the police before the pimps could murder them. Another time she'd announced that they needed to halve their carbon footprint, and had started biking to the train station, using only the library computer, reading by candlelight. But her most depressing cause by far was Lee.

If anyone's a cause for compassion, he allowed himself to think, *it's me.* He hadn't asked to be born to a liar and drug addict, a "father" who since Leland Jr. could first remember was either furiously mercurial or self-righteously "clean." Whenever Leland Jr.'s mom had forced Leland Sr. into an NA meeting via final ultimatum, he'd whiningly dragged his ass there only to lie through the first meeting and skip out on the second, privately confessing to Leland Jr.—as if they had the kind of relationship where they confessed things to each other—that a whole army of pathetic ex-junkies couldn't keep him away from his medicine. Leland Jr. had taken up the mantle of manhood very early on and he'd fought like hell. And on the morning when his mom woke him up crying and showed him the note Leland Sr. had left them—"This became too impossible for me to withstand; I cannot live like an automaton any longer"—Leland Jr. knew he'd won. Well, almost: he would've truly won if he got his mother that divorce he knew she wanted, or at least convinced law enforcement that they'd been robbed.

Lee was very different from Leland Jr. He was a Kool-Aid drinker: the way he cried in his shitty child's suit at the funeral, the way he gave his little eulogy—"He was the best dad I coulda asked for, he did the best job he could [sniffle, sniffle]"—the end of which Leland Jr. could scarcely hear over the sound of his own grinding teeth.

When he had arrived at the stepwitch's trailer-bungalow after the funeral, he had seen what he'd expected to see: the stepwitch, heavy-lidded and made up, looking like she was late for third-period algebra. She was holding a cat that smelled as if it had recently and messily evacuated its bowels; the kitchen still bore significant evidence of the previous night's dinner and possibly even the dinner before that; the living room was littered with dirty plastic toys that were too young for the nine-year-old boy who sat, in order to avoid everything, with his face glued to the TV. If it had been possible to live worse than Leland Jr.'s family had, this family was doing it.

"Don't disturb him while he's watching TV," was all she said as she let Leland Jr. in.

Leland Jr. nodded, confident that he owed this woman absolutely nothing and that after today, he'd never need to speak to her again. He turned his attention to Lee. The boy's skin was thin and yellowish. He wanted to say, "So you're the son he loved more?" but he didn't. Instead he walked past him and felt the glare on his back and then, unable to resist, turned around and said: "I'm just gonna run upstairs to grab a few things."

The boy turned, and out of his mouth came the words "Fuck you," quiet enough for only the two of them to hear. Leland Jr. smiled and said, "I'll be finished very quickly," and then proceeded to retrieve his and his mother's life from the house's smoke-filled, shaggy crawlspace.

He could remember wishing Jocelyn had been there with him at that moment. What little kid is warped enough to say something as megalomaniacally sophisticated as "Fuck you" when his stolen things are being repossessed? "Please don't take anything," maybe, or, "Who are you?" But "Fuck you"—those are the words of a proper son of Leland Sr., and such a son couldn't be a person deserving of compassion. Lee had already been beyond reform then, he was cast in his father's mold, and so would probably inherit his father's taste for shitty behavior and nose candy. That had been a good day—Leland Jr. had been smiling the whole time during the drive back to the hotel.

He broke stride under a streetlamp and paused the timer on his watch. He wasn't exactly sure where he was. His pacer said four miles. Four miles was usually nothing for him, but something about tonight was making things difficult. It was the idea of Jocelyn and the e-mail—the idea of a problem that should've been solved a long time ago, a bunch of nasty backwash still sluicing around in his brain.

He'd explain to Jocelyn about the "Fuck you" he'd heard that day. He'd tell her things Leland Sr. had done to the family that he'd been too embarrassed to tell anyone; he'd tell her in plaintive, pity-seeking detail how Melinda had built herself back up after being destroyed by Leland Sr.'s abandonment. Jocelyn had gotten all this in piecemeal fashion, and clearly she hadn't understood. He'd tell her as many times as she needed to hear it.

It's Lee's fault, he thought, his mind clamping conclusively around the idea. He imagined the jaundiced boy's face and aged it until he was staring into the sad, skinny eyes of a teenaged burnout. Leland Jr. had known kids like Lee in school: ur-nerds and wannabe thugs. The nerdier faction had some enthusiasm for books involving trolls and wizards and proudly congregated at the fringes of the playground. The fifteen-year-old thugs were patient observers, often stoned out of their minds on cough syrup. The mediocrity of those kids had always made Leland Jr., who'd run track all throughout high school, bounced between the first- and second-tier popular groups, and gone to Northwestern University on scholarship, extremely angry. It made him even angrier to think that he was related by blood to such a person, and that this person had risen from the anonymity of his putrid, narrow, meaningless life—a life Leland Sr. had spent a good chunk of his time on earth trying to condemn Leland Jr. to—to demand money from Leland Jr. now. It was pathetic. Was this supposed to intimidate him? Was this supposed to take him down?

Of course it would never take him down.

He looked up at the moon, which was fingernail clipping–thin. He smiled angrily. If this is the other shoe dropping, *Dad*, then this is nothing.

"You hear me?" he barked to the sky. "This is fucking nothing!"

CALEB MARSHALL

(1970–)

1985–1990
Cleveland

Caleb and his moms fulfilled their destinies around the same time, at least in his opinion. Within a week of his turning fifteen, he won the 1985 Cleveland Chess Championship in the fourteen-to-sixteen division and then his moms left to teach American literature at Dover College in Ontario. His trophy, fought for by hours of studying old strategy books and busing to a library fifteen miles away to squint over microfiche of Bobby Fischer interviews, went under glass in his school's hallway. His moms's position—fought for by Dr. Ellyn Marmeloy, who had told the Dover faculty that she'd resign in protest if they focused on his moms's background and ignored her "dexterous and brilliant critical mind"—was tenure track and well paid. That week, watching her cook breakfast for himself and Aaron, her pumps clicking, her skin clear and eyes bright, Caleb had the distinct feeling that he and his moms could have conquered the world together.

The final round of the championship took place in the Tower City Center. He was facing off against Magdalene Pyari, who lived in the south suburbs and was the only girl in the league. She'd beaten him in round three last year and had then been ousted in round four—now they'd both clawed their way to round six and the reporters (two of them—more than last year) were eating it up, snapping photos every time one of them hit the clock. Magdalene had always been aggressive with her offense—Caleb once watched her sacrifice both bishops and her queen in order to lure a weaker player into an improbable-looking checkmate—and she was no different in this game, incinerating half her pawns in the first ten minutes and then swiping at Caleb's power pieces with a rook-knight combo that Caleb had nicknamed Starsky and Hutch in his head. Starsky came galloping across the board G8 to F6, F6 to G4, Hutch crawling along next to him, the two of them staying what appeared to be one to one and a half moves ahead of Caleb's creeping pawn defense. Caleb was an extremely defensive player—he knew this about himself, had spent far more time than he'd cared to getting chewed up and spit out by offensive nutjobs—and he knew Magdalene knew this about him as well. This was how she'd beaten him last year. But in that great year 1985 he brought new sleight of hand to the table: something Dr. Loren Barsfield of *Chess for the 20th Century* called "compartmentalization." It was a strategy that required the patience and tedium-endurance of a true defensive player, and it basically involved playing two games. By the time he'd set up the fianchetto that beat Magdalene, she'd left all the royalty on her side of the board vulnerable, assuming she was a few moves away from a checkmate. And she was: if Caleb had whipped his bishops into position one move slower, she would've crushed him the same as last year. But instead it was Caleb slamming the clock as his stomach dropped with excitement and the judge shouting "Checkmate!" and Magdalene standing up to shake his hand, the announcer guy with the microphone onstage belting, "A victory for Marshall, who really stole the show this year!"

Sitting onstage in the fourteen-to-sixteen division champion chair while the head judge talked about their bright futures, he could see the two of them in the audience: his moms waving from the third row of folding chairs and his brother on her left with his arms crossed, one leg out in the aisle, wearing the blank, mirror-eyed look he always did when he was about to fall asleep. Caleb waved back at his moms a little so it wouldn't look like he was ignoring her, then he scanned the audience for anyone else he knew. Almost all the kids were white and from other schools—faces he'd seen across the room during district championships, meets, and drills. None of the kids from the Central Chess Club had turned up, nor had Coach Allman. Allman didn't like losing and Caleb didn't like his strategy, so no love lost there.

But down in the front row was a face from so long ago it could've come out of his dreams: Lu. The big guy he'd gone to school with since fourth grade, who'd stolen his lunchbox twice, whom Aaron had beaten up once— how Aaron had managed that was beyond everyone's imagination. Everyone had been terrified of him because he had been a foot taller than anyone in the grade the minute he turned ten. He had a girlfriend when he was twelve. But then Aaron had whooped his ass, left him on the floor crying. Then, days later, he puked at an assembly. All the kids were sitting cross-legged in that ratty old gym while Principal Clemens talked about violence, how the school was a peaceful community and didn't need any more violence than they'd already had, and when he said "violence" for the sixteenth time Lu grabbed his gut, looked across the floor at Aaron and Caleb, and puked everything in his stomach up onto his lap. Clemens sighed something into the microphone like "This is a mess right here" and as soon as all the kids started laughing and pointing, Aaron was on his feet, shouting, "This mother-fucker just PUKED all over the gym!" After that, Lu was Pukeboy in Caleb's mind, tall and stupid instead of tall and threatening.

Caleb went up to get his trophy still thinking about all that, watching Lu watch him, and when they all posed to take the photo, Lu just sat on his massive hands and stared straight ahead. Caleb jumped down from the stage and landed directly in front of Lu. Caleb smiled, offered his hand to shake. Lu stood up: still massive, still vacant-faced.

"Thanks for coming, man," Caleb said. "I don't really know anyone else here."

Over Lu's shoulder, he could see his moms and Aaron making their way to him. Lu's features now bore a look of incomprehension, and he shook his head a little, stuck his hand out, too. Caleb thought about apologizing for the Pukeboy shit but decided he'd wait for Lu to say something. Something about the lunchbox would be good. Or just "con-gratulations." The head judge came over and gave Caleb a warm squeeze on the shoulder. Caleb looked up, thanked him, looked back at Lu, who seemed angry now. He grabbed Caleb's hand and squeezed so hard that Caleb felt a pop.

"Fuck you," he said, and walked away.

Caleb didn't think of Lu again until five years later, when he read his obituary. Lu's death had been a shooting death, the perpetrators "unknown," and he was survived by his father (a mechanic) and his grandmother. By then Caleb and Aaron were living in the house with Jamal and JT—two levels, paint flaking off, growling heater. They were sitting smoking hand-rolled squares in front of the TV, Sabrina in Caleb's lap and a bag of chips in Aaron's, C-SPAN, which Sabrina was obsessed with, glowing bluish in front of them.

Caleb threw the obituaries on Aaron's lap and told him to read the one on the bottom right. Aaron did and then rolled his eyes and asked, "Are you surprised?"

"I'm not surprised," Caleb said. "Why would I be surprised?"

"Surprised about what?" Sabrina asked, and then she grabbed the obituary, read it, too, and said, "That's sad." Caleb felt her warmth shift on his legs—she was lying with her head against the sofa's arm—her ass teasing the inside of his thigh, and he bit his lower lip and shook his head, unwilling to make a scene about it. He put his hand over her stomach and felt her breathe. She was back to watching C-SPAN, the obituary on the floor beside her. Whatever desire he'd had to keep the Lu conversation going was erased by the rhythm of her breath, her little groans of disagreement whenever a Republican senator spoke.

He would marry her, he was sure. He'd met her at their new school between Fairfax and Shaker. She was the top student in their grade, fine-featured with dreams of being a marine biologist. He wouldn't have met her if he and Aaron hadn't gone to live with Aunt Debbie and Dennis after their mom left for Dover, which he'd hated at first: the four of them crammed into that shitty condo in the weird Italian neighborhood, the whole place stinking of Dennis (combination tar, sweat, and rotten sour cream), having to say grace before dinner every night, the paint-smelling new school where neither of them knew anyone. Aaron had taken the move as an opportunity to start "building an empire," drafting Caleb to help him sell fifteen-dollar dime bags to underclassmen who didn't know what they were paying for. They pulled in two hundred dollars a week, they got reputations, Aaron got locs and dyed some of them gold, asked people to start calling him Hammer—he never explained the nickname, and Caleb let it go.

The worst part about that time before Sabrina was the Nervousness, which Caleb told no one about. The Nervousness had come one day when he woke up before school, a feeling like a charley horse but in his mind, like one part of his thoughts strained and ached whenever accessed, but it was relentlessly accessed, and so his brain had no choice but to limp along struggling despite the straining and aching. The charley horse part of the thoughts was about him, who he'd been before, and how he was doomed to fail now. He'd once been the little kid who stood up onstage in the Tower City Center and claimed a division champ trophy, but that had been when Moms was around. *Something like that wasn't supposed to happen in the first place*, the Nervousness told him. *You were always worthless in that department. You know that, right? Just look around and the world will tell you that.* And the world did: it'd been a fluke, he could see that. Maybe he'd studied some strategy books but he didn't have the game in his blood, not like Magdalene, not like any of the others who won after him, white and suburban and described as "gifted" by the reporters who interviewed them. His math grades weren't even that good. He needed to work his ass off to make anything halfway decent happen—the world wasn't built for him, and it was exhausting to push against that, like that Greek myth where Sisyphus had to roll the boulder up the hill. It was endless, it was heavy. The Nervousness assured him that he was still smart, but his confidence had just been misplaced. He was his father's son. He was his brother's brother. The best thing he could do would be to follow their lead. *Follow their lead, stay in your lane*, it told him. And though it ached to hear, Caleb began to see how it might be true.

Then they had expanded from dime bags to benzos, which, he found, were an effective way to quell the Nervousness. Pop one and he felt the same but better and better, the kind of high you didn't think existed until you were thinking about it, and the Nervousness was done messing with him for the next few hours. Pop two in the space of four hours and he could make that last half a day. It was a nice trick, although it did fuck with his grades. He spent his junior year happy like this, upping his dosage as necessary, ignoring Aaron's weak threats to cut him off. And risk losing a business partner? Caleb had to laugh about that.

He met her in the spring of their junior year, at a party where he was dropping some shit off. It was crowded and he could tell she didn't belong there, had only come because she knew she needed to have some "fun," was sitting bored on the ledge of a big, burnt-out fireplace with the grate missing while some guy talked to her and she tried to drink a beer. The guy throwing the party paid Caleb and invited him in, told him to play whatever he wanted on the stereo, and asked him when his brother was coming. Caleb pushed past the kid and dug through his music until he'd found something serviceable—*Critical Beatdown* by the Ultramagnetic MCs; because of this he still broke out in an excited sweat whenever he heard "Watch Me Now"—and waited until the talking asshole got up to get another beer before sitting down next to Sabrina.

"Why you here?" he asked.

"Why am I here?" she asked back softly. "I got lucky. The better question is why're you talking to me?"

Caleb shrugged and blushed warm at the idea that she thought of him as occupying a social register higher than her own. She had the kind of mind that he could feel working from a distance: uncompromising and observant.

"You're beautiful," he offered.

She shook her head and laughed, snorted a little.

"I'm sorry," he said.

"It's okay." She was still laughing. "It's just really direct."

"I like to be direct," Caleb said, though he didn't.

When they began dating, she set herself up as a counterpoint to the Nervousness, insisting that he was a talented critical thinker and should apply to Axel Renfroe with her. But he knew that wasn't going to be possible—there'd been the whole thing with his moms and his grandpa, plus his grades had gone to shit. She scanned his report cards and said they weren't that bad, some Bs and Cs, but still plenty of As and A-minuses. He told her the only thing he'd been good at was chess, and that was math, so he'd probably have to major in math and how could he do that if he was making a borderline C-plus/B-minus?

"I could help you!" she said. "You could have it up to an A-minus by the end of the semester!"

Whenever she said something like this once they were together, the Nervousness shot a dark, inky substance into his brain that made his stomach clench. He smiled and told her he loved her, started kissing her neck, and soon she was sighing and forgetting—or choosing to forget—about the whole conversation. He managed this for almost three years, long after they'd graduated and she'd started at Axel Renfroe and he'd moved into the house with Aaron, Jamal, and JT, expanded their operation, started working some odd jobs. He'd done it again the night before

Lu's obituary ran, the Nervousness held back by a snorted milligram and some pulls from Aaron's piece.

"I want you to meet my parents," she said, a hand on his chest. "I want you to play my dad in chess."

Caleb laughed. "I wanna get married to you," he said.

But instead of nodding and kissing him she turned onto her back and looked at the ceiling. "Then you've got a lot of work to do."

A lot of work to do. Caleb didn't like remembering that sentence, especially now that they'd all been talking about Lu's death. The TV still droning, Aaron finished the bag of chips and said he was going to leave them alone, gave Sabrina a hug good-bye—he was already treating her like a sister-in-law—and wandered out the front door. They stayed watching C-SPAN for a few minutes after he left, then she looked up at him and smiled, said, "I've been waiting for this all day."

With more force than he'd anticipated, she sprang to her feet, straddled him, pulled off his shirt. She was wet as hell through her tights: he could feel it on his leg. But he held it together. Undressed her, held her waist as she enveloped him, shuddered, suppressed a groan as Senate Majority Leader George Mitchell droned on in the background about school vouchers. Soon he lost all hearing, sight, and touch that was not in some way related to her pliant body, forgot that it was nighttime in the fall in Cleveland in the United States on earth, inhabited a world that was just Sabrina, just her uptilted head and her parted lips and her involuntary noises, and then saw the inside of his skull, saw stripes of color, saw his future with her.

She left two hours later and didn't call the next day, which was unlike her. She didn't call for a week and didn't answer his calls. Several nights in with no call from her, not even four fat benzo rails could put him to sleep, could keep his heart from making a dent in his chest whenever he thought about her. He biked past her parents' house but didn't dare knock on the door. He biked past Axel Renfroe at eleven o'clock, two o'clock, five o'clock and never saw her. Aaron said she was fucking with him, testing his loyalty, and that she'd be back. He said he was surprised she hadn't pulled some shit like this sooner. Sleepless, Caleb called in sick to the drugstore twice. She finally called after ten days, her voice thick.

"Have you given it any thought?" she asked.

Relieved to hear her voice, he wanted to say yes, but he had no idea what he'd be agreeing to. "Given what thought?"

"The work you need to do?"

"Yes!" And when she remained silent he felt anger closing his throat. "Yes, but what the fuck? You disappear so I'll do anything for you?"

She was still silent.

"What work is it I need to do?" he asked, exasperated. "Be respectable? Go to college? Start making real money?"

"I missed my period last week," she said. "I'm gonna take the test tomorrow. You have to promise me you'll make some changes. Then we can get married."

Holy shit, said the Nervousness, upset for the first time in its life. *You fucked up.* Caleb's brain found a way to speak more clearly than he had in a long time.

"I love you," he said. "I'll make whatever changes you want."

She came over the next day red-eyed, the pregnancy test in her purse (negative). She told him her mother had seen the test and ordered her to break up with him or else she'd stop paying for college. She held him and said she loved him and would always love him and that she'd send letters. She told him please not to cry and left.

The Nervousness had never been happier. *I fucking told you, man! What did I tell you? What did I tell you? You shoulda listened to me, because you're in some deep shit now.* But Caleb had listened to the Nervousness, had followed its rules, and the one good thing about his life had gone away. *Well, good point,* the Nervousness said. *Maybe it's just that you didn't follow the rules right. The rules in your own motherfucking head. Maybe now you gotta die.*

Tall, quiet Jamal was the one who'd found him sobbing powder-nosed on the floor and went upstairs to get JT, who, upon seeing his sad state, made him a banana-and-peanut-butter sandwich and poured him a shot of whiskey. Aaron got home and said, "What the fuck happened here?" Caleb listened to the gulps and warbles of their conversation like it was coming at him through a lead wall. Aaron sat down at Caleb's feet and said he needed to get fucked up, pulled Caleb into a sitting position, and poured four more shots.

Some time passed—too much, according to the Nervousness—and Aaron announced they were going down to the flats by the river. Someone got Caleb's arms into his coat and said, "Shit, man, just stand up." Caleb stood, and the room rotated a few inches ahead of his vision. *That's all right*, the Nervousness said, voice sharp through the fog. *That's how it's supposed to be.*

JT said he was the least drunk so he drove and blasted P-Funk in the deck, parents' music. They parked and Caleb got out, buoyed by the car's momentum, running up the side of a giant pile of gravel above which was poised the yawning mouth of a hydraulic excavator. Pebbles at his hands and feet came dislodged, rolled away from him. *You need to get higher up*, the Nervousness said.

He turned around and slid down the side of the pile, everyone on the ground asking what the fuck he was doing. Then he ran ahead of them toward the Innerbelt Bridge. *Yes*, the Nervousness said. *Now you're thinking right for once.* He was starting to sober up as he ran but that didn't matter—it was useful, even. *Climb up that motherfucking sand*, it said. *If you're good for one thing in the world, it's to climb up that motherfucking sand and get on top of that bridge.*

Caleb climbed, the world around him silenced except for the blunt, deep sound of Aaron's shouting. He jumped from the top of the sand pile to the top of the bridge leg and began climbing up the steel gridwork. He felt like Spider-Man. He was Spider-Man. *This is gonna be the greatest moment of your pathetic life*, promised the Nervousness. *And it won't even be downhill after this, it'll just be nothing.* He climbed.

He was almost on top of the bridge, looking down and behind him at the Cuyahoga, cars rattling the pavement above him, seeing for the first time in what felt like a year the desperate-looking ant faces of Jamal and JT jumping and waving. Aaron's voice from somewhere closer: "I'm gonna kill you, you stupid motherfucker! You jump, you dead!" He put his head to the steel like he was praying, hearing the Nervousness say *Too late to back out now. This has to be it. If you don't go through with this, I don't know what I'll do.* "Probably something bad," Caleb whispered. "Something really bad." And there surged from the depths of his memory his father's funeral, six-year-old Aaron punching him in the jaw, Moms cooking sweet potatoes. He pushed himself from the gridwork and fell.

Until he snagged. His hand snagged on something, his wrist popped and strained. He looked up and there was Aaron clinging to the gridwork, heaving and sweating, grabbing him by the hand. From behind gritted teeth he hissed "Asshole" and "Crazy motherfucker." Then he swung Caleb toward the gridwork and yelled at him to grab on or they'd both die, and did his crazy ass really want to be responsible for killing himself and his brother? Caleb hit the gridwork once, twice, his nose bloodied, his brain cleared, and the Nervousness said, *Well, what the fuck is it gonna be?* And Caleb grabbed on.

They never spoke about that happening—the way Aaron acted, it was like it never happened. Caleb bandaged up his nose and did his night shift at the drugstore the next day, threw himself into his other work the day after. Caleb wrote a letter to his moms—he resolved to write at least once a week. She wrote back: *I miss you both and am looking forward to Christmas.* She always was. *Each year it seems the faculty gets more progressive—my eyes are further opened to social issues of great importance. I can easily see you teaching here, or at some other fine college, one day in your future.* Cowed by recent events, the Nervousness didn't dare speak, but Caleb still kept the benzos coming in the event that it did.

One day, in addition to the usual lavender-scented letter from his moms, he got a package. There was no return address, and the sender had shaky handwriting. He cut the box open and under the flaps of cardboard was a note balanced on top of layers of tissue paper. The note said *You have great potential. Go to college. Leland Bloom-Mittwoch Sr.* Caleb smirked. He never forgot a name. That white guy his moms used to sleep with.

Aaron hated him, but Caleb mostly pitied him—he was an aging addict who was clearly losing his mind. What the hell would this guy want with him now? Leland Bloom-Mittwoch was supposed to be in California or some shit, someplace crazy people with no money went to pretend they could "make it." He snorted laughter through his damaged nose, quietly thanked this clown for intruding in his life again, providing some much-needed levity. Then he dug beneath the tissue paper and found ten thousand dollars in unmarked bills.

May 8, 2009
Chicago

At eight forty-five in the morning Caleb Marshall had just debarked a bus on Chicago's West Side, having recently flown in from Cleveland to meet with an unusual client. Now he was looking at the blind kid who stood across the street from him. The blind kid—midteens, head-twitchy—seemed to be watching the traffic with his ears. He was unaccompanied. He was too young to drive, which—that was stupid, Caleb knew. He was obviously younger than sixteen and he was alone and unsupervised. Caleb produced a bottle of Xanax from his pocket, shook out a pill, swallowed it, and watched him.

The lights changed and the crosswalk man lit up and there came a rhythmic beeping from overhead that Caleb had heard before but had never bothered to contextualize. The blind kid heard it and produced a retractable white cane from his pocket, which he magicked open with a flick of his wrist. He began to cross. Caleb crossed as well. He watched the kid approach him. It was clear by the way the kid moved (semifluid, confident, with only some hesitation) and his reluctant use of the cane that he had not been blind since birth. The kid tapped past Caleb and Caleb craned his head to look behind him. He watched the kid find his way onto the curb and retract his cane.

Caleb crossed the street and re-rechecked his watch. It was now eight forty-nine and he was standing in front of the Rush University Medical Center, where, inside, Leland Bloom-Mittwoch Jr. was waiting in the psychiatric ward. Caleb hated Chicago, its segregationist North-South binary, the mirrored surfaces of its well-oiled downtown, its permanently fucked criminal justice system. He'd won none of the cases he'd taken on in the city, and all of them had been about the wrongful conviction of black juveniles in South Side shootings. He regarded the steel face of the university and thought about places he'd rather live if he didn't live in Cleveland. The Bay Area was his first choice: one of his biggest regrets was that he hadn't stayed longer when he had the chance. His second choice was a Massachusetts island near the Cape Cod Bay, someplace where he could wear dyed sheep's wool sweaters and learn how to fish. The only thing keeping him in the Midwest was inertia. Inertia and what psychotherapists would probably call a savior complex. He wasn't afraid of admitting to it. Better to be a savior than a sociopath. He should have that embroidered on a throw pillow someday. He laughed and then hung his head as he approached the hospital.

He pushed through the front doors and was greeted by a smiling receptionist at a wide desk. She was young—early twenties, unplucked eyebrows—with glasses and rosy cheeks. She'd been writing something with a pen that appeared to be made of the same material as the building's facade, and now she stood at attention, holding the pen with both hands, nodding pleasantly as he approached.

At the front desk of the Adult Psychiatric Unit, Caleb was told Leland Jr. was in group therapy and that he could wait in the waiting area. He assented, surrendered his briefcase and cell phone, and followed a nurse to the waiting area. And there she was, sitting in the chair closest to the single, trapezoidal window. Unchanged since the funeral, mostly. She'd gotten bangs—that was the biggest difference. Her eyes didn't bear even the suggestion of crow's feet. Her mouth was unlined. When she saw him, she sprung up from her chair and hugged him. He shouldn't have been surprised, but he was. Was this okay?

Jocelyn held him at arm's length and smiled. She told him he looked good. He shrugged and said he tried his best. He twitched out of her grasp and held her hands in his, then let go of them as if expecting a reprimand. He asked how she was doing. Now he could see the shadow of a massive bruise on the left side of her chin, blooming up ugly and fearsome beneath her concealer. Watching his eyes, she touched it and nodded. She said she was doing as well as she could be given the circumstances.

"He got a diagnosis of bipolar when we were in college," she said, looking out the window behind her, "but he didn't tell anyone except for me, and he never took the medication, and he's never had an episode since."

Caleb sighed. This would've been helpful information to know a week ago when he'd agreed to take the case. He looked back at Jocelyn, who now seemed shrunken and unappealing to him, inexperienced in defending herself in court. Or anywhere, really. He was reminded of Maggie, a girl he'd dated during his first year at the firm: she was small, like Jocelyn, an Oberlin graduate, nonprofit employee, child of professionals. The kind of white girl social justice princess he, a few years earlier, would've tortured with requests to say the N-word "for him" (he himself had written it out of his vocabulary years ago, a move he doubted Aaron would respect), delighting in her guilty squeamishness. Whenever he had spent holidays with her, the entire family used to crow about how good they looked together. Maggie had been fond of saying, "Everything happens for a reason." Which, he should've pointed out, was patently false. There was no reason for a six-year-old girl to be raped by her father or a fourteen-year-old boy to be shot by a twenty-five-year-old man: shit like that just happened, needed to happen, in fact, so the system could remain intact and smooth-running, so Maggie could go to a good school and "explore her interests," could get a nice, "impactful" job. If all Maggie's things happened for a reason, then all of Jocelyn's things certainly did, too.

"What caused the diagnosis?" he asked.

She looked back at the window, still hedging.

"What was it?"

"I don't know," she said. "One night in the dorm—well, he came to my dorm, which was actually on the other side of campus from his."

Caleb let out a sharp exhale of breath, tried far too late to soften it.

"Keep on going," he said.

She looked at him.

"Joss, you know I told you to tell me everything potentially injurious to your case."

She nodded energetically. "Yes, I know," she said. "But it's honestly such a small thing that I really didn't see it even being a part of whatever came up with the lawsuit. The doctors said this is paranoid schizophrenia, not a trace of bipolar."

"This constitutes a history of mental illness, though. It means he should've been taking meds and Lee had nothing to do with it."

She waved her hand at him as if at a bad smell. "He came to my dorm, I remember it was in the middle of the night, and it was on a Thursday his senior year at the beginning of the winter quarter. So I hadn't seen him for two days, which makes sense, because he was working on his senior thesis that quarter and always worked straight through the middle of the week. Oh, I forgot to say this—his roommate called me and told me Leland hadn't been asleep in two nights—"

Caleb shook his head and snorted. It was almost a little funny how much this fucked things up. He'd been talking with her for a week about Leland and his case and she just remembered all this now? She probably expected him to absorb the information and bury it. He imagined himself a gardener in her front yard, tossing dirt on her evidence while she looked on through the bay window.

"—he hadn't been asleep for a while, I guess, but I guess I just assumed he was working really hard, forgoing sleep for work, and the roommate made this little noise like 'mmh' and said if I knew anything that calmed him down, I should speak up. Like he was trying to get advice out of me, because Leland was walking around his room."

"Pacing?"

Jocelyn swung to the side, hugged her shoulders, and shrugged, all of which left her looking cranelike. She was obviously still dedicated to keeping herself thin, hadn't changed at all since he'd first seen her at Leland's funeral ten years ago. She was someone who had spent, as he had, a lifetime contorting herself to meet the expectations of a dominant culture. To him, the pattern of worry on her face was recognizable: he'd also worn the purple smudges he now saw under her eyes, the active culture of blackheads circling her chin, her inflamed and bleeding gums.

"You could call it that," she said, clearly uncomfortable. "Anyway, I didn't make anything of it, because his roommate was kind of an asshole if I'm remembering this correctly, I figured he was just trying to mess with both of us. So I told him to take Leland out for some drinks or something and then send him my way. By the time it was eleven and Leland wasn't there, I figured it was over. But then there was a knock on my door at four a.m. and there he was, stinking of grain liquor." She paused, held her hand to her mouth, and Caleb helplessly remembered every moment he'd daydreamed about her, every surge of warmth he'd felt for her. "He really did stink. And he just sort of staggered into the room like Frankenstein's monster, calling out for me, like, I don't know, like he was getting little shocks of electricity. And he saw me and just started talking instantly, like he'd been telling me a story for hours, picked up in midsentence. It was about how his suicide 'would close a logical loop.' And then my roommate ran out screaming. I told him to be quiet but he wasn't hearing me. He did that for an hour until I called the campus police."

"Close a logical loop?"

"It was something about how his father was illogical, or invalid, like a math problem. And Leland not being alive closed that loop somehow? The one Leland Sr. opened up by being born."

"Okay? But who gave the diagnosis?"

"The campus psychiatrist."

Caleb felt his muscles slacken. "A licensed psychiatrist? Did he have to pay to see him? Did he bill his insurance?"

"No, um, back then every student received free counseling. We just had to pay for the meds."

And he hadn't taken the meds. No paper trail. Absolutely no paper trail. As if to commemorate their sudden good luck, there flickered across Caleb's mind an illustration from a magazine article, a pastel brain with a bundle of dynamite at its center. It was from a story he'd read in *Time* about how environmental factors could "activate" symptoms of mental illness. He'd read it bored in the dentist's office, quietly congratulating himself on having his first root canal at thirty-eight. If he could get some doctor who could testify that drugs were one such environmental stressor—he already had a few ideas in mind—then he could use the bipolar to his advantage, build a case for Lee "awakening" a disease in Leland that would've remained dormant without his malicious interference. That was a great term: "malicious interference." Maybe he could even argue that the disease had progressed in some way—schizophrenia was worse than bipolar, from what he understood. He would look up EDM, see how many people had died from taking it, or at the very least lost their minds. There had to be more than a few.

Jocelyn was standing close to him now. His resolve thawed and he shuddered. The way she was basically pressed against him, the flurry of e-mails she'd sent him, the looks she'd given him in his rental car at the funeral all those years ago: he knew women well enough to know she had some kind of fantasy where he got debarred for having sex with her on the judge's bench—he could tell she was the kind of woman who was obsessed with professionals, whose kinks probably involved the sacrifice of a six-figure salary for the chance to eat her out. The obviousness of her dewy e-mails had made him smile: "Just checking in to see how you're doing" (right after the funeral), "Saw your photos on your mom's blog—so handsome" (when he'd graduated from Berkeley), "We know we'd be in capable hands with you" (a little over a week ago). He wondered how much she was keeping track of. His juvenile justice work in Cleveland? All his unsuccessful lawsuits against those racist cops? The Good Samaritan cases he'd filed against slum landlords, the meager ten- to fifteen-thousand-dollar settlements— the stuff that was turning his hair gray? He was like Obama, barely in office a year and already showing some silver around the ears. How many hours had Caleb spent in the mirror, inspecting the errant sprigs of old-man hair interrupting his seamless fade? How many women had mewled for him to please come back to bed, asking if he'd "fallen in"—only for him to respond that he was fine, just last night's Tanqueray. Because for some reason puking up Tanqueray was less embarrassing to him than the idea that he was getting older and had not yet accomplished the thing for which he would be remembered, had instead busied himself chipping away at the system brick by flinty brick, assuming he was comforting the afflicted and afflicting the comfortable, leaving instead an inches-deep concavity easily paved over after his death.

She'd earmarked his face at that funeral ten years ago and now she'd finally found a safe reason to bring him into her world. Her husband needed help, had suffered a psychotic break, and had been in the hospital for nearly a month. The toxicology report implicated the punk half brother, the little eulogizer from Leland Sr.'s funeral. Yet it was a case riddled with conflicts of interest—if he were a perfect attorney, he wouldn't allow himself to take it. But he knew that these were the kind of people who always thought their choice of legal defense was unquestionable. They were used to being right and would pay any amount to prove it. Case in point: he'd said something about having to factor in the cost of the commute and Jocelyn had offered to pay him double his hourly rate with a Pavlovian rapidity he'd rarely witnessed in clients.

Trying not to think about what was happening, he squeezed her hand once and let go. Self-conscious now, she backed away from him and sat down in a chair below the room's single window, worrying her little bird-hands in her lap. A nurse appeared, indicating that Leland had just finished group therapy and was now receiving visitors. Caleb turned to Jocelyn.

"Go in without me," she said.

He took a seat at a centrally located plastic table. Of course Leland Jr. would find himself in this country club after having a psychotic break, the walls painted orange and yellow, the nurses musing pleasantly about the warmer-than-usual spring. No state-hospital screaming, nobody held in six-point restraints, no women begging for someone (him) to believe them that they were being raped. He suffered a tight bolt of anger down his throat, then relaxed into his exhaustion.

If his mom was here, she'd harp on the fact that white folks went to this place and everyone else went to prisonlike psychiatric hospitals. She'd harp on the wealth disparity and how one of the side-effects of oppression is mental illness. She'd be right, of course, but she wasn't a lawyer and now she'd lived in a country with socialized health care for quite some time.

Leland Jr. was being led by two orderlies, looking far more state hospital than country club, pilling his fingers, licking his lips. He was too thin, his cheeks sharp and almost dimpled from it, and his hair was a fuzzy, silvering nest that Caleb realized, with more pity than awe, made him look young by comparison. Leland Jr. had clearly been working hard, or drinking hard, or something in the years since Caleb last saw him at Leland Sr.'s funeral. The nurse deposited him at the table across from Caleb and left.

"I know why you're here," Leland Jr. said as he shifted his eyes from the table to meet Caleb's, his words uninflected.

"I never doubted that," Caleb said.

Leland Jr. then pressed the heels of his hands into his temples and shouted, "NO! NO ALREADY!" Caleb jumped, then felt guilty for jumping even though no one else had seemed to notice. Leland Jr. raised his eyes and said, "You ever get ringing in your ears and you're terrified it'll never go away?"

"When I'm sleep deprived, yeah."

"Imagine it being a small voice," Leland Jr. said. "Like a child's voice."

Unsure where this was going, Caleb diverted the conversation. "I'm here to talk with you about your brother."

Leland Jr. laughed. "My brother? The victim? What is there to talk about?"

"He may have given you something."

"Of course he did! He absolutely did—that's what I've been arguing more or less all along." He threw up his hands, a long-suffering defendant finally exonerated. "But I don't hate him for it, and I'm not suing. Do you understand? I don't hate him anymore."

"That's all well and—"

"Hating him the way I did made me sick. It made me a nastier shade of the person I really am. I don't hate him because there's nothing left in me to hate him. There's no hate left in me. Look at me and tell me that you see a vengeful man who wants to sue an eighteen-year-old kid."

Caleb sighed. This was news. "Your wife has power of attorney," he said. "And she's suing."

"Well, tell her to stop. They have nothing. My brother wasn't as lucky as I've been. He didn't grow up with my comforts."

"He wasn't as lucky?"

"Right—he hates me, but he doesn't mean to hate me, he just hates the circumstances of the world that make him hate me. The things that put him in his place, which is a place he didn't ask to be in." He made a spinning gesture with his index finger that seemed to encompass the entire room. "That's what I've learned here."

"Leland, I'm going to ask you to remember whatever you can about your visit to Southgate."

Leland Jr. closed his eyes and whispered, "Stop it." Caleb could now smell a waxy, unshowered scent coming off him. "I went to Southgate with my wife, at the urging of her, to make up with my brother. She had offered him a job at Lefébvre because she felt bad for him. She has a very big heart." He shot a heavy-lidded look across the table that seemed to suggest Caleb, too, was a beneficiary of her very big heart.

"Do you remember Lee acting suspicious in any way? Do you remember the dinner you had—Jocelyn said it was at an Italian restaurant?"

"Of course he was acting suspicious!" he said, but more over his shoulder than to Caleb. "Yes, he was stoned out of his mind, he's a kid, he's poor, his father was poor, his whole family's poor, okay?"

Caleb had long learned to tune out clients who acted like Leland Jr. Instead he studied Leland Jr.'s face for traces of his father's. They had the same incipient widow's peak, the same beaked nose and converging eyes. Even their voices were similar—Caleb couldn't believe he remembered this after all these years—the same reedy baritone that always sounded a little like it was about to crack. Leland Sr. had called him monthly during his first semester at Berkeley, wanting to just shoot the shit at the time, hear about Caleb's classes and friends and girlfriend prospects. He'd always wanted to ask point-blank what role his mother had played in all this, but didn't for fear she'd done nothing, that his going to college was a bizarre, one-time arrangement between himself and a cokehead who used to cop from his dad in the seventies. He didn't want to think why he had been chosen instead of Aaron. Still, when he got notice that he'd been accepted to stay on and get his JD, he'd gone directly outside to the sticky pay phone on Hearst Avenue and called Leland, whose reaction was a breathed sigh and the words "Phenomenal. Just phenomenal."

Caleb was within inches of waving over a nurse, was already thinking about how he'd handle Jocelyn in the car, but Leland Jr.'s eyes betrayed what seemed like superior knowledge, and he stopped.

"I should've let them have the briefcase," Leland Jr. said. "The briefcase *at least*. I shouldn't have robbed Diedre and the boy, I see that now."

"You didn't rob anyone. If anything, you've been robbed—"

"Shut up," Leland Jr. said. "You've got to shut up, man. Please."

Caleb made accidental eye contact with a nurse.

"What briefcase?" he asked.

"TAKE IT BACK!" Leland Jr. yelled, and shoved himself from the table, nearly tipping over in his chair. "TAKE EVERYTHING BACK I TOOK, PLEASE, GOD!"

The nurse glided toward them, smiling apologetically at Caleb. She put her hand on Leland Jr.'s back, asked him if he wanted to go to his room. Leland Jr. swatted her away and a larger male nurse sidled up behind him and held his hands at his sides. They both whispered things to Leland Jr. in either ear, things that, judging by the sudden slackening in his posture, Leland Jr. was actually hearing. He looked over his shoulder at Caleb and hissed, "Take it all back, or else my blood's on your hands."

Caleb emerged from the ward to a pert and optimistic-seeming Jocelyn. They walked to the parking garage and she told him the whole story: the haymaker to her jaw, the Milwaukee hospital, the discharge and transfer to Rush, where she'd persuaded Leland Jr. to "voluntarily" commit himself for as long as it took to quiet his psychosis, the unknown whereabouts of Lee and some other kid, an accomplice.

"They got kicked out of the school, as far as I know," she said. "They're probably at Lee's mom's place in Cleveland."

"No warrant out for their arrest?"

She shrugged. "Well, no. And I think they managed to take a lot of their paraphernalia, so it's clearly their drugs—"

Caleb smiled. "Not the restaurant's?"

She smiled back, looked down, pulled her massive sweater tighter around her hips. He thought what he should've been thinking as he replied to that first e-mail she'd sent asking him to take on the case: *Should I be doing this?*

"Not the restaurant's," she repeated.

In her Prius, Caleb was reminded of his shitty rental at the funeral— either an ancient Civic or a Yugo, he knew only that it was cramped. A strange thing about the human brain was its homing instinct, as reliable as a roosting bird's: he could be with her now and feel the same catch in his throat he'd felt ten years ago, could anticipate that catch happening again ten years down the line. He placed his hand on her thigh—the first time they'd touched this way—and she fidgeted with pleasure. She asked him how things had been in Cleveland all this time, and he said they'd been fine.

She drove him directly to their River Forest McMansion, unbolted the door, and walked in ahead of him. Their winter coats were by the door—Leland Jr.'s and hers, hung on adjacent pegs—their laptops on the kitchen table, their laundry in a wicker basket abandoned halfway up the front steps. She didn't apologize for the place being a mess, just kept two or three steps ahead of him, kicking aside shoes, shirts, cardboard boxes, bubble wrap. She opened a pizza box sitting on the kitchen island and shoved a piece in her mouth, then offered him one. He declined and set his briefcase on the counter behind her, watching her. What did he know about her? From Googling, that she was the daughter of the former lieutenant governor of Connecticut (current Woodward Foods CEO), that she was a marketing executive at a French ad agency who'd sung in a female a cappella group at Northwestern University. He knew that she came up to his shoulder, that her scalp was pink at her part, that her upper lip bore the impression of an old pockmark. From kissing, that she had a quick tongue and a tiny creature's thrumming heartbeat, that she wrapped her legs around him nimbly.

They fucked once and he had to pause for just fifteen minutes before they fucked again. He wasn't thinking too hard about what any of it meant. He didn't owe this family any hard thinking. He was, essentially, responding to a distress call from a bunch of rich white people, suing a half brother who'd caused a half brother mental anguish. Mom would call these his reparations. He took them over and over again, from every crevice Jocelyn made available to him, took them until she was sweating and laughing, laid out on her back looking up at him, saying could he please just give her five minutes in the bathroom to tidy up, she'd honestly never gone that long before. So he let her go and picked up his phone. A few messages from an intern about a class-action suit against the Cleveland Division of Police. An e-mail from a client begging for a waiver of the already low consultation fee. Then his phone was buzzing with an unknown number. He let it go through, as he always did. Five minutes later it was buzzing again. And again one minute later, the same number. On the fourth call he picked up. He heard ragged breathing, throat clearing.

"Hello?" Caleb said. "You've called me four times now. It would be great to know what exactly you want."

"Caleb," the voice said. "I've missed you. This what you sound like now?"

He held the phone away from his ear, then put it back again. "Who is this?"

"I been wanting to hear how you sound for years," the voice creaked. Then the sound of tears. "I knew it'd be different but fuck if it isn't a full-grown man's voice."

Caleb was sweating. "Tell me who you are or I'll hang up and block this number."

"It's Reginald Marshall," the voice spat through its tears. "It's your dad, goddamn! Just take a blessing when the world gives you one, boy."

JOCELYN WOODWARD

(1973–)

1991–2009
Boston and Chicago

Unlike other girls, Jocelyn hadn't papered the walls of her childhood bedroom with photo collages. In fact, most of the bedroom walls were beige and bare—she'd expressed a vague desire to her mother to paint them light pink when she was eleven, and they'd never gotten around to it. She had a poster of her crush, Ian Curtis from Joy Division, on the wall across from her bed, and a butterfly made of wire and glittery pink mesh hanging from her ceiling—a gift from her grandma on her third birthday. It wasn't until after her high school graduation that she finally put something on the wall next to her bed: a photo of her and her friends at the party she threw when she graduated from boarding school.

In the photo, taken in 1991, big-haired Jocelyn stands in the center of the frame, all high cheekbones, bow lips, and long legs underneath her party dress, face pinched in imitation of a self-satisfied smile. She's flanked by her friends, fellow Bostonians: all girls, all white, most of them like her but with bigger-than-normal hips, a mole, jagged bangs. Sandy (the big-hipped girl) had invited her younger brother—who went to Allenton Prep, St. Josephine's brother school across the lake—to Jocelyn's graduation party. He'd shown up foggy-eyed and had spiked the lemonade with vodka, getting everyone drunk in the middle of the day. Most of them had only been drunk once or twice before, and the novelty of it, plus the fact that they'd just graduated, had them through-the-roof ecstatic. The adults at the party, Jocelyn remembered, sort of just shrugged their shoulders and joined in. Her dad had gotten a little sloppy at the grill, putting a hand on her mother's chest when she came over to kiss him. Her friends' parents, seeing the lieutenant governor act like a teenaged boy, had followed suit. The party lasted until long after sundown.

That night she was supposed to sleep on a cot in her parents' hotel room a few blocks from the St. Josephine campus, but she didn't bother to stop by and they didn't bother to check up on her. St. Josephine was built on a hill that rolled down to a small, man-made lake, on the eastern shore of which stood Allenton. She and her friends paddled a rowboat across the lake, Sandy's little brother at the helm shouting in his pubescent voice: "Land ho! Land hoooo!" They landed at the Allenton dock, received by a bunch of horny sixteen-year-olds in navy blazers who knew Sandy's little brother. Jocelyn brushed one of their cheeks with her hand and gave his forehead a kiss. That made everyone cheer. His eyes big underneath her protective hand, he said, "I can get cocaine if you want. I know a guy on campus."

"You do that," Jocelyn said.

The blazer boys scattered off somewhere and Jocelyn and her friends ran across campus, which rumor had it was more religious than St. Josephine and very strict. They ran silently, doe-like, communicating through muted giggles. They hid for twenty minutes behind the senior boys' dorm while Sandy's little brother went inside and negotiated with whomever was upstairs, then he came back down and told them they should wait for the signal and he was going to go hang out with his friends because he didn't want to watch his sister being kissed. It had begun to rain, or at least to mist, and their hair had flattened, their dresses clung to their bodies. Eventually a big-headed guy with perfectly parted hair leaned out the window and waved them up. They snuck in the back door, which was being held open by someone named Corey. His skin was brown and he had hair that was buzzed short and curly, and his smile seemed to be for Jocelyn alone. She followed Corey upstairs, close at his heels, watched the bend and pull of his capable legs ahead of her. The dorm was older than theirs, oak everywhere, stern portraits of high-collared, patrician men hanging from the walls. Behind Jocelyn, her friends laughed and asked inane questions about how many dicks were in this building and why it smelled like old gym socks. Her drunk made the halls dizzyingly bright, made Corey's shoulders seem broader than they probably were. She thought of how many people she'd met in her life who looked like him, and the answer was few to none. Who looked like him? Their mailman at their old house in Beacon Hill, who sometimes made small talk with her dad while he signed for packages. She watched Corey's calves beneath his Allenton slacks, the way his waist swiveled as he moved, the smile he threw back at her as they climbed the stairs. He led them into a room where a bunch of guys were standing, as many as there were girls. They cracked their necks, adjusted their blazer cuffs. An auburn-haired one unbuttoned the first two buttons of his shirt. There was a thunderclap outside, then the hard staccato of rain.

"There are six of you and six of us," the big-headed one observed unhelpfully. The auburn-haired one punched him in the shoulder and said, "Shut up, man!" Jocelyn threw her head back in laughter, and the other girls followed suit. Then Sandy leaned forward and stage-whispered to Jocelyn, "Your party, your pick."

Jocelyn scanned the assembled. She picked Corey. There was a hum of approval from everyone in the room, surprised approval. One of the girls said, "Jungle fever, huh?" Jocelyn smiled coquettishly and ignored her, eyes locked with Corey's. He offered her his hand and she took it. They left the room, everyone cheering, and began ascending a flight of stairs.

"I can't believe we haven't gotten caught yet," she said.

Instead of shushing her as she expected, he laughed loudly, heartily. "Graduation day is the one day a year the administration turns a blind eye and we get to—um—sow our wild oats, as I bet the rector would say."

She laughed, too. "He knows what a shitty deal lifelong virginity is."

He grabbed her hand and they ran up flights of stairs until they were at the top of the building. His room was the first on the left—his roommate had cleared out, mercifully. They stood in the center of the room kissing, his hands around her still-damp shoulders, their nose-breathing loud. She was embarrassed about the lifelong virginity joke because she was a virgin herself. Now she thought maybe he'd expect her not to be. She brought her hands to his chin and kissed him harder, and he picked her up like in the movies and deposited her on his bed. Standing there above her, he had the ready-to-pounce electricity of every teenaged boy she'd ever met, but the cut of his jaw and tone in his arms suggested he knew something about being an adult. He took off his shirt.

"I'm a virgin," she sputtered.

He laughed good-naturedly. "Well, then do I have permission to take your virginity?"

She thought the question was strange, but she had nothing to compare it to. She used to want to give it up to someone special, someone she was going to marry, but in the past year she'd gotten antsy as other girls shared their stories and had started to think that anyone would do. She nodded and slid out of her dress and they started. It was more painful than she thought it would be, but she smiled through the pain and kissed him and put her hands on top of his head. He asked if this or that felt okay, if she was happy, if she was comfortable. The questions sobered her, forcing her to think about what was happening as it happened. None of her friends were going this far, probably. She wasn't on birth control. She had a sick feeling that confirmed she was taking an unnecessary risk: if her mother found out, she'd be dead. Pregnant and dead. And it'd be Corey's baby.

He groaned and shuddered, and then there was a wetness between her legs that wasn't her own. He collapsed onto her, sighing, his arms around her. "Shit," he said. Then, as if remembering she was still there: "You were good. That was incredibly good." He rolled off her. She was almost completely sober now as she stared at the ceiling. He turned to her, propping himself on his side.

"Did you like that?" he asked.

She nodded. She was thinking, but none of her thoughts made sense. "What are you?" she asked.

"What do you mean?"

"Like what, um, what're your parents?"

He sighed a little and folded his hands over his chest. "My mom's white, Jewish, and my dad's black. That's the usual combination—black dad, white mom."

The usual combination. She had no idea what he was talking about. It was still wet between her legs. She felt herself on the verge of extreme anxiety. "So you're on scholarship?"

His face darkened. "No. My dad's a business consultant in New York and my mom's an artist. She came from money."

"I don't usually hang out with blacks," she said. "I'm not racist or anything. I'm just saying I've never kissed a black person. I never thought I would, I guess, until tonight."

She figured this information would have little to no effect on him, reportage of the truth that it was. But he was silent a while, staring at the ceiling, breathing tensely. "Thanks for taking a chance on me," he said.

"You're, um, you're a really good kisser," she said. He said nothing in response.

Now something cavernous had opened between them, something deep and awful. What was it, even? She rushed to close it: "You went to Allenton. I bet no one even sees you as black."

He sat up, his face in his hands. "Holy shit."

Sitting up was something to do, something mildly distracting, so she did it, too. She put her hand on his shoulder and he flinched away.

"Was that, like, weird for you?" he said. "You basically wanna say it's so weird fucking a colored, don't you?"

Her breath caught hard in her throat. "What?"

"Are you gonna say I raped you?" He was looking at her with his eyes narrowed. "Dumb bitch."

She reached for her dress and put it back on in silence. Crying, she left.

☐

The real reason she'd hung that photo above her bed was to purge all memories of that day, which had quickly shrunk to something hard, painful, and malignant tucked away deep in her brain. If the photo stayed in her room, so did everything else associated with it: Corey, the sex, etc. A month later, she wasn't pregnant, she didn't have any warts, she wasn't peeing blood. She was, for the most part, the same person she'd always been.

That fall, she had gone to Northwestern, where she'd dedicated herself to liberal causes. She marched in a protest to get the university to divest from the apartheid government of South Africa. She joined the Environmental Club and planted trees around the campus perimeter. She was the big sister to Lucia Milagros, a soft-faced girl from Chicago's South Loop who had a sick mother. Jocelyn told Lucia that if she stayed in school and kept on learning, everything would get better. Lucia nodded obediently and gave Jocelyn big, desperate hugs after every tutoring session.

From the muddle of memories and impressions that had been her precollegiate life, she felt her worldview beginning to take shape. Helping others was good work—better work than doing things exclusively for yourself. There was potential for goodness in everyone, even criminals, and extensive time spent with any member of a maligned population could reveal this. She volunteered at a local women's shelter. She answered phones at a rape crisis center. She reassured every aggrieved caller that she believed her, that she shouldn't blame herself for what had just happened, that the biggest task ahead of her was to heal.

She and the other volunteers who worked at the rape crisis center had a weekly meeting to process difficult calls. Many of the women who worked there had been sexually assaulted themselves, and some of them shared their stories during meetings, talked about unsympathetic parents who didn't believe they'd been raped by their boyfriends or husbands, about friends both male and female who told them to just "forget about it," about policemen who said they were asking for it. During one of these meetings, Jocelyn found herself overcome with awful memories. She stood up and said, "I was sexually assaulted my senior year of high school. At the time, I didn't think of it that way, but now I'm realizing that's what it was."

Her stomach churned uncertainly, but maybe this was just her body's process of acknowledging what had taken place. The other women around her leaned toward her, kind-eyed, compassionate. "It happened at a party," she had said, and could say nothing else. She sat down. Her face was hot in her hands. She could feel another woman's arm across her shoulders, pulling her in for a side hug. The head volunteer was announcing something about a potluck; soon, the discussion was brought to a close.

If asked, she would have said, "It happened at a party. He was a popular guy and he kissed well." But something in her head objected to this. It throbbed and rattled horribly. She thought she'd left it in her room, stuck to the wall along with the photo from her graduation party. He'd admitted to it, hadn't he? Why would he say something like that otherwise? He'd admitted to it and he'd been dagger-like. She was drunk. Maybe he was, too. She saw flashes of his face. She thought of herself at the center of the photo in her bedroom: tallest, happiest, prettiest, tipsy and powerful and young.

Her dad had encouraged her to continue with the French she'd so loved studying in high school, so she stuck with it in college. She met Steve Millheim in a Flaubert class she took during the winter of her freshman year. He was a physics major but he was good-looking, more interesting than the sloppy-drunk packs of frat boys who hounded her at parties. His French was almost perfect, and he wrote a poem about her called "*corps et âme*," which he had slipped into her backpack after a class one day. They went on one date, then another. They saw a student theater production of Tom Stoppard's *Arcadia* and ended up back in her bedroom, her room-mate out for the night with her boyfriend. He started taking off her bra and she told him she was a virgin. He said he'd be gentle and she said that was fine. She put in the diaphragm she'd bought at the student health center. After that, they were officially boyfriend and girlfriend. She saw him first thing in the morning and last thing at night. He came out of his shell a little, joked around more, spent a few more nights a week with the other juniors getting sloppy at Nevin's.

When she flew home to Boston for Christmas break, her father picked her up from the airport and said he was so sorry, but he was going to be in board meetings until Christmas.

"But you and Mom will have some time to catch up," he reassured her.

She nodded, her head against the window. She told him she was look-ing forward to it.

So she and her mother sat in the living room watching *Hill Street Blues* reruns. Jocelyn ate chocolate pudding that she could tell her mother disapproved of even if it was sugar-free, her mother sitting in the cap-tain's chair adjacent to the couch, wrapped in a Coach bathrobe, her blue eyes—unlined by crow's-feet, wide as a child's—turned impatiently toward the TV. She drank from a tumbler of bourbon with two loaf-shaped ice cubes that rattled softly whenever she took a sip. Jocelyn thought she and her mother had always been at their best on practical matters: food, the arrangement of furniture in a room, which events and rehearsals for events they needed to attend and when. But now that she lived over a thousand miles from her mother's home, they had nothing to talk about.

"You seem different," her mother said without looking from the TV.

"Well, I'm in college, Mom."

"Mm. So you are. I never understood why you had to go so far away."

Jocelyn swallowed another spoonful of pudding and shrugged. "I just liked the look of Northwestern."

"Yes, but you got into Brown, too. You could've been closer to your father and me."

"I didn't like it," she said. Which was kind of true. Really she'd just wanted to leave the East Coast—had felt this way since she was a child, when adults began to ask her what she wanted to be when she grew up. *Not you.* The only adult she wanted to be like was her dad, and he'd always encouraged her to travel, broaden her horizons.

"Well, what matters is that you're happy," her mother said, although Jocelyn knew this didn't especially matter to her mother at all. "You should be able to get your degree in a place that makes you happy."

Jocelyn nodded, and the noise of the TV dominated the room. She was getting used to it when her mother spoke again.

"But you really do seem different," she said.

"I don't think so."

Her mother hugged her elbows as if she were cold. "More timid."

Jocelyn licked the chocolate from her lips. "I have no idea why you'd think that."

Her mother shrugged. "A mother knows."

Jocelyn failed in her attempt to suppress a squeaking laugh. Her mother's eyes narrowed. "Do you find my caring for you funny?"

"No," Jocelyn said. "I absolutely don't."

"Is there a reason you're laughing, then?"

"No. I don't know. I was nervous, I guess."

"Well, if I didn't know better, I'd think this Steven Millheim you keep talking about isn't the first boy you've been with."

Jocelyn's core temperature shot up. *How was this happening? How the hell did she know?*

"Mom, I wouldn't lie to you."

"Yes you would. Every child lies to their parents." She smiled punishingly.

"I was raped," she said, or heard herself say. "By a boy at Allenton. The day of my graduation party."

Her mother froze. "What?"

"I didn't want to tell you."

Her mother closed her eyes and shook her head, then rubbed the bridge of her nose. "What was his name?"

"I don't know."

"Surely you do."

"I can't remember."

"Just try to."

"Corey," she said.

Her mother's eyes widened. "I know who you're talking about," she said, and then turned back to the TV.

That night as Jocelyn lay half-asleep in her childhood bedroom, she thought of a call she'd received at the rape crisis center during one of her volunteer shifts, a call she probably should've brought up at one of the debriefing meetings. The woman on the other end of the line was sobbing, and in order to speak at all she had to shout through her sobs. "They won't listen! They! Won't! Listen! They! Won't! Listen!" Jocelyn, tiny-voiced, kept asking her to explain who "they" were, and what it was they wouldn't listen to, but the woman hung up on her. Jocelyn turned over on her side in the dark and brought her knees to her chest. She hadn't needed any clarification. She'd known exactly what the woman meant. No one believed her, and everyone believed Jocelyn.

Straight ahead of her the open bedroom door let in a long square of light glowing turquoise blue in her sleep-limned vision. And in that light was a man's silhouette. The man had his arms crossed and stood with his shoulders slightly hunched, sullen, leaning against the doorframe for support. Seeing that she'd seen him, he righted his posture, began walking toward her, arms swinging, the same loping walk she'd admired from behind as Corey climbed the stairs in his Allenton dorm. She held her breath.

She turned her bedside lamp on. Her father stood in her doorframe, tie loosened, coat over his arm.

"Did I startle you?" he asked.

She shook her head, then looked at her clock. It was a little past one in the morning. "Why are you here?"

"I was working late," he said. "I needed to rearrange some personnel. May I sit?"

She nodded, scooting back, and he sat, shifted his hands out of his pockets, sighed with exhaustion. She followed his eyes to the butterfly still hanging from the ceiling.

"Glad to see you never got tired of Grandma Mimi's butterfly."

"It's like my best friend."

He laughed and rubbed his upper lip with his index finger, a thoughtful and good-natured tic that still pleased her as reliably as it had his constituents. He had a gentle face, the recessed eyes, long, blunt nose, and aquiline cheekbones of Richard Gere.

"Joss-Sauce," he said, and wrapped his arm around her. "How are you, kiddo?"

"I'm good." She traced a patchwork tessellation on her bed quilt. "You haven't called me kiddo since before high school."

His eyes got large. She thought he might be lost in some fit of existential panic, and then she realized it was a joke. "Are you really that old?"

"Daaad," she mewled.

"Really, are you not in high school anymore?" He checked his watch. "I didn't get that memo. Did a memo even go out?"

"No memos went out, Dad."

"I think memos should go out daily, and I think I should get a carbon copy of every single one!"

"Dad, you're gonna wake up Mom."

"No I'm not—she sleeps like a stone."

Jocelyn giggled.

"Okay, well, I just wanted to check on you," he said. "Your door's open and everything. I was in the neighborhood, et cetera."

"Thanks for checking on me."

He leaned in close to her. "Nothing bad storms this castle, okay? I promise you that." Then he kissed her on the forehead, stood up, and left.

It wasn't until long after she'd broken up with Steve, after she'd met and fallen for Leland, after she'd graduated college and married him and taken the position at Lefébvre, that she put together what her father meant by nothing bad storming the castle. She was three years out of college, three years into her job at Lefébvre, and had been in New York to meet with a client. Leland had flown in to spend the weekend with her. They had gone to a St. Josephine reunion on the Upper East Side, which had been in a velvet-lined gastropub overlooking Central Park, swarming with exfoliated women and their rakish Allenton husbands. She was unbothered by them because she was with a husband who fit her to jigsaw perfection, who saw the best in her and in whom she saw the best as well, who had ascended to the same heights the Allenton men had achieved but without their privilege. She loved him and felt she would always love him. She thought his presence would be enough to deflect whatever strangeness occurred that night, but she was wrong.

Late into the party, when everyone was the kind of civil drunk that was enough to get them dancing, Jocelyn and Sandy sat at the near-empty bar drinking Cuba Libres, a drink Jocelyn thought nobody ordered anymore. Sandy's hips had gotten wider over time, and gravity was already starting to have its way with her face and chest. But she seemed to be the same person she'd always been, still happy to rest her soft chin on Jocelyn's shoulder and say something like "Tell me everything and spare no detail!"

"So I know you don't live around here," she said, smiling sloppily into her drink, "but you'll be happy to know Corey's family's finally gone belly-up. His mom used to be Page Six and now it's all over for them."

Jocelyn hadn't allowed herself to think the name in so long that she heard it as a strange combination of clicks and hisses. She asked Sandy to repeat herself.

"You don't remember Corey Louis? The kid from your graduation party? When we snuck over to Allenton?"

"Yeah. I do."

Sandy's face softened in pity, which embarrassed Jocelyn to the point of breathlessness. "I'm really, really sorry. I didn't mean to bring it up. I just thought you'd be happy."

Jocelyn wanted to venture a why, but she didn't. The realization lodged in her throat with the frightening weight of a foreign bolas, dimmed her vision.

"His dad contracted with Woodward Foods," Sandy said. "You didn't know?"

Jocelyn took a long swig of her drink. When she finished, Sandy had apparently remembered that the mood was supposed to be celebratory. "Ugh, sorry, I'm drunk. I'm so drunk! I'm just surprised, is all." Her eyes narrowed mischievously. "After what he did to you, though—they're all wearing the mark of Cain."

Jocelyn steeled herself. "Tell me what happened."

Sandy leaned forward, chin in hand. "The Louis firm's bankrupt. There was a divorce. The dad's out of work and Corey can't get hired. He might be on the sex offender registry; I could check if you want me to."

Jocelyn drained her Cuba Libre. "No," she said. "No, thank you."

When they got back to Chicago, she put in a special request with her team lead at Lefébvre to be taken off the New York account for at least six months. She had already proven her talent to be leveragable, and her clients fell in line without resistance. She busied herself with the firm, Leland's emotional needs, and biweekly phone calls back home. She volunteered at an after-school program in Chicago's Austin neighborhood and went to awareness-raising meetings about child trafficking in the Midwest. Sometimes she did want a child, but Leland didn't, and neither did the tough little knot in her head.

In May of 1999, they flew to Florida for Leland Sr.'s funeral, which Leland said he wanted to attend out of "cosmic justice for the wronged." The hated Diedre had organized it cheaply. This was Jocelyn's first time seeing Lee—disheveled, disoriented little Lee, less a criminal in the making than a character out of a Dickens novel—and his inexplicably striking mother. They stood across Leland Sr.'s casket from them, Leland scowling, his arms crossed and Jocelyn's arm looped through one of his elbows. Next to her stood a tall black man, arms crossed as well, glasses tortoiseshell, eyes downcast respectfully. To look at the rabbi would be to risk looking at the black man, and to look at the casket might be construed as some gesture of respect for the deceased, which would upset her husband. Looking at Lee and his mother was out of the question entirely, and Lee's translucent child-skin plus the pair's mucusy sobs added up to something too pathetic, anyway. She looked at her feet.

The last prayer was said and the casket lowered. The assembled dispersed, Leland falling into aggressive lockstep with Diedre, who buried her face in her hands at his approach. Lee clung to the bottom of her coat as Leland spoke to her. Jocelyn could hear her husband barking "lawsuit" in a wolfish tone she had never heard before and didn't care to hear again. Diedre started walking faster, but Leland kept pace—eventually the three of them were a distance away, far out of Jocelyn's earshot.

Jocelyn had walked slowly through the swampy heat, sponging at her moist forearms with her palms. She found herself wondering how many months on average it took the coffins to sink through the marsh loam and float out into the Atlantic. That had to be something that had really happened, one of those old wives' tales that started out as the truth. She imagined a herd of Floridian coffins headed for Cuba, one of them popping open en route. There were footsteps behind her.

Up ahead, leaning against the trunk of the old Saab they'd rented, Leland shouted, "I'm going to follow Diedre home, hon!"

Diedre ran ahead of him to her car, Lee clumsily kicking up gravel as he trailed her. Jocelyn felt a bloom of warmth in her lower stomach and realized it was embarrassment about her husband.

"Okay," she called back.

"What?"

"Okay! Go ahead!"

"Let me drive you somewhere so we can call a cab for you!"

An entire shouted conversation. She rubbed her temples. The footsteps behind her stopped. The black man was standing over her right shoulder. "I'll drive her," he said.

She saw Leland squint up at the man, vision obviously hampered by the damp, oily sun that she suspected had already begun to redden the back of her neck. There was a moment of recognition, she could tell, then a visible shift in Leland's mood: he cocked his head, then hung it apologetically.

"Is that okay with you?" he called to the man.

The man shrugged, tossing up his hands as if to demonstrate that he was weaponless. "It's not a problem, honestly."

Diedre peeled out, Lee's somber little face pressed to the passenger-side window. Leland watched them go, then jumped over to the driver's side of the car and began fiddling with the door. "Okay—that sounds fine, I guess. Babe, just call me when you get to the hotel!"

"I will," she said, though he couldn't have heard.

"I trust you!" he shouted, and slammed shut the Saab door.

The man was standing next to her now, arms folded. "Was that for you? Or for me?"

"I'm not sure," she said. "I think it's a very emotional time for him—he's saying a lot of things he wouldn't normally."

"Of course," the man said.

They stood facing each other now. The man extended one of his hands and she took it. It was damp, or hers was.

"My name's Caleb Marshall," he said.

"Jocelyn Woodward. I—um," she stumbled. "I didn't take his last name."

He nodded and gestured to a cluster of mangrove trees farther down the gravel pathway. "Shall we?"

They walked to his rental, which was tiny, and got in. The seats were convection-hot, and Jocelyn could feel the backs of her thighs burning through her dress. She gave him the name of the hotel and the cross streets. He switched his glasses out for sunglasses and sat straight-backed, chin in hand, which struck her as strange until she realized he must be considering the route. When he finally shifted confidently into drive, she felt light-headed, as if she'd left one dream to enter another.

"So he's mad?" Caleb asked, looking not at her but the contents of his rearview mirror.

"I'm sorry?"

"Your husband's mad about Leland Sr.?"

She searched her lap, then the dashboard, as if for a misplaced pocketbook. "I'm not sure what you mean."

Caleb shrugged. "He doesn't like his father."

This was a strange postmortem of a funeral. Maybe she should make that joke. But how would that make her look, making a joke right now? "They didn't really get along, no."

"I can imagine. Our families were . . . entwined in certain ways."

"I'm—he never told me."

"Oh, please." Caleb laughed a generous man's laugh. "I don't know if he even knew."

They drove in silence for a minute or two. She had the distinct impression that she was being deceived, but she didn't know exactly how, or why. She recalled a ballet recital when she was six, standing behind the black velvet curtain at the rec center, the pathetic trickle that stained the tulle around her thighs. She felt like that now, remembering her mother's anger when she never took the stage.

"Why did you come?" she asked.

Caleb nodded as though he had been anticipating the question. "Because Leland Sr. paid for my college," he said. "And he left me some money for law school. Between him and scholarships, it's been a free ride."

"He left you money?"

"Cash, yeah. Unmarked bills. I had to deposit it very slowly, but I managed to pay everything off."

"Does Leland know?" But of course he didn't. "I'm sorry—where did the money come from?"

"I don't know," he said. "My guess is drugs."

Caleb looked at her dead on, though of course he wasn't really looking at her, there were sunglasses between them. He looked away, to his right, then back ahead. "Well, I respect him. He did what he could with what he had."

The conversation had become bewilderingly intimate. She wanted out. They passed a gas station, then another.

"I'm not going to share my father's profession with you if you don't know about it already," he said, and it sounded like a judgment.

They drove on in an extended silence, the longest of her life. Who the fuck was this guy? Did Leland know him? He must, from Cleveland. She thought of her mother's tight lips, her folded hands.

She realized now that her dress was too hot, black wool. He was wearing a well-tailored suit with a turtleneck; he must've been boiling, too.

"My father was Reggie Marshall," he said. "A friend—so I'm told—of your late father-in-law."

The name was unfamiliar; maybe she would've heard it if she'd been paying better attention to Leland's family saga.

"I'm really sorry about your father, whatever happened with him," she said, "but I have no idea about any of this. I'm just here to support my husband. We'll be gone tomorrow."

He nodded as if to music and seemed to back off. "I understand," he said. "I understand completely."

The hotel parking lot came mercifully into sight.

She told him he could drop her wherever he wanted. He stopped abruptly and started looking for something in his wallet. She waited for his permission to leave the car. He pulled out a piece of paper and wrote something on it, then gave it to her. It was his name and e-mail address: c-marshall@berkeley.edu. "Keep in touch," he said. She took it from him, shivered from the car's air conditioner, and nodded politely. She decided she would throw it away when she got back up to the room. She would tell Leland what happened and Leland would shake his head and say, "Everyone at that funeral was scum. Absolute scum. Don't let any of them fool you." Then he'd hug her and reassure her of her sanity. They'd make plans to move to a nicer neighborhood when they got back to Chicago. Leland would tell her that he couldn't bear to bring a child into a world as ruined as this one, and she would tell him that his feelings were certainly justified, but maybe he should consider x, y, z. She would call her father. She would sit in boardrooms at Lefébvre and speak in French with other young professionals.

But she didn't throw out the piece of paper. She hid it in her purse for reasons unknown. When Leland got back to the room that evening, a trunkload of recovered goods in tow, they didn't talk about Caleb Marshall at all. Instead Leland lay on his side on the bed and cried about himself and his mother, told her about the paintings and the jewelry and the yellow briefcase he'd recovered, the one he was scared to open, and why hadn't Diedre opened it already? Jocelyn spooned him and kissed the back of his neck and promised that everything would only get better after this, that all people had at least some good in them and that there was no amount of emotional damage that couldn't be undone. And as she said this she was imagining Caleb Marshall leaning across the divider between the driver and passenger seats, taking her face in his hands to kiss her.

Since that night, she'd thought about Caleb more than she'd have liked to, followed his career online, sent him the occasional e-mail. She told herself she was doing this because of his strangeness, the things he claimed to know about her husband and his father. She was doing her job as a wife. In 2005, she saw that Caleb had graduated from Berkeley Law with high honors—his mother, a woman named Natasha, kept some kind of black-identities-in-academia blog and wrote a post about his graduation. At the bottom was a photo of her and Caleb on graduation day: he in a variation on the cap and gown (a gold-brimmed hat with a blue tassel, gray-looking felt stripes on his sleeves), and she in a striking red dress. He was hugging her and she was wide-eyed, mid-laugh, clearly euphoric. The caption read: "Uhuru! My beautiful son fulfills his destiny, 6/6/05."

She set up a Google alert for his name. She watched as he joined a firm in Cleveland—they made a small announcement on their website. Shaker Heights *Pioneer Press*: "Young Lawyer Fights Ludlow School Closing." "Beachwood 2007 5K Run for Life, Finishers: Caleb E. Marshall." *Cleveland Plain Dealer*, a picture of Caleb onstage in a ratty-looking school auditorium: "Lawyer Tells Central Teenagers About Racial Profiling, School-to-Prison Pipeline." When he got a Facebook, she considered friending him but didn't, worried that he'd forgotten about her. He used no privacy settings, so his profile was visible to anyone. There he was with some girl, Meggie or Maggie (Jocelyn never bothered to read the tag) at a party. They had parties in Ohio? There he was at the gym, posing with someone he claimed was his personal trainer. Dancing—he was always tagged, he posted infrequently—at someone's wedding, at a christening.

The Internet was an incredible tool, she reminded herself repeatedly as the years wore on. Entering these new worlds de-stressed her. There were so many ways to use the Internet to de-stress: trolling through photos of Sandy's recent vacation to the Cayman Islands (her husband had always been husky, was starting to look fat), photos of the second wedding of one of her NU a cappella sisters (Jocelyn hadn't been invited, wasn't insulted), photos of the Lefébvre CEO's birthday party at which she'd developed a huge headache and had to drag Leland home early. But Caleb's photos captivated in a way she hated and loved. He broke up with Meggie or Maggie, dated another girl, broke up with her, went mountain biking somewhere, and claimed to be enjoying "the single life."

She wasn't friends with Lee, but she trolled his Facebook. His goofy grinning with a black-haired girl who could've been Italian, could've been Latina; his pretending to play the drums in someone's garage; an old, awkward preadolescent shot of the side of his face likely taken by a mischievous peer, his cheeks still chubby. In early 2008 she had even written to offer him a paid position at Lefébvre, which she knew he'd never take and over which she knew Leland would explode if he did.

A few weeks ago, just before Leland's breakdown or episode or whatever it was, she had persuaded him to visit Lee at college on the way to a business meeting in Milwaukee. The deal was she would accompany him on the business trip and to his meeting—which she thought was weird but he claimed bolstered his confidence—and he would give repairing things with Lee a chance. She had told Leland it would be good for them both, good and healing for him especially. He'd agreed with a wild look in his eyes, and she was momentarily reminded of that night in college when he had burst into her dorm at four in the morning after almost forty-eight hours without sleep. He'd been raving, but it was during finals and their friends just called it seniorphrenia. He hadn't acted like that since.

What did she know about brothers, never having had one? The visit had been tense and nightmarish, Lee not at all the sweet, grinning, Cheeto-fingered dork from the pictures or her memory. He was angular, agitated, clearly high. He had sexually objectified her at dinner and then spent the rest of the time exchanging barbs with Leland, who ended the evening by bribing him to never contact them again. In the car on the way to the hotel, Leland had gloated while her back ached, and she had popped a hydrocodone and wondered if maybe he was right, he and everyone who was always telling her to be more skeptical of everyone, to watch for evil even among the less fortunate, to stop believing everything happened for a reason.

He had wanted to have sex when they got back to the hotel and she had felt like she owed it to him. She had told him to give her a second and went into the bathroom. She splashed her face with water and then sat on the ground between the sink and the toilet and cried. As she did this, she thought of the past decade of her life—the four-hour board meetings that she clock-watched like a high school kid, the bewildering and frequently alienating sex she and Leland were having, had been having for longer than she cared to admit, the steady evaporation of all the Molière quotes she'd lovingly stockpiled in her memory, the lonely moments on vacation when she woke up to find he'd gone running without her, all the too-human-smelling panhandlers she'd avoided making eye contact with in the Loop, all the excuses she'd given for taking sick and personal days, her father's aging voice on the phone. She tried to cry quietly but couldn't: she sobbed instead and couldn't stop shaking. Then Leland was there with her on the floor in his boxers, holding her by the shoulders and saying her name.

"Babe," he said when she didn't respond. "I'm here."

She nodded, put her hands over her eyes.

"I'm here if you need to talk."

"I think I'm just coming down with something," she said through grunts and sniffles.

"You're sick?" He felt her forehead.

"No, I mean—I just feel nervous."

"Anxious?"

"Yeah."

He stood and left the bathroom, came back with an amber pill bottle. He squatted and flashed the label at her.

"Ativan," he said. "A friend of mine from work didn't need the rest of his prescription."

Another "friend of mine from work." He had so many friends of his from work who were willing to let him take their anxiety meds and pain pills: that's how she'd first gotten hydrocodone. These same friends from work were the guys who went out in a pack to party on JägerThursdays, who made her husband sick with their stamina. She accepted a proffered pill, drank from the metallic-tasting glass he'd filled at the bathroom sink. Without prompting, she asked for and took a second one. They sat there together for a few minutes in silence and she watched him scratch his stubble. She was thankful for him. Here was one reasonable person in a mass of unreasonableness. Here was the man who held the key to her future.

Later, they had sex on the bathroom floor. She showered and slept, the glow of his laptop sneaking into her dreams.

She was a little hungover from the Ativan as they drove to Cisco Drugs the next morning. They didn't talk about the dinner with Lee. Instead, Leland crowed about what a success Dithalmithor/teraflin was, how the trip to Cisco was less a corporate pulse-taking than a confirmation of his wizardry. He'd nudged Jocelyn awake at six o'clock and admitted that he'd been up since four, too excited to get a full night's sleep.

"There are a ton of kids out there slitting their wrists because of rapid cycling mood disorders," he told her with confidence in the car, driving several ticks above the speed limit. "And Cisco somehow got this patent— it was like a German patent, a drug synthesized at the Freie Universität."

She nodded, noting that he hadn't shaved that morning. Was he talking faster than usual? She put on her sunglasses, rubbed her temples.

"Whatever genius got this patent, congratufuckinglations to him and gravy for Winn Maxwell."

"Kids slitting their wrists?" she asked.

"Yeah. Childhood suicide's climbing. Kids get thrown in mental hospitals, get stuck on lithium, hate lithium, beg to go off, go off, kill themselves. Really, really sick kids. And then you have anxious bedwetters, you have depressed loners who've already made attempts, you have people looking for an atypical antipsychotic that won't cause their child to gain weight or put them at risk for diabetes, et cetera."

"It's so hard to imagine," she said. "It feels like something different from when adults do it."

He wiped his nose on his windbreaker. "I know."

Cisco was headquartered in a dome-like building made of highly reflective green glass in the city center—it hurt her eyes to look at it. Most of the PR department was composed of fresh-pressed, neatly bearded kids who Jocelyn guessed were all very recent liberal arts graduates. The kid who met them in the lobby was blond and chiseled, the kind of boy Jocelyn's mother would've approved of instantly. She forgot his name right after he said it, flashed instead on Leland's sleep-puffed and compassionate face last night. When she paid attention again, she saw the kid was wearing a Harvard Crimson pin. It shone as he spoke.

"As you can see, Cisco is committed to recruiting the best and the brightest." Harvard was now leading them across an observation deck, below which were men and women in lab coats and goggles, most of them sitting on high swivel chairs and flipping through dense texts. Only one of them was actually working with scientific equipment of any sort—a beaker and some kind of stand.

"This is the very lab in which teraflin was synthesized after we purchased the patent," Harvard said. "Dr. Hommeyer tweaked one hydroxy chain and—boom!—Dithalmithor."

"Amazing," Leland said, and put his arm around Jocelyn.

"Mr. Campbell will be meeting with you in the boardroom," Harvard said to Leland. He looked at Jocelyn. "Your wife is welcome to attend."

"Do you want to, Joss? You can wait outside if you'd like."

A numb cog, Jocelyn told him she'd like to attend. She watched the technician remove the beaker from the stand, rearrange it, replace it. "Which receptors does Dithalmithor act on?" she asked Harvard.

Harvard seemed taken aback. "That's a great question, Mrs. Bloom-Mittwoch."

"I'm Ms. Woodward."

"Right! Sorry." He followed her gaze downward to the struggling technician, who seemed to have gotten things in place, and was now adding what looked like grainy salt to the beaker under the supervision of another technician. "So it's not really something we know for certain. I mean, we know for certain that it doesn't work like normal SSRIs and SARIs, and that it does actually tend to block dopamine pathways, like clozapine, which you may know as Clorazil."

She nodded, though she was certainly out of her depth.

"Right. So those dopamine blockers can have a lot of negative side effects: tardive dyskinesia, cardiac difficulties, stroke, et cetera. Dithalmithor's got none of that—we know because we've been testing it for years now. That's why we think it's doing something else besides dopamine inhibition."

He paused, and she sensed a cockiness in his gaze.

"It's a magic bullet," she said.

"That's right, Ms. Woodward. Everyone's prescribing it." He touched a slim Bluetooth that she just now realized he'd been wearing. "Looks like Mr. Campbell will be seeing you both. Right this way."

They rode up in the elevator, Leland making small talk with Harvard about his education, his clubs, his sports. Right as they were getting out, Harvard turned to her and asked, "I'm sorry, but have we met before?"

"What do you mean?"

"I just—your name, your face—maybe our families have met before?"

"Our families? Where would our families have met?"

He backed off, stung. "I don't know—you just seem so familiar, and I remember the name Woodward."

"Maybe you guys are distant cousins!" Leland offered, and she couldn't tell if he was joking.

Harvard didn't acknowledge this, just nodded politely and left them with the CFO's secretary. The wait was long enough for Jocelyn to turn pointedly to Leland and say, "When I was a kid, he was probably in diapers. Or not even born."

Leland bark-laughed. "Seriously? We're not that old."

She said nothing.

"Are you feeling better?" he asked.

"What do you mean?"

"Are you still agitated from last night?" He squeezed her arm—too tight. "Lee seems to have a really awful effect on people."

The secretary told them they could head in. Dean Campbell, CFO of Cisco Drugs, big-bellied and pink skinned, was sitting at the head of a giant conference table. Leland shook his hand enthusiastically.

"And this is my wife, Jocelyn. She's an ad executive at Lefébvre in Chicago. I hope you don't mind if she sits in. I brought her along for good luck."

"Ah, good!" Campbell said. "Pleased to meet you!"

She watched him eye her ass as he pulled a chair from the table to seat her.

"Mr. Campbell," Leland began. "Winn Maxwell is more than excited to capitalize on this investment. We're so thrilled with Dithalmithor. I for one could barely pay attention on the tour, I was so dazzled by your facilities."

Campbell chuckled wetly. "Well, I hope you paid some attention—we've got state-of-the-art equipment here."

"Oh! Haha! Of course!"

"I paid attention," Jocelyn said, and for some reason this made both men laugh.

Leland leaned toward Campbell conspiratorially. "We've got something golden here, don't we?" He began drumming his fingers on the table.

"Yes," Campbell said. "Absolutely. It's remarkable, isn't it?"

Leland said nothing but continued drumming his fingers. A few seconds went by. The drumming grew louder, more noticeable. Campbell looked at Jocelyn. She looked at Leland. Leland was still looking at Campbell, drumming his fingers.

"Mr. Bloom-Mittwoch?" Campbell asked.

"Leland?" Jocelyn said. A surge of guilt shot through her. She leaned forward and tried to catch her husband's eye. But his face was vacant, she could see that his pupils almost entirely covered his irises. "Babe?"

Campbell looked at her, obviously embarrassed by the shift in the room. "Is he broken?" he joked. He leaned forward and spoke to Leland as if he were deaf. "Mr. Bloom-Mittwoch? Are you all right?"

Jocelyn pressed herself to Leland's side and whispered in his ear: "Leland. Babe? What's wrong?"

Leland jumped momentarily in his seat, which made both Jocelyn and Campbell jump as well. And before they knew what was happening, they heard a low growl, a sound that seemed subhuman. He leaned back far in his chair and released one loud bark and then another.

"Leland!" Jocelyn screamed.

His chair tipped over and the back of his head hit the ground with a terrifying smack, and now something was coming out of his mouth, foaming saliva, and then his face went slack, and then the rest of him, and he shook like there was a high-voltage current going through him.

"He's having a seizure!" Campbell shouted, halfway out of his seat. "Get his tongue!"

Jocelyn wrestled Leland's wallet out of his back pocket—slim enough, Italian leather—and stuck it in his mouth. His pupils expanded further. She turned to Campbell.

"Get someone in here!" she yelled at him. "Call the police!"

Campbell sped from the room, shouting for his secretary. Jocelyn held Leland's shaking, sputtering head in her lap. She whispered to him, "Help will come, babe. We'll get through this. We'll get past this. I'm really sorry. I'm sorry about last night. Please try and stay still."

And then he locked eyes with her. He let out a wallet-choked scream and punched her in the jaw.

NETTA MARSHALL, NÉE BAROCHIN
(1980–)

1985–1990
Chicago

When Netta was ten, an old man's pocket watch fell off its fob and onto the street and Netta picked it up, said *excuse me excuse me* and ran to him. He took it from her, looked at it and thanked her, hooked it onto the fat, snaky chain again, and walked away from her, and she watched from behind him as it swung back and forth, back and forth with every step, swung until it snapped right off the chain and fell on its face and cracked. Netta called *hey* so the old man would hear and he turned around and looked down. He was old enough that it showed all over his face—the corners of his eyes and mouth, his flappy ears, his lumpy nose—and she felt bad for him. He was the kind of person she was supposed to respect, but she probably already knew more than he did about the way the world was.

He stooped down low to pick up the watch, and when he stood he wobbled a little and had to take a step back. From the side, he was skinny but still strong, she could tell. The man's suit was black-gray, or black-blue—it bothered her that she couldn't tell the color, that never happened. The old man turned the broken watch over in his hands, pushed the little pieces of glass on the ground with his foot. Then he tilted his head up to the sky and wailed, wailed so hard and loud as he shouted a name—Marissa. Or Melissa? She couldn't tell. Netta ran away.

At home in her room she drew him. She put knobs at his elbows and knees and made his beard a little longer. She drew a second version of him where he wore a bowler hat. She made his nose smoother than it had been. Under the drawing she gave him a name—Marlon—and his birthdate according to the angle of his stoop: 2/15/30. Behind him she drew a little far-off square of blue that was supposed to be Lake Michigan. In his hands the watch became a toy, then a baby doll, then a limp-looking baby body, and he arched his mantis back and howled, and she wrote *Marissa Melissa!* coming out of his mouth.

The last and best picture she drew of him was so gross and sad that she jammed it in the sliding drawer in her desk so she wouldn't have to look at it. She thought she'd probably get in trouble if her mother found it, would be made to say one of her poems: "No evil thoughts in my mind, no wicked bindings in my heart, no intentions ill-devised, a pure home awaits a world apart," or "Speak not for the dead in me, the time to heal is long since passed; mine is the tongue of righteousness, mine is heaven's soul alone, at last." If Netta asked her where the poems came from, her mother's lower lip swelled and her eyes got mean and she said, "From me! Where else?"

Her grandma had died when Netta was four and her mother got sick right after. Before she got sick her mother had been a nurse and made good money. Netta's father was a Spanish teacher and a translator and made less money than her mother. He told Netta he had no idea where her mother had gotten the nurse gene, especially considering her own mother's hatred of modern medicine. That had been how Netta's grandma died: denying a big knot of cancer in her brain, refusing to see doctors, ignoring everyone's insistence that she check herself into a hospital.

She had shaken her head, her eyes weak and wandering, and said she'd leave as she was intended to leave. For the last few weeks of her life she sat in a big chair in the corner of their TV room, singing to herself and praising Netta's baby crayon drawings and sipping rumless cremas through a plastic straw. She died in that chair, Netta's mother watching from the opposite side of the room as she took her last breath. That day, by the time Netta woke from her afternoon nap, the men had already come to take her grandma's body away.

Netta believed her grandma's spirit was in the water, in the sea somewhere, or in a glossy puddle, or in the faucet's cough-cough-gush. Her grandma being in the water made her mother very sick. When her grandma's body was taken away, Netta's mother sat in a corner on the ground and didn't move for two days. After that she moved into the bedroom, where she stayed for a week. Netta listened to her talk with her father, their low adult tones, sounds that swelled and contracted in her ears like a frog's throat. After a week, her mother came out of the bedroom and sat for almost a whole day in the big chair, then called Netta's uncle to help her move it out of the house.

The next day she went back to work and held Netta in her lap like she always did and made up little stories and rhymes for her about a dragon whose mouth the fire on the stove came from or the tiny wind fairies who turned the blades of the fan. During the stories, Netta leaned back as she always did and closed her eyes and saw the colors that described her mother: her voice was peach, though her personality was more yellow, and now she was saying "dare," whose first letter was cocoa brown, and now she was saying "baby," which would be pale green if not for the *y* on the end, which made it turquoise. Her mother's heaving breath—the breath of a busy woman, an important woman—had no color to it, but the feeling of it on her cheek was a deep mauve, a color she'd learned about from a book Grandma bought her called *All the Colors in the World*. Deep mauve in, deep mauve out. Netta dozed while her mother told the stories, seeing the colors and feeling comforted by the way her mother flipped through magazines when she held her in her lap—not bored, just capable.

Then one day her mother was telling a story when her body went stiff, which made Netta go stiff, too. It was a Saturday morning, which meant her father was giving Spanish lessons. Her story that day had been about talking flowers, so when she said, "Did you hear that?" Netta had laughed with relief and said, "It's a dandelion saying hello!" But her mother had said nothing in response.

"Listen!" she said, and Netta sensed something wild in her voice, something her mother clearly couldn't control. "Stop it!"

Netta stopped moving in hopes that she was the one her mother had been speaking to, but she knew with a white-hot dread that this wasn't true. Her mother pushed her off her lap and began walking toward the window, batting her hand in front of her face and shouting, "Stop!" She turned and looked at Netta and her eyes were dark and flat and gray. Netta screamed and ran to her room.

Her mother stayed this way for days: not sleeping, not eating, not letting her father near. She mumbled in a nonsense language about her feet sticking to earth while her head was in heaven. She told Netta to count everything in the house and see if it was an even number or odd—when her father objected, she made a little cut in her right arm with a knife. That was her father's limit.

She went to the hospital for a week and came back angry-eyed and puffy-cheeked. She now took three pills a day and spoke to no one. Netta understood that she was well enough to go back to work at the clinic—which she did—but couldn't tell whether the mother she knew would remain wedged deep inside whatever this new woman was, this flat-haired woman who breathed slowly and sighed loudly and hissed that she wanted to die.

The time Netta's father used to spend with Netta's mother talking and laughing he now spent with Netta: he watched TV while she drew a picture at his feet, he ate long dinners with her while her mother slept, he read her a bedtime story and she woke up in the middle of the night to find he was still there, reading a book of his own. Netta knew that this meant he was scared, which scared her more, because what did you do when the people who knew the most about the world became frightened of it? What hope did she have, knowing nothing? She drew pictures of a dark-eyed dog, a floating house, a crying bird. Everyone who saw the drawings said she was gifted. Before, her father would have smiled wide and said they should all get her autograph before she got famous. Now he just looked down at the ground and rubbed her back, so she said, "Thank you for the compliment."

It went like this: her mother got better enough to wake up early and stay up until after dinner, started taking Netta in her lap again. There were no more stories, though Netta held out hope, and then her mother would get sick again. One night they were eating dinner and her mother dropped her fork and said the room was getting tight. Netta looked in her mother's eyes and cried out in panic, and her father pulled her to him and put a hand over her mouth. Her mother flung her plate and stomped around the kitchen, shouting at whatever else was in the room to stop making so much noise. She went to the hospital again and came back a week later with a different handful of pills. Forty days later, it happened again. And thirty days after that. Netta felt worry like bugs in her stomach, crawling up its walls and buzzing with hatred.

They took Netta's mother to see Michel, who'd been Netta's father's roommate in college. Michel was studying for his doctorate in biochemistry at the University of Chicago, which made him the unofficial family doctor. Even though he was the same age as her father, Michel looked ten years younger, light-skinned with sandpapery hair. He had a bendy face that Netta liked and wide ears that he could wiggle whenever he wanted—when he wiggled them he raised one eyebrow, too, and even Netta's mother laughed. He never tried to cure Netta's mother. Netta wasn't under the illusion that he could. Instead he spoke with her about modern medicine, long conversations that Netta listened to as she pretended to watch TV and her father dozed on the sofa behind her.

"By the time I die, I don't want there to be any room left in the world for nonscientific belief," Michel had said one night, and Netta heard her mother make the nodding sound she made when she agreed. "I want people to have come to their senses, to exist as rational agents in a totally knowable world."

His words seemed important: *rash on all agense in no ibble world.*

"Is it totally knowable?" her mother asked, and Netta recognized the challenge in her voice, a tone she only took with someone she respected. "Is science the end?"

"The end of what? Of all knowledge?" Netta felt Michel move behind her so she was sitting propped up against his side. "Of course it is. You should open a door and there should be nucleotides standing behind it, and behind that door atoms, and behind that door subatomic particles."

"I know there should be, but I've seen things I can't ignore."

"You've seen things?" He laughed.

"Yes," her mother said. "I've seen things that shouldn't be real only to me."

Michel was silent then. He ran one of his big, goofy hands over Netta's head, which for some reason made her shudder.

Netta's mother lost her job and they had to get a smaller apartment. Michel found them a beige-walled one in Rogers Park, close to Loyola, where her father tutored. When Michel showed it to them, Netta's mother walked around with her hands folded over her stomach—thickening since she'd left the hospital; her cheeks and thighs, too—and squinted her eyes and shook her head, looked at Netta, and whispered, "Seven steps down," which made Netta feel prickly and nervous. Within two weeks they were living there.

During the gray time after Netta came home from school and before her father came home from work, she was trapped alone with her mother, who would wail about ghosts Netta couldn't see no matter how hard she tried. One night, she turned on the faucet in the sink and splashed the water at Netta and asked her if this water didn't contain hundreds of spirits, if Netta couldn't feel them screaming in the air, landing prickly on her skin. By then it had been more than a year and a day since her grandmother's death, and Netta didn't know where her spirit had gone. But her mother's blank face and low whine made her anxious, and she said yes, she could feel every spirit.

"I want to die," her mother said, and walked slowly from the room into her bedroom.

Two days later, Netta's father was already home when she got back from school. He said her mother was in the hospital again. He made Netta a grilled cheese and they watched cartoons together and he told her during commercials that her mother would be cured for good now. Her mother stayed in the hospital for thirty days and Netta felt the apartment brighten from dark green to the purple she sometimes saw on the undersides of clouds during sunsets, felt her body get lighter, felt herself paying attention to the kids she was meeting at her new school. There was Leticia, who was pure pink, and Satvika, who was orange-red, and Elise, who was bright blue. Satvika once punched a steel-colored boy who called Netta a dirty monkey. Netta went to sleep at night thinking of them and felt a flush of orange the color of Satvika's name as she slid into dreams.

But sometimes when Netta was falling asleep, a dark green thought would come with an image of her mother in it, and Netta's eyes flickered open and her heart pounded hard. *No, no, no, no.* Eyes open or closed, she couldn't get rid of the dark green, where the floating image of her mother said, "I loved you so much, so why couldn't you love me back?"

"I loved you too!" Netta said, then caught herself: "I love you! I love you!"

But her mother, bathed in the dark green in her mind, just shook her head and cried, and Netta would wake crying, too.

When her mother did come back, she was flat again, had pills again—more than she'd ever had before. The doctors said she had a sickness in her mind and that she would always have to take the pills if she wanted to stay healthy.

After that, her mother didn't get sick again. But she also never went back to being the laughing-eyed woman who sat Netta on her lap. Her face looked longer, her posture better, her whole person shifting from yellow to off-white in Netta's mind. She had never cared about safety from beggars or the poor before, but now she did, instructing Netta to stay away from anyone who looked dirty or homeless. She said those people had fallen like they had for a reason, and that they would bring Netta down with them if she let them. She told Netta to be proud of who she was and not give white people a reason to hate her the way those beggars had. She got a job at the Loyola cafeteria.

After ten-year-old Netta drew the picture of Marlon she drew one of her mother's poems, two stanzas about how important it was to be clean. It started out as one of the Queen of Hearts' guards from the *Alice in Wonderland* movie: a playing-card body and a snooty white face. Then she drew a businessman's suit buttoned over his flat card-body. She gave him a mustache. She gave him a hat. She changed the sword in his hand to a scepter, then a walking cane. She put expensive Nikes on his feet. Then she erased a hole in his center so it looked like he'd been shot. Beneath him she wrote: "I am so pure, I am so good / I am the noblest dickhead, in all the hood."

1990–2004
Chicago

She grew up and did well in school, managed to get into a magnet school on the North Side (to her delight, so did Satvika and Elise—Leticia went to a Catholic school in the suburbs), won a scholarship to study figure drawing at the School of the Art Institute of Chicago. She did all this by ignoring her mother, who grew fat and bitter at Netta's happiness. It had been her father who framed the drawings, who showed them to Michel. It had been Michel who had arranged for a showing at an arts and cultural center in Hyde Park, the kind of place run by well-intentioned middle-class people who thought pastels and parchment paper were real antidotes to the city's gun violence. It had been Michel's friend Peter who'd seen Netta's drawings and offered to mentor her at his South Side studio. And it had been Netta herself who made the drawings (ten to fifteen a week), who for four years had taken two trains and a bus every Wednesday to Peter's garage-studio, where he taught her line, form, and contour, who had saved up the money she made working at the Indian restaurant on Devon to pay for pencils and charcoal and gummy erasers. Once a week Netta laid new drawings on the kitchen table for her father to admire.

At SAIC Netta was called "beautiful for a black girl" and "exotic," which made her feel a weird bluish violet she'd never felt before. She felt the need to make her adult body thinner than it already was, to wear the chokers and hair clips the other girls did. Satvika had left the city to go to college in Vermont and Elise and Leticia were both at DePaul. She tried to meet them for lunch in the Loop every other week, but by the winter of freshman year it felt as though they'd run out of things to talk about. Netta could tell with a navy-tinged sadness that they'd grown too boring and practical for her. Elise was studying to be a social worker and Leticia an accountant: they never had anything interesting to say, never attended any parties or gallery openings or concerts, and so relied on Netta to keep them updated on what drugs she'd tried and whom she was sleeping with, which exhausted her. She didn't want her friends to live through her, hustling around in their boxy sneakers and fringe bangs and outdated lipstick, fat purses bulging with tissues. She canceled on them twice, three times—by the fourth time, they'd gotten the message. She still sent them birthday cards and added them on AOL chat, but they never talked much beyond an occasional "Hey."

Her friends at SAIC were Chloe and Danielle. Chloe was in fibers and Danielle was in fashion. They were both from the rich northwest suburbs and lived in massive condos on the Gold Coast: the doormen knew them by name, and their bedrooms had views of Lake Michigan. But they both considered Netta the most interesting person they knew. They called Netta the Queen, and Netta's heart swelled and then shuddered in a way she didn't want to understand. She spent long weekends in Chloe's condo, which was the bigger of the two, and where there was weed and champagne and ecstasy. By the end of her freshman year Netta knew that ecstasy was her favorite drug, that rolling was one of her favorite things to do. The thin, bright faces of Chloe and Danielle would glow like white-hot klieg lights, divine and perfect, and their hands became the grabbing hands of playful children, eager and innocent, hugging Netta and holding her, offering her cheese and almonds, touching her cheeks and hair. She touched them back—all warm, all ecstatically warm and lovely, all bright mauve and rose and cyan, shifting like the blocks of color she remembered from her favorite Disney cartoons—and she felt loved and safe. She usually felt angry with her mother (and even a little with her father) for keeping her so sheltered. But when she was rolling she just pitied them, or collapsed on Chloe's settee and cried for them, and Chloe and Danielle would be at her feet, asking her what was wrong, why someone so beautiful and perfect should be so sad. And then Netta's tears would become tears of joy and she'd hug them to her, promise that she was crying because she was so incredibly happy, make them swear to only create beautiful things for the world's most beautiful people and tell all their enemies to fuck off.

"You're amazing!" Chloe said.

"You're a poet-goddess!" Danielle said.

And again the weekend after that, and the weekend after that.

She slept with Chloe and Danielle separately a few times, then all together a few times. She had blue-and-gold orgasms that she hadn't known were possible. She dated around in their friend group—white and Asian kids from Highland Park and Evanston and Lake Forest—and then got serious with Danielle's best friend from high school, a bisexual performance artist named Greg who wanted to be called Elmer after some character in an old movie. One evening after he'd made her come twice during sex, Elmer said he'd never imagined himself getting serious with someone like her. Something about his words had given her the old bluish-violet feeling, but this time she knew it must be wrong, must be some ghost from the beige apartment rattling the cage she'd sealed it in long ago, because Elmer was smiling so kindly as he said it, running his hand up and down her thigh.

Over winter break of their senior year, the six of them gathered in Chloe's condo on Christmas Eve: Netta, Elmer, Chloe and her boyfriend Damien, Danielle and her boyfriend Luke. Chloe's brother, Eric, a married architect in New York, had procured a drug called purple mox-c for her birthday. It was supposed to be twice as powerful as ecstasy. Chloe and Eric and Eric's wife, Annette, had done it once in Manhattan on Chloe's birthday, then Chloe and Eric had done it again during a family vacation to St. Maarten. The dark purple pills were stamped with yellow smiley faces. Chloe promised that she and Eric had done mox-c from this same batch, but no one really needed any reassurance. Elmer swallowed his without water, then tipped a glass to Netta's lips so she could swallow hers. They kissed while the others cheered them on.

Netta felt it first (she always did, the smallest and most sensitive): a fullness in her ears, a tightness at the front of her head. The feeling was so sudden and blunt that she tipped forward, hands at her chest, fearing she was having a stroke. She heard Elmer asking if she was all right, then Chloe, and her feet swam out of focus and a film crept up over her eyes. She imagined herself on a gurney in an emergency room, imagined Danielle and Chloe holding her hands as she lay comatose on an operating table, and she wished she'd spent the evening with her father like he'd wanted. She could picture him sitting in front of the TV in the living room in the houndstooth cardigan she'd gotten him last Christmas, wearing it all wrong with a pair of thick-waled corduroys, trying to read the newspaper. Then in the background "Wannabe" started playing; her parents were listening to the Spice Girls. She started laughing, felt something light and incredible fizz up from the tops of her thighs, a feeling close to an orgasm but not quite. When she sat up her eyes were clear and her mind was focused and she was singing "If you wanna be my lover, you gotta get with my fri-eends!" Danielle burst out laughing, then Chloe, then Luke. Elmer stood up and found *Spice* in a pile of CDs—which was in itself too perfect, too funny— and put it on Chloe's stereo and Damien got up to dance. The dance seemed so spot-on, so touchingly for her, that Netta laughed and cried and said, "I love you! I can't believe how much I love you!" and then Elmer was in her lap kissing her. When Netta looked up (just minutes later, she hoped) they were all kissing, the make-outs melting into one another, getting passed around like a cold. Luke held Damien's hand as they kissed their respective girlfriends, then they turned and kissed each other and Danielle was coming to kiss Netta, so she pushed Elmer off her lap and opened her mouth for Danielle, and Elmer went to kiss Chloe.

Danielle's body on hers suddenly felt indistinguishable from her own, Danielle's mouth so soft and her tongue so dexterous, and Netta imagined a womb's skin closing over them, twins floating in amniotic fluid. She looked up (Danielle's eyes were still closed) and the walls of the womb pulsed around her, the thrum-thrum of a mother's heartbeat just inches from the top of her fetal head, and she thought how incredible it was, what a medical miracle it was that a black twin and a white twin could not only share a womb but also fall in love. She thought, *Finally: a womb of their own!* and laughed through the kiss (Danielle didn't seem to notice or care, just shaped Netta's lips back into a pucker with her own).

An electric ding sounded from outside the womb's walls and then a vibration from within, and Netta asked Danielle through the kiss if she'd brought her vibe to the party. Danielle pulled away just long enough to laugh and say how Netta was too perfect, too funny. The dinging and vibration pulsed again, then again, and Netta realized it was her mobile phone in her back pocket. She fished for it and put it on the couch next to them, thinking of how to stop it so she could go back to Danielle's blue-gold mouth and the bright yellow feeling of those hands on her body, on her nipples (already hardening in anticipation of the sex she was sure she'd soon be having), and flipped it open to turn it off only for it to ding and vibrate again, "Dad" on the small screen.

"Just one minute, love," she said to Danielle. "I want to tell my dad how incredible he is." And Danielle nodded and sat back patiently, looked over her shoulder at Elmer and Damien as they touched each other's faces.

When Netta picked up the phone and said, "Hey, Dad, I love you," he was already talking. The way he was talking didn't make sense—not for the night, not for this moment in the night—and she sat up and said, "Dad! Dad!" which made everyone stop what they were doing and look at her.

"Your mother's tried to kill herself!" he wailed. "I found her in the shower with her wrists open. She's in the hospital now."

The words were like a crack to the head with a baseball bat.

"No," she offered. "I'm not sure you remember that right."

"Where are you?" he said. "I wanted you here tonight!"

Elmer sat down next to her and began rubbing her back. Then he made a snorting sound and laughed, and the others laughed, too. "Are you speaking an alien language, babe?" he asked.

Netta half heard him and shuddered, because her body couldn't withstand a second crack to the head. She dug her fingers beneath her ponytail, feeling for a patch of scalp on the back of her head from which she was certain was leaking dark crimson blood. Her vision was the darkest green it had ever been.

"Netta," her father said, his voice well modulated now, "this is serious. They said it was lucky I found her. I was teaching—I don't know how long it was she'd been there like that."

Netta ground her teeth. Now he's acting calm, of course. Then came an image of her mother in the shower and she vomited on her dress.

The next time she was aware of her body in space, it was much later in the evening and she was in Leticia's studio in Uptown, her hair and chin still smelling of her own vomit. Leticia was getting a sweatshirt and sweatpants ready for her and pulling her soiled dress off her head while Netta said something about how she had missed her mom's death, how she was such a horrible daughter that she'd driven her mom to kill herself. And Leticia was assuring her that she was wrong, telling her multiple times that she'd spoken with her father and that he said her mother was alive at the hospital and sedated and stable, saying she could call him again if Netta wanted. But Netta didn't want to talk to her father again—she wanted to take a shower, and then she wanted to go home and lie in her childhood bed and cry for her father and mother, cry for how small and sad and scared of the world they were, cry for how she'd traveled far from them without inviting them along. Leticia listened as she talked, and Netta knew that if she let herself think about those years of unanswered AOL "Hey"s, those lunches during which Leticia had sat silently while Netta told some stupid story about tripping at a Pearl Jam concert, she'd vomit again. How smug Netta had been! How sophisticated she had thought she was! But she knew nothing of the world, and Leticia in her shitty studio apartment with her washed-out jeans and accounting textbooks knew more! Netta couldn't tell whether it was worse that Leticia had always known more or that she'd kept her knowing more a secret.

Then Netta was out of the shower and in Leticia's strange clothes, pushing open a door that was the entrance to her mother's hospital room. She was watching her father speak with a nurse wearing a Santa hat while her mother slept noisily against the hum of the machine that was monitoring her heart and helping her breathe. Netta's father hugged Netta, then Leticia, and Netta wept helplessly, dirtied her father's shirt with snot and tears. She approached her mother's bed and realized with horror that she was still high, that she had been high for hours and would probably be high for many more. She was just a frightened little girl come to share her mother's bed in the middle of the night, and she nudged her mother awake, the nurse saying, "Careful!"

Her mother blinked and sat partway up and her hands, mittened with bandages and restrained at her sides, tensed as she tried to move them.

Then she looked at Netta in confusion that Netta watched change to anger, then to something between pity and fear. She was sea green—the color of a child.

"Why are you here now?" her mother asked.

Netta bit her lower lip and shook her head. Her mother watched her.

"Speak up," she said. "Why are you here, Netta?"

"Oh, Ma!" Netta said, and threw herself across her mother's lap, the nurse pawing ineffectively at her back. "I'm sorry!"

"What the hell are you sorry for?" her mother asked, and laughed.

Netta felt her mother's little pink burbles of laughter and clung tighter to her, pressed her face into her mother's needles and tubes.

"I thought I was ready to leave, but I'm not." Her mother said this lightly, as though they were discussing running errands. "I thought I was all alone, but I'm not."

"Of course you're not," Netta repeated, not knowing what she was assenting to. She felt far off, like an object in the lens of a telescope. Her mother was the victim of a world built to hate her, to deny her existence—her grandma had been as well. And so was Netta herself, sitting on her ailing mother's hospital bed in her twenty-dollar choker and United Colors of Benetton, her brain dyed a fucked-up purple from the mox-c, and she hated to think about who she'd been, about who she would eventually become.

That March, Netta graduated from SAIC. Her mother was still in the hospital. She broke the lease on her River North apartment and moved back into the beige apartment with her father, slept in her sixteen-year-old twin bed, and began a freelance job as a figure drawer for a small publisher of anatomical textbooks, a gig she found through Peter. She'd broken up with Elmer in January after they had a fight about whether she was "too emotional": he maintained he'd tried to help her that awful night but she'd called him a fuckstick and told him to get away from her; she had no memory of any of that and didn't really care.

In the weeks after her mother returned home, Netta spent most of the day at her bedside, reading her the literature she liked: surrealist poetry, magazines in which decorated writers were interviewed at length by overeager journalists. Sometimes she would ask for *Popular Science* or some obscure medical journal, and Netta would have to dig in a cupboard in the kitchen where her father had stored all those magazines, the oldest ones yellowed and bound together with a rubber band. But she never read long from these—Netta's mother would tolerate four or five paragraphs and then demand to be returned to the author interview. After a month her mother's depression lifted enough for her to get out of bed in the morning, and Netta would walk with her to Hollywood Beach, where her mother scattered stale Saltines among flocks of desperate-looking seagulls.

At SAIC, Netta had abandoned her drawings of people for representational surrealism like Ernst's and Magritte's: a fire hydrant with human hands, a white woman emerging from the mouth of a panting dog, a *mise en abyme* of birds' eyes. But now she returned to people, to her charcoal and her parchment paper. She took the train to Cabrini-Green and drew the old women wheeling their metal carts in and out of public housing, drew a coked-up young man from the neighborhood who approached her almost daily asking for a date. She babysat every other week for Michel and his wife, took the two bougie Hyde Park kids (by then Talib was a first-grader and Shalia just out of diapers) on walks through Englewood and Auburn Gresham, where she would take photos of bored-looking young women behind convenience store counters, of teenaged boys on their bikes trying to act bigger than they were. When Talib tripped and skinned his knee, she preserved the mental image to draw later: a little boy on his stomach at the corner of Sixty-Seventh and Halsted, hands splayed at his sides, mouth open wide in pain.

And she drew her mother. Over and over and over again she drew her mother: waking up in bed, counting empty jars in the kitchen, searching for employment on the ancient computer she'd finally talked her father into buying. She did studies of her mother's ankles, feet, hands, arms, neck, ears, face. She drew her mother in situations she had never been in, was unlikely to ever be in: dancing, playing basketball, conducting a train. A homeless woman under the Lake Shore Drive overpass became her mother. A cheerful docent at the DuSable Museum of African American History became her mother. A woman taking her order at Lou Malnati's became her mother. The best of the drawings she copied onto canvas with the best acrylics she could afford. In six months, she produced more drawings than she had in four years at SAIC. She stacked them on every available surface in the apartment—those she couldn't fit in the apartment she stored in the closets and dressers of Leticia and Elise, who had now begun the decent-paying jobs they'd been studying for. She called Satvika, who was starting work as a public defender in Montpelier, and told her about the drawings, about her mother.

"It sounds like you're ready for your first show," Satvika said, her voice the same orange-red it had always been.

And of course Satvika was right. Michel's wife, Sandra, who was a professor of art history at the University of Chicago, said Netta's work reminded her of later Loïs Mailou Jones. Soon after that Netta was offered a show at the South Side Community Art Center in Bronzeville, and she invited everyone she knew to attend—even the old women from Cabrini-Green and the convenience store girls in Englewood—promised everyone free food and wine if they'd just stay and look at the pictures she'd painted of them. The show, which she called *The Big Heavy World*, featured twenty of her character studies and thirty-five twelve-by-fourteens of either her mother or other women as her mother. Her father came and cried with pride; her mother said she was too tired to attend.

Netta sold all but five of her paintings from *The Big Heavy World* and began work on a new series the next day: pictures of black Chicago women of all ages and stations, some commissioned portraits, some drawn from memory. She didn't tell any of her clients that she was really just drawing her mother over and over, hiding her dimpled cheeks, wide nose, and sleepy eyes in theirs. It took her only three months to finish the series, which she titled *Alo, Manman!* (In Haitian in honor of her grandma's roots.) The second show was at a gallery in Wicker Park, even better attended than her first. People noticed common features in the women's faces and attributed them to Netta's "style"—one reviewer went so far as to write, "As the artist develops her work, we will come to recognize a Barochin in much the same way we do a Botero: a diversity of character communicated through the same plump face, the same almond eyes and rounded nose." An agent approached her and suggested she move to New York. She told him he could represent her, but she had no interest in leaving her hometown.

One of the portraits in *Alo, Manman!* had been of a girl named Shanea McQueen and her mother, Roxane, a cherubic pair from Cabrini-Green whose round faces both nicely concealed and revealed Netta's mother's features. Roxane had been the beauty of her family, it was easy to tell: she walked with confidence, commanded both the respect and fear of her children. While Shanea had inherited her mother's looks, she often hid them. She hugged herself whenever she sensed she was being watched, pulled her large T-shirts over her knees while sitting cross-legged on the couch. Roxane had asked for the portrait so Shanea would understand not only how beautiful she was, but that she came from a long line of beautiful women. At the opening, the portrait, titled simply *Mother and Daughter: Cabrini-Green*, had drawn plenty of praise, and had left Shanea biting her lower lip with embarrassed joy.

Two weeks later, Shanea and her older brother were walking home from school on Hudson when a policeman asked them where they were going. Her brother had offered the truth. Shanea had asked the policeman what was so suspicious about walking home. The officer said there was nothing suspicious, said she'd need to calm down and let him do his job, asked her to show him some ID. Shanea said her name was Shanea McQueen, she was fourteen, and he could speak to her mother if he wanted. The officer withdrew his gun and said she'd better produce some ID. Shanea sighed and reached into her jacket pocket and the officer shot her.

Netta followed the story obsessively. The McQueens sued the city for $3 million. The officer—Albert Kowalski, whom the media kept describing as a "family man," "proud Polish immigrant," and "father of three"— hired the same lawyer who'd defended Mayor Daley's nephew after he killed David Koschman. In court, the lawyer claimed Shanea had been aggressive and argumentative; Kowalski feared she was about to withdraw a weapon, so he'd acted in self-defense. In the testimony, Shanea's brother became a suspected gang member and Shanea became a disruptive delinquent. The judge ruled in Kowalski's favor.

Netta lost sleep over it. She ignored her agent's phone calls and went back to making detailed pen sketches of the backs of hands and neck tendons for the small publisher. She drew her mother again, but this time more out of rage than curiosity: her mother with monstrously large teeth, her mother with a bolt through her head, her mother aflame. She saw her life as a sad downward trajectory from clueless child to leeching adult— she should have stayed in that penthouse with Chloe and Danielle, reading *Cosmo* and getting fucked up and making fake art for rich white people. She called Chloe and Danielle for the first time in a while and they snorted some coke, went to a bar in Wrigleyville, snorted some Valium, made out, passed out. She felt like shit: she knew now that being with them had always made her feel like shit, but before it'd been gold-leafed shit. When she woke up the next morning she had a voicemail from her friend Ray Simon, failed artist turned community organizer turned real estate entrepreneur, who said there was going to be a protest and remembrance ceremony for Shanea in Cabrini-Green on Saturday and could she come?

Of course she could. It was September and getting cold again; she wore long sleeves and a vest, a pair of baggy jeans that had once belonged to her mother. As always, men hassled her as she walked, asking her what she was so mad about, why she couldn't just give them a smile. She had no patience for them today—she spoke back, swatted them off, told one old piece of shit who claimed Shanea had been sleeping with Kowalski to cut off his dick. He leered at her but she didn't care—she was feeling reckless. Let one of these assholes shoot me, too, she thought.

At the corner of Sedgwick and Erie there emerged from the crowd another man, heavy-browed. This one seemed lost. She didn't care. She was so fed up with him. She was so fed up with all of them.

"What's this?" He locked eyes with her and didn't break his stare—the "this" could've been her or the protest.

"It's a protest," she snarled. "A fourteen-year-old girl was murdered by a cop."

"Oh." He nodded, glanced around him. "I parked a few blocks away. I was wondering where—"

She jammed a spare sign in his hands and told him to hold it. He smiled and snorted a laugh, both of which wore on her patience.

"I don't know where the fuck you're from," she said, "but people in Chicago get murdered for acting confident."

That seemed to sober him up, and he held the sign and marched alongside her. He, the man she'd fall in love with, didn't speak to her all the way east on Erie and south down the Magnificent Mile. She pretended she was alone and not guilty, a little girl whose understanding of the world still involved magic, who listened to her mother's stories in a big, bright kitchen.

LEE BLOOM-MITTWOCH JR.

(1989–)

1996
Florida

When he was just six, Lee Bloom—he didn't want to bother with the *M* part of his name, it was too hard to say—had a whole back-yard to himself. The trees in his private backyard went curvy like elf-trees and had long palm-hair and swayed when he came close to them and stood still when he went away. There was a mud path that led from his backyard to the swamp, and if you walked along it your feet sunk deep and the mud was warm and soft and gross because it sometimes felt like a person's hands. One time, he walked down the mud path and stayed still for a very long time—days and days—next to the swamp and he saw one alligator eye on the first day and another on the second day and then on the third day he saw alligator teeth and on the last day he saw a whole alligator mouth. The alligator mouth opened and snapped shut at him.

His mom was named Diedre and she was pretty; she wore makeup most of the time but in the morning her face didn't have any makeup, and sometimes it looked softer but sometimes it looked sleepier. She carried him around the house in the night when he was a baby and he couldn't stop crying. She carried him upstairs and downstairs. When he was big-ger she stopped carrying him but sometimes he walked behind her around the house and she told him "Here is where we keep the mops, here is where we keep the orange juice," in case he ever had to show anyone. She drank bad-smelling vodka with orange juice, in a chair outside. She smoked outside—she told him not to do what she did. His dad told him her life had been a very sad one before, but he didn't say why it was sad.

His dad was named the same as him: Leland. But he didn't get called Lee, he just got called Leland or Senior. His mom sometimes said, "Don't be so stupid, Senior," and kissed him on the nose so then there was lipstick on his nose. He laughed: he had a deep laugh. He was taller and older than she was. His skin was tan-colored but hers was white like the 2 percent milk that Lee had in the cup with the alligator on the front of it. The alligator wore purple shorts and said "Aloha from Miami!" She said to Lee, "Someone spilled milk all over me and didn't get your dad." And his dad said, "Lee's going to tan like his father," and Lee said, "I can't get a tan." But his dad said, "You've got cinnamon skin already. That's how all the Bloom-Mittwochs tan." Lee didn't know about any other Bloom-Mittwochs, except for his dad's other son, but he'd never seen him. Sometimes Lee thought maybe he was adopted from a different mom and dad because he looked different from them and tanned different from them. Sometimes his dad talked fast and sometimes he talked slow. Sometimes when his dad talked really fast his mom talked really slow.

His mom's name was Diedre Bloom-Mittwoch but before it was Diedre Mifkin. She didn't like her mom and dad, who were Lee's grandparents. They lived far away in another part of Florida; he hardly ever saw them. She told Lee his grandma Mifkin used to be very proper but now she saved everything in bins in her house and the whole front part of the house where the kitchen and living room was had bins full of twine and newspapers. Lee's dad's parents were dead. They used to live in a dark forest-city on the other side of the world that his dad called the Vald. When Lee thought of the Vald he thought of yellow eyes in the trees and animals that could talk. He asked his dad if animals could talk in the Vald and his dad looked at his mom and said, "Good question. Nazis could talk, couldn't they?"

They lived in Paradise, his mom said. Because they lived in Florida. It was sunny in Florida, but not anywhere else in the world. In the summer it got hot so there was sweat between his toes. When it got really hot in the summer he played in the sprinkler and his mom sat on the patio behind the screen and she drank orange juice and vodka and his dad smoked cigarettes and filmed Lee with the video camera that had a mirror in front so it looked like a monster eyeball. One day when it was really hot Lee made the Sprinkler Olympics. It was a special day because he just saw a crocodile eye and he was going back and forth from the sprinkler to the water to check to make sure the crocodile eye was still there. His mom thought it was funny. She said, "A watched crocodile never surfaces." She laughed.

Lee jumped through the sprinkler and he screamed because it was cold on the soft parts of his legs. He said, "Watched eye never surfaces!"

His dad laughed behind the camera. "Tell the audience what you're doing, Lee."

"Sprinkler Olympics!"

"Do you think you're going to get the gold this year?"

Lee shook his head. "I dunno. I dunno . . . depends." He went back to look at the crocodile eye and then came running fast through the sprinkler. He screamed again.

"Depends on what, Lee?"

He jumped back in and screamed so that he felt it in his head but also going down his spine into his stomach and the tops of his legs. His mom said far off: "Depends on whether he's on steroids. He has to be if he's a six-year-old gold medalist."

His dad's face got really serious, and he made his voice deep like a sports announcer guy's. "Are you on steroids?"

The ground was hard on Lee's feet where there wasn't mud and soft where there was. His feet went down and down and up and up. Sometimes when he jumped they went one-up, one-up, and then one-down, one-down. He landed hard on the ground in mud and it didn't feel hard. Through the water there was a big sun.

His dad gave the monster-eye camera to his mom so she could point it at them and then his dad came growling like a monster into the sprinkler and Lee ran away to look at the alligator eye again, but it wasn't there.

"I got you!" his dad said real fast, and lifted him up.

Lee was getting tickled like crazy, and trying not to laugh made him laugh harder and harder.

"Rrrrrr," his dad said. "Rrrrrr, I'm the Sprinkler Monster."

"This is the Sprinkler Olympics!" Lee said.

"I'm attacking the Sprinkler Olympics!" his dad said. Then in a weird voice: "I ehm ze Svprinkler Munster fruum Rooshia!"

They were back in the sprinkler and it was wet and sunny and the

Sprinkler Monster tossed Lee high in the air and Lee screamed and his mom said, "Looks like you'll have to forfeit, baby." Lee fell down from up high and the Sprinkler Monster caught him strong under his arms and Lee kicked his feet because he wanted to go again, so the Sprinkler Monster tossed him up again even higher.

2008
Cleveland

And then baby Lee was stopped in midair and hung suspended in the grainy, greenish fuzz of Diedre's decades-old TV screen, the similarly ancient VCR humming quietly with the effort of the pause. The camcorder's timestamp read 7/6/1996, the last of Lee's baby videos. It was twelve years since then and nine years since Lee's dad jumped, and here he was with Maria Timpano, watching the video on the couch in the living room of the Cleveland apartment where he lived with Diedre (whom he rarely called "Mom," but more out of habit than disrespect), through whose windows one could see a billboard advertising Pall Mall smokers on a beach, a loud bottom-left surgeon general's warning announcing that SMOKING IS BAD FOR YOUR HEALTH. And so was Cleveland, Lee thought, but Diedre had been under the impression that moving here would mean a "fresh start" after his father's death. Starting fresh in the dead man's hometown.

It was Lee's Senior Ditch Day and he'd talked Maria into ditching with him—which she didn't need a lot of persuading to do, only marginally in school was she anyway ("was she"? God, he was fucked up), her genius ass already off taking classes at Case Western—and they were high and a little hungry but intent on ignoring both those feelings in favor of sex. Lacking a proper childhood of her own, Maria was a sentimentalist for kid arcana, always demanding to flip through Diedre's old photo albums of Lee and watch video after video after video of him learning how to walk and eat and sound out the words in his board books. Diedre had been a dedicated videographer—that much he had to give her credit for—and his father a committed performer. But the videos were pretty boring (kids are stupid, Lee knew, and prone to repetitive behaviors), and even Maria got bored after they'd incinerated a nug or two, and they usually moved on to undressing pretty quickly thereafter.

This Senior Ditch Day would go on to earn a top-three ranking among the worst days of Lee's life. The number one worst had been the day he learned that his father had committed suicide by jumping off the roof of a hotel in Tampa. The second-worst had been the day of his father's funeral, when his Sith Lord half brother had followed them home and rummaged through his life and repossessed all the things in their house he thought they owed him. The third-worst would be this day, because it was on this day that he fucked things up with the love of his life.

They began doing what they'd intended to do right there in the living room, raven-haired Maria asking him if maybe they should be more careful because his mom was about to come home, Lee reminding her that Diedre had seen much worse in the span of her strange time on earth. And Maria—who was actually kind of a freak when she wanted to be—had rolled her eyes and stood, stripping naked and beckoning him to the floor. When that was over he'd lain in a fetal position at her side, whispering that he never wanted to get up. But one of her friends from drama club was having a party later and she had to go back to her place and sober up and get ready. Which meant he had to get up as well, to try to draw out their good-bye kiss for as long as possible.

When she left, he'd gone into Diedre's room, in the drawer where she kept her Xanax, and had ground up a pill with the butt of his lighter and snorted it off her dresser. He then walked across the complex to his friend Max's apartment. Unlike Lee, Max—just as poor ("economically challenged," as the Shaker Heights mayor had once said of Ludlow) as Lee, with the same genre of "seen it all, done it all" mother, though buoyed financially and sexually by his social status as quarterback—had an Internet hookup, a dial-up one that made those weird late-nineties sounds like telegraphed Morse code. Lee didn't really mind Diedre's unwillingness to pay for Internet: they had TV; he was content checking out books from the library (currently it was Eastern European fiction in translation) and playing old N64 games. She was feeding and clothing them both on a $13.50-an-hour managerial salary from OfficeMax, so it would be asking a lot anyway. And it wasn't like he'd been the perfect son, either.

He was going to Max's to check his e-mail, which he'd abused on his eighteenth birthday—December 15, 2007, the drunkest he'd ever been—to write to Leland Jr., demanding reparations for the goods he'd stolen after the funeral. Leland Jr. had taken jewelry that would've looked nice on Diedre, he'd taken pictures that hung in the hallway, he'd taken the car and sold it for parts. It occurred to Lee on the eve of adulthood that the virtuous thing to do would be to get everything back. Not just for the money but for the principle of it. He would show Diedre and Maria and everyone who'd ever known him that he was in no position to be pushed around by the Sith Lord. But secretly he was, because it was months later and he'd been dreading Leland Jr.'s response since he'd woken up with a brain-throttling hangover on December 16.

He offered Max a Xanax for his troubles and sat down at his outsized monitor while Max played an ancient version of Doom on his laptop in bed. Lee saw—as he thought he would—the bolded **re:** that indicated Leland Jr. had indeed read and replied to his e-mail. To get his courage up, he searched through his inbox for the e-mail from Jocelyn: **Hey, do you think you'd want to work at Lefébvre?** In it, her apologies for replying to Lee's (incoherent) e-mail that Leland Jr. had obviously forwarded her, her modest and unrealistic offer—forty hours a week, $8.25 an hour; how would he live off that, wherever Lefébvre was, and didn't she know he had school?—her desire to get to know Lee better, her promise that Leland Jr. wanted to extend an olive branch as well. He'd wasted his time crafting a response, feigning interest for reasons he couldn't explain to himself, and never sent it. Now he reread the e-mail that had started it all:

> from: "Lee" <bonemachine@gmail.com>
> to: "Leland Bloom-Mittwoch" <lj-m@winnmaxwell.com>
> date: Sat, December 15, 2007 at 2:13 am
> subject:
>
> Leland Jr.,
> I am your half brother Lee writing to ask that you please sur-
> render the asets that rightfully belong to m e. My mother, Diedre,
> whom yo u will probably rememmber from the funral, and I have
> been living in a state of near-povertty since you executed my
> father's will. Diedre defaulted on the morgage of the house in
> FLorida and I am now living withher in Ohio, where our father
> hasd friendss. Yo u have personal assets belonging to us which
> you thought belongged to you. I dont think im being rude when
> I ask: why do you need these assets? II believe I have a right to
> know. You are well-off, as is your mother. Yur job is high-paying

and has security. Ths is not the case with Diedre, who works at Officemax. What do u need this money to buy, exactly?

I wuld like to remmind yu that I am Leland Sr.'s son and he is my father just as much as you are his son and he is your fathe.r I believe that you are obligated to at the very least fairly divvide the assetts between us both if you will not aknowledge that I am the rihtful inheritor. If you do not comply with these requests I woill be forced to pursue legal action.

Sincerely,

Lee Bloom-Mittwoch

And now he had no choice but to read what Leland Jr. had written in response. He sighed, held his breath:

from: "Leland Bloom-Mittwoch" <lj-m@winnmaxwell.com>
to: "Lee" date: <bonemachine@gmail.com>
date: Wed, April 23, 2008 at 4:19 am
subject: re:

Lee,

Let me start by saying that your kind words regarding myself and how I choose to live my life and what I choose to do with my money (and where it came from) are much appreciated. The last and only time I saw you, you were a kid at your father's funeral; you seemed like a charming boy then and it's obvious to me that you've grown into a young man of equivalent charm. I didn't respond to your e-mail sooner because I promised myself I wouldn't, but eventually I realized that you had a good point when you insisted that you have a right to know about "the assets." Here are some answers to your questions:

1. I have zero doubt that you are your father's son. You are probably more his son than I am; I gladly surrender him to you.
2. I settled your father's estate in the way I did because (a) he didn't write a will, and I'm assuming if he had, he wouldn't have had testatory capacity anyway; (b) the sum of heritable assets included no property (you may not realize this, but the house you lived in in Florida was mortgaged beyond belief)

216 of Rebekah Frumkin

and so totaled under $100,000; (c) many of the more valuable possessions in that house were stolen from my mother. If I remember correctly, you and your mother retained the assets that rightfully belonged to you and then some: your father's savings including the money he took from my mother (I remind you that this sum was bequeathed to you at my mother's request, not my own), valuables belonging to your paternal grandparents, etc.

3. Your threat to sue, while certainly intimidating, doesn't seem like the wisest course of action for you.

Regards,
Leland Jr.

Worse than he'd expected. His heart's thrum sped up and he stared into the screen, then at his hands. Then he propped his head in his hands and stared at his lap, his be-jeaned knees. Max's voice asked from far off what was wrong and Lee let him look over his shoulder at the screen, then listened as Max went into the kitchen and came back with a bottle of his parents' whiskey. They took burning pulls from it and smoked again, Max saying that none of this was Lee's fault, that he was dealing with a truly fucked-up person here and it was probably better to sever ties than keep on dealing with him. Lee nodded and nodded and said nothing, because anything he said would cause the fireball of anger at the base of his skull to supernova throughout the rest of his body, and then he'd have no choice but to cry. They smoked again to sober up and then Max mentioned he had Oxy, which they agreed they'd take before getting in Lee's car.

He saw Maria had texted him three times, all some variation of *when are u coming to pick me up??* She liked arriving places together—he loved it—and her friend's house, if he remembered correctly, wasn't within walking distance of hers. He was twenty minutes late already. Normally he'd do something—jumping jacks, stretches, deep breathing—to get soberer, but he was in a hurry and the weed and Xanax had already canceled out the whiskey and he was taming the Oxy's head-float by chugging water. But when they got in Lee's car (which was really Diedre's car), Max had asked feebly whether Lee wanted him to drive. Lee glimpsed himself in the rearview mirror and saw that Max maybe had a point, but knew as well that accepting Max's kindness would cause him to feel embarrassed, so he just shrugged and said, "Nah, man, I'm fine."

This was how they ended up in the bottom of a ravine next to Maria's house fifteen minutes later. Stern old Papa Don Timpano had seen them, called 911, and promised Lee he would never be allowed within a mile of raven-haired Maria Timpano again.

Late April 2009
Wisconsin

Lee sat at one tip of an ovoid formation of boys passing around a Pascal. He was thinking once again about Devi and how easy it would be to walk across the hall, say a sad-sounding and noncommittal hi, and drill her. This was an idea he'd been tossing around in his head all day, a head now dense and furry with THC in a way he liked to refer to as a "Mary Jane maze." The ovoid formation went like this: Lee, Dallas (real name Jeff but he was from just outside Dallas), Abel (last name), a rando named Donny (possibly a friend of Abel's?), and Lee's best friend at Southgate College, Tarzan Phillips (Christian name: Edward Jonathan Phillips). Although Tarz claimed unparalleled expertise with most drugs—cannabis especially— and sometimes (albeit needlessly) assumed a parental or instructional role with Lee, it was Lee alone who'd thought of the Cockneyesque nickname: Pascal as in Blaise Pascal as in blaze, the former being far afield from words like roach, spliff, and blunt and their washed-out, mildewy associations with the early seventies. Avoided entirely was the noobish and embarrassing word "joint," which you often heard deployed by adults who'd only ever taken one puff in their lifetime, or had felt briefly cool for a moment at some party when they were offered some burning paper and didn't decline.

The Pascal was now being passed around with the sort of mad-loud enthusiasm Lee imagined must have prevailed in Heorot right before Grendel broke in and slaughtered everyone. Everyone in the oval (excepting Lee and Tarz) had done the Four-Twenty Challenge and was treating this afternoon like a Deadhead Christmas morning, delighting as they never had before in Tarz's rolling ability, his strip-of-index-card roaches, and the foul tobacco he'd purchased in preparation for their catharsis. Midterms had been over for more than thirty-six hours and they'd all been drinking since around noon. Add to this the fact that since most kids at Southgate were pretty much scared of their own shadows and had gone home already to spend spring break playing video games, Lee et al. had the school to themselves. Lee had initially balked when Diedre pressured him to move away for college (*You're bored and restless and it's annoying*), but now he conceded that it had been worth it.

And across the hall, Lee knew Devi was sitting in her little jean shorts (jorts) in her chair in front of her bathroom vanity and fixing and refixing that bland-as-all-hell overstraightened hair. Lee held the blazing Pascal in his lips and began texting her: *hrny as fuk.*

Tarz plucked the Pascal from Lee's mouth and licked his own lips, leaning toward Lee's ear in a way that gave him goose bumps. Tarz sometimes acted like a little kid, and depending on who you were you found this either endearing or annoying. Lee, of course, would defend whatever Tarz did or said to his dying day.

Tarz opened his hands and inside were some shriveled mushroom caps. "For Hitler's birthday," he said.

Two texts on Lee's phone. The first from Devi and the next from Jocelyn: *ya me 2 cum oer*

We're at the rest stop with the Starbucks before the last exit now so it's going to be maybe another 30 minutes.

Everyone in the oval excepting Tarz, Abel, and Lee was majoring in physics; Abel had gone for chemistry and Tarz was computer science. Lee was English, which had been a foregone thing for a while. They'd had the grades and the test scores to get into Southgate (no. 23 in the nation), and Lee just had the test scores and a sufficiently depressing admissions essay.

Another text from Jocelyn: *Did you get my last text?*

Jocelyn, pathetically innocent, had been trying to broker a peace between Lee (Palestine) and the Sith Lord Leland Jr. (Israel) for a little under a year now. Lee knew she loved thinking of him as her charity case, had tried to intervene in that nasty e-mail exchange that fucked over Lee's life (his emotional life at least) senior year of high school. She had sent tons of e-mails after that apologizing, calling Leland Jr. "moody" and "very defensive of his mother." Lee tried hard to feel bad for her, but then he remembered she was a thin, rich white woman who had offered him what would very well have been the shittiest stir-my-coffee-and-file-these-papers job of his life. He was about to cut off contact with her and be done with the whole thing. But then he told Tarz about it.

The plan had started as a joke: wouldn't it be funny to see Leland Jr. tripping against his will? Then Tarz pointed out that Jocelyn would make a fine Useful Idiot if they ever wanted to make it happen for real. All they'd have to do was guilt her via e-mail into coming to campus and bringing her angry little husband. And what, Lee wondered. An eyedropper of acid in his coffee? Ground-up mushrooms in his rich-man's kale shake? Something better, Tarz said: a hallucinogenic Shulginesque polymer that he had learned about in some chat room and ordered through the Silk Road. It was supposed to be a modification of a mood stabilizer called teraflin that was being prescribed in trial doses to unlucky bipolar patients across the United States. Tack on a hydroxy chain and the patient could be left hallucinating for weeks. Tarz couldn't figure out how this worked and was within inches of trying the substance himself, but Lee knew that the Sith Lord would be a better guinea pig.

Now, just hours before the Sith Lord's arrival on campus, Lee and Tarz each took a small palmful of fungi and bottoms-upped. Lee texted Devi: *k*.

Tarz, glassy-eyed and smiling, took Lee's right hand in both of his. Another strange fact about Tarz: his nickname came from a wardrobe malfunction he'd experienced in a mandatory physical education class, when a spontaneous fight during a game of dodgeball had resulted in his shirt getting mostly ripped off his body. He seemed to like the name more than Edward Jonathan Phillips—who could blame him?—so it stuck. More facts about Tarz: he wore *Cowboy Bebop* wristbands to partially cover up giant scars on his wrists, and he had some nerve damage in his left hand. But none of that kept him from virtuosic mastery of the Zelda games, Grand Theft Auto, and Metal Gear Solid.

Sooner than he'd expected, Lee's brain experienced a surge of euphoria. The room's colors became oversaturated and those with beards (Abel, Donny) looked bearlike. Lee excused himself, stood up, and took two steps back. There was a chorus of "Where are you going?" which he ignored. He went out, turned right, and walked just a few feet to the door with the whiteboard and pink pom-poms. Devi opened it.

What made Devi desirable (his phone was ringing—it was Jocelyn, he ignored it) was just how far she hadn't come since high school. She had the daisy bras and B-cups of a fifteen-year-old who still read Judy Blume. She straightened her hair mercilessly, just as the popular girls had done at Shaker Heights High, and she wore furry boots in the wintertime. Her taste in movies ran along the lines of Ryan Gosling, Zac Efron, Jake Gyllenhaal. She barely read—she was a prospective biology major and, to Lee's disappointment, could not say with any confidence who Thomas Hardy or E. T. A. Hoffmann were. She was clueless about irony, listened to Maroon 5. Obviously she had done really well at some rural high school somewhere, but now it was clear she had missed the boat. Her glory days were over, and she was all Lee's.

Their encounters always ran like this: drunk/stoned/balls-out tripping Lee pressing sober Devi against the wall and being pleasantly surprised by the anger with which she shoved her tongue in his mouth. Then she would undress him and they would go to her bed. Her face never registered pleasure of any sort, but she had boundless energy, clawing at his chest as she screeched. Now, with his phone ringing again ("Jostle In"), and the oval in the next room and the dorm virtually unoccupied, she was scratching up his body. He imagined what this would be like if she were a boy—a frail, scarecrow-tall, lanky boy with long-fingered hands who sighed like a girl as he worked Lee over.

He finished and she made no attempt to get off him. Seven missed calls. A text from Tarz: *Get back here.*

Now would be the time to stand up, get dressed, cross the hall, and begin undressing again in his room. That would give everyone the unsubtle hint that the party was over. It would be faster and easier than wrapping his tongue around the words "You need to leave." Devi was still on top of him and he was holding her, one hand at her back, one at her ass, as though she were in a front-slung papoose. He had the staticky, hippocampal impression that they were trapped in a snowdrift. She was breathing heavily. The room's palette was set on a higher saturation than it had been when he and Devi had started, if that was even possible, and he had the vivid and rather uncomfortable impression that she was thinking about how fucked up he was, and how fake he was, and how little he deserved her. She was no doubt imagining what a kindness she was doing him, letting him rest her light and tight little body on top of his pale, loose one. He was getting a shitty Pygmalion vibe from the whole thing and gently pushed her off him.

"Were you asleep?" he asked.

She made a face at him, grunted, and got up, going to her vanity.

Always fighting, always bickering, the goddamn chemicals in his brain;

this he was being told by the two doctors he'd been forced to consult after driving his car into a ravine, both of whom seemed to agree that he had bipolar disorder. Watching Devi get dressed sent him racing back through the hypersaturated tunnel of his thoughts to the day when he was all wired shut in the psych ward in Shaker Heights. In the fucking psych ward because he'd totaled his car! With a wristband that claimed he was a sui-cide threat! All because his former best friend Max, himself barely recov-ered from being concussed, had told someone important that Lee was a danger to himself. And Maria had come to visit Lee—Don Timpano wait-ing angrily, no doubt, in his Honda Accord right outside Lee's window—and give him back his sweatshirt with all the Bart Simpson heads and break up with him. There she was standing over him again, small and raven-haired, eyes blank and breath coming quickly.

His jaw, shattered after making contact with his steering wheel, had been wired shut and he'd had to write out what he'd wanted to say to her that day. He'd written—laboriously, with his right hand—something for her about getting better. He'd written: *this won't happen again—it was a fluke.* He hadn't wanted to die so much as he'd suddenly found himself in the process of dying, and if he'd known a way to immediately reverse that process he obviously would've. He'd change now: for her, for Diedre, for Max, for all the other people he loved and who loved him.

"I know," she said, leaning over his face, her hair falling across his cheek. "Remember when we met in the band room?"

He nodded and then winced. *Of course I remember,* he thought.

"I really had no idea who you were."

I knew exactly who you were. I knew it instantly—I saw you and I knew it.

"But right away I liked you—I still like you. You were a source of inspi-ration." She bit her lip. "Which is why I wanted to tell you I'm going to do the philosophy PhD at Princeton."

He wrote something about being proud of her and loving her and knowing she'd always succeed no matter what she did. *I'll just move wher-ever you go. Fuck Southgate.*

"My parents don't want me to see you anymore."

That's their problem.

"I'm really exhausted, Lee."

Of course. Me too.

"I loved you," she said.

Oh fuck. That was past tense, wasn't it? She loved me?

Rethink it oh God Maria please rethink it.

"I loved you so much. But you're an addict and you have to stop doing drugs before you can give any love back. That's basic human psychology. You can't give real love back now."

The fuck? His body ached. (Even today, even remembering it, his body ached.) *Addicted to what?* He suffered hot splinters of pain as he tried to open his jaw.

"You can look me up one day," she said, her mouth shrinking in his vision, her chest shrinking, her body looking sunken and skeletal.

You changed my life.

But no, Maria, see—you completely changed my life.

Maria, if you shrink and go away you know what will happen?

Maria, we will both die if you shrink and go away.

His phone rang again and shook him out of the memory, and he was shocked into a cold sweat. He answered it, watching as Devi reapplied her makeup.

Jocelyn's young Meryl Streep voice: "Lee? I've been trying to reach you for about thirty minutes now."

"I know. I'm sorry." He realized with mounting anxiety that this conversation with Jocelyn was the only thing grounding him in bread-and-butter reality.

"Your brother and I are actually just about to get off the highway at Janesville," Jocelyn said. So we're gonna be maybe another fifteen minutes."

"Okay."

"Leland's had a rough day. He's kind of tired. So we need you to be ready to get a pretty early dinner."

"At like three thirty in the afternoon?"

"More like four thirty." Her tone was sharp and exhausted. She sounded haggard. He understood that it had been an insolent question. He understood this through the kind of sad fog that had prompted him to long, cathartic crying jags as a child.

"Yeah, sure," he said.

"Are you okay? You sound a little preoccupied."

He watched Devi, who was making a show of not watching him. "I'm looking forward to this," he thought he said to Jocelyn.

"Lee? Are you still there?"

He hung up. That was going to make things worse. The last tie to the shores of sanity severed. *Shit, that could've passed as Samuel Taylor Coleridge.* Now he had a very small window of time to recover himself—his superego—before Jocelyn called back. He would start by being honest with this girl-shape that was obviously Devi as a wolf, not a boy. That was her species—he couldn't put his finger on it before.

"I think you're beautiful," he said.

She blinked those alien eyes and snarled her girl-muzzle as if to say, *Go on.*

"I like sleeping with you. I could date you. It would really help me forget about someone else." He shook his head, as if this would refresh the sentence. "I mean—I genuinely want to date you, sorry. But you don't give me many concrete reasons why I should date you. You're not in the reason-giving business, I guess."

This last line was especially Bogartian, and he regretted it, but he also didn't. "As Time Goes By" began to run through his head—he'd seen the movie so many times. He was Rick and she was Ilsa. *Casablanca* with an all-alien cast.

She grunted cheerfully, her face now totally transformed. He couldn't expect a similar declaration of devotion from a wolf—that much should have been obvious. Still, he kept on watching, waiting for one.

"Fuck off, parasite," she said.

His phone rang again and that set the ground pounding at the same rate as his heart. At an impossible-to-sustain rate. He left the room.

He was in the hallway, on the wrong side of it. He had, he felt, exactly the same distance to cross as Hannibal had when he first surveyed the Alps on his Gallic campaign. The ground shifted and surged in a way that would have been pleasant had he not had to walk across it. A door opened down the hall and out popped Tarz's head. His face was extremely sad. Cartoonishly so. It was clear he had really wanted to be with Lee for the entire time they were tripping, to sit side by side and talk about their sense impressions. He had wanted it to be their little secret: Them v. World.

"I'm a bit ineebs," Tarz called to him. "What about you?"

Lee made a noise of assent. He looked at the ground.

"Your phone's ringing," Tarz said.

"Yeah."

"Do you want me to get it?"

Lee realized Tarz was approaching him and next thing he knew Tarz had answered the phone and was carrying on what appeared to be a lucid conversation with Jocelyn. Lee watched the ground rise and fall in a way that would've bewildered Hannibal's elephants.

"They're basically here," Tarz said, handing him his phone back. "They're in Janesville." When Lee said nothing, Tarz grinned and assumed a secretarial tone. "I'm sorry, ma'am. Your son can't come to the phone right now. He's tripping balls. Yes, most unfortunate. Thanks for calling and have a great day!"

"Why are you not getting any of this?" Lee asked.

"Any of what?"

"Is like the ground moving up and down." He'd forgotten how to properly inflect a question.

"Yeah. It usually does."

"Is anyone any kind of animal or interspecies being."

Tarz let out a belly laugh that lasted too long for Lee's liking. "This is like your second time doing this. Just calm down. It gets better."

Lee could feel himself metabolizing the drug. It was as though he'd swallowed a radioactive paste—the kind whose phosphorescent progress he could just as easily trace with his mind as with an X-ray machine. Tarz was hyperaware that Lee had done this only once before and that it'd had no effect on him: either he'd metabolized the psilocybin too quickly (*was that even a thing?*) or Max had gotten bad shrooms or they'd taken too little and because of that Lee thought he could handle it today, of all days. But now Tarz seemed worried.

"I'm not her son," Lee said.

Tarz, who had been staring intently down the hallway, turned to face him. "What?"

"I'm her half brother-in-law."

"Does that make me her fourth niece twice removed?" He paused, seeming to give it serious consideration. "Because you and I are nieces-in-law, right?"

"Fuck."

"What?"

"They're coming soon. I have to get dressed. Get those guys out of my room."

Tarz did as he was told. Lee crossed the hallway using the surge of adrenaline his awful realization had prompted. The oval stood and dispersed, Tarz bidding them good afternoon as he ushered them out.

"Want me to sit on this bed and tell you a few things about the real world?" Tarz asked.

Lee nodded. He got corduroys and a button-down shirt from his bottom dresser drawer. He noticed that Tarz was messing with iTunes on a laptop that was probably Lee's. Norman Greenbaum's "Spirit in the Sky" began playing, an embarrassing favorite of theirs. This was a good and old song. The happiness they felt about this song was genuine, earnest, unironic, and Lee repeated this to himself in his head. It made him sad to think there were so few feelings like this.

He locked himself in the bathroom and began to change. There was no time to shower. As he changed, he listened to Tarz's voice. It was talking about how they both had parents:

". . . moms and dads, and as far as I can tell they all love us a lot. That can be a pain in the ass, but it's also pretty nice at times. There's at least two people who guaranteed have to love you and two who guaranteed have to love me."

Lee felt something on his face that he suspected was a tear. He touched his cheek and confirmed his suspicion. Sweet Greenbaumish Tarzan understood so little about Lee's life, his father.

"And of course I love you, and of course I need not specify it's not a romantic love, but I love you very deeply and care about your future and I don't wish any car accidents or personal tragedies on you."

"That's sweet of you," Lee said. The bathroom was getting smaller. He was crying while brushing his teeth. The song started again.

"There will always be a part of your brain that knows where it is, which is earth, and knows who you are, which is Lee. And that part of your brain can't ever die, because it's pretty much linked up with your soul."

Lee thought of the pineal gland, which he'd recently learned used to be the Cartesian site of the soul. His pineal gland was on fire right now. Thinking about it made it hurt. The room beat with his heart and breathed with his lungs. It would have been nice to vomit, but he'd never felt less nauseated in his life.

"What part of my brain can't ever die?" he called out to Tarz.

"The one that's linked up with your soul," he heard from outside. He grabbed the edges of the sink and shook his head, still crying. He raised his eyes to the mirror but saw nothing.

"Tarz!" he called.

Tarz entered. "What's up?"

"Look in the mirror," Lee said, his hand trembling and spindly looking, a Dickensian villain's.

Tarz looked in the mirror and then looked back at Lee. "It's you."

Lee looked again and there he was: giant-eyed, gray-faced, crying with relief. There were his fake front teeth, both bright white porcelain, hollow when he tapped them. He laughed. That had actually been pretty funny.

Tarz ushered him out and they sat on the bed. The song was still playing. This made Lee feel better. As a matter of fact, this made Lee feel great, almost sober (or at least baseline—because he'd never really be sober again, he knew that much). Tarz produced a little baggie full of black powder.

"That's what it looks like?" Lee asked.

"Yeah. They didn't have any pictures of it online." Tarz shook the baggie and they both watched the powder jump.

"What does EDM stand for?"

Tarz shrugged. "No one knows, at least not on the forums. Electro-something, I think."

Lee pocketed the baggie.

They walked together to the student union, which was in a building called Cowling. Tarz was half skipping and focused not at all on their present task, saying instead how excited he was about having a black president, how appealing his politics of hope were. As a southern boy he'd caught a lot of flak around the water fountain for his infatuation with Obama bin Laden (his school was Republican, his bullies were conservative). Fuck you and your Muslim sympathies, and so on. Lee listened obediently. He wondered if he looked more like his mother than he usually did. She looked a little like Marlene Dietrich, who had the perfect face for an O RLY? image macro, the kind you used to see a lot of on Reddit. Marlene Dietrich, like his mother, gave zero fucks. But then Diedre had been born without fucks to give. Jocelyn, by contrast, had the kind of face that was all fucks-giving, like *Oh yes thnx I am everso pleased to be at ur everso deliteful dinner party lol*. And Leland Jr. just basically had Lee's same face, just on the body of a Sith Lord. Lee was so impressed by how real the faces of Jocelyn and Leland Jr. looked in his imagination that he was shocked to realize he was now, in fact, looking at Jocelyn and Leland Jr. themselves.

Tarz introduced himself as "Lee's best friend" and made some small talk with Jocelyn. Lee locked eyes with Leland Jr. and did something he hoped looked like a smirk. Leland Jr., his face receding down a dark tunnel, his eyebrows like a badger's, crossed his arms and didn't move. Lee imagined him holding this pose in a coffin: he imagined his eyes still open in mad little scalene triangles. *Serves you right, motherfucker*, he thought. *You don't just steal from a kid.*

Then Tarz was gone and it was just Jocelyn and Leland Jr., who was rubbing his scalene triangles with his thumb and forefinger.

"Leland's really tired," Jocelyn said to Lee, nervous-smiling. "He was up early this morning. And you know how much he works."

Lee nodded. Her words had an evanescent echo.

Jocelyn started fishing around in her purse. She pulled out a piece of paper on which she'd written something. She held it up, considering it, and beatific rays of light shot out from it.

"Have you heard of Toscana?" she asked.

"Yeah, of course," Lee said.

"Okay, so you wouldn't mind eating there?"

"It's the only decent-looking place around here," Leland Jr. said in a weird baritone.

"You're looking really nice," Jocelyn said to Lee. "You clean up well, my friend."

They got in the car and Lee realized that the trip had only just begun, that the shrooms were clearly stepped on. Jocelyn was asking him quaint things from the front seat. Stuff like "How was your trimester?" "What classes did you take?"

Leland Jr.'s eyes were in the rearview mirror. "So you're going back home this week?" He asked this as if it was a reasonable thing for the two of them to talk about.

"Yeah," Lee said, meeting his stare. "They don't close the dorms down officially until Wednesday. Midterms just ended I think on Sunday. So we have like today to kind of get stuff together. Get stuff arranged for departure."

This was a longer answer than Lee had intended to give. He watched Leland Jr. react to it. "Do you talk to your mom a lot during the school year?"

"Yeah. I mean she calls every so often."

"Hm."

"Oh, that's good," Jocelyn said.

Leland Jr. did a hard sniff and then said, "Yeah, it is.".

"She's still at OfficeMax," Lee said.

"Really?" Jocelyn said, leaning over until Lee saw her eyes in the rear-view mirror with Leland Jr.'s.

Leland Jr.'s eyes narrowed. "Why?"

"She likes it there." This conversation really should've been harder to have, but on drugs it felt just like straight-up autobiography. "I mean, she's really well liked there. She's working really hard, and it's really paying off for everyone. It shows in how she talks, too. I can pretty much hear her smiling over the phone."

There was a silence, and he knew he'd given a problematic answer. Up until now he'd been doing a brilliant mimic of a sober person. "Well, yeah, the phone smile is immaterial," he said, unable to stop. "I guess it's really the work that's what matters."

This was the Fat Man of sentences. The car was funeral-silent. Then Jocelyn said: "Are you doing better? You seemed pretty freaked out when I talked to you earlier today."

Then it made sense. Leland Jr.'s gaze. Had been at his pupils. He was suspicious. He was doing some detective work. Of course he was. That e-mail, those heritable assets, were sitting all dense and petty in the air between them.

"Oh yeah," Lee said. "Sorry. That was just a really bad connection."

At Toscana they went around the table submitting their orders to a Boswellian waiter with no chin and big eyebrows. Lee was no longer capable of the high-level paranoia that would have convinced him the waiter wanted to administer a drug test. He just smiled at everyone. *Something great is going to happen*, he kept thinking. The setting and the people in Toscana couldn't have been more perfect. It felt like an exclusive club with its dim lights and red velvet drapes, and Jocelyn and Leland Jr. looked like a viscountess and her creepy viscount after a long day of hunting. The whole thing was very lush and restrained, very bourgeois-European. He felt like he was in *Rules of the Game*, a movie he'd once watched with

Diedre on VHS when, one year, there had been nothing else to do on Christmas Eve. He had the idea to text Tarz about it even though Tarz would never get the reference. Well, but this was older than *Rules of the Game*, this was like Tolstoy territory. He took out his phone and discovered he had three Tarz-texts awaiting him:

fuuuckkk amazing visuals

so, in conclusion, all is dank and to all a good night

y/n: I will either go to Heaven soon or prob hell?

Lee texted back: *heaven*. Then, before he knew what he meant: *ur heaven*.

Here we go. This was going to start off blunt. He turned to Jocelyn, resisted the urge to take her hand in his and kiss it, and said, like Karenin pretending to be a passionate Frenchman: "I hope my brother realizes what a privilege it is to be married to you."

Jocelyn put a hand to her blanched bosom.

"I'm not your brother," blurted Leland Jr., stroking the demonic beard he'd just sprouted.

Lee leaned forward. He recalled one of Tarz's mantras: *Life is a series of minibosses and death is the final boss.*

"Death is the final boss," Lee quipped, and laughed.

Jocelyn did her best to laugh along. Leland Jr. remained in a stormy humor, stroking his beard, his fist around a diamond cane.

"I'm sorry—I must've read that somewhere," Lee demurred. "Or made it up entirely. I don't remember. 'That person that I was— / And this One— do not feel the same / Could it be Madness—this?' "

"Oh!" exclaimed Jocelyn-as-viscountess. "Dickinson?"

"The very same." Lee felt for the baggie in his left pocket. "Not impressed?" he asked Leland Jr., who leaned forward and glowered across the table. "Am I a thorn in your foot, brother? Is Diedre a thorn in your foot? Is Dad a thorn in your foot?" Leland Jr.'s face hardened. "You've got a thorny foot, bro."

Leland Jr. breathed in deeply, as he'd likely been instructed to do in whatever anger management seminar Jocelyn probably had him taking.

"Are you angry about Dad throwing himself off a roof and loving me more?" Lee politely inquired.

Leland Jr. turned with a neck-snapping motion to his wife and gestured at Lee. The viscountess continued to clutch her pale bosom.

"I've about had it with your fucking antics," Leland Jr. hiss-whispered. "You are not my brother, and I owe you nothing."

"What?" Lee made like he was hard of hearing.

"He stole my life to build yours, you ungrateful twat. And everything he tried to give you was gonna get snorted up your nose, anyway. Everything in that sad little house of yours. Like father, like son."

"Okay, Leland—" Jocelyn started to say. "Not right now. Not like this."

"No, no!" protested Lee, the very picture of equanimity. "Do go on, Leland. I'm curious to hear!"

"Why the fuck are you talking like that?" the viscount asked, rudely breaking the fourth wall. Lee ignored it, maintaining his own gentlemanly composure as the light in the room pulsed in his peripheral vision.

"Stop swearing," Jocelyn said.

"I'm doing it quietly!"

Scandal, Lee thought.

"I have no interest in using my mother's money to fund your drug problem. It's a miracle you made it to college, Lee."

"I'm flattered!"

Leland Jr. tried to physically brush this sentence off like one would a gnat, rapidly adjusting the front of his still-buttoned waistcoat. "But you're going to piss this away if you're anything like your father, and I'm going to do you a favor by not being a party to it."

"For Christ's sake," Jocelyn exclaimed, a distressed and delicate hand across her pale brow.

"I'll pay you a thousand dollars to never speak to me or my wife again," he said. "I think that offer's more than generous, considering what your father owed me."

Jocelyn was gesturing nervously in the direction of the waiter. "Please," Lee said, his hand on her forearm. "There's nothing to worry about."

She looked at him a little confused but still smiling. "I was just hoping we could at least get some bread."

The viscount was staring darkly at Lee. If he was a miniboss, then he was a huge miniboss. Lee extended his hand and they shook. "So it's agreed. One thousand dollars for you to stick your pretentious, bitter, ego-swelled head directly up your ass." Lee smiled and folded his napkin jauntily in his lap.

Leland Jr. wrested his limp hand away as though he'd touched a furnace and looked incredulously at Jocelyn, who said, head bowed, "I heard it."

"Unbelievable," he said to Lee. "You can't hold it together for one dinner. We're treating you, and you can't even keep your shit together!"

"That more than makes up for everything you took from me, brother! And if I didn't know better, I'd say you're actually enjoying our little back-and-forth here."

"That's it!" Leland balled up his napkin and left the table, and Jocelyn (now more baroness than viscountess) gave Lee an apologetic but angry glance and followed her husband.

Happily, the food arrived before the viscount and viscountess did. Happily still, Lee mixed the EDM into the viscount's fettuccine, praying that Tarz had been right about it not tasting like anything. With the surety that comes with the successful commission of a wholly justified crime, Lee texted Tarz the following three texts:

the ants r in the soup

no visuals for me just nine centurion Europe

*ninteenth century Europe fuckin autocorrect

Seconds later, Tarz texted back: *did u mean "you're heaven" or "your heaven"*

The viscount and viscountess returned to the table, the viscount in a determined huff. He withdrew his checkbook from his snakeskin purse and then gestured, palm open, to his now blushing wife for a pen, which she provided. Lee smiled at her, but even his charm was insufficient to calm her vaporous anxiety. The viscount scribbled a check, tore it off, and thrust it in Lee's direction.

"One grand, you cretin," he said.

Lee didn't take it, just smiled.

"Of course," Leland Jr. huffed in a tone of hypothesis-confirmation.

"What?" Jocelyn queried.

"He's high! Look at him!" He pointed to Lee's pupils.

"I took mushrooms," Lee confirmed.

"Jocelyn!" Leland Jr. roared. "Is this proving my point? Have I proven my fucking point?"

"Let's just eat," Jocelyn said.

And they did, Lee watching in pleasure as Leland Jr. slurped his meal. "You," he snorted through his wet, noodled mouth. "You little shit. You couldn't even show up sober to your own arraignment if you had one."

Lee tossed up his hands. "I plead not guilty, Your Honor!"

"This isn't an arraignment," Jocelyn said, evidently near tears. "This was supposed to be an opportunity to make peace."

Leland Jr. turned to her on his elbow, smiling for the first time since the evening had begun. "You thought it could all be solved over dinner, didn't you?"

"That's never what I said."

"You assumed we'd hug and make nice?"

"I never said that, Leland! Keep your voice down."

"This is who I'm dealing with, Jocelyn." He flung a broad hand in Lee's direction. "This is my 'family.' Do you understand?"

"Has he proven it to you, my leggy baroness?" Lee said, whatever filter he'd had completely vanished. "Or will he prove it to you later tonight?" He made a soft thrusting motion, smiling at the horrified viscountess. He was feeling more pleasant than he had in a long while, his eyes departing from her gaze and lolling across the beige-white tablecloth, fixing pleasantly on the bread basket: the bread, its shape, its flakes, its ridges.

Lee was instructed to wait in the restaurant's foyer while the royalty took their leave. He dug his hands in the pockets of his corduroys and smiled. "I can't say it's been a delight," he said, waving the check instead of his hand.

"Neither can I," Leland Jr. shouted back, hurrying his wife to their SUV. "This is the last we'll be seeing of each other, ever. I'll take out a restraining order if I need to."

Lee watched them drive off, sated. He withdrew his phone and texted Tarz:

mission accomplished

I now have the means to woo Baroness Maria von Timpano

Tarz: *wtf*

I'm rich, Lee keyed in, *so im getting Maria back.*

TARZAN/TWEETY/NEW PERSON
(EDWARD JONATHAN PHILLIPS)
(1990–)

2007–2008
Mississippi

Edward Jonathan Phillips was spending the morning slumped over the screen of the Hackintosh he'd recently built, darkening once again the e-door of a Reddit Ask Me Anything whose URL he could've typed from memory. The AMA read: "I am a gay man who was married to a straight woman for twenty-eight years. Ask me anything." The question Edward Jonathan Phillips wanted to ask was: "Did you ever play house with your male friends in grade school and suggest that you be the mom and/or that there be two moms?" But the question didn't seem relevant to the AMA and asking something that personal would, he was sure, humiliate him unspeakably.

Edward Jonathan Phillips (Fucken Eddie to his enemies, EJP to friends) had the unique daily pleasure of being exactly like himself. Whereas someone more normal could probably go to high school in Braxton, Mississippi, and float by relatively unnoticed, any under-the-radar deformities (big teeth, Judaism, lack of a gun license, liberal parents, fascination with Satan) earning him at most a nickname and some light ostracism, there was something about EJP's battleship board that was embarrassingly conspicuous. Today, December 15, was the day Joey Gipson had very solemnly warned him not to come to gym class, but EJP had to go to school and he had to show his face at every period because last week he'd been truant for the last time he could be before the school district (and then his parents) would have to get involved.

It was five forty-three in the morning, which was a good time for it to be. He began pulling on a few strands in the gray patch of hair just above his right ear. He was starting to gray on his left side, too, and he'd overheard his mother asking his father—who was Alexander to everyone but EJP's mother, who called him Father—about it one night while EJP was walking stoned past their bedroom to the bathroom on the other side of the hall. It wasn't really a time to eavesdrop (he had messy, load-blown hands, the fingers of which he couldn't really feel because of the rare California medical in his bloodstream), but his mother was saying, "Maybe we should move," to which Alexander said in response, "I think the hair's genetic. There's no way he's graying from school." And then his mother hiss-whispered, "Of course he is! You're not even gray now." "But," said Alexander, "my dad was completely gray by the time he was forty. That's pretty unusual."

Now EJP's strategy was to just try and pull the gray hairs out before they became too noticeable. But he couldn't do it fast enough. Andy Stockton had started calling him Snowbird, and EJP was unsure of the meaning of this insult until Dennis Delpiere accused him of loving to eat snow. "Don't eat the yellow snow," Dennis told him one day at lunch. "You'll get the clap, Snowbird." It could've been his imagination, but the gray hairs came out a little more easily than the other ones. He'd had ample time to do a study of this. Time needed for removal of six gray hairs=time needed for removal of two normal hairs.

The first question on the AMA was the most obvious one: "Why did you stay with her for so long if you are not physically attracted to women?" The answer began: "She was my best friend since childhood and I thought I could change my—" EJP stood up and walked to the other side of the room. He checked to make sure the crack at the bottom of the door had been sealed (it had been since last night, with a beach towel) and then went to his closet and got the pipe he'd made out of his broken N64 controller. He packed the bowl where the joystick should've been with some gummy mids he kept in his desktop drawer. Then he did a long hit while reading the rest of the answer: "—orientation because I knew that no one I loved would understand or approve of who I really was. Ironically, I think my wife was the only person who was able to accept that I was gay. You have to keep in mind that I'm talking about Alabama in 1979; we live in a world that's a lot more progressive than it was back then."

Before taking his second hit, EJP looked up at the disabled smoke detector on his ceiling. He scrolled back up to the top of the AMA and reread the first question and the response. He didn't want to scroll down in case a troll had ruined the thread by linking to photos of a horse's dick or something. But the second question seemed legitimate, and so did the third, even though it dissolved into a tangential thread about marriage licenses in Vermont. Maybe this Addled_Astrolabe dude once had a shot at stopping it. As in maybe his wife knew and cared enough to help him, and that was how she loved him. This woman is a hero. There should be a whole forum for her: r/thiswoman.

He took another hit and tilted his chair back as far as it would go. He tried to think of another question for Addled_Astrolabe. This one would have to be on the nose. "Is this something you thought would actually work?" What was the "something"? The question sounded accusatory, which was exactly how he didn't want it to sound. "Did you think you could change your sexuality by marrying her?" Sexuality is fluid. He'd seen those words on the Internet somewhere and in that combination they'd produced a weird reaction in him, like the sudden addition of warm water to a cold bath. "Would you actually recommend doing this?" To who? Another hiccup; it was getting to the point where grammar errors produced system-wide stutters if he was high enough, as if English were as finicky as Java and wouldn't give him results unless he thought in it correctly. To whom? Who was asking for the recommendation? He stared hard at the Eye and could almost see a heavy, wrinkled lid, a furrowed eyebrow. A saggy nexus of Old Testament judgment: Who wants to know?

Link wants to know.

One of his favorite Ocarina glitches was something the Internet had nicknamed Crooked Cartridge. Performing it was potentially damaging to the entire system, but it was worth it. What you did was you made Link run around the Kokiri Forest while you simultaneously lifted the left side of the game cartridge out of the console—slowly, slowly—until Link either glitched out or disappeared altogether. If he wasn't invisible, the new Link was a fibrous bundle of color or an anamorphic outline or half-bodied— and he could run through anything: people, fences, rocks, trees. EJP had this theory about himself that his cartridge had been fucked with at birth, and that was why he was the way he was. This was at face value a bad thing, because an error in the code was an error in the code. But if he could be more like Link, it could be a good thing.

And this morning he was thinking he could've actually proven it if his mother hadn't called him downstairs. It was six thirty. Time was not on his side. The little situation in the N64 pipe was not cashed. He blew off the smoke and put the whole thing in a shoe box and put the shoe box under his bed. Then he shouted down to her that he was coming and Visined his eyes in the bathroom. He thought for a moment he could smell what he and his mother were going to cook. She would say "waffles, eggs, and peanut butter toast" as soon as he entered the kitchen.

"Eggs and bacon, sweetie," his mother said, looking hard at his eyes. "Start on the toast."

He felt like he was looking through Vaseline, which was kind of funny, but he resisted making the joke to his mom. He put the bread in the toaster and thought, *I'm sorry, Mom.* Her back was to him and saying something like *What the fuck is wrong with you?* in response. The idea of his mom saying "fuck" was too funny to him. She was working diligently on the bacon. She had an unpleasant day ahead of her, he knew: she had to go pay Grandma Alice a visit, which meant reading the newspaper aloud to herself for a few hours while listening to Grandma Alice's ventilator.

"What're you laughing about?" she said, turning around. She said it like she used to say it when she tickled him as a child. She hadn't used this tone of voice with him for a while—probably because she was afraid she'd embarrass him—and now that she finally had, it made his stomach drop. He and his mother would never again be in a situation where she was tickling him; instead she would only sound like she was tickling him and he would have to remember the feeling of being tickled. He swallowed, and the sobering reality of the day came into focus: Joey Gipson, gym class, his truancies, the fact that Addled_Astrolabe was born gay, the uselessness of his high, how quickly they'd eat breakfast.

"Nothing," he said.

In the car on the way to the high school Alexander said: "Your mother thinks someone's bothering you at school." He said it quickly, as if it were the last item on a meeting agenda.

"Nothing's happening."

"I didn't think anything was. Boys will be boys, right?"

EJP nodded: "Right." *Boys will be boys* was Alexander's way of acknowledging the bus incident. During the bus incident, EJP had gotten punched twice in the stomach, hard enough for some bile to come up, and then Dennis Delpiere had held a pencil across EJP's throat while David Olson, a bit player who was trying to cozy up to Joey Gipson, had written the word "faggot" in black Sharpie across EJP's forehead. It hadn't taken long. They'd done it in the back of the bus, between cul-de-sacs in a subdivision, and EJP had stayed quiet as instructed. The bus driver pled innocent and EJP's mother refused to let him back on the bus until "reforms were made." (The word "reform" didn't exist in Braxton High's data set.) EJP stayed home from school the next day, his thrice-scrubbed forehead still ghostily projecting "faggot" in every mirror. The principal was the one who'd told Alexander that boys will be boys, "especially on the bus."

"Maybe we'll get you back on that bus soon," Alexander said. Then he reached across EJP to open the passenger door and EJP stared at the front steps. "Thanks," he said, and got out. He stepped into the school's intake valve and was swallowed by the building's Soviet-era interior. He stood there a few seconds holding the shoulder straps of his backpack. Kids were going to their lockers, eating muffins wrapped in napkins, taping posters to walls. Abe Verdega, who walked with a limp and always smelled a little like gasoline because his dad owned the Quick Pump, was getting head-smacked by some biggish male tormentor unknown to EJP. Julie Cosworth, who sometimes spoke to herself and wore long dresses, was looking in a mirror stuck to the inside of her locker. *Them and not me*, thought EJP. *I can be invisible.*

He walked down the hall to his locker. There were no notes stuck to it telling him to go fuck himself. The janitor had scrubbed off the very real-looking, very hairy dick Dennis Delpiere had drawn on there last week. Inside, nothing had been disturbed: not his Portal poster, not the potted cactus his mother had given him. He thought hard about it: he was at the very least still a little high, and if he wasn't a little high, he was stoned. This was a good way to feel, morning-stoned. This was as good as he could feel in a hallway of Braxton High. Then there was a flash of the Thought, and his brain's electricity went momentarily haywire. He silenced it. *Better today's problem be*—hiccup—*It's better if today's problem is the Thought and not Joey Gipson.* He closed his eyes and hung his head in the safe metal module of his locker. *Today's problem is not Joey Gipson.*

He would see Gipson, Stockton, and Delpiere during gym, which was fifth period. First period was biology, which was too easy to waste time doing the homework (C-minus), and then calculus, where he at least did the homework because it would've been embarrassing not to (A). Nothing happened in either class. Well, he was blinking too slowly in biology and got called a burnout by Denise Earlwick, but no one cared about her opinion. People were already organizing Senior Spirit Week, he realized as he walked under banners that read SENIORS '08 CELEBRATE! It was weird to think that the group "Seniors '08" also included himself, Abe Verdega, and Julie Cosworth. They, too, were technically being encouraged to "celebrate." Another occurrence of the Thought. Another.

Here were two questions he didn't think Addled_Astrolabe would've been too thrilled to see asked: "Do you/did you hate gay people?" and "Do you/did you hate your own thoughts?" These were both true enough of EJP, glitching through the hallways of Braxton High on September 17. He really did dislike the idea of a man sleeping with another man, though he would never hold it against Addled_Astrolabe for being born like that. Many people would, though: Grandma Alice always used to call homosexuals "them" and "unnatural." It was an unpleasant, even dangerous, way to be born. EJP pitied gay people the same way he pitied anyone born with a disability: the world wasn't made for them. It seemed unfair that the world was made for other people and not for them.

As far as high school was concerned, there were correct ways to be born and incorrect/deformed ways to be born. And without question the worst and most disgusting deformity was gayness: regardless of your skin color, your weight, or the size of your house, it was an absolute nightmare to be born gay, because it had to do with nothing but your own perversity. Which was why EJP always deleted his browser history and hated the Thought and pitied gay people but didn't—because he couldn't? because he was too weak?—hold it against them.

Third period was English, where he functioned as the class dictionary (*import class: dictionary* was a joke he sometimes made to himself as he walked in the room), and where they were halfway through a book he hadn't started. Third period was prime fuel for the Thought, because in the absence of a seating arrangement he found himself always sitting behind

Chris Finn and Eliza Strobeck, who sat next to each other. The two of them made this period the worst of the day—worse than history and gym, worse than the bus rides home used to be—and yet every day he forgot about it and went home thinking the Thought was manageable, and had to be reminded again the next morning that it wasn't. *This day's only problem cannot be the Thought.* In a more just world, he'd be able to sit through third period with a blunt smoldering between his lips, blissfully thinking no thoughts at all.

Here is how the Thought began: Chris Finn and Eliza Strobeck were the exceptions to every social rule. They were not popular and they were not unpopular. Chris ran track and was in mostly AP classes except for science and calculus. He was black and had a double-peaked upper lip and was maybe five inches taller than EJP. He always wore his varsity jacket, which fit him perfectly. Eliza was in all APs except for government and she did drama, though not in a high-profile way (she was usually given the female supporting role, but once or twice [*Guys and Dolls, Oklahoma!*] had managed to steal the show). She was white and about EJP's height, with rosy cheeks and good, but not great, taste in clothes. The two had probably met in class—nobody really talked about where they met. But that was exactly the thing: nobody talked about them. They had been dating for a year and were very public about it and had no major social support network and thus no specific roles to fill—not the Tough Black Kid, not the Hot White Girl. They were a sovereign country. They kissed in the hallway. They held hands. He drove her to school. What was it about them that set them free? EJP had a theory: it was love. A glitch can't be in love, but a glitch can recognize it from miles off.

Late last year was the first time EJP noticed how they looked when they kissed. When they were both sitting, Chris sort of cupped her head in his hand and pulled her to him and she leaned in, smiling, and then met his mouth with hers in a two-halves-of-a-whole way. Sometimes when they were walking in the hall she'd skip in front of him and pull on the open flaps of his varsity jacket and his head would droop a little so he could kiss her. EJP's favorite was when he stumbled in on them after they'd already started making out, which happened most frequently in English before the bell rang to start third period. It usually took a few seconds for them to realize he was in the room, but when they did they pulled apart and waved at him. He wasn't used to the feeling of waving back, but he enjoyed it.

After a few months of watching them kiss, it occurred to him that it must feel a certain way to be receiving that kiss. He thought about how it must feel for Chris to be kissing Eliza, and then he wondered how it would feel for Chris to be kissing anyone he loved. He'd probably get hard. Chris, who had a handsome profile, who had a very strong jaw across which there was already a dark swatch of stubble, would get hard and kiss more with his tongue, would go deeper into her mouth, would pull her head closer, would pull EJP's head as close as possible.

That was the first occurrence of the Thought, and in the following months there were more: Chris is about to have sex and he's standing over a bed on which someone is lying prone and hairless and it turns out that person is EJP. Chris is running track and there's EJP sitting in the bleachers in a miniskirt and a skintight sweater, cheering Chris on. Then they kiss under the bleachers. Then they both undress and Chris touches the palm of his hand to EJP's bare stomach. The shitty, shitty fucking Thought. The Thought that was ruining him, making him spend so much time on Reddit, making him avoid conversation with his mother and Alexander. He tried to find small ways to keep himself from thinking the Thought, but they were almost as bad as the Thought itself. Once he bought a shirt with a pink-and-white unicorn on it and wore it under the Sewanee hoodie his mother had given him. That kept the Thought at bay, but not for long. Another time he'd stolen a black dress from the back of his mother's closet and worn it in his room while getting high and playing Donkey Kong. The thought hadn't revisited him for three days after that, and his mother never missed the dress. Another time he'd gone into a wig store and in the back tried on a girl's blond wig with bangs and a bow above the right ear. That worked wonders for keeping the Thought away.

The worst occurrence of the Thought had been on a night not so long ago: he'd imagined Chris and Eliza kissing in front of the lockers and then tried not to let his brain swerve. But that was giving him blue balls so brutal he thought he'd maybe die, so he allowed himself for the sake of his own health to imagine Chris was kissing him. And then before he knew it, Chris opened his eyes during this particular kiss and pulled back and said: "I love you, Eddie."

Most of the time all his thoughts re: the Thought were focused on its disgusting nature, but in his more private, stoned moments, he was embarrassed and a little infuriated that it was for Eliza and not him that Chris was a human being. A human being with things he loved and hated, a human being who changed his underwear and probably felt nervous about some track meets and excited about others, and who'd probably had Eliza over to meet his parents more than once. He and Eliza had certainly talked about what colleges they'd apply to and whether they'd get married before or after they graduated. But to EJP he was just a pair of lips and a washboard stomach and the Goddamn Thought and nothing else. Not a human being, and especially not a human being who would ever come close to loving him.

Pathetic motherfucking glitch.

He had fourth-period lunch, which was too early to be hungry, so he went to the bathroom and ate half the bologna sandwich his mother had made him and listened to Abe Verdega whimpering in the next stall, as he often did. It was a postcrying whimper, the worst kind. EJP pounded on the wall of the stall. The whimpering quieted and Verdega's feet left the floor.

If it was true of the Metal Gear Solid games, then it was true of the world as well: your enemies know you better than your friends. He imagined his grandma Alice, breathing through her ventilator in the hospice in Mendenhall, finding out that EJP had thought the Thought. She'd be horrified; it'd probably hasten her death by a few months. But more important, she'd be surprised that EJP was capable of such a thought. Gipson wouldn't. Gipson had grown up with him, had been watching him on the playground since 1996, could anticipate everything about him. Gipson was an undefeatable boss because any attempt on his life amounted to an attempt on EJP's own. He was a plague of locusts, Omega Pirate played on hard, the lung cancer that was killing Grandma Alice.

The bell to end fourth period rang and EJP walked in a zombified shuffle to the locker room. When the doors were in sight, he Z-focused on them. He opened them, was met with a burst of pressurized mold, and walked in. He could already hear Delpiere's voice coming from somewhere in the maze of lockers ahead of him, whispering and then laughing. He passed through the cluster of B-list lockers. All eyes were on him: a conspicuous irregularity.

"Excited for the showers, Phillips?" someone said.

Anything would be better than this. He was an idiot for not staying home today. If he'd been suspended for ditching, if both his parents had never spoken to him again, it would be better than this.

He began worrying the combination on his locker. His hands were shaking. He had a minute until the fifth-period bell rang. He could feel Gipson behind him. Gipson's hand, large and veiny, flat against the lockers, suddenly right next to EJP's face.

"Phillips," Gipson said.

EJP turned around.

"Are you worried about being late?" He was tall, big shouldered, with hair that he'd let grow a little long since quitting football. He smiled. "Andy and Dennis are in coach's office bullshitting about why we're running late. So feel free to take your time."

EJP suddenly started talking even though he didn't want to. The locker room had emptied of everyone except the two of them, and the lack of a noise cushion made his voice sound desperate and prepubescent. "I had to come in because I'm going to get suspended if I don't—" The bell rang. Joey Gipson stroked his chin and nodded. "I mean, I had to be here," EJP said.

"Right."

"I'm saying because you told me not to be here, but I had no choice. Like seriously, I had no choice."

"Uh-huh. Rock and a hard place."

"I'm not gay," he blurted. It was like a dagger to the stomach to put the words "I" and "gay" together in a sentence, even if it was that one. "You think I am, but I'm not. I swear I'm not. I hate gay people."

Those words didn't do good things to Gipson's face. His mouth got hard and tense. His eyes got wide. "I thought we were going to have a real conversation here. But apparently you don't want to."

"I'm sorry."

Gipson put his face close to his. "Fuck you."

Not knowing what else to do, EJP nodded.

"I told you not to come in today and you did."

And then he punched EJP in the stomach so hard he crumpled immediately. Joey Gipson kneeled across his chest and punched him one-two-three, bloodying his mouth. His mind went blank with pain, but he tried to hold his tongue back so he wouldn't bite it off. Gipson stood up and kicked him one-two-three in the ribs and then one-two-three in the back when he rolled over. Then EJP heard panting and it stopped: he didn't look up. He pressed his face to the ground. Gipson was gone.

For a while, EJP lay on his side and explored with his traumatized tongue the gap where his left front tooth had been. The tooth had skidded across the floor to the middle of another locker bay. It killed him to stand up and get it, but he knew he needed to, and he did. He put it in his pocket and winced and began to cry. *The motherfucking glitch is crying.*

There was blood down the front of his shirt and on the floor. Gingerly, he changed into his gym shirt and shorts and held his old shirt in his mouth to stanch the blood. No bones were broken as far as he could tell. He had to go home. He had to walk home. He tried to shoulder his backpack, but the pain made him dizzy. His idiot brain reminded him that Chris Finn would never be there to help him back up.

"Shut the fuck up!" he screamed. The locker room was eye-of-the-storm quiet. Maybe Coach Arnold was seconds away from running in and finding out about what happened. Then Joey would get detention, blame EJP, and the horrible cycle would continue.

He limped out of the locker room, gasping at the pain, dragging his backpack. He'd forgotten how eerie the hallways were during class periods—even more unpleasant to be in than they were when crowded with people. He heaved himself through the fire exit next to the locker rooms, a loud buzzing sounding behind him.

He was running across the lawn with the mad stagger of an escaped convict. Miraculously, no one came after him. He'd either get a month of Saturday detentions or be suspended. His vision narrowed from the pain. The more adrenaline he could conjure, the faster his broken body could move. He was getting close to losing all the blood his front tooth-space had to lose. He broke into the most excruciating jog of his life. The few cars rumbling around Braxton at one twenty slowed, but none of them stopped for him. They must have been scared. He was, too. His brain was flashing bright white with the kind of realization that was so persistent and painful precisely because it was so true: he had been born the deformed way. All this time Gipson had just been showing EJP what EJP already knew, that he was a fraud and pervert, that he was an embarrassment and danger to the human community.

He was passing Cisco Drugs. He thought of Alexander in his lab, adding chemicals to other chemicals. He thought of his mother at Grandma

Alice's bedside, reading aloud to the constant beep of Grandma Alice's vitals. He felt momentarily bad that they didn't know him as well as Joey Gipson did, but then who would want to? Look what the burden of knowledge had done to Gipson. He would never wish that on his parents. He started crying again, which snotted up his nose. He bit down on his shirt and wailed. *Keep running, asshole.*

Another thing: he wasn't even good like Link. He was supposed to defend the weak from Ganondorf and protect the Triforce. Who were the weak? Julie Cosworth and Abe Verdega? He'd done nothing for them. He knew that if given the chance, he'd put on Dennis Delpiere's monkey suit and dance for Gipson and Stockton. He'd do it in a second. He'd flip trays and beat up gay kids and call people fat and poor and insane to their faces. At least he'd be safe. If it meant he could be safe, he'd act however they wanted him to act. However anyone wanted him to act. If he could've kept himself safe, he would've used the bought time to fix himself. But now it was too late. He was totally beyond repair. He was a real fucking glitch. They'd all been right about him. Some people were Chris Finn and Eliza Strobeck, and some people were glitches.

He had a mile and a half to go, then just the length of his subdivision, then there was his house. It didn't feel like he'd been run-stumbling for long, but he had and his guts burned. He keyed in the garage code and dropped his backpack in front of Alexander's tool shelf. There were certain items that looked grabbable and certain items that looked programmed into the background. Grabbable: the door to Alexander's study. He coughed his shirt out of his mouth and opened it. When he couldn't unlock the gun cabinet across from the desk, he opened the right-hand desk drawer and took out the hunting knife Alexander had gotten as a graduation gift. The handle was embossed "Fight for your Ole Miss '72!" EJP stared for a second at the knife before taking it upstairs to the kitchen sink, where, with unbelievable pain and surgical precision, he opened the artery at his right wrist, and then, blind from the shock of the initial pain— which was worse than anything Joey Gipson had made him feel, a prelude to what he was now feeling—he turned on the faucet and prepared to take on his dominant hand. Which was when his mind did this weird thing where the pain was so incalculably bad for him to feel, so disorientingly and terrifyingly unlike anything he'd felt before, that he became immune to it.

He thought about a game his mother used to play with him when he was very little, when she had curlier hair and bigger eyes and when Alexander would still sometimes cook his pot roast and the summers were longer and the house was brighter inside. She'd hide one of EJP's stuffed animals behind her back and then produce a different one, making him believe that his elephant had turned into his toucan and his toucan had turned into his puppy and so on. And then eventually he'd pounce on her and find all the animals behind her back and she'd say, "You found me out! You found me out!" And she'd tickle him and he'd laugh and try to run away.

But he'd never really wanted to get away. He'd definitely never actually wanted to get away. *Oh shit oh shit oh shit.* On the floor, his back against the dishwasher and his wrists bleeding in rhythm with his heartbeat, EJP realized weakly and then strongly that it was better to be a monster and see the toucan become the puppy than it was to never have been a monster at all. The kitchen sink was spewing water and he howled, his voice thick with regret: "Ma!" Then a second time: "Ma, please!"

And like an apparition there she was, just as if he'd summoned her, opening the door from the garage and stepping into the kitchen, a copy of the newspaper in one hand. She looked up and saw him and gasped, and he said "Ma" again, but this time only with his breath, and for a fraction of a second there was just the sound of running water while they stared at each other.

May 2009
Wisconsin and Ohio

Jocelyn had made a phone call to the dean at the college about her husband, who was apparently locked in a psych ward in Chicago, foaming at the mouth. The college confiscated all the paraphernalia from Tarz's and Lee's rooms and suspended them both (this counted for both strikes one and two of Southgate's Three Strikes Drug Policy). They left campus together in Tarz's car—he knew he'd driven to school for some reason, and it turned out that reason had been to drive away. They didn't wait to hear back from their parents or eat any more of those pasty liberal arts cafeteria meals or sit around being given lectures by all their friends about how they were dumbasses who should've been more careful. And now here they were in a car together, driving from Wisconsin to Princeton, New Jersey, where Lee thought he was going to win back this girl from high school who had dumped him while—this was Tarz's understanding—he was in the hospital in a full-body cast after a car accident. It wasn't exactly Tarz's place to comment, but if it had been, the comment he would've made was, "Why the fuck would you mess with someone like that?"

The thing was, just sitting next to Lee in the shitty Honda felt good. Of course Lee could drive manual transmission. There seemed to be nothing he couldn't do. So Tarz let him drive and pretended to look for something in the little glove box between their seats so he could brush against Lee's hand as Lee toggled the transmission. Lee liked to drive with the windows down regardless of the weather, and the wind made playful cowlicks of his hair. Sometimes they stopped at oases and Lee got a cheeseburger from McDonald's and a side of fries and Tarz got a McFlurry that tasted like chlorine but which he nursed so Lee wouldn't think he was some kind of health-food hippie extremist. Then he'd open his laptop and work on a game he'd started designing.

The game was a love note to Nintendo's golden age, a basic platform setup wherein Birdo of Super Mario Bros. 2 starts level one as male, becoming increasingly feminine until she ends level eight, the final level, as female. He'd written the script and done the graphics himself, in the style of a late-eighties sixteen-bit scroller. The game wasn't supposed to be that challenging—it was easily winnable if you were playing with a keyboard on a PC—but he knew the gender-change element would appeal to hipsters who wanted to subvert their warm-and-fuzzy memories of nineties Nintendo. The best part about the game was the cameos: in the second level, Luigi accompanies you through a cave in a dress and heels; in the sixth level, muscle-bound Falco limps on-screen in a sequined shift and begs to be carried on your back. The game was supposed to look like someone hacked the original Donkey Kong, releasing all the Easter eggs of code the creators had planted there for the benefit of extremely patient nerds. Tarz wanted to give the players of this game the hope that this alternate universe lurked beneath the pixelated surface of every game they'd ever played. If they just knew the right buttons to push, they could see Princess Peach shaved bald and dressed like a biker, or play Doom from the perspective of a ruthless five-year-old girl, or watch Mario finally consummate his relationship with Yoshi. He'd titled the game Birdette's

Universe. Lee was always trying to look over Tarz's shoulder, but Tarz would shut his laptop and insist it wasn't ready yet.

"Is a game like a painting?" Lee asked. "Is it like a book? Are you a tortured artist who can't show your audience your beautiful little jewel until you've finished carving it?"

"It's something like that," Tarz said. He liked how much Lee talked. He always had. "Nobody would even like playing this game until I'm done making it."

"I'd like playing it."

As far as Tarz knew, Lee had only slept with girls. He hadn't asked him about it, but he'd seen him with them. He had a type, too: girls who were smaller than his own small frame, who wore their hair in bangs and looked like they were always about to cry, who'd gone through life without being told that anything was wrong with them. They dangled their little pink purses off their wrists, unbuckled their heels whenever they came to visit Lee, tried to get advice about Lee from Tarz. Tarz pretended he didn't know anything, but he knew so much. He knew, for instance, how Lee had a secret fondness for old-people music, especially acoustic rock. He knew which memes Lee found the funniest (faildogs), which he found needlessly gross (most things originating from 4chan), and which corners of the Internet he spent the most time on (TVTropes.com). He knew both he and Lee had fake front teeth, though he had one to Lee's two. He knew that Lee was ticklish on the bottoms of his feet—he'd found this out by accident one night when they were both sitting on Lee's bed, Lee barefoot and Googling something they were both too stoned to remember. Tarz leaned to look over his screen, the zipper of his hoodie lightly brushing the bottom of Lee's foot, and Lee had squealed and whined something like "Buy a girl a drink first!" which made Tarz laugh.

But Tarz wasn't about to tell any of this to the girls who came looking for Lee. Neither was he going to tell anything to this Maria Timpano person if they ever found her. Tarz himself hadn't been with anybody ever. Lee had never asked him about it—they maintained an eerie, fragile silence around it. One night when Lee was getting ready to see Devi at some party, rolling back his cuffs, he had asked Tarz if he was going to be lonely and Tarz had responded by busting out his scale and grinder and saying he actually had a few customers stopping by. Which wasn't a lie—he turned $160 that evening—but it wasn't the truth, either. He'd liked the muted pop of Lee folding and unfolding his collar, the rustle of crisp linen against his skin. "I'd go if the right person asked me," he said, and Lee got a sad look on his face and said, "There's no person right enough, Tarz." He didn't know if Lee meant it as a compliment, but he took it that way.

Now it was just the two of them: Tarz's parents had given up trying his cell phone, and Lee's mom had only called once to ask him to come home eventually. "We're on a friendly vacation from reality," Lee said. "We might as well use it to get shit done." Truthfully, Tarz had been meaning to get his degree done. But then he was a white boy who wanted to go into game dev—his kind didn't exactly get turned away for lacking a college degree. Although Birdette's Universe wasn't the kind of game any studio would be knocking down doors to publish, either. If he had a college degree, he could just settle into some corporate software engineer job pulling down six figures a year. Lee was the one he was worried about. Who hired English majors, and what did they hire them to do? Teach other English majors usually, but you needed a degree for that. Maybe Lee could live with Tarz; Tarz could provide for him while he got back on his feet.

"What's all the shit we've been meaning to get done?" Tarz asked.

"Well, you can finish your game. And I can win back Maria. And maybe we can go to Mexico or something after that and live like Tony Montana?"

They still had weed, at least Tarz always did. It was necessary for him to get through the day. They had tried to give him mood stabilizers and antipsychotics in the hospital, and then benzos and an SSRI when he was finally discharged, but he had started cheeking the pills doctors gave him and flushing the rest as soon as he became lucid enough to understand where he was and what was happening. When he was discharged, he just hit his piece as regularly as possible.

"I never liked Tony Montana," Tarz said. "He was all show and no substance."

Lee laughed, slamming the steering wheel. "All show and no substance! Okay, then who do you like?"

"Like which drug lord do I like?"

"Yeah. What else would I be asking?"

"Well, I mean, El Chapo at least has a system of patronage that helps his friends and family."

"El Chapo's a scourge! And Tony Montana would do the same!"

"Yeah, but he's like, this weird lone wolf. If I had all that money and power I wouldn't be like 'Ooh I gotta fuck a bunch of women, I gotta bury my face in a mountain of cocaine.' I'd be thinking of who needed my money more."

Lee nodded. "That's considerate."

"I guess the drug lord I'd really like doesn't exist. Maybe someone somewhere in Latin America selling drugs to bankroll a socialist commune where, um, the needs of the disabled and women and children are prioritized."

"Be the drug lord you wish to see in the world," Lee said, making a grand gesture that seemed to include every car on the road. "There's nothing stopping you."

They took an off-ramp to a little town near Fort Wayne, Indiana, where Lee decided they'd find the nearest consignment store and make "disguises." Lee liked playing dress-up, but not in public, and certainly not in consignment stores. Doing this meant he sincerely thought ditching their clothes and wearing other people's would protect them from being arrested. Which was entirely unrealistic, a belief too childish for Lee. Which meant he was panicked. Now Tarz was nervous. Why would Lee be thinking like this? Did the law extend beyond the college campus? Southgate was world-adjacent, if not its own planet. He'd always thought he could do whatever he wanted in that little microcosm and the worst punishment he'd suffer would be suspension. Then Lee flashed a sun-spackled smile and Tarz forgot what he'd been thinking about.

These were the things Lee had only admitted to Tarz in the privacy of their dorm room: how much he'd loved the smell of Diedre's perfume, how he'd imagined himself as an exotic bird in Florida, how he'd liked going to temple just because he got to wear a pair of old tap shoes his dad had bought on the cheap to look like dress shoes. And Tarz in turn told him about his stuffed toucan, about drawing endless crayon portraits of Princess Peach, about drawing himself as Princess Peach. He even told Lee about the Thought. He never talked about the time with the Ole Miss knife after Joey Gipson beat him up: he hadn't tried to wrap words around that for a long time, and he didn't particularly want to. Lee listened to his secrets and absorbed them. Tarz did his best to do the same: Lee's past was an effective window to his eccentric present, and there was no denying how much Tarz liked that present.

The store was called Annie's Closet and it was run by the pursed-lipped, plastic-glasses-wearing, old owl lady archetype who usually worked in high school cafeterias. When they walked in she offered to take their coats and bags and stow them behind the counter so they could shop with their hands free. Tarz wandered around the store and made his way back to the dressing room, where Lee had piled a stack of clothes outside the curtained stall. He walked out wearing what looked like army fatigues: a green jacket, camo pants, a black beanie. "I'm deploying to Baghdad tomorrow," he said with a salute.

"Too soon," Tarz said. "You're the guy riding the bomb in *Dr. Strangelove.*"

Lee found a pair of aviators and tried them on, looking from the mirror to Tarz. "What do you think of Buck Stronghold as a name for me?"

"Well, if we're doing disguises it has to be realistic."

"Buck Strongman. A nice Jewish boy." He messed his hair up in the mirror, then fixed it again. "Now go find yours."

Tarz escaped from the military section, then from the men's section altogether. He turned around to see if Lee was watching him. He went to a rack of women's dresses and selected a green crushed velvet one, then a red polka-dot one with a ribbon tie under the bust. He tried them both on in a little dressing room at the other side of the store. They fit smoothly, the red one snagging on his hip bone just a little, nothing some Spanx couldn't hide. He liked the crushed velvet one better because it brought out his eyes. He spun around in it and a small part of his brain said he should stop, registered the danger he was in. He countered that he wasn't doing this because of the Thought. He was just wearing some clothes he wanted to wear.

"Do you like it?" he asked. "The girl who'd wear this would be called Tweety."

Lee looked him up and down over his aviators, then slid them up his nose and smiled. "That would make you Tweety, wouldn't it?"

They paid and left, the owl woman less friendly now that Tarz was wearing a dress. But what the fuck was she going to do about it? They drove fast on the highway, blasting *Demon Days* all the way to Toledo, where Lee finally declared himself in need of a nap.

"Buck Strongman's had a long day on the road," he said, hauling their bags into the elevator of a Comfort Inn while Tarz followed. "He needs to relax."

"Tweety needs to relax, too," Tarz said, though he was speaking like she would. "She does declare, she's not feeling right in the head."

"Oh, is she a southern belle?"

"I'm a southern belle," Tweety said.

Buck Strongman came off with the military fatigues, but Tweety didn't come off, not then. She shaved her legs in the bathroom, plucked a few blond hairs from her chin (she'd always been fair-haired and could never grow a beard), trimmed anything that gave off the remotest suggestion of a sideburn. Then she packed a bowl and hot-boxed the bathroom, packed another bowl, and brought it to Lee, who was lying on the bed watching Cartoon Network. Lee turned to look at her, then sat up.

"Damn, Tweety," was all he said.

He took the pipe from her, into which Tweety had sprinkled a little ketamine she'd managed to save after the raid, and then kept on watching TV.

"So, you don't talk that much about Maria Timpano except to say you love her," Tweety said.

Lee nodded. "Yep."

"Well, maybe you can tell me a little about this seductress."

Lee sighed and rolled onto his side, his hand cupping his ear. "She happened to be the first person I fell in love with in high school. That's just how it worked out. And now I just want to—I don't know. I want her to tell me her dad was the one making her say all that shit."

"What shit?"

"About how she didn't love me anymore."

This made Tweety unspeakably sad and she feared she knew why.

"I do love her, I just feel weird about it," Lee said. "You know what I mean?"

Tweety shook her head, though she knew exactly what he meant.

"I don't know, dude." Lee turned onto his back and made binoculars of his hands, stared at the ceiling. "I'm not doing any of this right."

It would be the boldest move of Tweety's short life, what she did next. She kissed Lee quick on the mouth. She pulled away and looked at him, breathing hard, while he looked at her. Then he smiled and pulled her to him and kissed her back. Tweety had imagined before how this would happen, when and where and who would start it, but she'd never imagined it would be in a Comfort Inn somewhere in Ohio while she wore a crushed velvet dress she'd bought at Annie's Closet. She'd imagined fumblings in a dorm room, both of them so drunk and high that they would ignore what had happened the next day. She'd imagined Lee lying about it to his other friends if they ever found out. She'd imagined being bad at sex, it being something she'd never had with anyone besides herself, so bad that they'd stop halfway and Lee would say what a mistake they were both making. But she wasn't bad at sex, at least not with Lee. They did it twice in one night.

After Lee kissed her on the cheek and fell asleep, Tweety started to come off. She was naked under the sheets, neither the boy who'd made a bong of his old N64 controller nor the girl who'd worn the crushed velvet dress—just a someone lying very still, breathing, wiggling their toes, flexing their feet, realizing for the first time how their body responded to being loved. This person, this once-Tarzan, once-Tweety person, wanted to spend their life hanging suspended between two poles. It could've been the horse tranquilizer, but some part of their brain that stayed sober always, even in the most extreme of circumstances, knew it wasn't the horse tranquilizer. There was no telling how the brain hitched its reins up to the body, especially not after sex like that. They wanted the hotel to last forever, the night under the clean sheets with Lee sleeping naked by their side to last forever, but then Lee's phone started buzzing. Lee didn't stir.

The New Person reached over to pick up the phone and answered, "Hello?"

"Lee?" a woman's voice said, sounding thick and desperate. The New Person felt bad for this woman. They wanted this woman to know that someone cared about her in her state of crisis.

"Yes, speaking," they said.

"Lee, I'm—I don't know where to begin. This is Melinda, your half brother's mother."

The New Person's eyes widened. "Okay."

"I'm, um, calling because the Marshall family came forward, Reggie Marshall, actually, I'm not sure if you'll even know who he is. But he's reached out to let us know that your father had some money that belonged to him, and he'd be willing to um, divide up the inheritance at this point, if we can locate it."

The New Person nodded. This all made perfect sense. "Sounds good."

The desperate woman sputtered with joy. "Lee, thank you, I'm so sorry, I could've been so much better to you. I wish I'd reached out to you, but I was fearful. He wouldn't grant me that divorce. He was a bigamist, your father, but his sons were never all bad. Lee, anyway, we couldn't find the money anywhere so I had the idea to check that temple in South Florida, he wrote to me about it so much in his letters. The one where you used to go as a child. He never mentioned the name. Can you remember the name?"

"Not off the top of my head," the New Person said.

"That's fine, that's fine. I'm just so thrilled you answered the phone! I'm trying to do right by everyone, and your brother—well, I know you're not on the best terms—but your brother had a briefcase in his basement and we took a look in it and there were just bricks and packing peanuts."

"That's very like Dad."

"Right, yes, he was very paranoid about his possessions. He left decoys everywhere. Especially toothbrushes—he used one he kept hidden under his pillow and kept a perfectly clean one in the bathroom, you know, just in case I used it on accident? That sort of thing. He was a sick man, I'm sorry to be saying this. I bet you don't want to hear it, and I know perfectly well how you feel."

The New Person couldn't help wanting to hug this woman. The world hadn't done right by her. "I don't mind you saying any of that, Melinda. I appreciate you calling me."

"Bless you, Lee."

Lee stirred in his sleep, flipped onto his stomach.

"Will you call me when you remember the name of the temple? You have my number."

The New Person smiled. "Of course I will."

MARIA TIMPANO

(1992–)

May 2009
Princeton

No matter how broad the taxonomy of definition-bound "human-ness" grew, Maria knew there would always be some human whose existence served as a counterexample, whose life would be constantly questioned by authorities and defended by advocates. There is no system big enough, loving enough, to catch us all; and aside from that there's just individualism, loneliness, tribalism. Certainly now—trying and failing as they were to make their lives in the landscape scorched and cratered by their parents' culture wars and economic crises—she and every other irregular member of her generation deserved the utmost compassion and patience. But she was only one woman, and she didn't know whether she had the resolve to be compassionate or patient.

She and her ex-boyfriend were obvious counterexamples to respectable "humanness": he had a mood disorder and she had a brain disease. He had called her for the first time in what felt like years and was speaking with the drugged-up certainty she was so used to hearing from him, the gibberish-in-a-baritone she'd come to associate with white maleness. He was saying he missed her and he was on his way to her, and when she told him that wasn't such a good idea he agreed that it wasn't because he might be in love with his best friend, too. She asked him if he meant Max and he said no, it was Tarzan, well—it was Tweety, she didn't know him, but he was beautiful and they'd fucked twice in a row a few nights ago and had been fucking pretty steadily ever since. He was sorry to be saying all this so quickly, he just missed her so much and also could she remember the name of the temple he told her about visiting when he lived in Florida? He didn't want to call Diedre and ask because maybe she'd be mad, but he really had to know the name of it ASAP.

Why had she picked up the phone when he called? Why did she still have his number, even? She had, contrary to what she'd told him when he was in the hospital, never fallen out of love with him.

She had, on the other hand, fallen out of love with Princeton. Two or three years ago, tiny teenaged Maria would've gotten—as her mother, Amanda, liked to say—"dinner-plate eyes" at the idea of coming to a real Ivy League university, the wood-paneled halls bustling with the world's future public intellectuals, cancer-curing research scientists, Nobel laureates. She would've imagined a place richer and greener than gray-brown Cleveland, where all the parched grass in her front lawn could be folded into a tumbleweed and bowled down the street. The Ivy Leagues made you a person of consequence. She loved the idea of that, and of the purported daily rigor of such an environment. But now she felt differently. And that wasn't because the appearance of the place failed to match the campus of her dreams: the lawns were cut daily and freshly irrigated by sprinklers that sensed changes in the barometric pressure, the dining halls were Waldorf Astoria–beautiful, the thick-trunked trees had been growing for centuries, and a wall of the Yankee Doodle Tap Room bore framed images of Princeton grads who'd grown up to become people of consequence.

But the campus population had come up short. Well, that was unfair—it was the spirit in which the campus population was being molded. The celebrated alumni on display in the Yankee Doodle Tap Room included Donald Rumsfeld, and with the exception of Michelle Obama, they were overwhelmingly white. Though Maria was white herself, whiteness wasn't something she'd ever bothered to notice. Nonwhite people were all around her at home, and she'd known since she was a child that their lives were historically regarded as things of lesser consequence than her own. But she'd never sat down and really considered the syrup-thick, ectoplasmic dominance of whiteness everywhere, the country's best-kept secret. Not until she'd arrived at a place like Princeton did she realize that whiteness was a cudgel being used to keep everyone in their proper place. Whiteness was being thrust in her face every day, rich whiteness, the kind that people of all races on Princeton's campus aspired to, where Aryan investment bankers walked around in boating shoes and pink Lacoste T-shirts and made a big deal about Manhattan real estate and drunk brunch. Regardless of who you were, you kept your hair straight, sipped champagne out of cut crystal glasses, and loved Kanye West's music while thinking him "insane." You pledged the right eating club and stuck with them, your kind. Even the kids who pledged the "creative" club knew and respected the right collection of white male writers and filmmakers: Thomas Pynchon, James Joyce, David Lynch, Andrei Tarkovsky.

Among these people, Maria was a fixer-upper, a cultural infant whose whiteness had gone to waste on a Cleveland childhood and clothes from Target. Even her friend Gourav, who spoke bitterly about being one of only two brown kids in his Montessori school in West Texas, was shocked that Maria had never traveled to Berlin or Paris, had never at the very least kept up with the lives of the Olsen twins. "It was like yesterday they were on *Full House*, and now they're modeling and one of them dated Heath Ledger," he said, shaking his head. "I would basically kill to be their childhood best friend, like their guy friend who they grow up with and realize is actually really likable and virile. Is that a bullshit fantasy?"

It was a bullshit fantasy.

Most of her students in the freshman seminar she taught hadn't noticed she was a year or two their junior, so eager were they to prove themselves to one another. The class was meant to weed out candidates too weak for the philosophy major, a swift and brutal tour of Descartes, Kant, Hume, and Berkeley with a special focus on the transcendental arguments. It was nearly nine-tenths male, shoulders hunched, looking over their tortoise-shell glasses and talking over the two women, who sat next to each other in the back row and were forced to ask the clarifying questions none of the men would. Maria was grateful for the two women, and answered their questions about Cartesian space and the foundations of idealism as patiently and thoroughly as she could. Most of the actual teaching she'd accomplished that morning came in the form of responses to the women's questions, corrections of the men's statements about "its intangibility" and "its ubiquity" ("it" was sometimes "space" and sometimes "the study of metaphysics" and sometimes nothing), and the dousing-out of one brush-fire between two guys in the front row about whether or not Nietzsche was influenced by Kant (which—what the hell?—everyone was influenced by Kant). The ninety minutes had worn on tediously. At the end of class, no one said good-bye to her, and she forgot to remind them that all the readings were posted on the class module online.

This was the first time she'd been around college students since Case Western, but she hadn't forgotten about collegiate sangfroid, the way everyone treated the formulation of successful hypotheses as validations of themselves instead of ways to strengthen others' understanding of—and comfort in—the world around them. Why else would people debate the existence of an external reality with so much passion? You had to love yourself more than anything to be happy about proving skepticism true. The kids at Princeton were exactly the same, debating big ideas in order to fill small careers, scuttling across campus with their messy hair and briefcases, minds full of proofs and pure math that they planned to someday share with students who looked and acted just like them.

She had never thought of this before. Here was a set of Western rules and conventions and ways of being and seeing and so on and that was designated "philosophy," and then here were all these non-Western ways of being and seeing and they were called "religion." She spent an afternoon Googling the parts of the world she knew nothing about. She read about obeahs in the West Indies, the mixture of Yoruba and Roman Catholicism that resulted in Caribbean Santería. She looked at pictures of Jagannath, Hindu Lord of the Universe, his wide eyes carved into the surface of a temple in Uttar Pradesh. She scrolled through reams of images, imagining them flattened and compacted and printed on the pajama pants of white girls in Ivy League dorms. Atheism and empiricism were de rigueur for a very small, very isolated set, and she was an element in that set. For years now she'd been debating nothing among a substanceless group of people who'd deluded themselves into thinking they had a better relationship with capital-T Truth than anyone else. As a consequence, she hadn't attended the first meeting of her graduate seminar, preferring instead to spend the day in her room eating Cheerios, watching YouTube videos, and thinking about how she'd broken things off with Lee.

The exemplar of this winner-take-all-and-I'm-the-winner attitude was G. E. Moore's tongue-in-cheek proof for the existence of an external world:

1. Here is one hand.
2. And here is another.
3. There are at least two external objects in the world.
4. Therefore an external world exists.

What jackassery. That was the kind of proof by fiat that made every-one feel embarrassed about arguing in the first place. Like everyone has to stop hair-splitting because this dude just showed up and proved them all irrational with his immensely clearheaded thinking. How many times had she been at a party or sitting in the cafeteria and heard something like: "The Arctic Monkeys are easily the best band producing music today, and that's in large part because most other bands are channeling their influence." What the hell was that supposed to mean? "The Arctic Monkeys are the best band because other bands know they are the best band." The external world exists because G. E. Moore sticks out his hands. As if his existence were enough to make anything real. The kind of proof Maria would've submitted, if she had even wanted to participate in a skirmish as trivial and exhausting as the logicians' debate over whether everything is real, would likely have been participatory: Stick out your one hand, and stick out your other. See? You've borne witness to two external objects in the world. You have authority to claim the existence of an external world. But of course that proof wouldn't hold water with Moore. Of course it wouldn't, because each subject's individual confirmation of an external reality could amount to nothing more than a series of imagined realities, independently "confirmed." All rational subjects needed was some agreed-upon epistemic landmark to demonstrate the existence of some reality independent of them. And that landmark was G. E. Moore's hand—he'd even offered a second landmark, his other hand! There can be no "private Moore's hands," everyone knew that. His hands are the Hands; they are the primitive by which the rest of the world is defined. Gloves would be "the things that fit on G. E. Moore's hands," food "the stuff that is eaten using G. E. Moore's hands," Africa would be "the continent that is hun-dreds of thousands of miles from G. E. Moore's hands." Maria's hands would be "the hands that are not G. E. Moore's hands." He'd colonized everything. And, as far as Maria was concerned, colonization could go fuck itself.

So that's how she found herself sitting outside the Firestone Library one night with Lee on the other end of the phone. She conjured from her mind's recesses all the Lee memories she dared to: his galumphing shaggy-haired around his mother's tiny apartment, his bringing his face between her thighs (this one made her wince with its intimacy, made her tingle just thinking about it), his listening patiently as she explained about being-in-the-world. They were still friends on Facebook, and he hadn't taken down any of their photos together. In her favorite, she is smiling directly into the camera (the photographer must have been Max), her mouth parted midjoke and her eyes red-ringed. Lee is at her side, eyes closed, head resting on her shoulder. Another guy might have found the photo embarrassing—her assertiveness, his submissiveness—but Lee had made it his profile picture for a while. His current profile picture was of a red dwarf exploding.

She wondered if she'd grown weak, desirous of the heteronormative predictability afforded her by an admittedly powerful high school romance? Was she using Lee's un-Princeton person as the vehicle for her rebellion, attaching herself to him under the false assumption that low-income, drug-addicted white people weren't the white people she hated—the white people like herself? Was she in love with Lee in an undeniable and sometimes panic-inducing way? *All are true*, she thought as his phone-babble continued, and she wondered how much of what he said was true and whether he was on cocaine. Her own experiences living in her own mind had disturbed and disquieted her so much that nothing he was saying sounded remotely out of the ordinary. He was just being alive, the way he'd been alive since the night he stumbled out of the ravine shout-whistling her name through the bloody gap in his teeth.

Now she was letting her mind drift from the conversation, thinking about the criteria for humanness—her philosophical training had taught her to think this way, which she resented. Surely people who wanted the rehabilitation of all criminals would be hard-pressed to defend a serial murderer and rapist? A child pornographer who repeatedly exploited infants? Or what about the matter of disability, the right to life? Was someone with multiple disabilities, with zero brain activity, still human? Should someone for whom light and sound were excruciatingly painful be made to live in the world? Someone so horribly depressed that death suggested itself as relief? And when did someone like this require defense over self-determination, and who was to decide? Maria was aware that she was a healthy seventeen-year-old pacing back and forth in front of a copse of New England trees, listening to Lee's monologue on the phone. She was aware as well how fragile this state of being was for her: how she, too, had once been a near-death vegetable, how Lee was probably driving as he spoke to her and at risk of becoming a near-death vegetable himself.

But oh God, she hated this way of thinking. She hated her fear of everything, her logician's obsession with universality (or the Western simulacrum thereof). There was no metaphysics of morals. The right to die was a case-by-case-basis kind of thing, as was criminal rehabilitation. But then there was no metaphysics of the world, either: mathematical and scientific axioms meant nothing for billions of people living on the sides of mountains or dodging bullets or pedaling rickshaws, so why should they be the universal indicators of truth?

She knew this much: she was Maria Timpano, she was alive, she was who she was because of a brain disease, not in spite of it.

"Lee?" she said. She said it again and again until he'd finally stopped talking.

"What?"

"The temple's name was Chaim Sheltok," she said. "And if you're gonna go, I wanna go with you."

1992–2008
Ohio

When Maria Timpano was born, rain was slapping loudly against the fiberglass windows of Case Western Reserve Hospital, loud enough that Amanda Timpano, who'd refused an epidural because she was against taking drugs if she could avoid them, had noticed it. Don Timpano was holding her hand, and he felt her squeeze his hand a little tighter. This began a pattern of squeezes where she alternated between very tight when the rain picked up and slightly slacker when there seemed to be a lull in the noise. There was a distant rumble of thunder and a flash of lightning, then both again, louder and brighter. Don registered people in the hallway talking about a possible Code Black. An RN himself, he knew that a Code Black meant severe weather, but this wasn't information he was about to share with his wife. Amanda, her lower half grinding brutally against itself in an effort to dispel Maria, felt a hot, sweaty shock of cortisol burst out from the base of her head and wreak its sludgy havoc in her already messed-up body. She screamed in panic and pain, and Don tightened his grip on her hand. The sky outside their window was green.

"You're fine, Amanda," an RN said behind her surgical mask. "Keep pushing and you'll be okay."

The Code Black talk in the hallway got louder. The obstetrician hunched forward between Amanda's spread legs, chin in hand, and announced that she was dilated about five centimeters.

"Is there gonna be a Code Black here?" Don asked. Neither the RN nor the obstetrician responded, so he repeated the question.

"Don't worry, Don," said the RN, Lucy, whom Don knew personally because they'd both gotten certified at Case Western two years ago, and whom Don resented a little because she'd proven herself far more gifted in the medical sciences than he was. "We're not gonna call a Code Black tonight."

Amanda made a groaning, crying sound, her body taken to the absolute hilt of its physical capabilities. She'd been an athlete in high school—a gymnast well known for her flexibility and endurance—which had cultivated in her an extremely high threshold for pain. When she was eighteen, she'd torn her Achilles tendon while attempting a vault routine without stretching; the only way anyone had known she'd been hurt was by the grimace she'd made on her landing. She had been a thin, double-jointed girl with messy long hair and ovarian cysts, her periods heavy or nonexistent. When she did bleed, it was accompanied by the kind of pain that would make other girls blanch and run to the nurse's office. At the advice of the family doctor, Amanda's mother started her on a diet of protein shakes to help control her periods and build her strength. Now a twenty-nine-year-old woman, Amanda still drank High-Protein Pony Powder mixed with juice twice a day, and she was certain had she not done this, she would never have gotten pregnant with Maria. She'd worried about Maria's conception more than she'd worried about labor and delivery, assuming her brutal puberty and short-lived gymnastic career had exposed her to every awkward and painful torment of the body, and that there remained no pain that wasn't beyond her imagination. Now she knew she'd assumed wrong, because every nerve in her body had fried itself with the effort of feeling. With Maria's every tug and slide, Amanda's vision flickered a little. She screamed and then cried because her screaming sounded jagged and horrible to her.

The obstetrician announced six centimeters, then seven. Amanda felt whatever progress she'd been making stop, the momentum now confined completely to her distended uterus and building up in a series of Maria's frantic kicks.

"It's not working!" Amanda shouted.

The obstetrician looked up at Amanda and Don, the look on his face one Don recognized well from nursing school: professional cluelessness. "You really can't push?" he asked.

"No, she can't," Lucy said. "It's okay, Amanda."

A voice came over the PA announcing the Code Black. The sky was at this point spitting rain against the windows, and the thunderclaps sounded like God in a fistfight, which was what Don's mother used to call thunder. Another RN came in the room, one Don didn't know.

"Code Black!" the new RN shouted at Lucy.

"We're in the middle of a delivery," Lucy said.

The obstetrician paged someone and gave that person quick, tense instructions. Lucy reached across Don to grab Amanda's hand and tell her that everything was going to be fine, she just needed to hold on, hard as that sounded, and take some very deep breaths. The obstetrician walked up to Amanda's left arm with what Don realized was a syringe.

"What're you giving her?" he asked.

"Phenergan," the obstetrician said, and injected Amanda, who shut her eyes, winced, and didn't reopen them until Maria had been delivered via C-section.

For the remainder of Maria's life, the questions most frequently asked of her, Amanda, and Don would be about her early childhood: what she liked and disliked, how she expressed herself, whether any of them suspected then what they all knew now. Maria learned quickly that no single answer was satisfactory, that people preferred to hear her story and draw from it the conclusions that best fit their (emotional, spiritual, journalistic) needs.

From the start, it looked as if Maria would be completely developmentally normal, if not slightly precocious. She spoke her first word at seven months, not "mama" or "dada" but "chair." She skipped crawling altogether and began walking at thirteen months. She could speak in two-word sentences by twenty months and was speaking in five-word sentences by twenty-four months: in one video, Amanda holds her at the waist on their front lawn while Maria bounces up and down, shouting, "I like a red car!" Doctors told Amanda and Don to expect great things of Maria. They had on their hands a future straight-A student, a potential doctor or lawyer or veterinarian. Amanda took Maria on walks to the end of the block and back, pointing out trees, birds, and bikes and then showing her their corresponding versions in picture books. According to Amanda, Maria's favorite thing to do at night was to sit in her crib surrounded by board and picture books and pretend to read them until she fell asleep. Sometimes she twirled a chunk of her hair around her right index finger and fell asleep like that, her sectioned finger turning bright pink, then purple. Amanda grew to anticipate this, checking on Maria around nine o'clock and gently unwinding the hair from her finger.

At around twenty-five months, Maria's development plateaued and then began to regress. Amanda was reading *What to Expect: 2–5 Years*, which she'd checked out from the Shaker Heights library, and which told her that around this time Maria should be peppering her with questions about how things worked, like why the sun went up and down and why it only sometimes rained and how cars could go fast. But Maria seemed content to play with her plastic figurines—the only questions she asked were "Milk?" if she was hungry and "Bedtime now?" if she didn't want to sleep. Her vocabulary had started dwindling, too. Whereas she'd once said "tree," "book," and "stairs," she now said just "this" and pointed. She couldn't talk about anything that wasn't in her immediate vicinity. She fell asleep at the drop of a hat, nodding off in the car, in front of the television, in her crib long before lights-out. At first Amanda thought it was an extended cold or flu, but Don ruled that out with a basal thermometer and an ophthalmoscope from work. They took Maria to a pediatrician, who could find nothing wrong with her. On the car ride back from the pediatrician's office, it seemed Maria had stopped talking altogether. Don kept on asking her if she was sleepy or sick or angry, and she said nothing. Amanda begged Maria to say something to them, and Maria just grunted wildly and looked at them, her face pained.

They brought her to the Rainbow Babies and Children's Hospital. She had lost the ability to walk, crawling like a child half her age, and instead of talking she made only a series of grunts and squeaks that didn't sound human. She was admitted immediately, and brain scans revealed lesions covering 20 percent of her brain's surface. If the lesions stopped growing right then, Maria would be permanently disabled. If they continued for any extended length of time, Maria would be dead.

Was it true that both Don and Amanda thought of killing themselves and Maria during the awful week she was in Rainbow Babies and Children's Hospital? The answer was yes, absolutely. Amanda fantasized about checking her floppy infant-toddler out of the pediatric ICU, buckling her into her car seat, and driving them both into the Cuyahoga River. Don imagined setting the house on fire after dosing his family with a lethal amount of potent sleep-aid. Don and Amanda didn't share these fantasies with each other for obvious reasons. Instead, they took turns waking up from nightmares and sobbing into their pillows. The most common reassurance was "We'll get through this," which was, of all things that could possibly be said during what Don and Amanda would eventually describe as the worst month of their lives, the least realistic sounding.

One day at the hospital, Maria had a series of seizures and stopped breathing. She was placed on a ventilator and remained in a coma for a week. At that point, her diagnosis was "neurodegenerative disorder." No one had seen anything like it in the history of Rainbow Babies and Children's Hospital. They planned to fly in a neurologist from Columbia University in New York, a Dr. Boza whose interest in the situation, everyone knew, was more scholarly than lifesaving.

Meanwhile, Maria was dreaming in shapes of white and maroon. There was nothing about the days-long visual of these shapes that suggested meaning as human beings are commonly taught to think of it: no narrative and no opportunity to ascribe them a narrative, regardless of how abstruse such a narrative would be—the shapes never changed in size or color or dimension, never moved faster or slower across Maria's injured brainscape. The only intelligible things about them were that they were the colors white and maroon, and that they were moving. The fact that these shapes existed confirmed for Maria that she was alive. They preserved her higher-order thought, frozen though she was by her hundreds of lightning-fast seizures and her breathing tube.

When she arrived, Dr. Boza looked at Maria's brain scans in a room full of interns, all of them awaiting her diagnosis. The scans revealed nothing to her, so she ordered another CAT scan and asked about Maria's history, specifically her exposure to encephalitic diseases. She learned Maria had a clean bill of health prior to this hospitalization. But Maria's karyogram revealed something Dr. Boza never thought she'd see in her lifetime: a chromosome-four deletion associated with Déphines's disease. If this was, in fact, what was causing Maria's illness, she would only be the fourth sufferer in the history of modern medicine. The disease—first detected in 1862 by a Belgian doctor called Rolande Déphines—was a condition of the brain suffered by children under the age of four, where developing brain tissue turned degenerative and cannibalized healthy tissue. Déphines's two cases had been the landmark ones, and there had been another one in Israel in 1987. None had survived.

Meanwhile, in the pediatric ICU, the two nurses tasked with staving off pressure ulcers shifted Maria's small body ever so slightly, emptying the contents of her catheter bag. The maroon and white shapes moved across Maria's inflamed brainscape as they had done for the past week. Then—and this would end up being Maria's first conscious memory of her time alive—the shapes stopped, and her head opened and was flooded with light. There were noises that sounded like speaking and then noises that sounded like screaming but she couldn't see much. Her vision was grainy and glazed, black and white, and then finally colors in meaning-signifying shapes. The first combination she saw was green and light brown and black: a nurse in green scrubs, her skin light brown and her hair black, her hands up over her head waving, shrieking. The sound of her shrieking something Maria could understand: "She woke up! She woke up!"

"All of you seem really nice," Maria began, addressing the circle of nurses and interns around her, "but I've been here long enough without being able to speak with my mom and dad—I think that's long overdue, don't you?"

Breanna, the nurse who'd first seen her awaken, nodded in astonishment. "We've called them both."

The amazed reaction of the nurses and doctors startled Maria. She asked to see her file and another nurse handed her a clipboard, his hand trembling. Maria read: Maria Timpano, female, DOB: 5/8/92. She read that she was risk-negative for any number of heritable and lifestyle diseases. She read that she'd suffered several grand mal seizures and had been stabilized on a ventilator. Her diagnosis was Déphines's disease.

"What's Déphines's disease?" she asked.

"We don't think you have it anymore," an intern said.

"Then why am I here?" she asked. "I want to go home."

She tried to climb down off the bed but Breanna rushed over to her and picked her up. "You can't leave the room yet, sweetie."

Behind Breanna, a few other nurses were telling her that they didn't think she was allowed to pick Maria up. Maria squirmed in Breanna's arms. "It seems like if I can walk, I should be able to walk on my own," Maria said.

When Amanda and Don first saw Maria up and walking around her room in the pediatric ICU, giving exploratory tugs to IV tubes and messing with the gauze in the lowest drawers, they at first didn't believe this was their child. Maria was intelligent, it was true, but this child, this Maria clone, had the purposeful curiosity of an adult scientist. She was not yet three.

"Mom!" she said. "Dad! Hi!"

Dr. Boza was now obsessed. She wanted to know how this child had beaten certain death, and whether her genetic tenacity could be distilled, bottled, and administered to the numerous ventilator patients in ICUs across America. Maria was photographed in her bunny T-shirt and diaper only (toilet training was somehow not a part of her rapid development), standing against a whitewashed wall in the pediatric psych ward, smiling mischievously, hands behind her back. In the printed version of the case study, a black bar appears across her eyes to protect her identity. Don and Amanda were invited on *Good Morning America* and then *The Oprah Winfrey Show*—they accepted both invitations and consented to the use of footage of Maria completely destroying a Stanford-Binet administered by Dr. Boza, scoring somewhere in the two-hundred-plus IQ range. Oprah particularly loved a clip of Maria's response to an offering of green Jell-O in the hospital: "I think if everyone had to eat hospital food for six months, they'd understand exactly why I'm making the face I'm making."

Maria spent much of her early childhood in the pediatric psych ward. Sitting on the bed, kicking her legs and looking at the far-off ground, listening to RNs talking, Maria could feel time's passage as the future slipping grain by grain into the past. The present was a thin, habitable sliver of things where they sat now. These slivers made all the difference, these sharp little knife's edges. Maria balanced herself on them, listened to what happened around her, submitted herself to scans and X-rays and the chirping sound of Dr. Boza's voice, knowing that whatever moment she was living in was only that moment for so long, until the future leaked in a little more, and then it was the past. This would happen, she knew, until the future had emptied itself out entirely.

She was released from Rainbow Babies and Children's in October 1996 to much fanfare from all peds staff. Dr. Boza wore a plastic tiara with pink stars attached by springs—she put it on Maria's head, kissed her on the cheek, and said, "Thank you. Thank you so much." By then the hospital could have been wallpapered twice-over with scans of Maria's small body. Don and Amanda told every curious news outlet that their daughter was going to live a "normal life," which was, because of all the media attention Maria's case had now attracted, absolutely impossible. Weeks after her release, the family appeared on *60 Minutes*, Maria with her black hair in red-ribboned pigtails and a plaid dress with red plastic apples as buttons. They all went out to dinner with Mike Wallace before filming, at a mahogany-toned place in Manhattan that served a lot of chargrilled red meat. Don ate heartily—Amanda, who was still a vegetarian at that point, ordered a house salad. Maria ate a plate of pasta with chicken Bolognese and answered Mike Wallace's patient questions. He was smaller than he looked on TV, but his face was wide, awkwardly tan, and shiny. She could sense a very private sadness in him.

There wasn't much else to the story, at least not according to Maria. She grew up in Shaker Heights with her parents (whom she'd begun to call Don and Amanda because she didn't believe in naming anything or anyone a second time) and homeschooled herself. She was finished with the seventh grade by the time she turned five, was done with high school by age seven. She took classes at Cleveland Community College—English and German, in which she'd developed an interest after digesting a copy of *Grimm's Fairy Tales*. At CCC, Maria was the eager mascot, the affable sidekick, the pleasantly intelligent freak. Stringy-haired college kids in sweaters and Doc Martens playacted as parents, lifting her up into tall desk seats, nudging her with pride when she got an answer correct. For five years, Maria kept herself occupied with the accrual of knowledge—facts she could manipulate and implement in unexpected ways. A class on early Christianity dovetailed well with a seminar on John Milton. A drama class in set design complemented a class in Newtonian physics. Her Achilles' heel was math; she wasn't particularly bad at it so much as she found it tedious (combinatorics) or restrictive (Cartesian planes), and so she did it up through Calc III and washed her hands of it—except for symbolic logic, of course.

For five years, she was an observer. If someone asked her what her favorite thing to think about was—and tons of people did, because she was a line item for good parenting or good medicine or whatever—she'd say "why people see the world the way they do and if the way time moves is a part of that." Dr. Boza sent the family a yearly Christmas card, a picture of herself and her mustachioed husband sitting together on a porch swing in Sag Harbor, New York: "Wishing You and Yours a Joyous Christmas and a Happy New Year." Her papers on Maria had won her an endowed chair in neuropsychology at Columbia University.

Maria was lonely—Don and Amanda worried that she was lonely, and she worried that they were worried—but it couldn't be helped, and she had no hope of acting purposefully if she was going to spend her time distracted by other kids. She could sustain a kid conversation for a few minutes (anything beyond thirty seconds was because of her exceptional, self-abnegating empathy) before politely excusing herself to cry somewhere in private, wondering what it was about the combination of her thoughts and the thoughts of the kid that made for such an epistemic disaster. Amanda bought her plastic figurines like the ones that came in Happy Meals and Maria told elaborate stories with them when she wasn't reading or otherwise working: she sat on the cement steps in front of their house and made the Cookie Monster and the Hamburglar speak to each other about how much they loved each other and where they were going to go for lunch. Sometimes she looked up from these storytelling games, having noticed someone walking past or the degree-by-degree descent of the sun, and thought about what a busy and complex place the world was and how she scarcely fit into it.

She entered Case Western's undergraduate philosophy program at age twelve, determined to accomplish actual work beyond the wide-eyed accrual of information. She was going to prove first and foremost that there was an external world about which she could make meaningful claims. Then she was going to prove that measurements of that world were respective to their measurers. Amanda drove her to and from class every day.

No longer was she the friendly, benign kid she'd been at CCC. Now she refuted arguments, debated those stupid enough to take her on, drilled through Hume and Descartes and Wittgenstein, and cheerfully demonstrated her superior knowledge of what she'd read in front of the class. She mastered the Cambridge School, worked her way through Bertrand Russell's proofs, got as solid a grip as she could on contemporary metaphysics. By their logic—G. E. Moore, Hilary Putnam, David Lewis—she could prove the existence of a world that needed to be spoken about meaningfully, could wade her way through all the hemming and hawing about what yellow really was and whether we're all talking about the same thing when we say "dog." There was no private language. The physical world was real and observer-independent. Maria couldn't understand why the other students didn't need to believe this as much as she did: what had happened to them that they were so casually detached from all the comforts of being alive? Didn't they know what a privilege it was to wake up, get dressed, and walk around the lawns of Case Western, to just do that like it was owed them? To do it in the company of others, and to have others know, more or less, what you're talking about when you relay these experiences? To walk the earth without others who shared your thought-concepts was to be utterly alone. You might as well be dead. Did they want to be dead?

She wrote her undergraduate thesis on Hilary Putnam's Twin Earth thought experiment. She slid it into the department head's wooden cubby and then sat in a chair outside her office, head in her hands, surrounded by the kind of noises she never would've heard at CCC: soft, scuffling moccasins on the boys, wedge heels on the girls, hushed conversations, promises politely broken, parties scheduled and rescheduled. Maria had never been invited to a party because there was always alcohol there and why would her mom drive her to something like that? Hair swishing, backpacks rustling, someone talking to a professor in a confident voice. Her classmates were entitled to the world, and they took it for granted. It was their plaything, its existence questioned for sport. The idea hit her hard in the chest, sent her lurching forward and gasping. She could either leave the field and be done with their glibness or she could get her PhD and prove conclusively that the external world exists. No counterexamples, no combative papers, no oppositional panels at conferences: she would give them nothing to debate. The question was whether she was strong enough.

Now began the part of the story that no one knew about except for Maria, Amanda, and Don: Maria's second deterioration. At age fifteen, she stopped sleeping. She was up for five, six, seven nights in a row, pacing the house, hands at her elbows, shivering. Her mind, scarred and healed, a tool deftly trained in the acquisition of data, was now misfiring, furred with loud static like TV snow. She snapped her jaw at the air, she tensed her feet and arms in frustration, she lay still in her bed only to roll out of it. She didn't attend her college graduation. Instead, she was in bed, Don and Amanda ministering to her like she was a sick child who needed chicken soup and Pedialyte. Her old psychiatrist prescribed Risperdal again, which Maria took after brushing her teeth, laughing at the dim face trapped in the mirror.

She slept only for a few hours every other day. Amanda would lie in bed next to her, holding her hand and whispering that this wasn't going to be forever. Maria heard this but would keep on squirming and screaming, her body heaving with frustration. Don and Amanda were terrified that their daughter had never been cured, that her illness had just been in remission for thirteen years. Maria became convinced that she wasn't a person but the freak-vessel for a noxious disease.

Dr. Boza flew in from New York to examine her. Maria flipped around in her bed to lie on her back and look up at Dr. Boza. She was a small fifteen-year-old, knock-kneed and barely taller than five feet. She'd spent the first part of her life absorbing facts for the sake of fact-absorption, the second part of her life engaged in a project intended to leave people feeling basically optimistic about the existence of the birds in the sky and the ground under their feet, and this new third part gruntingly miserable with the horrible realization that the world's existence was a thing to be debated at all, that skeptical unreality was so deeply woven into academic discourse—and even into the pessimistic talk of laypeople like her mom and dad—that the fight-for-your-life shapes that'd roused her from her coma might not have existed at all, much less the coma, much less herself, that she might have been foolish and even stupid to stay alive for a world that wasn't real. She kept all this from Dr. Boza, who could find nothing Déphines-related wrong with her. Her lab work was normal, her psychological evaluations betrayed no immediate suicide risk.

Maria's sleepless nights were impossible to medicate, so Amanda ended up staying awake with her, whispering words of encouragement until she herself fell asleep. Don would often stumble out of the master bedroom around four in the morning to check on them both.

"Mom," Maria said one night.

It was around two o'clock. Amanda was half-asleep. She sat up abruptly, as if she'd always been awake, and said, "Yes, sweetie?"

"I want to be done with this."

"Done with what?"

"This part of my life."

"Okay," Amanda said. Her voice was small and exhausted in the darkness, trembling in a clueless attempt to be careful. "I'm not sure what you mean."

"I don't know," Maria admitted. Her eyes were swollen from crying. There were harmful chemicals running the length of her, corroding her veins, junking up her bloodstream. "I was actually hoping you would."

Called upon for the first time in thirteen years to know something her daughter didn't, Amanda sat forward uneasily, head in her hands. "You don't want to get the PhD?" she asked.

Maria arranged herself on her bed so her feet were pressed against the wall, pointed up at the ceiling. "I don't know," she said.

"But you were so excited about getting it before. You'd get in anywhere you applied."

Maria took her feet down, put them back up, took them down again. She curled herself into a cruller shape, her nose above her knees. She closed her eyes hard and saw bright lights, electric yellow and blue snake-shapes. She was suffering from the manic energy of indecision and exhaustion, was host to a brain that did not have her best interests at heart. Because that was the awful difference between Maria and most people: there was a her and there was a brain and they were distinct in ways that did not bode well for her survival.

Amanda's voice came soft across the carpeted room. "Sweetie?" she asked. "Do you want to just take a break for a while?"

Maria starfished herself in her bed, exhaling raggedly. "Yes."

Then began another major shift in Maria's short history. She stopped all nature of academic work. She started watching Cartoon Network, a bowl of Pringles balanced on her stomach, wiggling her feet in pleasure at the arcane jokes intended for parents and babysitters. Amanda bought her a flute and Maria learned quickly, playing Mozart concertos alone in her room while watching the TV Amanda had set up for her in there. Don, confounded by his daughter's sudden lack of ambition, kept himself from asking questions about her plans and progress. "She's only fifteen," the other RNs at the clinic told him, "no matter what she does, she's still gonna be Maria Timpano."

Amanda suggested Maria join the orchestra and drama club at Shaker Heights High School. Maria auditioned and won first chair easily. Walking through the hallways of the high school after her audition, flute case hugged to her chest, she felt pleasantly anonymous. She was dressed in a turtleneck and khakis and she was being ignored and the fact of it relaxed her.

She was sleeping better. In the orchestra rehearsals at the high school, she was, for the first time, surrounded by girls who understood their bodies well enough to ornament them perfectly, who wore purple lipstick and wedge heels and teased their hair into gorgeous updos. And, much to Amanda's joy and relief, Maria wanted this for herself, asked to be driven to the mall so she could buy low-cut jeans, a red-sleeved jersey shirt with an eagle screen-printed on it, a blue polka-dotted bikini for summer. Although she was not there for typical reasons, she was still a part of student life at Shaker Heights High School. She had to lower her flute to her lap in order to listen to an obnoxious PA announcement in the middle of practice, had to use the lye-smelling girls' bathroom with the stall that had "I like thick dicks" written confidently on the door. She helped paint the set for *Into the Woods*, an amateurish azure backdrop.

The orchestra had a percussionist, a Rimbaud-looking kid with permanently bloodshot eyes. He was popular, in a manner of speaking. When orchestra was over, kids were always flocking around him, following him out the door—guys especially. He encouraged the attention, flipped up the hood of his hoodie, jerked his head in the direction of the parking lot. Maria understood she was either supposed to love him, as many of the grungier girls seemed to, or hate him for his confident dirtiness, which appeared to be the consensus of Shaker High's upper crust.

Out of curiosity one day she followed him—Lee was his name—and his crew out the door after orchestra. She stood at the pickup curb in the parking lot, pretending to be busy cleaning her flute but really focused on what was happening behind the first row of cars to her left. There was Lee, flanked by a kid she knew was named Max, a football player. The rest of the kids who'd followed Lee out of the rehearsal room had queued up and were giving him money. Then Max gave them something in return.

Maria had never seen something like this, but she knew exactly what was happening. They dealt drugs. When Amanda pulled up to the curb, Maria told her to drive slow past the first row of cars. So Amanda did, and the kids dispersed like panicked geese; Max jammed his hands in his pockets. Lee looked up and made eye contact with Maria, who threw her head back, laughing. Drugs seemed like a pleasant waste of time if you had the time to waste.

One day the orchestra director took an extra-long break, leaving them alone in the classroom. They were rehearsing *Clair de lune* and the kid on the piano started riffing on the opening bars. Some of the woodwinds joined in, then the brass instruments. Maria played a few arpeggios, her eyes closed, moving her shoulders in rhythm with the music. Then someone was behind her, tapping her on the shoulder. She turned around.

"You're bad for business," Lee said.

"What?" Maria put down her flute. "What're you talking about?"

"I can see you watching us outside. You drove our customers away that one time."

She laughed. "Plenty more where that came from."

He squatted, rubbing his nose with his thumb in a hyperaffected manner, turning around to see who was looking at them and who wasn't. "You're a genius or something, right?"

She shook her head.

"Yeah, you are. I've read about you in the paper. Like practically my whole life I've been reading about you in the paper."

"Don't use that word with me."

"Paper?"

She didn't say anything. She felt herself smiling.

"All right." He looked around again. "How do you like high school?"

She shrugged. "It's what you make of it."

"What're you making of it?"

"I dunno. Flute and drama, I guess."

"Can I see your phone a second?"

Against her better judgment, she gave it to him. He punched some keys and gave it back. "You've got my number now. So we can hang out."

Something warm bloomed in her chest, and she crossed her ankles involuntarily. "Okay," she said.

She didn't tell Amanda about it. She started an application to Princeton's PhD program in philosophy. It was the highest-ranked program of its kind and she'd corresponded with some of the faculty while she was still an undergraduate at Case Western. She submitted it well before the deadline.

Lee called, like a dispatch from another universe. He called again and she picked up. He told her it was going to be his birthday next week and asked if she would mind hanging out with him. She said she wouldn't mind, and he picked her up in his mom's car, rusted out above the wheels, and drove her to University Circle. She'd grown an inch or two in the past year, but he still had several inches on her, especially when she wore the flat-soled winter boots she'd been wearing since she was twelve. His head dipped low, his hand was on her cheek, there was a warm buzzing in her chest, then her throat. They kissed awkwardly, then smoothly, snow falling down around them. Maria smiling involuntarily behind the kiss, finding it very funny that this thing was happening between them, remembering him as she'd first seen him: hair in his bloodshot eyes, banging on a drum.

They started spending time together. Maria lied to Don and Amanda about having "extended tech work" for *Into the Woods*. Every day after three o'clock, they went to Lee's apartment, where he lived with his luminescent mother, Diedre. In his room—the room of a real teenager, bepostered, messy—Maria got high for the first time on what Lee claimed was the "best and stickiest sativa-strain there is." She choked immediately, but the second drag was successful, and her palms felt a little sweaty and light, her heart raced a little, her head buzzed happily.

Maria liked this new way of living. She poured her energy into increasingly elaborate lies for Don and Amanda. (Both were graying a little now, Don thickening but Amanda still thin, both mystified by their daughter's blossoming social life but also thankful for it, confident that she knew better than they did the right thing to do—she always had, anyway.) At one point Lee asked if she could stay at his place overnight, so Maria made up a fake sleepover. Then she brought an overnight bag to orchestra practice and Lee drove her back to his place, lighting up a blunt at a red light, Maria smoking most of it as they drove, her mind blissfully free, distracted by how Lee's car was a simple and pleasant reprieve from the cold, how Lee nuzzled her whenever they were stopped.

They sat on his bed, and Lee put his icicle hands up her sleeves and kissed her. Then, half-warm, half-cold, they stripped down to their underwear and slipped under the sheets. He kissed her collarbones. He kissed the skin just above her bra. Trembling, he peeled back one cup of her bra and kissed the skin there, too, which made every relevant part of her body tighten and sigh. She rubbed her feet together rapidly. She put her arms around his neck and looked at the crown of his head. He stopped kissing her, pulled away, and was kneeling on the bed. "Hold on," he said, and bent backward to find something in one of the drawers of his night table. He produced a condom and showed it to her meekly in the bedroom's post-sunset light. "I've technically never done this," he said. She told him she hadn't, either, and she nodded when he asked her if she'd like to.

"I love you," he said.

Relieved for some reason, and giddy, she breathed back, "I love you, too."

She told him about herself after that. She asked him for reassurance that she was more than a disease, because the problem of her identity was likely to rear its head if she got too high: she would've been average or averagely above-average if she hadn't developed lesions on her brain. But, he reminded her, she would've been dead if she hadn't thought in white and maroon. Those white and maroon shapes were her, not Déphines.

It was true—and she'd always known this—that she was the complex series of chemical reactions that comprised Maria Timpano, would always be made of ever-changing Maria Timpano phenomena stabilized by the fact of her persistence over time. Her elements may have changed, but she persisted. She endured. Eating breakfast sausage and chocolate pancakes with Diedre and Lee, she endured. Writing, reading, cleaning her flute's mouthpiece, messying her hands with oil-based paint, touching her bare feet to grass, exposing her face to the winter wind and the distant sun: she endured, she endured, she endured.

And of course she endured irrespective of the changes in things and people around her—she'd always known this, too, and that's why she kept her mind at a distance from any attachments she couldn't help, Amanda and Don being the only attachments she couldn't help. She experienced a weeklong flinch when she realized she was starting to form an attachment to Lee. She felt droopy if the subject of college came up—he'd only applied to places in the Midwest, meaning they'd have to do long-distance if she got into Princeton—and she hated it when he lost himself in obsession about the wounds of his past. Sometimes it seemed as if his world consisted only of her, securing reparations from his older half brother, and drugs. Drugs smoked and snorted and washed down with liquor filched from Diedre's kitchen cabinet.

One night in April (she was about to turn sixteen and he was about to graduate), they had plans to attend a party thrown by her friend Stella from drama club. Stella was, like most of her friends not shared by Lee, a self-identified "nerd" and rule-abiding optimist. The party would likely consist of crudités and the nostalgic viewing of Disney movies. Lee and Max had promised to give her a ride there and bring some beer.

As she waited for them she'd stretched out on her bed, half reading Adrienne Rich and listening to Don and Amanda discuss a movie they'd watched earlier that night. The movie had been a Western, and Don hadn't liked the protagonist: too violent, he thought, too angry. Amanda wasn't exactly trying to defend violence and anger, but she thought the movie called for it, because it was "stylized and hyperbolic." Don didn't have anything to say in response to that, and then Amanda laughed; maybe he'd grabbed her around the waist, or kissed her ear like Maria sometimes saw him do. They were happier now, she could tell. Now they had conversations they would've considered superfluous five years ago: was this a good movie, did this place or that place have better coffee, would Maria like to come with them to see a show or was her new social life keeping her too busy? Maria felt guilty for whatever her sickness had taken from them that time had finally restored.

Lee and Max were almost thirty minutes late, which was egregious even for them. She checked her text messages, saw nothing. Then there was a screeching and some abrupt metal-on-metal grinding outside. Maria felt the reverb in her bed, and it dawned on her with a panic that the metal-on-metal could've actually been part of their house. Don and Amanda had stopped talking. She went to her window and looked out. Don was running toward the ravine at the edge of their property. There were lights coming from the ravine. A car. Lee's car.

She stayed at the window, heart swelling with panic. Soon there was an ambulance in their driveway, Amanda standing outside in her windbreaker. There was a tow truck pulling the ruined car out of the ravine, and there was Max on a stretcher, his face full of weeping welts. And then there Lee was scrambling up the ravine, his left arm hanging uselessly at his side. She looked and looked at him and saw only a parody of someone she knew: his face was blood-drained and ghostly, his front teeth were gone, his left eye was swollen shut. He was stumbling past the EMTs trying to apprehend him, pushing past Don, who finally held him by the shoulders and asked, "Who the fuck are you?" And when he told Don his name and how he knew Maria—she winced hearing it—Don roared, "Stay away from my daughter!" But he ignored Don and turned his damaged face toward her window, opened wide his bloody mouth: "I love you, Maria! I love you!"

REGGIE MARSHALL

(1945–)

May 9, 1973–1985
Shaker Falls, Ohio, and Independence, Indiana

His eyes blinked open and he was awake. The first thing he saw was a canopy of trees above him. The first thing he felt was thick mud-sludge around his chest. The first thing he heard was a bird squawking, perched somewhere not too far.

And then his head hurt. His vision went white, then fuzzed to gray-black. He touched the left side of his head, the source of the pain. It was soft and pulpy and when he pulled his fingers away they were covered with blood. He brought his hand to the wound again and found something hard and round lodged there. When he applied pressure, he felt nothing. But when he tried to pull it out, his head seized with bright, unbearable pain.

Next to him floating in the sludge was someone he recognized as Sunny. His vision blinked black to white to red like a TV changing channels. When it stayed still for long enough, he saw that Sunny was dead. He screamed and climbed out of the sludge and scrambled up a little leaf-covered hill. Then he sat there, holding his legs close to his chest, looking down at Sunny's body floating in what he now knew to be the swamp. He vomited, mostly greenish bile. His stomach, emptier than it had ever been, clenched in protest. Nearby (shockingly nearby, now that he'd noticed it) was a road.

Sometimes walking, sometimes crawling, he followed along the road but didn't leave the cover of the woods. If a car passed, he stopped moving. He was sure he was hidden but wanted to be safe.

He followed the road until the woods ended and a bristly thicket began. He stopped, still on his hands and knees, and lowered his head to the ground. The blood rushed to his forehead. It felt good and he stayed there like this for a long time. Finally, he stood up and his vision flashed and settled into a static fuzz bathed in pinkish light. He left the briars and started walking alongside the road.

As he did this, he realized something: his wife and children were probably dead. He'd come from a bad place, he remembered. From Shondor's massage parlor. Shondor didn't play. If he was supposed to be dead, which he assumed he was, there was no way they weren't. He didn't have much time to think about why it was he wasn't dead, so he didn't. He tried walking faster, but after a few steps, his right leg gave out and he collapsed. He looked up at the sky and saw a fighter plane's jet trails. When he shifted, his back protested, and he could feel the round, tight knots of new bruises forming. Someplace close to his head it felt like there was a piece of flint between his skin and his spine. He got back up and walked slower than he'd ever walked. Then he started crying, because even if he could run that wouldn't keep Tasha, Caleb, and Aaron from being dead.

He was crying and walking slowly like an old man, the stabs in his heart coming from how he was alive and they weren't, or how much his body wanted him not to be alive, or maybe a piece of flint stuck there like the one it felt like was stuck in his spine—he couldn't tell. Cars were going past him, a few of them honking for him to get out of the way. One slowed down and a kid shouted something out the window Reggie had heard before but chose not to hear now, because he was tired of the world wanting him dead. He agreed with it finally: *Take me.* But the world wouldn't even let him be taken. Fuck that. A red flatbed truck was approaching from the distance. He could stand in the middle of the road. Or jump out right in front of it, though his legs felt too useless to jump. Right as it was about to pass him, he threw himself in the road and the truck screeched, the sound just about blowing his ears out, one of the wheels almost crunching his right hand. He could hear the car door opening and someone getting out. He was ready to be beaten, but when he opened his eyes he saw an old white woman with braids that had been pinned to the sides of her head like a crown. She was bending down next to him, blinking at him through glasses that made her eyes huge.

"Sir?" she asked, shaking his shoulder. "Sir, are you okay?"

Reggie grunted. It was the best he could do.

"Sir!" she shouted.

"I'm not deaf," he croaked.

She leaned her arm against the car bumper. She wore the kind of quilted vest white people wore when they called themselves "outdoorsy." She adjusted her glasses, then crouched closer to him. "You threw yourself in front of my car." She grabbed his chin, tilted it so she could see the bullet hole. "Oh my God," she gasped, then stood and staggered away.

"I think I got shot," he said.

She nodded and made her lips tight. She was small but strong, lifting him like she would an infant and loading him into the passenger seat of her station wagon. She said her name was May.

"What's yours?"

Eyes closed, Reggie could only think of two first names. "Richard Edwards," he said.

"I'll call you Rich for now, how's that?"

He grunted, turned his head to the side, and murmured, "I don't care."

"What's that?"

He didn't hear her because he'd fallen asleep. When he awoke, it was out of what felt like the deepest sleep of his life: he was still in the passenger seat of May's truck, May was still driving them somewhere, listening to what sounded like AM radio. The voice on the radio was saying that if God saw you sinning and didn't see fit to punish you right then and there, your punishment would come later. Homosexuals, for instance, may appear to be living happy lives in cities across America, but many of them end up dying of AIDS. "And those who don't will die of cancer or heart disease, let me tell you," the voice went on gathering steam.

May looked over and saw that he was awake. "How're things, Rich?"

It took Reggie a moment to understand that she was talking to him. He felt a cloth around his head and realized she'd dressed his wound.

"I always keep some first-aid things with me," May said. "Doing the kind of work I do."

Reggie didn't care what kind of work it was she did. He wanted to die. He was thinking of his days on the block with Cookie, those January afternoons when they were standing out there in their Browns jackets and their boots talking about anything—the fuckability of girls, the dainty way Cookie ate chips, how Nixon was like Hitler without the mustache— the buyers lighting up on the corner, basically asking for a beatdown from the cops. Why had he been so stupid? Why had he thought he could do the same thing he always had but on a bigger scale, with a real family? He was born to die quickly and brutally and he wanted it over with already.

"I want to die," he said out loud. "I think my family got killed and they tried to kill me, too, and my worthless ass survived."

He looked at May, who was staring hard at the road.

"I said I want to die," he repeated. "Stop the car, let me out, and let me take care of it."

"No."

He slammed his fists into his thighs, surprised he was suddenly capable of such strength. "Let me do it or I'll open the door myself."

"Go ahead."

The door was locked. He unlocked it, opened it partway. May was still staring at the road. He slammed it shut.

"Please will you stop the car."

"I'm just trying to get where I'm going," May said.

Reggie sighed. "Where are you going?"

"Someplace you can rest."

They drove in silence then, Reggie's mind wandering in and out of sleep. When they finally stopped, it was in front of a steel barn surrounded on all sides by trucks exactly like May's. It looked like something from the future. He thought that maybe it was the future and he'd been asleep for years.

She shut off the truck's ignition, got out, and started walking toward the barn. Reggie didn't know if that meant he was supposed to stay in the car or follow her, but he did know it meant he could escape if he wanted to. There were woods around the barn, what looked like a pond to the left of it from where he was sitting. The woods looked dense, but they had to lead somewhere. He could walk into the pond thinking about Natasha and Caleb and Aaron as he'd last seen them, at home. The boys running around in their pajamas. When he was dead he wouldn't be able to think about that anymore. The way Aaron had pouted whenever Tasha tried to feed him applesauce. The way Caleb sometimes tried to wear Reggie's shoes.

He got out of the car and followed May into the barn.

The barn was lined with cots, rows and rows of them. Some of the cots were filled with sleeping people, some were empty. Some people gathered in a corner, talking quietly. They all wore white T-shirts and blue overalls, just like May, except she wore a red flannel shirt, too. At the back of the barn someone had built what looked like two little plywood rooms with flimsy doors, and a man wearing a white doctor's coat came out of one. May turned around to look at Reggie looking at the place.

"This is what we call the Stay," she said. "It's a place for troubled folks."

The doctor walked past May, waving, and ignored Reggie. Most of the people there were white. A few were black, a few brownish. Reggie both wanted to leave and to lie down and fall asleep for hours. May grabbed his hand. "You can get better here," she said. "We know what brought you here, and we know how to fix you."

Then he was in the plywood room getting examined by the doctor, who was—just like May—a thin and white farmer-type who looked as if he never slept or ate but could still lift a cow. The doctor peeled off Reggie's bandages and made a hissing sound as if he were looking at roadkill.

"Sir—"

"Richard," May corrected him.

"Richard, um, you seem to have a bullet lodged right in here. I can actually see it, right here in the left temporal lobe."

Reggie nodded, his eyelids heavy. The doctor moved to stand in front of him. "Richard, you survived a bullet to the head. At what appears to be fairly close range. That bullet should have traveled through your head. You should've been dead instantly."

"I'm sure he realizes," May snapped.

The doctor withdrew apologetically. "I'm sorry, of course you probably do. I'm just saying this is, um, this is nothing short of miraculous."

Reggie sighed. "It happened in Cleveland."

"I picked him up in Ohio," May said.

The doctor made his lips tight. "We're in Independence, Indiana, now. So it's better that you leave Cleveland behind. Leave all that behind, Richard, and get better."

He was rebandaged, allowed to shower (the doctor offering him soap from behind the curtain), and given a pair of overalls and a white shirt, which he wore. He wanted to die but something he couldn't name was keeping him alive.

He slept on his cot, woke up, helped the other people on cots plant vegetables in a garden and milk cows in another, smaller barn. He helped sow a field with soybeans. He ate breakfast (oatmeal), then he ate lunch (ground turkey and mashed potatoes), and then he ate dinner (ground beef, green beans, and mashed potatoes). He held hands with them as they said prayers. They prayed that God would assume them into heaven and punish vengefully those who did not see His light and follow His way. After a few days, Reggie learned the prayers and started saying them with them. He couldn't do it without smiling at first, because it was some of the stupidest bullshit he'd ever heard in his life. But then the words stopped meaning so much. He said them syllable by syllable until it didn't sound to him like he was saying anything.

After this had gone on for a little while, May took him aside and told him that he could take a day off from the farm because the doctor was ready for him. She brought Reggie back into the plywood room and sat him down on the old barber's chair he'd sat in before, but this time they'd rigged it to tip so far back it was almost like he was lying down. She asked him if he could lie on his right side, so he did. Then the doctor was back, wearing a paper mask, a flannel shirt, and latex gloves. He sat down on a stool next to the chair and said, "I'm going to get that bullet out of you, Richard," some of the best words Reggie had heard in a while. In this makeshift clinic, with this pretend doctor at his side, he was pretty sure he'd die. Then the doctor put a plastic mask attached to a big metal canister on Reggie's face and he took one big gulp, two, and was asleep.

Just his luck, he woke up. He was still in the chair and his head was throbbing so hard his vision was fading again. He tried to sit up but the pain made him want to vomit, so he didn't. His left eye blinked on and off and his right eye saw pink, red, white. He could hear the voice of the doctor, who was saying to someone else, a man going "Mhm," how incredible it was that Reggie had survived.

The chute of his mind narrowed and dumped him at a specific point: the night with Sunny. Sunny in the room talking about the bomb that killed his family. The briefcase full of money. And that was it. Nothing else. Reggie began to sweat. Was it Sunny who shot him or Shondor or one of the other thugs? Was it really night or had it been early morning or the middle of the day? He could remember everything before then, every single detail of his doomed life, but the night of his death was out of reach.

The doctor wanted him to stay in bed for the next two weeks and said they'd give him something called "first induction rights" while he was asleep. He showed Reggie the bullet he'd pulled from his head and offered to let Reggie keep it; Reggie didn't want it. The doctor said he'd bury it somewhere around the farm and Reggie ignored him and tried to think about the night he'd been meant to die. The doctor told him not to think too hard or strain to remember things he couldn't remember, and then he smiled with his thin lips and cracked eyes as Reggie asked how the doctor was capable of reading minds.

"I'm not a brain surgeon, but I'm still a doctor," he said. "I know a thing or two about the way people work."

After two weeks, Reggie was permitted to go to something called Group Circle, which was a time once in the morning and again in the afternoon when people talked about why and how they came to the Stay. May led every Group Circle, beginning by saying that she'd been a heroin addict who turned tricks for money. She had a child named Alice whom she lost to a man who threatened to kill May if she ever came after them. There was a man there whose face was tight with clay-looking scars because he'd burned himself cooking meth. There was a teenaged girl there who'd eaten balloons of cocaine to smuggle them from New York to Canada.

"We're all sinners," May said, "and we're all drawn closer together in our willingness to purge ourselves of our sin."

They didn't make Reggie tell his story in Group Circle until he realized he wanted to. He talked about his momma going away and his dad taking him to Hot Sauce Williams. He talked about the fights he got into with the cops. He talked about stealing from corner stores when his dad drank the rent money. He talked about Cookie and the block, the postal service, seeing Tasha in the window. He talked about Sunny, the money, the people he'd killed. He figured he'd killed at least ten people in his life, all men, none innocent. He was a murderer and he was a druggie and he was a sinner, he said, and it felt good to say it.

"You're welcome here, Richard," May said, and Reggie felt bad for still lying about his name. But maybe Richard was a better name. Maybe Reggie was dead and now Richard would live a good and virtuous life.

The farm produced soybeans, corn, beets, arugula, milk, cheese, eggs, and butter in the warm months. In the cold months the pigs and a few of the cows were slaughtered and the meat was preserved. May said it was best to eat in cycles of vegetarianism: cleansing one's body of meat was beneficial, but only for short periods of time. The doctor checked on Reggie daily, removing the stitches from his wound, applying ointment to it, breaking it to Reggie that his head would never heal right. When he saw himself in the barn mirror, he saw a man with a caved-in temple, a slightly slanted face. So this was Richard. He began to think of himself as Richard Edwards, a God-fearing farmer who was redeeming himself through hard work.

There was a rule against having sex on the cots in the communal barn, but there was no rule against having it elsewhere. After a few months at the Stay, Richard and a girl named Audrey, younger than Tasha, would go into the woods next to the farm and fuck from all angles until they were dirt-covered and exhausted. Audrey had run away from home at thirteen and joined an anarchist gang in Indianapolis: they blew up buildings and beat up the racists who beat them up. But then one of the men in the gang had gotten her pregnant and she'd given herself an abortion with a coat hanger. She'd bled for days and almost died, and she hadn't been able to get pregnant since. Of all of them, Audrey was the one who reminded Richard the most of himself: doomed to suffer while young and repent while old, the best years of her life wasted as his had been on antics that could easily have resulted in their deaths. Audrey was too young to know about the music he liked or the movies he'd watched, but they would lie together naked in the woods, legs threaded, talking about the things they'd seen and done before The Stay.

"May drives all over the country on special missions rescuing people," she told Richard. "You're so lucky she found you when she did."

"I am," Richard agreed, and tickled her foot with the bottom of his.

He wasn't in love with Audrey: he didn't think he could ever be in love again. He liked her very much. He liked having sex with her. She was shorter than he was by just a little and had broad, flat feet that she always said she thought were embarrassing. He kissed them and told her she shouldn't be embarrassed. When May saw them holding hands, she didn't say anything, just smiled. Audrey worked the fields with him in the warm months and slaughtered the animals with him in the cold ones. He liked the way she could chop off a chicken's head in a single, swift stroke. He liked the way her back muscles strained and swelled as she lifted hocks of slaughtered livestock and bags of grain. He liked the way she found something new to work on every day: some sin buried so deep in her past that she hadn't even thought to uncover until the moment some sunlight through the window or the lowing of a cow or an expression he made triggered the memory, and her eyes would brighten and she'd say, "I remember something I did when I was twelve that was absolutely inexcusable!" That's what they called sins: absolutely inexcusable. It had been absolutely inexcusable of him to use drugs, to put the lives of his family in jeopardy, to conspire with thugs and pimps as though they were his friends and brothers. But with the help of Audrey, who had ropy legs that squeezed him like a soft vise, he was getting better.

May performed marriages for couples at the Stay who were sure of their commitment. When Richard and Audrey had been together for five years, she married them. The ceremony was large, with all the Stay members in attendance, even the doctor, and a great white canopy hanging from the ceiling of the sleeping barn. They said their vows, pledged their ever-enduring love to Jesus Christ, danced, and ate a steak dinner. While the Stay members danced and drank May's fresh-pressed cider, Richard and Audrey snuck into the cow barn and made love in the loft. Audrey called it making love, at least, because they were married—another sin struck from their earthly records. As they lay naked hand in hand in the hay, he was sad for a moment that none of these efforts would ever turn into a child.

Years passed. He and Audrey were allowed a private room, which they built themselves. He made love to her and worked the fields and went to Group Circle. He felt like he was swimming upstream toward his salvation. It was the longest he'd gone in his life without seeing a cop. It was the longest he'd gone in his life without getting in a fight. "Sinning is violent, and visits violence on the heads of those who practice it," May said. He hadn't realized until then just how right that was. The other members of the Stay had their children, the children learned to speak, learned to walk, learned to run. They became teenagers, then young adults. Richard and Audrey were known for their ability with kids: the childless couple who could always be counted on for fun and a handful of the toffee treats they sometimes picked up whenever they were in town buying supplies. The children loved him so much that May suggested he lead his own Group Circle for them, which he did, but there was so little to confess among them because they'd all lived such pure lives. So they spent hours discussing how Sammy coveted Courtney's carrot patch in the garden, or how Julia had stolen a toffee from the jar in the doctor's office when nobody was look-ing. May said Richard was a regular example for the children, a miracle man who'd survived a bullet to the head.

"It's because I think I always had love for God in my heart," Richard told the kids. "And that love, even if you don't know it's there—it pro-tects you."

Nobody ever left the Stay. Some first-timers tried to run away, but they always wandered back, hungry and delirious. Richard became co-leader with May, in charge of intakes and supervising physical examinations and first induction rites if the person in question hadn't been baptized (and like him, they often hadn't been). He got his own truck, his own set of keys to every room in the barn, a pair of overalls with *Stayer* stitched over the heart. Sometimes new residents tried to demand use of the red rotary phone May kept in her plywood office, and Richard always had to explain that calling the sinning world was counterproductive to the healing process. If they became antsy or angry, Richard let them try to run away, knowing they'd never get far.

He'd been at the Stay a little over a decade and he'd never driven with May to Ohio. That life was gone. There was no use dwelling on what he'd lost. Cookie was gone, his momma was gone, his dad was dead, and so was his family. May thought his decision to stay behind was prudent and con-gratulated him on his self-preservation. But every time she went to the city, he asked her to bring him a copy of the *Plain Dealer*. While Audrey gardened, he sat splay-legged in the grass reading it, everything from the front-page news to the obituaries. He told himself he wasn't looking for anything in particular. And then in the fall of 1985 May gave him a copy that had his son in it.

His son Caleb was alive.

Caleb was fifteen, the article said, and he had a face that looked a little wider than Richard's, long-lashed eyes that looked womanly. He wore a zippered sweatshirt with a T-shirt underneath. There were words on the T-shirt. He tried to breathe in and out slowly, tried to focus on what the words might say until a dam broke in his brain and he began sobbing. He turned away from Audrey so she wouldn't see him. His son had won a chess cham-pionship. There he was in the photo in the paper, pumping his fists in victory. There he was holding the trophy with his mother and his twin brother.

Tasha and Aaron. Tasha had aged. Her smile was forced, her eyes tired. His heart thumped. What had happened to her? Aaron offered a little grin, wore his hair in a hi-top fade. She had her arms around both of them.

How had he brought these kids, these almost-men, into the world? This long-lashed one and this grinning one, both of them in sneakers, both of them posing for a photographer? How had he managed to marry a woman that beautiful, with eyes that shone even when she was tired, with a face that kept the purity of her child's face? He was remembering her baby photos now, the box of them her momma sent her when they were living in University Circle: he was looking at this recent picture of his wife, the love of his life, and remembering the photo of her standing in a cotton romper in the grass in front of her parents' house in 1950. They'd photographed the boys in similar rompers years ago.

He pounded his chest as another sob shook his body. Audrey was down on the ground with him, holding him by the shoulders. He turned the page to the obituaries.

"Sweetheart, what's wrong?" she asked.

He pointed to the obituary for a woman named Pureena Mace. "She was my neighbor in Cleveland," he lied. "She made me cookies when I was little."

"Oh, sweetheart," Audrey said, nestling her head between his chin and his shoulder. "I'm so sorry."

May 8, 2009
Independence, Indiana

He had gotten old: they had a sixty-fourth birthday for him at the Stay. The party was as big as their wedding, and Audrey sat next to him the whole time, her graying hair in a loose bun, shouting at the kids so they wouldn't run into the vegetable garden. May and the doctor had set up a corn maze and they all wandered through it, Richard holding Audrey's hand, imagining he was finding his way from earth to heaven. He would be there soon—everything reminded him of his mortality: his swollen joints, his fragile memory. His wound still made a cave of his left temple, and his smile was still crooked, but now both looked appropriate on his gaunt old-man's face. He'd finally aged into himself. They ate cake—the adults slowly, the young ones hungrily, asking for seconds and thirds. Audrey squeezed his hand and told him she was going to go run through the sprinkler with the kids, left him sitting alone at the massive table with the doctor. The doctor moved chairs to sit next to Richard.

"I meant to say, I got you a present," he said. "You've been so busy all day I haven't had time to give it to you." He pulled something wrapped in a napkin from a pocket in his overalls. Richard unfolded it to find a blood-stained silver bullet.

"I never buried it," the doctor confessed. "I knew maybe you'd want to see it someday."

Richard thanked him and pocketed it. The concavity in his head twinged, as it often did when he thought about his injury.

"You're a miracle, Richard." The doctor stood up to get a second serving of cake. "Your entire life's a miracle."

Now Richard was alone at the table. He wondered, as he had for the past sixteen years, whether Tasha and the boys still thought about him on his birthday. He'd died on his twenty-eighth birthday, just months away from the boys' third. He doubted the boys remembered him at all, much less remembered his birthday. Tasha would. They'd celebrated his twenty-eighth a day early because he'd told her he had a big job coming up. She'd gotten him a cake in the shape of Bruce Lee, and he'd eaten Bruce Lee's forehead while she hummed the theme song from *Enter the Dragon.* They'd stayed awake until dawn while the boys slept in their cribs. Would she remember that on this day?

His life without them had been much longer than his life with them. A saner man would have simply accepted that returning to them would mean returning to Cleveland, would mean returning to Shondor, who would find out and kill all of them if he knew Richard was still alive. A saner man would have moved on, kept his nose out of the *Plain Dealer,* thrown himself into his life with Audrey. But Richard was Richard and as much as he wanted to devote his entire being to Audrey's soft and sensitive one, he couldn't keep himself from taking the newspapers May offered him. He couldn't keep from reading them cover to cover, carefully scanning the obituaries at the end. Aaron never made it in the paper, but Caleb would sometimes show up: a finisher in a citywide track competition, one of several finalists in a science fair.

When the Stay got a computer, Richard looked them up online. They'd grown into handsome men. Aaron was a real estate developer in California, wearing a tux at a benefit dinner next to a long-legged woman in a gold dress. Caleb worked at a small law firm in Cleveland and posted a list of all the cases he'd won on the firm's webpage.

And Tasha. She kept a blog, "Black in Academia." She posted less as the years wore on, and Richard could barely understand what she did post. A picture of her and the boys on Christmas in an apartment that looked like Cookie's old place. Aaron standing in front in too-big shoes and Caleb clinging to his mother's side. And then just photos of Tasha and Caleb: Caleb's graduations from college and law school, Caleb visiting Tasha in Canada for Thanksgiving, Caleb and a woman who could've been his girlfriend hugging Tasha on her birthday. The posts were about "interpretive texts" and "the performance of respectability." He could believe that the words were Tasha's, but he couldn't believe that she'd written them. He couldn't believe that she was alive somewhere without him.

Even on the days he managed not to think about them, he still dreamed about them at night. In one dream, he was struggling to see through gauze and Aaron was trying to talk to him but he couldn't talk back. In another he was having sex with Tasha and she had no face. In another he was trying to pick up the boys, swaddled babies, but they kept dissolving through his fingers like water. He woke up crying more often than not, and Audrey woke up with him. Sometimes she massaged his shoulders and reminded him that he was safe and a good Christian and she'd always be with him. Sometimes she threw her pillow over her head and demanded that he stop crying so she could get some fucking sleep. He would sleep again, dreamless, and awaken into dazed anxiety, watch the sun rise through the barn window. Then he would fake sleep as Audrey awoke and got out of bed, would guiltily receive her kiss on his forehead and wait until she'd left to open his eyes to their room full of pale white light. On the mornings after the nights he dreamed of them, he wouldn't be able to leave the bed for hours.

Audrey worked to keep what she called his "disturbances" secret. He figured they troubled her because she couldn't explain them. They weren't linked to any material sin and he described them in terms too vague for her to understand. She asked him to please not bring them up in Group

Circle. He didn't need any convincing—admitting to those types of dreams would reveal that he'd been lingering in the past, an offense that could get him booted from the Stay—but it was painful to keep them to himself, painful like a piece of glass in his foot. He once admitted to Audrey that some of the disturbances were about his old family.

"The family that got killed by Shonda?"

"Shondor," Richard said.

Audrey sighed. He saw her eyes go glassy with tears.

Then she was shaking in misery and he was comforting her. "Sweetheart, you know the dreams weren't, I mean . . ."

"I don't care what kind of dreams they were," she said. "I just don't want to hear about them anymore."

She stood from the bed without looking at him and ran out the flimsy door he'd built for their room. It didn't even slam shut properly. He pitied her fragility and envied her love for him. Why couldn't he feel the same way about her?

He turned the bullet over in his hands. He felt his blood surge, then settle. Why couldn't the doctor have buried it? What use was there dredging up the past?

Now Audrey was running through the sprinkler with the children, stepping her foot on the sprinkler head to angle the water in their direction. She waved at Richard. He waved back. Her hair was soaked. Water ran down from her forehead, between her eyebrows, off the tip of her nose. Her white dress, wet, hugged her form, revealed patches of her skin. She had accomplished a staggering amount in her time at the Stay. He remembered her as a scared kid who sat hunched over in Group Circle, who wouldn't speak about her past unless coerced by the Circle leader ("Audrey, you've been quiet for two weeks now. Maybe it's time you shared?"), who cried during meals and barely ate. Now she was his wife and he'd spent the better part of his life with her. She was vibrant, fifteen pounds heavier than when she'd arrived emaciated, a mother to every child on the compound. She believed in God.

And he didn't. It occurred to him just like that. After years of thinking he did, he didn't. Holding the bullet, he was now certain there was nothing meaningful and beautiful and Christian about a bullet in the head. Audrey and May and the doctor could pretend there was, but there wasn't. Nothing happened for a reason. Nothing was won by hard work and abstaining from sin. Nobody could redeem themselves through suffering.

He was a part of nothing greater than his pathetic life, which had begun in a water-stained apartment and would end on this farm in Indiana. The greatest thing in his shitty little life had been taken from him.

The greatest thing in his shitty little life.

He stood to get another slice of cake. The children mobbed him, dampening his overalls with their soaked clothes, singing a disjointed chorus of "Happy Birthday." He waited until they'd finished and sent them back in the direction of their parents, who sat at round tables by the vegetable garden. Audrey called after him but he pretended not to hear.

In the barn, he cut to the front of the cake line. May smiled when she saw him, handing him a slice.

"Here comes the birthday boy!" she chanted. "Here he comes!"

"Do you think I'm a coward, May?" he asked.

"Of course not. What makes you ask that?"

"I didn't save my family."

He looked at May, hoping she'd be soft-faced, understanding. Instead her eyes were flat.

"Now is not the time to think about that, Rich."

He shook his head. "I'm Reggie," he whispered.

"What?"

Reggie went back outside, pretending not to hear May calling after him. Everyone looked different to him, strange, like he was just meeting them all for the first time. He could feel himself settling into himself, sliding back into his skin. They were part of a cult. They all wore the same outfits and they sat in circles singing about Jesus and did whatever May and the doctor said. He had been living in a cult. He dropped the cake on the ground and balled his hands into fists. *What the fuck am I doing here?* His voice was back, his mind was back. He hadn't thought like himself in thirty-six years.

He stood in the sprinkler, grabbing Audrey by the shoulders and kissing her wet forehead. At arm's length she looked like an aged child.

"Richard, what's wrong?" she asked. "Why are you acting like this?"

He hung his head. He knew but he didn't want to say.

"Richard?" she asked. "Can we talk about this later?"

He nodded. He went to their room, where he listened to the sounds of his birthday party ending, confused residents asking Audrey where he'd gone. There was a knock at the door, probably May, and he didn't answer. He took the bullet from his pocket and rolled it between his thumb and index finger. The doctor had no idea what he'd done, giving this thing to him. If it weren't for this motherfucking two inches of lead, Reggie would've never been Richard. He would've gone back to Cleveland and, despite the danger of Shondor, the fear that had paralyzed him all these years, he would've saved his family.

His family. The money.

Everything from his old life was a puzzle. The money hadn't been meant for him—it'd been meant for the goons he'd killed, the fake-Irish ones Shondor and Sunny hired to kill him. The car bomb *had* been meant for Sunny's family, not Sunny. Shondor was always five fucking steps ahead. Shondor probably knew that if the goons didn't kill Sunny when they showed up to collect their payment, then Sunny would kill himself because his family was everything to him. He knew that on the offhand chance Reggie showed up instead of the goons, Sunny would kill him out of loyalty to Shondor. So worst-case scenario, Shondor has to pay some goons to take out Reggie and Sunny. Best-case scenario, everybody dies and Shondor keeps his money.

It was a good plan but it hadn't worked. Because they'd been thrown in a swamp. Shondor always gave bodies with no outstanding debts a proper burial, whether he hated them or loved them like family. If he'd gotten the money, Reggie and Sunny would've gotten their own plots and pine coffins. Which meant something had happened that not even Shondor could've anticipated. He'd gone over the details in his head before, but now one missing piece finally fell into place.

The junkie. Leland.

He lay on their bed staring at the ceiling, the bullet in his hand. Back when he was who he used to be, he would've done something big right about now. He would've kicked in a door. He would've fucked up someone who owed him. He would've gone down to the scrap place where Leland worked and fucked him up, too. The bullet felt hot; it hurt to hold. His temple twinged. His vision fogged and he massaged his crooked face. Audrey was lying if she said she loved this face.

□

She came back to their room after dusk, after extinguishing the campfire around which they'd all been roasting marshmallows, after helping the parents put their children to sleep. She didn't want to face him when he was possessed by his disturbances: she felt helpless and frightened and a little jealous of his dead wife. Maybe she'd tell the doctor he needed a sedative for sleep. Maybe she'd be more forgiving when he woke up in the middle of the night. He was a loving, righteous husband fully deserving of her compassion. She'd been stingy with it lately: her jealousy, her unwillingness to speak about what troubled him. She would change. She nodded to herself, picked a flake of burnt wood from her overalls. She would change. She knocked on their door and opened it, singing "Richa-ard! We missed you out there." But the room was empty. She found a note on the bed: *I'm sorry. Love, Reggie.*

EPILOGUE

June 12, 2009

Unlike the more modern synagogues in north Florida—the no-frills cement ones built by the Jewish retirees who'd floated south from New York and New Jersey, with Reform rabbis who wore guayabera shirts and kept kosher one day a week—the Temple Chaim Sheltok predated both World Wars.

Chaim Sheltok himself came from a clan of Jewish Hasidim who lived in a town called Heimsheim in the south of Germany. The Sheltoks were a family of tailors, then called the Schneiders. In 1861—ten years before German Jews would be granted full civil rights after the Franco-Prussian War—a group of Gentile students destroyed the Schneiders' shop and set fire to their house, leaving Chaim's grandparents dead and Chaim's father badly burned on the left side of his face. Shunned by the residents of Heimsheim as a freak and a cripple, Benjamin Schneider traveled to Belgium, where he found menial work as a cook on a fruit ship. He was paid thirty-five francs per trip, and the ship made four or five trips a year, often to the sorts of tropical places that only seemed possible in storybooks. After a few years of being beaten for refusing to cook pork, Benjamin scrambled off the boat in Havana, hid in the basement of a church, and stayed there for two and a half days, emerging only when he was sure they'd written him off as dead. He used the last of his strength to tear up his clothes, kick off his shoes, and begin begging for food and water in the street. If asked, his name was Benji Sheltok. The people of Havana took pity on him, and within a week he had a place to stay. Within two years, he'd opened a tailor shop, married a Cuban shiksa, and started a family.

Lore had it that young Cordaro Sheltok emerged from his mother's womb speaking Yiddish. Embarrassed by his apostate father and his own status as a half-caste according to the Halakha, Cordaro changed his name to Chaim when he was nine and began attending Jewish services every Friday. When the congregation sang their kaddishes in Spanish, he belted his in Hebrew or Yiddish. He knew his Talmud better than the community elders, and would sometimes even correct the rabbi on particularly difficult passages. Fortunately, the rabbi was a good-natured man who encouraged Chaim's passion. He considered the boy's gift for languages miraculous, his intellect messianic, and as Chaim grew, so did the rabbi's love for him.

The rabbi was an emotional man, frequently reliant upon his wife to ground him. He told her about Chaim, and even allowed her to watch them debate a passage of Talmud. She agreed that the boy was impressive, but pointed out that since his mother was a Gentile, he was not a Jew. The rabbi went to sleep that night convinced of her argument but when he awoke the next morning, he knew she'd made an error in judgment. Determined not to be on the wrong side of history, he assigned Chaim a Torah portion and gave him his bar mitzvah the following year. He told his wife that a truer Jew had never been born, and perhaps the occasion of Chaim's birth would someday prompt revisions of the Halakha.

When Chaim was fifteen, the rabbi told him he was a gift from G-d, the last true hope of the Jewish people, a potential prophet of infinite wisdom and compassion. He told Chaim that he had to strengthen the Jewish presence in America, the youngest and most powerful nation in the world. He said that for Chaim to do this was to fulfill his destiny. All the rabbi asked was that Chaim send for him and his wife when he got there.

After all these years of watching him grow, the rabbi and his commonsense wife, childless, had begun to think of Chaim as if he were their own. His wife had even relented to the idea that the Halakha might be wrong. Prudent though she was, she still believed in miracles, and if a boy like Chaim could be the son of ragged-faced Benji Sheltok and his goy wife, then miracles were perhaps more common than she'd ever allowed herself to believe.

At age sixteen, Chaim jumped on a tobacco freighter bound for the United States. By the time he was discovered, the ship was halfway to Miami and nobody had the heart to throw him overboard. He was put to work cleaning the decks and commodes: work that he did with alacrity, knowing that he was fulfilling a divine prophecy. When they landed in Miami, Chaim repeated his father's strategy of eighteen years prior, bolting from the boat before anyone could catch him. It was said he ran fifty miles without looking back, stopping only when the sun had finally set. He slept, his back to the trunk of a palmetto tree, and then awoke after five hours and ran another fifty miles. When the ground gave way to swamp, he began to swim. He did this for days on end, inexhaustible, guided forth by the hand of G-d. He was stung by mosquitoes, attacked by flying spiders, and nearly lost his left foot to an alligator, but he emerged from every night's rest with his wounds completely healed. On the tenth day, he stopped running. He knew he had reached the place where his temple would be built.

He called the place Heimsheim after his ancestral homeland and wrote to the rabbi with his good news, telling him to bring his wife and send for Jews from all over the world. Without his knowing, Chaim's rabbi had begun publishing essays about him—these he now sent to Chaim with pride. The story of Chaim's quest had appeared in *Dos Yudishes Folksblat*, a Yiddish paper in Europe, and he became something of a minicelebrity in the Orthodox community. An eager group of Lubavitcher Hasidim traveled all the way from Brooklyn to meet Chaim in Heimsheim, and by the time the rabbi and his wife arrived in Florida, aided by the donations pouring in from around the world, construction had already begun on the Temple Chaim Sheltok.

Although the assembled were of relatively humble means and their materials unrefined, the temple took on an elegant, palatial structure that Chaim attributed to the guiding compassion of G-d. As they worked, a small town sprang up around them. Hundreds of Jews—American Orthodox, European Hasidim, African Sephardim—journeyed to witness the construction of Temple Chaim Sheltok and to meet its overseer, the young messiah. Many of them stayed on to help.

On the evening of June 12, 1909, the rabbi and Chaim were dissecting their nightly passage of Talmud before Chaim repaired to his bungalow and the rabbi to his, where his wife was already asleep. The temple's outer structure had been finished, and the next day the crew was to begin construction on the roof. The rabbi asked Chaim what kind of roof G-d had told him to build, and Chaim responded that the roof would be dome shaped, like the Dome of the Rock in Jerusalem. Taken aback, the rabbi asked Chaim why and Chaim reminded the rabbi of the Foundation Stone at the Dome's heart. "Like the stone, my heart has been pierced by the lack of love in this world," he said. Impressed once again by his former congregant's wisdom, the rabbi blessed him and the two parted ways.

When the rabbi awoke the next morning, it was to a great commotion. His wife pulled him by the hand to their front door, telling him they were lucky to have lived in this age of miracles. When the rabbi laid eyes on the temple, his heart nearly stopped with disbelief. It had been finished overnight. What's more, the wood and plaster they'd used had been replaced by marble. He ran inside, where men, women, and children were rambunctious with joy. It was just as majestic as the outside, its most incredible feature an intricate image of Jerusalem done in blue, white, and gold tile on the temple's domed ceiling. The rabbi heard a child call out, "It's magic from another planet!" Everyone was too stunned to correct him. The rabbi's eyes filled with tears. "Chaim!" he shouted. "Chaim!" The other congregants in the temple heard the rabbi shouting and began to shout as well. In that morning's rhapsodic confusion, no one had seen him.

But Chaim was not in the temple, and he was nowhere in the town, either. He was gone the next day as well. The next week he was still gone, and then the weeks of his absence accumulated into months. The residents of Heimsheim searched the Everglades. No one had seen him. Some of the more morbid Heimsheimers began to whisper that the rabbi was a wicked man who had murdered Chaim in a fit of jealousy. Others suggested that Chaim had somehow been subsumed into the temple by G-d, and this was how the structure had been completed so quickly.

A year after Chaim's disappearance, the rabbi died of grief. In the vacuum of leadership, a young man named Abraham Kamzin stepped up. Kamzin had been first in his class at his Moscow yeshiva, and had been ordained by the Russian Orthodox rabbinate shortly before making the pilgrimage to Heimsheim at age twenty-nine. He was accepted by the community, and served competently as its rabbi until his death in 1939, when his son Abner took over.

By the end of Abner's tenure in 1968, the Temple Chaim Sheltok's miraculous origins were widely regarded as a hoax, Chaim Sheltok himself believed to be a legend cooked up by Hasidic mystics who refused to live in the twentieth century. Abner's son took over and told his congregants in his no-nonsense manner that the beautiful temple had been built by German-American plutocrats in need of a nice place to worship while they turned the Everglades into condos and resorts.

By June 12, 2009, the hundred-year anniversary of the temple's completion, the place had fallen into gilded disrepair. The rabbi was now Abner's grandson Ari, a young man who'd recently put a halt to his father's baffling and exclusive tradition of holding services in Yiddish and Hebrew. Although he'd been raised in the Orthodox tradition, Ari had rejected what he considered the Orthodoxy's willful parochialism, outrageous sexism, and snobbish, covenant-bound exceptionalism. He believed in the freer attitudes of Reform Judaism. He led his services in English and welcomed Jews from all walks of life.

As luck would have it, the temple's centennial fell on a Friday, so Ari had organized a small commemorative party for after the week's service. The party was over before sundown, and he was the one left to sort the uneaten cookies back into plastic Tupperware containers, fold up the tablecloths and retractable tables, and sweep the floor. As he was headed to the janitorial closet to grab a broom, a knock sounded at the front entrance. It was strange since it was late already, but thinking it must have been a congregant missing a purse or cell phone, he opened the door.

In front of him stood a kid who couldn't have been older than twenty and a girl who looked sixteen but whose intelligent eyes disarmed him. Between them stood a third kid who looked neither male nor female.

"Can I help you?" he asked. Just his luck that these people would wander in now.

The boy-kid nodded and then pressed his lips together, hesitant. The girl spoke for him: "Do you mind if we come in and take a look around?"

Ari had hoped to close up and head home to his wife, Shosh, and infant daughter within the hour—the two had gone home immediately after the service because his daughter had begun crying in a disruptive way—but the kids standing in front of him seemed so sincere. Where were their parents?

"Please, come in," he said. It'd begun to rain and he felt better about the charity of his decision. The kids pressed in, smelling of incense and grease and sweat. The girl thanked him profusely, and he told her it was no problem. "We've been on a road trip," the genderless one explained. (Ari was proud that he thought of the kid as genderless and not as a freak, as his father almost certainly would have.) "We went all the way to New Jersey from Ohio and then down here."

"I'm just going to head back there and grab a broom," he said, pointing in the direction of the janitorial closet. "But feel free to make yourselves at home. I'm happy to answer any questions you may have."

The kids nodded at him, and he headed to the closet, which he frequently had trouble opening. Stefan, who came to clean the place once a month, always managed to get it open so smoothly—how? They both had the same set of keys. Then, as he fiddled with the door yet again, he remembered with a small gasp that he'd forgotten to pay Stefan for last month's service. He'd gotten the invoice and put it on top of the computer in his office—why hadn't anyone reminded him? He shook his head, remembering that this was no one's job except his own. Just because he was the rabbi didn't mean his congregation had to do all the work for him. That was a holier-than-thou habit he'd picked up in yeshiva that he was determined to shake. The last thing he wanted was his child memorizing Torah for her bat mitzvah with some ideas about how being the rabbi's daughter made her superior to other children in the congregation. Or worse—how being an observant Jew made her better than, more faithful than the many secular and observant-but-non-Jewish friends he hoped she'd someday have. Broom in hand, he vowed to himself (as he had many times before) to work hard to unlearn all his old habits.

He reentered the sanctuary smiling. Across the room, the boy was being hugged by a very small woman, smaller than he was, who was whispering "You piece of shit" into his hair and crying what sounded like tears of relief.

"Hi!" Ari said, and they all turned to look at him.

"Oh, hi!" the woman responded, and he could tell from her response that she wasn't sober. He himself had never been drunk or high or in any way mentally altered in his life, not even on Simchat Torah, and his first thought was: *How is she feeling right now?*

"You must be the rabbi here?" she asked, her speech loose.

Ari, flustered, nodded.

"This is Lee, my son, and Maria. And this is Lee's friend—"

"Tweety," the genderless kid said.

"And I'm Diedre," she breathed. "Lee and Maria want to take a look around, if that's all right with you?"

"Of course! Did you know that today marks the hundred-year anniversary of the temple's construction?"

The Lee kid's eyes widened meaningfully at Diedre, who, now that Ari was seeing her up close, had some crow's-feet around her eyes, some wrinkles at the side of her mouth. He bowed his head and breathed in quickly, then bit his lips and exhaled, looking brightly at all of them.

"Listen—I have a little work I need to take care of in my office. Just give me a knock if you need anything."

"Thank you. Thank you so much, Rabbi—"

"Ari Kamzin."

"Thank you, Rabbi Kamzin. I'm Diedre, by the way, if I haven't already said."

"Great! Pleased to meet you all."

Two steps away and he'd already forgotten their names.

In his office, he booted up the computer, a desktop model from the early 2000s badly in need of replacement. As the computer ran a tedious virus scan, he thought about how much or little he should watch what the kids and the mom were doing. Maybe he'd offer to drive them home, or to the hotel they were staying at if they weren't from around Heimsheim. He furrowed his brow as the computer made its crinkly waking-up noises. His thoughts were punctuated by a loud thunderclap, and lightning illuminated the windows of the temple. His heart began pounding. Storms like this always served as a reminder of his insignificance, the horrifying possibility that everything he loved could be taken from him in an instant. He fished his phone from his pocket and texted Shosh: *Running a little late— some people from out of town came to visit the temple for the centennial. (Guess I'm the Shabbos goy!) Will be home w/in the hour. Love you and Lina.*

He shuffled through a stack of papers that he was sure contained Stefan's invoice. If it wasn't in there, it would probably be in the file cabinet, filed away already. He was always imagining he'd paid bills he hadn't paid, which made him look cheap, which made him worry that other people thought he was cheap. He tried to pay Stefan on time as much as possible, but there were months that he'd forgotten until halfway into the next month, and he found Stefan and told him how sorry he was and cut him a check for time and a half. Poor Stefan. He was always smiling and waving his hands and saying, "No sir, please don't worry about me, I know the money's coming." Which was incredibly generous of him, considering this was his livelihood and his whole family probably lived paycheck to paycheck. Ari couldn't imagine life without Shosh's salary. How would they buy Lina's clothes and food? How would they keep up with repairs on the house?

He found Stefan's invoice and remembered the woman and the kids. He groaned internally. These people probably wanted a tour of the temple. It was a historic landmark, after all. On more than one occasion people had wandered in looking for tours. Maybe he could make Stefan a tour guide and pay him double. It was a funny idea, not the kind of thing he'd actually do, but nice enough to think about. Some people actually liked that mystical stuff, paid good money to hear it. If they started charging for tours, would they no longer be tax-exempt? Shosh would probably know. She always knew about things like that.

He cut Stefan's check and looked at his phone: *We miss you, Shabbos goy!* She always knew how to make him smile, his Shosh. Back when they'd first met he'd been a nervous yeshiva student and she'd been the daughter of a prominent Miami rabbi. She wore a long black wig—it would take him years to find out that her real hair was dirty blond. He remembered when she'd invited him to her family's Seder. While her mother prepared the Seder plate, he'd watched as Shosh searched for bread crumbs under the couch. He'd asked if he could help at all and she'd looked up at him and said, "Yeah, could you check the bathroom door jamb?" He tried to keep himself from laughing. What family got bread crumbs in the bathroom doorjamb? But he did as he was told. He'd loved her way back then. He knew he'd marry her when she lay down on her stomach to stick a feather duster under the couch. He spent more time looking at her that day than he did checking anything in the doorjamb, so when she sat up and caught him she hissed, "Ari, doorjamb!" Years later it became a joke between them. *Did you hide the salt again, Doorjamb?*

He texted her back, *I'm not your Shabbos goy, Doorjamb!* And then for fear it sounded too harsh: *Hehehe.* It was strange to him, this family, appearing on this day. It would be a lie to say he didn't want them gone, which was ungenerous of him. He didn't want them gone, really. He just wanted a little quiet time before he had to pack up and go home and help

Shosh change and feed Lina. Just some time to apologize to Stefan when he came in to clean, some time to reshelve his books and tidy his desk and take a lint roller to the parochet in front of the ark. He had no idea why or how, but those curtains were always full of fuzz at the end of the week, fuzz and the stray hairs of congregants. Which was strange, considering how far from the ark everyone sat. It was like a fuzz magnet, that thing.

And then the mother approached him and spoke the name he'd grow to hate.

"We know this was probably before your time, but have you heard of someone named Leland Bloom-Mittwoch? He used to be a very devoted member of this congregation."

Leland Bloom-Mittwoch. It was a bizarre name. An unforgettable one. If his dad had mentioned that name in passing, Ari was sure he would've remembered it.

"I'm sorry, I don't think I recognize that name."

There was the sound of keys at the back door. Stefan was just arriving now, late from working his other job. How he worked two cleaning jobs was entirely beyond Ari, who usually couldn't be bothered to clean his room. Shosh liked to remind him how messy he was, which didn't exactly help motivate him to clean, but she did have a point. He was probably the messiest person he knew outside of his old college roommate Levi (he slept in his dirty laundry!) and his daughter, who was constantly puking on herself. *You complain about their spit-ups now, but you'll hate it when they get older*, his father had told him. Unlike his father, Ari had resolved to hate nothing about his child. Or children, if Shosh decided she was up for it.

"Are there any records we could look through?" the intelligent-eyed girl was asking.

"Records we don't keep, I'm afraid," Ari said.

He was getting agitated now. He had other things he needed to do. For instance, the mikveh bath needed cleaning—he'd be sure to tell Stefan. The drains had been clogged for a while and he'd done nothing to fix them. Plus the check, plus he needed to get home to Shosh and Lina ASAP. Why didn't he just man up and show these people the door?

"I wish I could be of more help to you," he said. "I have to go help the janitor quickly, but I'll be right back."

"Take your time," she said. "And thank you."

Stefan was in the janitorial closet in his white jumper, digging for supplies. Ari never knew why he wore that jumper, especially given that he didn't work at the kind of place that would require him to wear a jumper, but he figured Stefan had his work outfit and his civilian outfit and there was absolutely nothing wrong with that. Ari himself had a work outfit and a civilian outfit. His work outfit was his robe and his civilian outfit was a ripped T-shirt and a pair of sweatpants that said *Brandeis* down the side. He secretly hoped Lina would go to Brandeis, though he'd be fine with whatever college she chose. He wouldn't pressure her to be just like her parents.

He apologized for the late check to Stefan, who told him it was "no big deal." Stefan was too kind for his own good. Too kind and caring and selfless. He was the sort of guy who would be taken advantage of by someone other than Ari, someone who exploited foreign laborers by withholding an unethical amount from their paychecks.

As Ari left the back room he realized he'd forgotten to tell Stefan about the mikveh bath. No use beating himself up—if he'd let it go this long, what was the harm in letting it go another day? None of the women in the congregation observed *niddah* laws anymore, and those old enough to care about the mitzvot probably didn't menstruate anyway. A few of the young women had gotten into reclaiming it as a feminist ritual, but that had only lasted a few months and no one had said anything about the drains. It hadn't come to Ari's attention until he'd tried the bath out himself one night and found a giant knot of hair floating over the mouth of a drain. Why he hadn't made a note to himself then and there to get the drains fixed, he had no idea. Maybe it was because the mikveh was old-fashioned and putting time into it would make him look like a man overly concerned with women's cleanliness, like the nonfeminist he didn't want to be. His phone buzzed, probably from Shosh.

"Do you folks need any more help?" he called as he made his way back to the sanctuary. He stopped at the entrance, eyes wide. In just the few minutes he'd been gone, the room had been torn apart: benches opened, cushions flung willy-nilly, the rug rolled up, tiles dislodged from the floor. And the family had disappeared.

"Stefan!" he yelled. "Stefan, we've been robbed!"

☐

A week later he still hadn't recovered from the embarrassment of crying wolf. He couldn't look Stefan in the eye: all Stefan would see, he was sure, was an overdramatic boy-rabbi with absolutely no street smarts. It had taken the two of them ten minutes to determine that no valuables had been stolen, that the safes in Ari's office and the programming office were both uncracked. The place was a mess, but Stefan had put it back together speedily, insisting all the while that he didn't need overtime. Ari decided to pay him time and a half just to be safe. Ari hadn't gotten home until ten that night, Lina long asleep. He tried watching TV with Shosh but lost track of the plot and fell asleep on her lap. She was forgiving, his Shosh, but he knew there was only so much coming home late and passing out she could tolerate. She had told him when she was pregnant that the fact that her hours were more flexible than his didn't mean she wanted to raise the kid on her own. He had been so obliging, so in tune with what she was saying, but now he was slipping. And all because he thought he'd been robbed by three kids and a drunk lady. The height of stupidity. A side effect of male privilege, as his best friend at Brandeis, Shelly Ruderman, used to remind him. "You are a straight white man, Ari," she would say, "so if you make any decision without someone else's input, it's going to be stupid." Such as the decision to cry wolf to Stefan and stay late scouring the temple for "evidence."

A week after the centennial, he was leading the congregation through the *Aleinu* via muscle memory and using his mental energy to determine how to be a better father and husband. There were some men in the congregation he truly admired, men he could tell never disappointed their families. Like Ben Wasserman, who managed a Menards and whose twins Ari had seen through their b'nai mitzvah. Or Louis Rust, who had four kids under the age of ten and never forgot to bring his mother to services. What did the Bens and the Louises know about manhood that Ari had never learned? Was it how they carried themselves, shoulders back, hair parted neatly, beards well trimmed? Was it their salaries, their degrees? Was it how well they probably communicated with their wives? Would Shosh prefer to be with a Ben or a Louis, someone who would come home on time and put Lina to bed and then have sex with Shosh against the dresser like they did in the movies? Was Shosh secretly ashamed that she had chosen the gawky yeshiva student who fell asleep with his head in her lap? Would she make this clear to him by having a years-long secret affair with a Ben or a Louis?

Horrible thoughts. He was having horrible thoughts because that horrible family had torn up his sanctuary.

The Bens and the Louises were looking at him pleasantly now as they sang the *Aleinu*, their wives and children singing along, the youngest ones' eyes wandering as they pretended to sing. Ari had been young in temple once, a little boy in a kippah already memorizing prayers when he could barely walk. When you're young enough, temple is a soothing place, somewhere to go and chant and watch burning candles flicker in the distance, a place where it seems like it's perpetually bedtime but things are just interesting enough to stay awake for. Whenever he was leading services and saw that look of sleepy wonder on Lina's little face, he knew she was feeling what he once felt and his heart swelled. He wouldn't be like his father, interrupting that beautiful haziness between sleep and wakefulness with a command to sit up straight and pay attention. He wouldn't be the kind of father who made his child recite kaddishes in the car on the way to services. He'd become a rabbi in spite of his father, not because of him. Shosh was always telling him it was in his blood, which he guessed was easy to believe, but he really would never have cared about *tikkun olam* if it hadn't been for the way he'd felt in the temple when he was little, like G-d was whispering kind words to him through all the cracks in the floor and shining warm orange light through the stippled glass windows. That was all him, not his father. He told Shosh, "If I didn't believe in Yahweh, I don't care what my father said, I would've been the rebellious son who went into orthopedic surgery or dentistry." That always got a laugh out of her. When she laughed at his jokes he knew he must be doing something right. Could a Ben or a Louis make her laugh like that? He doubted it.

He scanned away from the Bens and Louises to the other congregants, like Tim and Isaac Rosenberg, whose wedding he'd officiated. He'd like to see his father marry a gay couple. He'd like to see his father do a lot of things, like recognize the existence of black and brown Jews, or make the temple wheelchair accessible, or buy art for the walls that wasn't all European-Ashkenazi, or do more to restore the temple than install gray-brown shag carpets in the offices.

His father was everything about the faith that Ari hated, all the oppressive and exclusionary rules he was trying to unlearn every day. Luckily he had the grace and patience of congregants like Tim and Isaac to help him in the unlearning process. If it wasn't for congregants like them, he'd be at risk of becoming one of those bearded, bifocaled rabbis who was always

quoting Talmud to make people feel bad about themselves and their decisions. So what if someone is gay? Or doesn't want to be a boy or a girl? Or
can't afford to stop working on Saturday? Who was he to judge? He was
just a spiritual vessel whose profession it was to make some incredible
people, Jewish people, aware of their unique covenant with G-d and their
earthbound duty to make the world a better place. He was like a mailman.
Or a garbageman. As long as he showed up and did his job and didn't make
waves, everything would run smoothly.

Who was that, though, sitting next to Isaac? She was a large woman,
very overweight, but he didn't mean that in a judgmental way. He himself
was a little plump in the middle and even though Shosh was sometimes
on him about losing weight, he knew that people can just be born a little
heavier and there's no harm in that. The woman had thick blond hair tied
up in a shape like a turnip. He didn't recognize her. Neither did he recognize the man sitting next to her, reed-thin with a patchy beard and huge
eyes like he'd been drugged.

After the service, Etta Gorstein held his hands in hers as she always
did and told him how beautifully he sang, and Tim and Isaac congratu-
lated him on another enchanting Shabbat. The overweight woman grinned
and introduced herself: her hand was thick and damp.

"I'm Melinda," she said. The thin man offered his hand, a disturbed
look on his face. "This is my son, Leland."

Leland.

"Pleased to meet you," Ari said, aware that he was doing his Unfriendly
Voice, which Shosh said was different from his normal voice in that it was
two octaves lower and made him speak slower.

"The synagogue is beautiful," the woman, who was clearly a goy, said.
"I've never been in a place this, um, majestic before."

"Mom," the son said under his breath.

"It's very old," Ari said quickly. "A lot of history here."

"I can only imagine," the woman said.

"Well, thank you for coming," Ari said. "I hope you enjoyed the service."

"Oh, but, um—" The woman tapped him lightly on the shoulder.

His worst nightmare. He touched his phone in his pocket. He would
call Stefan. He would call the police.

"We're actually here with a question for you."

"Mom," Leland said again, louder.

"We were, um, wondering if you remember someone coming here named Leland Bloom-Mittwoch?"

"No!" The woman, her son, and a few of the straggler congregants jumped. "No," he repeated, trying to say it cuttingly. "If you are in any way associated with the people who came here last week—"

Now the son was taking an interest in the whole thing. "There were people here last week asking about Leland Bloom-Mittwoch?"

Who *were* these people? It had been so tedious to get those tiles back into the floor last week, and it had taken Stefan a whole day afterward to regrout them. "Yes. And they tore up my sanctuary. I'll call the police. I'll actually call them if you try anything."

"No, no, no." The woman held her hands up like he'd accused her of having a weapon. Her son did the same. The son especially looked like he'd lived a hard life, had that hollow-cheeked meth-smoking face Ari some-times saw on shirtless young men pushing grocery carts along the side of the road. The grocery carts were usually full of nongrocery items: cans of spray paint and ashtrays and giant bags of rock salt. Why these young men were always in transit, Ari had no idea. He liked to imagine they had girl-friends (or boyfriends!) waiting for them at home, cooking meth like some people cooked dinner. He would teach Lina not to ignore these men, to give them whatever change she could spare, to offer them rides in her car if they looked particularly desperate. Well, maybe not rides in her car, that probably wouldn't be the safest. But at the very least compassion. At the very least a noncondescending smile. *Tikkun olam.*

"I'm sorry," Ari said, because now he felt guilty for ever having hated the woman and her son. "I just don't understand what you're looking for."

The woman looked like she was about to say something, but the son shook his head. "We're not looking for anything," he said. The woman turned to him, questioning, but he kept talking. "We just wanted to know if you remembered Leland Bloom-Mittwoch."

Without thinking, Ari made an offer he instantly regretted. "Would you like me to call my father and ask him if he remembers Leland?"

The woman nodded and the son shrugged.

This would be good, Ari reassured himself. This would be weird, sure, but good. He'd find out who Leland was (finally!) and get this mess straight-ened out in his head and he'd talk to his father, which he hadn't done in a few months. Now they'd have something to talk about. He could say, "These two people are waiting in my office with me, Dad, and they want to know about Leland Bloom-Mittwoch." His father would have to respond with more than the usual grunt.

The three of them crowded in his office, which made Ari realize how small it was. He barely had enough room for his books on the shelves: he'd had to start stacking them on the floor. His desktop was all computer and printer and papers and no pens. The landline phone buzzed. The mother and son were sitting in front of him, knees against the desk, the son peeling a sheet of dead skin off his thumb and the mother looking at Ari like he was the president about to drop a bomb on Al Qaeda. Nothing he was doing could be *that* important. He dialed his father's home number. He asked the woman where she was from and she smiled pleasantly and said, "Cleveland." Now there was a place nobody talked about anymore. Or had anybody really talked about Cleveland to begin with? What did he know about Cleveland, other than that people called it the Mistake by the Lake? He had gone to grad school with someone from Cleveland. Simon Yeltsman. Or had he been from Cincinnati?

The phone kept on ringing. His parents didn't even have voice mail. Leave it to the Kamzins to distrust any technology invented after the Cold War. He hung up and tried again. Then again.

On the fourth try his mom picked up.

"Ari," she said. "What's happening? Why are you calling so close to sundown?"

"Ma, I'm sorry, I'm just in a little bit of a situation here," he said, and the woman leaned forward in her seat. "Is Dad there?"

A raspy sigh. He remembered that sigh from her, the way she'd huff it in the mideighties after a drag from a Gauloise, Ari having just done something unforgivably stupid.

"Some people want to know about a member of the congregation. Do you remember someone named Leland Bloom-Mittwoch?"

"What? Bloom-Mittwoch?"

"Yeah, they're here because they think—"

"We think he might have left something," the woman whispered from her seat.

"They think he left something here many years ago that belongs to them."

"In the late nineties," the woman went on. "He died in 1999."

"He was here in the late nineties," Ari said.

Another raspy sigh. His mom was probably wearing a turtleneck and jeans over her boy-slim hips, chewing on the inside of her mouth and making that little scowl she always made when she had to think about something she didn't like. "I have no idea."

"I'm his ex-wife," the woman stage-whispered, and her son rolled his bulging eyes.

"I'm looking at a woman who claims she's Leland Bloom-Mittwoch's ex-wife," Ari said.

"Stop this nonsense," his mother hissed. "Put the ex-wife on the phone."

He did as he was told, and he watched the woman's face go from expectant to polite to miserable. She handed the phone back to Ari, who hung up.

The woman began crying. Her son held her.

"I'm so sorry to have bothered you," she said.

Ari reached across his desk to put a hand on her forearm. "Oh, um—"

"Melinda."

"Right, Melinda, please don't let my mom ruffle your feathers like that. She's a very matter-of-fact woman. I shouldn't have given the phone over."

"No, it wasn't her." She shuddered, massaging her cheeks. "It was just that it was, it was just chasing a lie." And then the son whispered something to his mother that Ari couldn't hear and she cried harder. What to do with these people?

"Would you prefer if I, um, tried to give them a call back tomorrow?" Ari asked. "Are you in town long?"

The son shook his head. "No need. Right, Mom? We're going to forget about this and go home."

The woman said nothing.

"For what it's worth," Ari said, "I think there must have been a Leland Bloom-Mittwoch in the congregation because you are two of six total people who've asked about him in the past week."

"Six total," the woman intoned.

"Okay, yes, we don't doubt that. What we doubt is literally anything else about him, especially rumors originating from the man himself." The son leaned forward in a way that made Ari uncomfortable. "Apparently he had a giant briefcase full of money and somehow hid it in this temple."

Ari smiled, finally understanding. More temple lore. Shosh was going to eat this story up when he got home.

He asked them if they needed a moment and the son nodded yes. He stepped outside: no texts from Shosh, just smiling baby Lina as his wallpaper. He would never change that wallpaper, no matter how old she got—he'd whip that phone out at her bat mitzvah and her sweet sixteen, "embarrassing" her with proof of how adorable she'd been. Her hazel eyes and little ridgeless nose and gummy smile. He could think of nothing better to look at. It wasn't fair that kids grew up, for their sakes or their parents'. Even he'd been adorable at one point in time, chubby-legged and quick to smile. He used to call his mom Mimi and his dad Poppy. Where he'd come up with those names, he had no idea. At least he had Shosh and Lina. Everything would be different with him and Shosh and Lina. Lost in thought, he hardly even noticed the mother and son walking past him on their way out of his office.

He called his father back again that week, during hours of the day he knew he'd be by his phone. No response. It wasn't unlike his father to act stoic or distant or gruff, but it was entirely unlike him to be unreachable. Were they now officially estranged? That would be a shame—not for Ari, for whom it would mean less grunting, less judgment, less haranguing about the progressive changes he was trying to make to the temple, but for Lina, who deserved to grow up with grandparents. Shosh's parents had passed of heart attacks within months of each other two years before Lina had been born. It had been horrible for Shosh, who lost twenty pounds and slept three hours a night and wore dark gray circles under her eyes. A grief-destroyed wife shouldn't be held accountable for maintaining a perfect Jewish household, so Ari had done everything around the house in addition to running the show at Chaim Sheltok. Seeing Shosh like that had made him realize how awful life must have been for his mother, expected to serve his father regardless of how she was feeling—no wonder she'd been so angry at Ari all the time. Where else could she vent her emotions? No one would expect any complaints from the rabbi's wife.

After a week of no response from his father, he stopped trying. Why beat a dead horse? So they were estranged—that would probably last as long as the High Holidays, and then his father would want something from him, and then the phone would start ringing again. He used to be envious of boys who seemed to have close relationships with their fathers, like Eric Shimmel, whose father coached the Little League team, or John Tao, whose father was leader of the Boy Scouts. Mr. Tao had a wide, kind face and always let Ari put double marshmallows in his s'mores when they went camping. John, who was tall and girl-graceful and constantly acted like he was better than everyone else, probably didn't appreciate his father enough. If Ari had been the son of Mr. Tao, he wouldn't have avoided being in the same canoe as him, or groaned when he was called on to be partners with him during CPR class. He was going to make sure Lina dodged the ungratefulness bullet. She would know from the start how lucky she was to have a home and two loving parents and a college fund.

He was preparing for the service while Shosh played with Lina in his office. Having the two of them there always made services better. All the congregants loved cooing at Lina, especially the female ones, and Shosh wasn't stingy about letting them hold her. The three of them made the temple homier, unlike his father, who had forced Ari to wear a tiny suit and shake everyone's hand as they filed out the door to the parking lot. Surprisingly, Shosh had been less interested in the Leland Bloom-Mittwoch story than he had, attributing the barrage of visitors to a recent full moon. She could get weirdly pagan, his Shosh, and there was no predicting how or why. She thought the tides controlled moods and crystals prevented illnesses and accidents happened for a reason. Ari had always been skeptical about that stuff, but who was he to judge? Plenty of people believed in those new age healing rituals, and far be it from him to question their beliefs. Probably a lot of people thought Judaism was a crock of ancient snake oil cooked up to make a group of regular people feel special.

He'd taken to the Internet: according to the *St. Petersburg Times* archive, Leland Bloom-Mittwoch Sr. had died jumping off the roof of a hotel in Tampa in 1999. He was survived by a wife and a son, Diedre Bloom-Mittwoch and Lee Bloom-Mittwoch. Other than that, there wasn't much information on old Leland Bloom-Mittwoch. He tried searching "Leland Bloom-Mittwoch Jr." and got a photo of the thin son looking considerably less thin, shaking the hand of someone whom the photo caption described as Winn Maxwell's largest investor. Winn Maxwell was some kind of hedge fund in Chicago. After looking at the Winn Maxwell website for a while, Ari got bored.

He'd just finished de-linting the parochet when he saw them. First came a tall old man with a head that looked like it had been badly dented and then reformed. He wrapped his arm around the hips of a woman who appeared to be his age, who surveyed the temple critically through a pair of black-frame glasses. Behind them were two men with the same face, one of them shorter than the other. The taller one held the hand of a woman Ari could have sworn looked like the painter Netta Barochin, but then all he'd seen of her had been a grainy photo in the *New York Times*. The shorter one held the hand of a nervous and birdlike white woman.

"Hello," Ari said, aware that he was maybe sounding overgenerous, like the dorky, mustachioed dad who wants to be liked by his teenager's friends. He hoped he wouldn't actually become that dad when Lina was a teenager, walking into the living room with freshly baked cookies and interrupting some gossip about hot boys at school, an apron tied around his growing paunch, asking if anyone wanted oatmeal raisin clusters (because of course as a dorky dad he wouldn't make the kind of cookies kids like, and of course he'd call them clusters instead of cookies). Lina would surely roll her eyes at him after he left the room. She'd say something like "Sorry about my dad, you guys, he's just a little . . . *desperate*."

"Hi," the shorter twin-faced man said, and separated himself from the pack to shake Ari's hand. The white woman crossed her arms and stood apart from the rest of the family—Ari had the feeling that it was less her wanting to stand apart and more the family's pushing her away. He couldn't blame them, which was mean of him to think, but she looked like a hard little person, the kind of person who would send back her steak at a restaurant because it hadn't been properly dressed. The older woman with the glasses took a seat on a bench.

"I'm Caleb Marshall," the shorter twin-faced man said, and gave Ari a business card that read *Caleb Marshall, Attorney at Law, Lewis & Mathers & Marshall*. "I'm here with my family. We made the trip down here together. It's a special occasion for all of us."

He introduced them: the man with the dented head was in fact his father, and he was named Reggie Marshall. Caleb's mother was named Natasha Marshall. They were obviously in love. As Ari spoke to them, Reggie massaged the base of Natasha's neck and she smiled at his touch.

They were a beautiful couple. He used to think that sort of thing was impossible, especially among the older generations, because his mother nitpicked and his father handled it with stony silence.

The white woman was introduced as Jocelyn, and she gave a terse little wave. The twin-faced man was Aaron, Caleb's brother. And his wife was Netta.

"Oh my God," Ari said. "Are you the painter? Netta Barochin?"

Netta smiled at Aaron, whom Ari saw give her a strong-jawed look and a shrug like *Whatever you want.* Why would Aaron be giving her this look and shrug? They seemed to be in love, too, but not like Reggie and Natasha—more recklessly, but maybe more passionately. Aaron and Netta were also tall and beautiful and made Ari feel like a schlub. Which he knew was unfair, was just his bad self-esteem talking, but it was hard not to feel that way.

"No, I'm not," she said. "I sometimes get asked that."

Was she lying? Ari liked her already, the soft way she spoke. He'd known a girl in grade school like her who was the tallest in class but also the shyest, and whom he would sometimes walk home and talk to about a collection of bugs she kept in jars under her bed. He couldn't remember her name. It started with a *T.* Why was he remembering a grade-school crush now? He figured if Netta was lying, he'd let her lie, because there was no harm in wanting to be modest. His mother used to say modesty was the best policy. Netta Barochin was well-known enough that people were probably always bothering her for autographs, and that had to be annoying, although Ari was such a civilian type that being famous seemed like a blast to him. How did rabbis get famous? There were no megarabbis like there were megapastors, which was probably good for the faith but obviously bad for getting famous. Ha, like he really wanted to be. He had everything he wanted in his life already.

"We're very sorry about this," Caleb Marshall said. "We don't really want to occupy any more of your Sabbath. The radically truncated version of the story is we all know a man named Leland Bloom-Mittwoch Sr. who was a member of this congregation in the nineties, and we have reason to believe he left a sum of money here. A donation perhaps?"

"It was in a yellow briefcase," Reggie Marshall said. "It belonged to me."

"You have something that belongs to him," Aaron Marshall echoed.

They knew this Leland, too?

Ari was realizing for the first time the magnitude of his ignorance about the Temple Chaim Sheltok's history. He didn't know, for instance, that his father had once tolerated in his congregation the presence of a drug addict named Leland Sr., an inconsequential person with a wild brain who'd shown up on the temple steps one evening begging for "spiritual shelter." He said he lived thirty-five minutes from Heimsheim but was willing to make the drive as many days as the rabbi would let him. Thinking he was doing the poor man a mitzvah, Ari's father sat Leland Sr. behind the women's cheesecloth so he wouldn't embarrass himself during services. He'd even allowed Leland Sr. to volunteer his free weekdays cleaning the temple. After some time of that, he let the poor man bring his family to Friday services, his pale ghost of a son and his strangely beautiful wife sitting behind the cheesecloth while he sat with the rest of the congregation. When Leland Sr. finished a volunteer cleaning session, the rabbi always left his office through the back exit and walked around through the front entrance, greeting the man as though he'd just arrived back from running errands or performing a bris, as though he trusted him fully.

The work seemed to calm Leland Sr., and he was always so eager to discuss scripture with the rabbi afterward. The rabbi would listen patiently to him, trying his best to chalk up the man's many inconsistencies to sloppy self-study. When Leland Sr. reached his limit discussing scripture, the rabbi would invite him to talk about personal matters. Then he'd try his best to mask his emotions as Leland Sr. told him about the first wife and son who hated him, the disappearance and likely violent death of his best friend in 1973, his unshakable need for "medicine." The rabbi asked him about the good in his life and Leland Sr. assured him there was plenty—his second wife and son who loved him, the fact that he needed only two doses of medicine a day now.

The rabbi truly pitied him. Although he knew no good could come from pity, he allowed himself to feel it thoroughly, allowed himself to imagine the unfortunate series of events that could have landed him in a pair of shoes similar to the man's.

"We all suffer traumas that threaten impurity in our souls," the rabbi said. "And we should be freed from them, not punished for them."

It wasn't until three years later, on the evening before his birthday in 1999, that Leland Sr. finally understood the rabbi's words. The true meaning occurred to him like a divine slap to the back of the head. That night he stayed up watching TV long after Diedre and Lee had gone to bed. Then he went to the basement, where for years he'd been hiding Reggie's money in a yellow briefcase (the money changed briefcases often, the old ones serving as decoys for those whom he wanted to throw off his noxious, cursed trail) to which he'd recently added a study Torah the rabbi had gifted him. He loaded it into his car and pressed his forehead to his steering wheel, whispered to G-d that he hoped his wife and son would be okay, that he even hoped his other wife and son would be okay, that he was very sorry for everything he'd done.

He drove to Heimsheim and pulled into the temple parking lot. By then the rabbi had made a copy of the master key for him, trusted him enough to come and go as he pleased. He silently thanked the rabbi for his trust, then thanked G-d for trusting the rabbi. The moon was bright over Chaim Shel-tok's high marble dome; the massive door screeched as he pushed it open.

Briefcase in hand, he walked across the main chamber, past the lectern, past the rabbi's office, and into the room with the mikveh bath. He had always loved cleaning this room: its damp, high-ceilinged echoes, the perfect blue of the bath tiles, the low whispers of people purifying themselves. He had never gone into the bath himself—the rabbi had urged him to, but he'd claimed a fear of water. Now, alone in the middle of the night, he stripped naked and walked the stairs into the mikveh, stopping when he was up to his neck in water. He thought about holding his breath and just sinking but knew he wouldn't be able to go through with it. Besides, would the rabbi enjoy finding his drowned body in the mikveh the next day? Would G-d?

He doggie-paddled to the edge of the mikveh and clicked open the briefcase. He lined up all the remaining stacks he had on the bath's edge. Two by two, he grabbed them and swam to the drain on the other side of the bath. He lifted the cover and stuffed the stacks down there, did the same with two more and two more until all the money was gone. He paddled back to the stairs and dipped his head underwater, floated up and spent half an hour watching the moon's progress through the massive temple windows. Then he climbed out and went back to his car. The night's heat made beads of the water on his skin and he thought, *I am pure now.* Now he could leave; he could be in Tampa by morning.

Ari's father had told him none of this. He hadn't felt the need to. Now, in front of these people, Ari could feel his blood heating up. Who were they, anyway? Why did he have to be the one to help them? He'd been through enough. He wasn't going to have his temple ransacked again. He had a life of his own, a congregation to lead! The service would start soon and here he was in the aisle, squaring off with more of these people. Lina was coming down with a cold: tomorrow she would probably wake up at six o'clock, crying, and Shosh would be grumpy. Maybe he and Shosh would have a fight over breakfast. Maybe they'd fight over breakfast every morning after that, and Lina would grow up thinking of her parents as combative, their marriage unhappy. Maybe she'd become a disagreeable and bitter teenager, constantly rubbing salt in their wounds, driving them further apart with her jeers. Maybe they'd divorce and fight over custody. No, no. It was too horrible to think about. He had to get on with what he needed to do.

"Sorry," he told them. "I don't think I can help you."

ACKNOWLEDGMENTS

I never would have finished this book had it not been for the generosity of the Guthrie family and the Richard E. Guthrie Memorial Fellowship. I am similarly indebted to the Meta and George F. Rosenberg Foundation for the Meta Rosenberg Scholarship in Creative Writing.

Many thanks to the Iowa Writers' Workshop. To Ethan Canin and Sam Chang for reminding me that I'm a writer capable of producing a full-length novel: I wouldn't have gotten by without Ethan's patient compassion or Sam's ruthless optimism. To Connie Brothers for helping me sort out my life when I was barely old enough to know what life is. To Tony Tulathimutte for offering me eighteen single-spaced pages of immensely helpful criticism and Okezie Nwoka for spending hours on the phone with me hammering out point-of-view issues. To Ashley Clarke, Deborah Kennedy, and Sinead Lykins for brilliant insights and hearty encouragement. To July Orringer and T. Geronimo Johnson for guiding this novel through workshops. And to Yuka Igarashi for helping my writing flourish.

This book would not exist without Ross Harris's muscular efforts as a literary agent. And it wouldn't make much sense without Sarah Bowlin's editorial skills. It wouldn't be on the shelves without Caroline Zancan or Jessica Wiener championing it. And it wouldn't be quite as queer without Kerry Cullen.

A special thanks to the great city of Cleveland for my visit, and the numerous Clevelanders who welcomed me with open arms. To Sidney

Mallory for letting me sleep on his couch and jumping on trampolines with me. To Tyler Lacor for wandering the woods with me and to his family for letting me overstay my welcome. To Steven Aviram for damn good pizza. To Lance Johnson IV and the Planned Parenthood crew for telling me everything I'd ever need to know about Cleveland. To Smitty's Seaway Barbershop for being an all-around great establishment.

I am lucky to have gone to India with the 2014 Critical Languages Scholarship in Hindi crew, and I was lucky to have gotten to know Caleb Christian, Benjamin Simington, and Annika Gage, all of whom helped me with this novel in ways they probably don't realize. I am similarly lucky to have gotten to know the talented Mimi Neathery, and to have graduated from the Compass program.

Shout-outs to my oldest friends who buoyed me with their goodness. To Julia Clark, Zarina Kamzina, Hannah Button-Harrison, and Alex Wennerberg for their help in making this novel happen. To Clare Costello, Jimmy Rothschild, Graham Schneider, Rachel Linder, Corley Miller, and the inimitable Vivian McNaughton for reading countless drafts and excerpts over a five-year period.

I am grateful for my family, both the Frumkins in New York and Florida and the McHenrys in Illinois. This book is as much for my grandma Doris McHenry as it is for my parents, Michael Frumkin and Melissa McHenry. There isn't a simple way to make clear how much I love you all.

And finally, there's Sharlene King, my life and love. This book is for her, too.

About the Author

REBEKAH FRUMKIN is a graduate of the Iowa Writers' Workshop and the Medill School of Journalism. She is a recipient of the Richard E. Guthrie and Meta Rosenberg Fellowships. Her fiction, nonfiction, and journalism have appeared in *Granta*, *Pacific Standard*, and *The Best American Nonrequired Reading*, among others. She lives, writes, and teaches in Chicago. This is her first novel.